SHOEMAKER'S WIFE

MYSTERIOUS ARTS
BOOK TWO

CELIA LAKE

SHOEMAKER'S WIFE

1920 should have been a wonderful summer. The Great War is over, and Clara's husband Owen has finally come home. All he wants is to set up as a shoemaker and enjoy a peaceful marriage.

Nothing about Owen's return is easy.

There's not enough money for Owen to start up his own business. Worse, he's having trouble finding work, like many other returning soldiers, and everything's getting more expensive. Clara's worried about running her aunt's apothecary shop while her aunt is away. Things at home are awkward and uncomfortable. Neither of them knows how to turn a wartime romance into a proper marriage.

When a lucky break gets him a new job backstage in a magical theatre, Owen is hopeful that his life - and Clara's - are beginning to turn around. Unfortunately, the new job brings new worries, and one of Clara's customers is taking a more personal interest in her than she's comfortable with.

There might be a way to solve all their troubles, if they can just remember why they fell in love in the first place, and learn to trust each other.

Shoemaker's Wife is a romance about falling in love for a second time and learning how to have a happy marriage. Join Clara and Owen for shoemaking, a winter pantomime, the challenges of rebuilding a life after war, and all the ways kindness makes a difference. The second novel in the Mysterious Arts series about the magical community of Great Britain, it can be read in any order.

CHAPTER 1

JULY 15 1920, TRELLECH

"You could go home." Clara looked up from where she was polishing the wooden counter yet again. She'd polished it twice today already, rubbing the beeswax into the wood.

She could. But she wasn't sure she wanted to. Or what home meant, today, compared to yesterday and the day before, and the three years before that. Four years. It depended very much how she counted.

"Thank you, Aunt Lillian, but he said he wasn't sure when he'd actually get back." To be precise, Owen had sent a postcard through. It said that he would finally be demobbed today, and that was it. Nothing saying he was looking forward to seeing her, no idea of the time, no details at all about what he expected. Nothing.

Clara fidgeted with the wedding ring on her left hand - a plain gold band - before she forced herself to stop doing that and go back to polishing the wood. At least that was vaguely useful, and it was less tedious than polishing the metal fittings or cleaning the glass of the apothecary shop's display cases. She was due to dust the hundreds of bottles

1

again, but she certainly didn't trust herself to do that today. She was entirely too fumble-fingered.

Aunt Lillian snorted and wiped her hands on her apron before going back to her work in the back room. That was where the actual magic happened, and that wasn't something Clara had any real skill with. She could do the simples well enough, blending up a skin salve or the most routine of powders. But she wasn't trained or certified for anything else, and so the front room was her domain. She did well keeping the books, at least, and handling all the ordering of supplies and bottling and labels.

Clara prided herself on having learned the seasons and cycles of when to stock up on certain herbs and waxes and oils, and when to snatch up a good deal. Even better, she felt like she'd finally learned when a deal was too good to be true. The shop did a solid business these days, even with everything the War had changed. Maybe because of everything the War had changed, and that was a depressing thought. The Healers and nurses were constantly busy with critical cases, and the apothecaries had had to pick up helping as many others as they could.

Not that it had helped Owen's Mum. The name ran together in her head, one word, Owensmum. She wasn't Clara's mum, and calling her something like Mother Hubbard was entirely too much out of a nursery rhyme, even if it hadn't generally felt ridiculous. Etta Hubbard had been a kind enough woman, always knitting and agreeable. And she'd been good to Clara, though Clara had felt it was out of something like a mutual unspoken terror, because what if Owen died?

Owen's Mum had been ill, after she'd had a problem with her heart in 1916. That was when Clara and Owen married. But she'd got better. That was when Clara had moved in. Clara had been working for Aunt Lillian for a couple of years by then, but it was easier to give up her room in the shop's attic to an apprentice. She'd enjoyed having a little space between herself and her work, not having it all tumbled in together. The scent of the herbs and the waxes and the oils would mingle in a chaos of smells in her room, making it impossible to feel she had put anything down.

Then, all of a sudden, half a year later, Owen's Mum had woken with a racking cough. Nothing would help, but it wasn't bad enough the Temple of Healing would give her a bed. And then one night, two in the morning, it had gone far too quiet and Clara had been all alone.

She'd had to sort out the practical details, changing over the lease for the shop below, and writing a letter to Owen then worrying it hadn't ever got there. When she'd finally heard back from him, a month later, he hadn't said much, a bare thanks. He'd enclosed a signed letter giving her the formal permission to do what she'd already done on the strength of the marriage certificate and a number of fussy oaths on her magic.

Clara had read that letter huddled up in three blankets - no sense spending money to heat the place when it was just her, even if it had been a bitterly cold and snowy winter that had extended nearly to May Day. She hadn't done more than tidy Owen's Mum's room, leaving it just as it was. Clara didn't need more space, either. She left it for sometime later, before Owen came home. If he ever came home.

Only now he was. Or at least, she assumed so, that nothing had gone wrong between wherever he was and Trellech itself. And that was the problem now, wasn't it? She wasn't at all sure what she felt about it.

She was glad that he was coming home with no horrible injury that would shadow him for the rest of his life. But it was an impersonal sort of gladness, the kind she felt for plenty of men who'd come through the War and come home. Most of them sooner than Owen, mind. He wasn't among the last to be demobbed, but he hadn't been early in the queue, either. Just a letter, every month or so, with just as a few details about the place or time as she'd got during the War itself.

Clara was sure, now, that she'd made a mistake of some sort, back when they'd met. She remembered it, more clearly than anything else in the last four years. Clara had been volunteering in the Temple of Healing, doing the ordinary sorts of things. She'd brought fresh water and hot tea around, to those who could drink it. She'd written letters or ticked off the proper boxes on the information cards that men could send back to families and sweethearts and wives. Clara had rolled endless bandages, and found it almost soothing.

Owen hadn't caught her attention, not at first. But he was there, on the ward, for a good two weeks. By four days in, during her second visit, he had a pile of small objects in his hands, working away at them between entirely necessary naps. Nothing fussy, but he'd fixed a loose nail in one of the nurse's shoes, apparently. Next he'd mended a lap table, then a string of children's toys. By the time she'd got round to his bed, she'd heard him laughing, more than a few times. That was a sound you didn't hear often, not in that ward.

It had been a whirlwind romance in the autumn of 1915. They'd had enough sense not to marry immediately, even that early in the War, Clara knew too many stories of how that went wrong. But then he'd come back for his mother's illness the next spring. He'd got enough compassionate leave to be home for a fortnight. An only son, no other family. That was the sort of thing that tugged at administrative heartstrings just a tad. Or, as Clara had come to think, more cynically, it was good for morale to let the men in the trenches see that kind of exception from time to time.

Clara had come to realise that the men over there were largely interchangeable. At least people like her, like Owen. No particular magic, certainly no posh training in arcane arts. Aunt Lillian had gone to Alethorpe, rather than just going straight into an apprenticeship, like Clara had. She was properly certified, with the framed paper on display to prove it. Owen had had an apprenticeship. He'd been out on his own making shoes for a year or two before he'd gone to fight.

They'd have to work that out, somehow. Their marital property was more steady than most people's. Owen's dad had owned the shop on the ground floor, the flat above, and storage above the flat. But the shop was leased out for at least another nine months, in an agreement that would be expensive to break. Clara had been floating through the flat, sitting in one chair in the sitting room, one chair in the kitchen, and using the second bedroom. Not Owen's Mum's room, not her chair, not her bit of the kitchen. She'd been like a ghost, flitting through the space, leaving no mark of herself except in her own room.

Which wasn't even hers anymore. Clara hadn't been able to decide what to do about that. But it wasn't as if she'd had time or the ability to move beds around in the five days since she'd known Owen was coming home. He could figure it out.

She'd figured out so many things for so long. He could decide about this. It had been his home since he was born.

She'd entirely rearranged the room that had been his, though. All his things were packed away. She'd brought down the trunk with clothes last night, but not the pictures and what-nots.

She didn't realise she'd stopped polishing until Aunt Lillian tugged the cloth out of her hand and nudged a jar into her fingers. "Go home, Clara. You're no good here."

It made Clara flinch, but she wouldn't argue. Instead, she curled her fingers around the jar. Blue glass, silver-coloured lid. "What's this?"

"It didn't set properly. Give it a good home." That would be the skin cream Aunt Lillian had been working on this morning. "The new one, it needed more wax."

Aunt Lillian had been working on alternate bases to the spermaceti ones. Clara largely approved, for cost reasons as well as all the others. Beeswax and lanolin and all that were less prone to changes in pricing, season to season. Especially if - as Aunt Lillian did - one had a friend with sheep and beehives up somewhere in Scotland. As opposed to whales, who tended to wander for one thing, and there were torpedos and such during the War. Both bees and sheep were much better.

"If you insist. Usual time tomorrow?" Clara turned to gather up her bag and make sure her hat was firmly on her head. She'd brought it out of habit, but she'd picked up food yesterday, on market day, enough to feed Owen and herself something for supper. Nothing fancy, but solid, eggs and some chicken and even some berries.

"You could take the day, you know." Aunt Lillian leaned against the door frame. "If you decide you want to, just stay home. I won't worry much." Aunt Lillian had had a reasonable enough marriage to Clara's father's brother, or so Clara had always been told. But she'd been a widow a very long time, all of Clara's life.

"I couldn't do that." Aunt Lillian had a steady schedule for making new items. Someone had to be tending the shop for that to work. Then she softened. "I'll drop a note with one of the messengers if I won't be in." She could spare the coin for that, if she actually did decide to stay home. If tonight meant staying home was sensible.

She didn't actually flinch, but she shifted from foot to foot. Aunt Lillian touched her shoulder once, almost hesitantly. "Tell him I'm glad he's home, too. And I'll see you when I see you. Off with you."

Clara nodded once before she made her way out of the door. She checked the displays in the window one more time out of sheer habit, then adjusted the hat one more time. She looked well enough, in a simple yellow day dress, a brown hat with a golden ribbon. And nicely sturdy shoes, if ones that were getting on a bit and needed resoling. Respectable, that was the right sort of word. The sort of person sensible people would buy potions and medicine from in a shop.

It was far earlier than she usually left work. She heard the Temple bells chime two as she turned down the street, so a whole three hours early. Three and a half, depending on how long it took her to tidy up and help Aunt Lillian figure out what needed to be ordered next. Half the time she'd eaten supper there, just to have company, and make sure Aunt Lillian wasn't alone either. She turned down the street, toward the flat, unsure how to face the rest of her day.

CHAPTER 2
JULY 15, CLARA'S FLAT

Being home hadn't helped. Clara took some solace in being right, though it was a bitter and sharp sort of solace. She washed up, tidied the kitchen again, and swept the floor, not that there was anything new to sweep since this morning. She was sitting in her chair in the sitting room, staring at the day's paper and not actually reading it, when there was a knock on the door.

Owen wouldn't knock, surely? Or would he? It wasn't like they'd talked about that, about anything useful, other than the date. Though she supposed he hadn't taken a key with him, and she'd taken to locking the door out of habit. Aunt Lillian's shop always had to be locked up when someone wasn't there, and the habit had come home with her.

Home. Right. She took a breath, brushed her hands on her skirt one more time, and went to open the door. Standing there was Owen. He looked the same and entirely not the same at all. The moustache he'd had last time she'd seen him was gone. His hair was the same darker auburn, though there were a few bits of white in it. And his eyes were that hazel she'd loved, from the start. Most of all, his eyebrows hadn't changed, the left with its quirk of an angle that made him look like he was always amused.

That didn't help now either. The rest of his face didn't give much away, not a smile, not a welcome, not anything. She ducked her chin. "Welcome home. Come in? Cuppa?"

She held out her arms, a bit uncertainly, before she saw he was laden down with things. A big bulky wool coat, over one arm, his uniform on, a battered fabric bag over the other arm. "Your things?"

Owen grunted. "Good to be home. Can I leave this out here? Needs to go back to an office, tomorrow, but it's all over lice."

There were a lot of things in those three bare sentences she wasn't sure about, but she was quite certain she didn't want lice in the flat. They would not improve anything at all. "Bath first, then? I can run you one."

"Hot water still decent, then? I'd like that." His voice softened a bit at the end, enough that she glanced over her shoulder as she turned away to go to the bathroom. "I'll stay here, it's fine."

She started the tap running, rummaging for the salts she kept for days when her shoulders and feet were sore. They smelled good, too. Nothing fancy, of course, mostly mint, but mint was refreshing. Rejuvenating. When she came back, she leaned against the wall where she could see him. "Master Tompson, across the road, has kept an eye on things. The hot water's fine, wood's a bit dear for heat, but the chimney draws well."

Then she ducked back into her bedroom. Their bedroom, probably. At least tonight, or she assumed so. She pulled out a comfortable pair of trousers and an older shirt, worn floppy, and slippers. Fresh pants, too, though they smelled a bit too much of cedar and the tang of the charm against moths that his mum had used. "Clothes on the rail."

Owen nodded once. "Let me have a bath, then. May be a bit. If there's something to eat after, I'm famished." That, at least, she'd planned on.

"Chicken and some veg?" Clara offered it carefully.

"Sounds fine." He then shrugged once, hung the coat on a hook outside, and then bent to undo his boots - big heavy things, badly worn. He left those just inside the door, to one side, before going off in his stocking feet to the bath.

"Towels on the door." Where else they'd be in this flat, she had no idea, it wasn't like there was storage to spare. "And there's bath salts, if you want them."

He made some noise she couldn't interpret as the door closed, leaving her standing in the sitting room with nothing much to do. Well, she could make some food. It had been cool last night, surprisingly so, so she'd roasted the chicken then. She hadn't wanted to fuss with it. But she'd kept aside some of the drippings, to make gravy with. And she could do something with carrots and potatoes, and a bit of butter. There was bread, she'd got a new loaf yesterday, and she'd remembered to up the milk order.

It would do. Nothing fancy, but she wasn't sure what he liked anymore. She wasn't sure what she liked, either, if it came to that, for a meal with anyone else. She had tea with Aunt Lillian sometimes, before she came home, but that was a different sort of meal. Or sometimes she'd eat with a friend, but that was rare enough. They had children or obligations or other family, and she'd never wanted to intrude on that.

Owen took a long time in the bath. Longer than she'd expected, and more than long enough for her to worry the gravy was going to do particularly unfortunate lumpy things. She set the table, then reset it, pulling out the woven placemats for a bit of colour against the faded shades of the curtains and the dingy half-white of the walls. They needed whitewashing again.

Finally, Owen came out, shuffling a little in the slippers. The clothes hung on him differently. He'd put on muscle in the shoulders, the fabric pulled there, but the trousers were looser. "All right?"

"Grand for now." His voice had a pleasant enough burr. Then, finally, he held out a hand to her. Only now, Clara was sitting, and it was awkward, she had to get up again, and then had no idea what to do with herself. He took her hand in his, then tugged her close.

Clara froze up for a moment. No one had touched her, not other than Aunt Lillian or a hand on her arm, in the market, in years. She didn't know what she was feeling, or what she felt about it. There was a jumbled sentence, all caught up. Then, thankfully, a bit of his smell caught her. Not just the mint - though he'd used plenty of that, and the lavender rosemary soap - but something that smelled just like him. There were hints of leather, and warm oils, and a thread of wood, not just the cedar from his clothes. Her breath caught for a second, and his arms tightened around her.

It wasn't bad. It wasn't like she'd been worried about. Clara wasn't sure she'd call it good, or splendid, or easy. But she took a breath and let it out, leaning against him, wanting to know more about whatever this was. He held on, steady, for quite a long time, before he kissed the top of her head. "Glad to be home. That smells grand."

"Nothing fancy, just chicken and carrots in a bit of honey, and mash."

"So much better than what I've been eating. Nothing

that's been near a tin." He didn't say more about it, just settled down in the other chair, glanced at her, and then tucked in. He certainly ate with a healthy appetite, near enough inhaling two-thirds of the plate before he said anything else. Then he looked around. "You've not changed much."

Clara shook her head. "The bedroom. I mean, not your Mum's." Now she flushed, she could feel the heat on her cheeks. "I didn't think I ought."

She was looking away when he made a noise, a low grunt. "I'll have a look. Tomorrow. And I need to see about finding work." There was something fiercely determined in that, but she couldn't argue with the need. The apothecary paid enough to feed her, to keep her in clothes, but it would only barely stretch to two. That was leaving aside any habits about cigarettes or beer or whatever else Owen might want.

He coughed, then. "The shop?"

"Leased through Lady Day." The end of March, one of the traditional ones. "They'd like to renew, I expect, but they understand things are changing again."

"We'll see about that, then. Any repairs needed? Anything I should see to?"

He hadn't asked her about her work, nothing about how she was at all. She waved a hand. "I have a list. I can show you. Nothing urgent, like I said, Master Thompson's been kind."

"I'll call round and see if I can lend him a hand in turn." Then he set his fork and knife on the table. "What do you usually do, of an evening? Or the rest of the day?"

"I leave for work at eight, the shop opens at nine, I'm there until five, usually, and noon on Saturdays. A half day or a day off here and there, depending on who wants a few hours of work and their schedule. Or if Aunt Lillian wants a bit of a break from the stillroom. If there's something you need me free for, I'm sure she'd sort it out." Clara looked up at that, and Owen nodded once.

"And the pay?"

"Enough for me, probably not enough for both of us, for long, but I've a little set aside." She hesitated, then risked saying something more personal. "You look like you need feeding up."

That got her another grunt, but reasonably good-humoured. "I do. But I can make up a fair bit if you keep me in bread and butter and maybe some jam. And I'll see about finding something." He considered. "You really didn't change much."

Clara shrugged. "I didn't feel like it was mine to change. Just the bedroom, I hope it's all right."

Owen tilted his head, as if he was puzzled, but he nodded just once. "Fine for now, and we can sort things out as we go. Mind if I go have a look around? And - you said you didn't move anything in Mum's?"

"All the photos and all are out. I dusted, that's it." It still smelled like her, like the medicines and the skin cream and the hint of wood. Owen nodded, pushing back from the table, and leaving her alone with a half-eaten plate. She left him to it for a good hour. She washed up, made up her own lunch for the next day, and counted out some coins for whatever he might need. Then she sat at the table and made a clean copy of her list of things that needed tending. She'd had it in her head, from the door that stuck slightly to the chair in the sitting room, to a bit of a nail that stuck up from the floorboard.

Then it was time she went to look for Owen, not that he could go very far. Clara found him sitting on the end of the bed in her - their - bedroom, staring at the space. She'd tucked his toolbox into the corner, the last time he'd gone, and set the trunk with his clothes in front of it. "I cleared out space in the dresser and the wardrobe, but I didn't know what things you'd want to wear." It sounded feeble, like she should have had them all put away, already. That a proper wife, welcoming her husband home, would have known what he needed without him saying. Or at least she'd have made a guess at it.

"No, it's fine. Some of it won't fit proper anymore, not good for going out in. I'll go through it, decide what's what."

Clara ducked her chin. "What would you - tonight, I mean? This evening?"

Owen looked up at her, quiet for an entirely too-long moment. "The paper. A cuppa. Some quiet. And then—" He glanced at the bed, then back at her. "If you want?" He didn't spell it out, in crude terms, but it wasn't the flirtation they'd had. They'd only had a couple of times, properly together, only after their marriage, when they'd worried about being loud enough to wake his Mum. Clara had enjoyed that, far more than she'd honestly expected to, for all the fumbling.

Now, she didn't know what to expect. She just smiled. "Paper. Cuppa. Let me put the kettle on again. I'll join you in one." The evening went well enough, and it let her get used to the sound of someone else in the flat again. He got up once or twice to use the loo or refill his cup from the teapot. She did the same. And then, around about nine, he stood, and held out his hand.

When Clara took it, he pulled her in for a kiss - a warming kiss, a reassuring kiss, though feeling skin and not his moustache distracted her far more than it should. Then he guided her along to the bedroom. The sun was finally setting, but you didn't get much light in the window in the bedroom even in the height of the day. The next part was a bit of sorting things out in the dimness, until she drew the curtains. His fingers undid the buttons of her frock deftly enough, hers fumbled on his shirt.

Then he was pulling her down to the bed, his fingers rough against her skin, all uneven callouses. She'd expected him to rush, for it to be over immediately, but it took longer than she'd thought it would. Some of that was that he seemed to want to touch her, more than anything else, the way he had always touched other things in his life. As if his fingers told him the most important things, not his eyes. Several times, that tickled, and she half-flinched away, before he tried something else.

By the time he finally pressed inside her, Clara was trembling, overwrought. The sensation was too much, and not enough, all at once, and she had no idea what to tell him about it, or even if she should. Before she could get any sense of it, he was moving, then faster and harder. He rocked her into the bed making it creak and bang a little against the wall. It all came to an end far too quickly, before she found her own pleasure.

Owen was asleep almost immediately, after one single kiss on her shoulder. Clara lay there, staring up at the ceiling, flat on her back. His hand was draped across her stomach, in an intimate possessiveness that made her shiver. It hadn't been bad. She'd quite enjoyed some of it. But whatever that was, it wasn't like she remembered, and it had a hollow ache to it she didn't care for at all.

CHAPTER 3
JULY 16, THEIR FLAT

Owen came awake suddenly, and he had no idea why. He held still, like he'd learned, not flailing or making a noise. There was always a reason he'd woken, even if he didn't know it yet. Once it had been gas, just beginning to filter in. Another time, it had been flooding. More than a few times, it had been rats.

The bed felt strange. Maybe that was it. It was certainly far too soft, it had give to it. Not at all like the floor, or a narrow bunk cut into a dugout. Or even those wooden frames with a beaten-down thing that pretended to be a mattress, all ticking and straw. It wasn't unfamiliar, it had been his bed before, even if Clara had apparently been sleeping in it for years now. It smelled like her, too, like the bar shampoo she had in the bath, and the soap, all optimistic herbs.

He held still, taking stock. He didn't think it had been a noise. The room was quiet now, at any rate, other than Clara's quiet breathing. She was curled on her side, away from him, the blanket pulled up tightly over her shoulder, nearly covering her face.

When nothing else changed or moved, Owen gave up on staying put, and got up, quietly.

He'd learned to be quiet enough in badly-made boots, it was much easier in bare feet. The floor wasn't even cold. He rummaged for a minute, finding the trousers and shirt he'd had on earlier and shrugging into them. It felt better to have clothes on, that was normal. Thirty seconds later, he was out the bedroom door, pulling it closed behind him. She'd kept the knob oiled, it was easy for him to make sure it latched without a sound. He'd been an obedient sort of son, but a man had a reason to be out of the flat from time to time without his Mum knowing.

That brought him across the hall into Mum's room. It really hadn't changed at all. He called a light into his hand, one of the tricks he'd been taught in his apprenticeship and had barely been able to use during the War. Owen would have to remember he was back in a space where he could do magic, and it was normal.

That was going to be a challenge, he could feel it already. It had been hard enough to navigate this afternoon, after getting dropped off at the train station. The demob camp had brought a whole host of them down in a series of big carts, and most of the boys had gone off to London, or Manchester. Owen had been on his own almost immediately. He'd taken the train just far enough to get an easy portal, before waiting for a chance to go through to Trellech. There had been a wait - something about sheep - and he mostly hadn't minded.

Mostly, though. Being out in the open countryside had unnerved him, more than he wanted to admit to. He'd had a few short leaves, the past couple of years. A minor injury or two, enough time to be in hospital near the Front for a few days. And then twice, enough time for three days in Paris. It hadn't been long enough to come back, nor even enough notice to let Clara know he could get leave if she wanted to meet him at Dover or something. He hadn't bothered to let her know.

Now, he took a breath, and looked around Mum's room. She really hadn't changed anything. Not Mum, while she was still alive. And not Clara, either, other than the fact that the flowers on the mantelpiece were silk, and not real. Changing out the flowers in a room no one used would be foolish. But the rest was the same, the knit blanket across the bed, another couple resting on the trunk at the foot. There were the various family pictures on every flat surface. Mum, Dad, Owen at various different ages, all to mark particular occasions.

The most recent was, of course, the wedding, with Clara in a smart frock, her hair in curls. Owen wore a suit that didn't quite fit anymore, but was the best one he owned. Mum was beaming in it. Owen stared at it, and tried to remember what that day had felt like. He remembered, dimly, through a fog, being happy.

The happiness had been partly about him - he'd loved Clara's practical humour. When he'd met her, in the ward at the Temple of Healing, she'd been stubborn about getting things done. Some of the VADs and volunteers would duck things they didn't know how to do. Clara was fearless about asking, and wanting to understand what to do in this case, and when she needed to ask again. And she'd had gentle hands, he'd needed that. So many of them had needed that.

Now, Owen stood, and took one of the blankets from the top of the trunk. It was one of Mum's less garish combinations, a royal blue and golden yellow that he remembered her making during his apprenticeship. He'd lived there, it was the only way to do some of the prep and cleanup efficiently. But he'd been able to come back for Sunday dinner every week, and often Wednesday tea as well. She'd sit and knit when she was done with the cooking, or after they'd finished eating.

That brought him into the sitting room, which also hadn't changed much. Mum's chair, left alone, and a small sofa. That was too low to the ground to be comfortable now, as he'd discovered earlier. Then the chair Clara had used, which had a few small things handy. He could see a pencil stub and a bit of smoothed wood to put her tea on, with a ring stained by the damp. But there wasn't much of Clara here, at least he didn't think so. Certainly the walls were the same colour and the furniture hadn't changed.

Owen ended up settling on the floor, first leaning his back against the sofa, and then curling up on his side on the floor. It was a far better floor than he'd had for a long time. The last six months or so, he'd had a cot, and it had been reasonably dry, but before that, this floor would have been luxury. It was dry, it didn't have awkward lumps, it didn't smell like mildew. It still felt like luxury, honestly. He pulled Mum's blanket around him, and stared up, at the light coming in through the window from the street. Around the time it was starting to get a bit brighter, he fell asleep again.

When he woke, there was something that made him freeze in place. A noise, this time, one he hadn't expected. Worse, there was utter quiet after, the kind that came before another blazing artillery attack, or the sound of a sniper. The moment where everything got worse, that was the way it was. The way it had been for as long as he could remember, now, even though he knew better.

Then there was a cough. "I - I thought you'd gone out. Sorry." Owen heard footsteps, retreating back to the bedroom, and he levered himself upright. He hadn't moved much, in his sleep, the table was still where it had been, the blanket still around him. He sighed, stood, and folded the blanket, before going to return it to Mum's room.

When he'd done that, he came to the bedroom and cleared his throat. Clara was mostly dressed, he could see her fingers twisting in the mirror over the dresser as she did up the front of her frock. This one was blue, yesterday's had been yellow. Colours, the wide range of colours on people, that was still new. That people around him weren't wearing uniform colours, in their limited rainbow. She brushed out her hair with a few fierce strokes, and then pinned it up with quick almost angry twists, before she turned round to face him.

"Sorry." Owen didn't know what else to say.

"I didn't expect." Clara stopped and swallowed. "You weren't here when I woke up. I assumed you'd gone out. Or something."

"I'm sorry I scared you." That was true enough.

It was also enough to make her take another breath. "Breakfast? Do you need pointers to anything, what's open, what isn't?"

"I thought I'd take the coat back, there's a man at the Veterans Club who has a listing for jobs, and - other things." They hadn't been well explained, in the gossip he'd got so far. But he could go round and ask. "You'll be home for tea? I might go to the Corwins." She looked blank, and he added. "My apprentice master and his wife." He hoped they were still well. He hadn't heard from them in a while.

Clara nodded once, and answered the question he'd asked. "Half five, probably. I don't usually eat much for tea, last night was an exception. I could do an egg for you now, and toast, when I do mine? And there's chicken and veg in the keep-cold box, if you want that for your meal."

Owen got the sense she was ticking off things on a list. It wasn't as if he cared a great deal what food he ate, so long as there was some and it wasn't half mud or worse. "That's fine. Can I pick up anything on the way back? Bread or I don't know."

"Beer if you want some for yourself. I've tea, bread, there's milk and butter. Jam." She considered. "A bit of cheddar, getting hard."

He just nodded. "Should I put the kettle on?" He could do that much, he knew where it was and how the hob worked.

The offer visibly startled her, and she answered with a jerk of a nod. "Ta. I'll be another minute or two."

Owen got the kettle going, but he wasn't sure what tea she liked or chose. There were four tins out on a little shelf, and none of them had been Mum's choices. Owen wasn't sure what to do with that, what to make of the chamomile and lavender, or the mint, in place of Mum's black. Two minutes later, Clara came out, with a few bits of cosmetics on, something that made her eyes stand out, not that he knew what to call it. From there, she put an apron over her frock, and fried up eggs, as well as slicing bread. "Do you want yours toasted? I can do the charm for it."

That, now, that was definitely a luxury. It wasn't one he'd ever learned. "Please."

She did something with her hand, and then put the bread on a plate, before flipping two eggs onto it, and one onto her own plate. As she sat down, she handed the plate over and waited until he was eating before she buttered her own bread and tucked in. They ate in silence, though it didn't feel as oppressive as last night.

21

Once she was done, she took her plate to the sink, rinsing it. "Right. I should get off."

He wondered, all of a sudden, if he should offer to walk her to work, or meet her to walk back. But before he could ask that, she hesitated, kissed him on the cheek, and turned to go out the door without another word. And it left him staring after her, unsure what to make of any of it. Starting with why she'd given him two eggs, and herself only one.

He didn't know what things were dear now, and what things there were enough of. Not plenty, Owen was quite sure plenty wasn't really on offer. Maybe he could wander by a grocer and get a sense of some of it, or ask the Corwins. He'd been grateful for the additional egg, but he didn't know anything about the household. That bothered him, a great deal, how much was the same and how much was entirely unknown.

Most of all, he wondered about Clara. They'd been easy with each other, before. Oh, they'd been rushed and not nearly enough time, but he'd made her laugh and smile. She'd teased him, with a comfort that was entirely missing now. Owen knew some men had come home to find a wife taken up with someone else, but Owen didn't think that was it. Not the way she was, the little he'd seen, with a strict set of habits and her own spaces. Certainly, it didn't seem like she'd have brought anyone round here.

That reminded him that she'd made a list of things that would be handy. He could have a look at that, check his tools, and see what he was up for tackling sooner than later.

CHAPTER 4
JULY 17, TRELLECH

Two hours later, Owen at least had a sense of the space. There was only a nominal toolkit, other than his shoemaking tools, and he made notes of what nails and such he wanted on hand. Sandpaper too, something properly coarse and something finer, to take down a rough edge. That would do for the door that was sticking, too. Linseed oil, he'd thrown his bottle out last time he'd been in the kit years ago, so at least it hadn't gone rancid.

Owen went through the kit of his trade then, checking to see what he had, what he didn't. No leather, he'd sold that all off, he'd have to see about picking more up. That would be expensive to get much, he was sure. He rummaged in the trunk in the corner, figuring out what clothing he had, and finding a pair of age-stiffened boots. But he'd made them to fit his feet, years ago, and his feet hadn't changed. He'd get the oil today, loosen them up, and go from there.

Another twenty minutes, after changing into a respectable shirt and trousers and a lighter-weight jacket, he was out on the streets. He'd done one more charm against pests, and tucked the greatcoat over his arm. That would be his first stop. He made his way downstairs, first of all. The shop was quite busy, really, in different ways than when it had been briefly his and his alone. People came in and out, to see the barber. It seemed to be doing decent business.

Owen waited a couple of minutes until there was a pause in customers. "Morning, Wilson."

"Mister Hubbard. Heard you were on your way back." There was something a tad defensive in the comment. Not rude, exactly, and Owen had certainly heard a lot worse in the past few years, but decidedly prickly.

He held up his hand. "Clara made it clear the lease is yours through Lady Day. I don't know what my plans are yet, I'll let you know if we'll be ending the lease with as much notice as possible." For one thing, he was sure the rent from the lease was going a long way toward keeping things going. Though of course there'd be repairs and fees and all that due to Trellech.

Wilson nodded once and visibly relaxed. "We do well enough, I suppose, but it's been tight. I suppose with more men coming back." He hesitated. "Trim for you? Or do you want to be growing your hair out proper?"

"I'd like to grow it again. But a proper shave, tomorrow? And if you'd have a look at my razor and all?" It was a gesture in the right direction, Owen thought, a nod to professional mastery.

"Sure. First thing or last are easier. More time."

"First thing. Half eight?" That way, if he did decide to go look for work, he'd be well prepared for it. "Usual precautions?"

Wilson grunted, amused, and gestured at the small

metal pan ducked into the downstairs fireplace. "After every customer, while they can see it's done. Sweep, summon anything that's gone astray, burn it all."

"Grand." Owen didn't think anyone would bother to want his hair in particular, but that was one thing that had nagged at him, all through the trenches. He knew well enough the ways you could act on the hair to act on the man, at least in general. That part didn't take a Schola education, after all.

Then someone else came in, chattering to a friend and hailing Wilson with a hearty complaint about some tiny matter. Owen nodded without another comment and saw himself out the door. Master Thompson across the street looked busy, so he'd come back there later. He wanted to thank the man and see if he could even things up with a bit of help. Instead, he turned right to follow the streets through to the centre of Trellech.

The city wasn't terribly busy at this time of day, or at least it didn't seem so. People came and went briskly but cheerfully, as if there'd never been a war on. Or at least it looked that way until he got closer. Plenty of men, his age and younger and older. Some were missing an arm or a leg, with a cane or limp. Others had the jerky movement that meant things had got rattled inside their heads. He nodded briefly as he went past, and they did the same to him, recognising something alike enough.

Soon enough, he found himself in the shop that had once been something else. Now it was a waypoint for the Army, with a counter and a desk and various drawers and filing cabinets where stock had been kept. He waited his turn, through the four people before him, each of them going away with a silent, inward-turned dejection that didn't suggest anything promising.

The clerk looked up briefly, then took in the greatcoat. "Just demobbed?"

"Yes." Owen had to resist tacking on 'sir'. "The great-coat to return, and I'd appreciate any pointers about finding work."

The clerk looked down. "Name, rank, where you served? And your discharge papers, please."

"Owen Hubbard. Second Army." He gave the rest of the details automatically. He'd repeated them over and over again. He unfolded the papers from his pocket and handed them over.

The clerk looked up once as he wrote. "Passchendaele?"

Owen nodded at that. The clerk sniffed once, something that Owen couldn't begin to make sense of, and scratched at the paper more forcefully with his pen. There was quite a bit of that before the pen paused. "Greatcoat on the hanger there, please. All four limbs, both eyes, no gas?" The man counted out a few coins, pushing them back across the desk as Owen returned from hanging up the greatcoat.

It was a blunt way to put it. "A few injuries, now healed. Nothing disabling." He'd somehow been lucky there, for values of luck that had kept him away for a full year beyond most. "I'm a shoemaker by trade. I don't know if there's work for me at the moment in that." He flicked through the coins. Not much, but it was something.

The clerk nodded once. "You qualify for thirteen weeks' pay, while you look for work. You must report here Monday, Wednesday, Friday, to get your payment. See, here." He counted out another few coins. "24 shillings a week, but I assume you want that in our coin."

"Please, yes." That would be another bit of help if Clara was worried about money.

There was a bit more scratching on the papers, and then

the man handed them over. "Present those each time you come in." Then he considered. "So, you're used to hand tools. Not much work for that. Willing to live away from Trellech?"

"Not for long. I've a wife with a job here."

"Do you?" Another sniff, though this one had a different and decidedly disapproving quality to it. "We might have some work as the harvest comes in, farm labour. Temporary, of course. I can add your name to the list." He flicked through a piece of paper. "The Veterans Club has a board for postings. Mostly skilled labour." Clearly, the clerk considered himself too busy for most of that sort of thing.

Owen knew when pushing wouldn't help anything at all. "I appreciate it, sir." He didn't salute, but it was a near thing. His wrist twitched. He'd have to remember not to do that. "I'll come by Monday. Any particular time?"

"There's a line first thing, clears out by half nine, gets busy again before and after luncheon. We're closed for the noon hour, of course." It was getting on for eleven now, and Owen could take that hint.

"Monday, then." He made the brief obligatory gesture at politeness and then turned to go out. Next stop, to see if the Corwins were about. That took him past the Temple of Healing's massive entrance, across the corner of Portal Square, and into the Crafting Quarter. He ducked down one of the streets and came up in front of the shop. There were shoes in the window, but the lights were dim inside.

Owen knocked once and then tried the door. A bell rang as he entered, but there was no one visible in the shop. A moment later, Master Corwin came out of the back, apron around his waist. He blinked several times, as if the world had beaten him down, and this was at least a pleasant surprise. "Owen. Come in."

"Master Corwin." They'd never exactly been close. Master Corwin certainly wasn't an effusive sort. He got on with the work and did it well. But he'd been a decent apprentice master, and he'd taught Owen well, and that mattered. "Demobbed, finally. Got home last night."

"Ah." There was a gap there, an odd echo. "Not much work going, in shoes. Hard to get supplies. Fair amount of the trade going to factory-made." It came out gruff.

Owen held up his hands. "I'd like to get back to it, but - things have changed. I've changed." He couldn't figure out how to explain how he felt, but there was in fact something in him that didn't much want to be pinned down to steady work. Not right now. He'd have to sort through that. Sometime. "May I ask after your family?"

"My wife's tending to her brother. The family farm." Master Corwin hesitated. "He lost an arm. He's been in a bad way."

Owen sucked in air between his teeth. "Sorry to hear that, sir. And no apprentices now?" He didn't see any of the signs of one. Things weren't well dusted.

"No. No one to take it on." Master Corwin shrugged. "You have your tools back?"

"Tools, yes, but I need more linseed. And leather, eventually." He rubbed his fingers together. "Coin being scant."

"For most of us, boy, for most of us. Your wife?" Master Corwin pulled a stool over behind the shop counter, without offering Owen a seat.

"She's well, sir. Working for her aunt, still. It's an apothecary, she minds the counter." That was, he realised, about all he knew about her work. He had no idea of her pay, or much about her actual tasks.

"They'll have been kept busy then. How are your shoes?" Master Corwin raised an eyebrow.

"The uniform boots are awful, sir. Twenty ways round. I need to oil and loosen up my old boots, though. I've a last, but do you have oil I could buy off you? A small bottle?"

"Ah, that we can manage. At cost." Master Corwin stood, going into the back room. He came out a couple of minutes later with a sealed bottle and named the price. It was fair enough, and Owen wasn't going to argue about it. "Anything else you need?"

"Perhaps another visit in a week or two, sir, when I'm ready to see about buying a bit of leather. Even if it's dear."

That got Owen a grunt. "Certainly. Anything in particular?"

"Comfortable pair of shoes for myself. We'll see from there. Something sturdy. I don't care much about the colour. Brown, black, that doesn't matter." He wanted the work of it, to feel the process once again, as much as anything. Besides, he'd need to replace some of his clothes. He could adapt them to whatever shoes he made.

"I'll keep an eye out." Just then, another man came in, and Owen immediately nodded and stepped back. He knew better than to get in the way of business.

That just left the Veterans Club. He made his way back out to the main streets, down south toward Club Row. First, he had to present his papers and get himself properly recorded as a member of the club. The man tending the desk passed across a pamphlet. "Rules, obligations, opportunities. We're still serving luncheon, inexpensive meals."

"Please." Owen didn't want to fuss with going somewhere else. "And who do I speak to about whatever jobs are on offer?"

"That's Peterkin, over in the alcove there. When you're ready." At that, he was shown off to a table in a long room. There were spaces for two or four to eat, and most of them were full. Owen was seated opposite a man with a space free, who looked up, nodded once, and went back to reading his copy of the Trellech Moon. The meal was, as described, inexpensive. It was just bread, drippings, a bit of roast in a thin gravy and more vegetables, but tasty enough.

When he was done eating, he counted out the coin for the meal, piece by piece. Peterkin, in the alcove, looked up as Owen approached. "Not met you before, sir?"

"Owen Hubbard. Just demobbed, looking for work. I'm a shoemaker by trade, but I've no workshop nor materials. I'd like a bit of work to get myself settled. I'm good with hand tools, anything similar."

"No mechanical skills?" Peterkin trailed his fingers down a list. "And did you apprentice?"

"With Master Corwin. He'll give me a good character but he doesn't have work for me."

"Most of the shoes are made by one of the factories now, or somewhat like." Peterkin looked up. "Can you do fine work?"

"I have in the past. Is that where the business is?" That would take more of an investment in the materials, and some practice. Fancy people wanted fancy shoes with decorative flourishes and cutwork, and a personal last, and all of that took a skilled hand.

"A fair bit of it. Especially if you can do charmwork for fit, or decoration." Peterkin finished going through the list. "Nothing right now. You're welcome to check in. You can put your details on file, too, in case someone is looking for a specific skill. There might be some work from harness makers, or perhaps luggage."

Neither of which were things Owen particularly wanted to focus on, but the skills could cross over, yes. "How do I let you know my particulars?"

Peterkin handed over a pamphlet. "Take that and fill it in at your leisure. Most people want to sleep on it, check dates and so on. Bring it back, and we'll file the details."

Owen nodded. "Appreciate it." He glanced over his shoulder. "Someone else to talk to you. I'll be back tomorrow, most like." With a nod, he went back out, circling through the streets to get a few dozen nails and that sandpaper. He stopped to pick up a bit of beer, and a modest hunk of cheese to replace the rather hard bit left in the kitchen. Finally, he came back to the flat to wait for Clara to come home.

CHAPTER 5
JULY 29, HESTER'S FLAT

"Sit, sit. Thaddeus, don't put that in your sister's mouth. Play nicely." The five-year-old boy looked up, blinked, and then set down the nut he'd been trying to get his younger sister, Marigold, to eat. The children settled into a less noisy bit of play in the corner. "Pardon, Clara, you know how it is."

Clara did not know how it was. Or rather, she knew how it was when she visited Hester. Three children, spaced two years apart - the youngest was sleeping in a bassinet, a few feet from Hester's chair. Hester looked well, honestly. Plump and well-fed, in a way that wasn't that common for most these days. And the house looked grand. They'd moved just before baby Phillipa was born into a larger flat. There were three rooms for the children and a pleasant and spacious sitting room with a lovely view of one of the gardens.

It wasn't anything like Clara knew, not directly. She'd grown up with an entirely different aunt, who'd packed her off to Aunt Lillian when she turned sixteen. She'd been old enough then she could properly handle some of the necessary registers in an apothecary. She didn't remember her parents terribly well. They'd both died when she was six, a boat that had gone down in a storm. Aunt Margaret was tidy and no-nonsense, and she hadn't been cruel. But she hadn't known what to do with a child, and it had showed.

Aunt Lillian hadn't known what to do with a child, either, but she did know what to do with a helper. Once - when someone had brought in a rather nice bottle of sherry as an extra bit of thanks - they'd got a bit tipsy. Aunt Lillian had suggested Clara could properly apprentice, but that it would take money. And of course, neither of them had that to spare. The apothecary apprenticeships were trickier than most, they wanted people not to apprentice with family. They would have had to negotiate the connections carefully. And usually pay a fair bit to make up for the fact that an apprentice wouldn't be able to take on much of the actual work for a bit.

Clara didn't understand all the restrictions, but she understood what they meant. Aunt Lillian would be in the back room, making things, and Clara would be in the front of the shop, tending the counter and doing the maths. She didn't mind it, generally, but it wasn't going to change. It wasn't going to give her space for things to change. If she hadn't moved in with Owen's Mum, if they hadn't already owned the building through a twist of fortune, she'd be living in a single room in a rooming house somewhere.

"Clara?" She'd missed something. Obviously. Hester didn't have a lot of patience with that.

"Sorry." She reached for the tea. "Wool-gathering. Or whatever you want to call it. You were saying?"

"You must be so happy Owen's back. And perhaps ready for your own little ones? Just such a blessing, you can't imagine."

Clara could feel herself freeze in place. And then she cursed at herself. She'd known perfectly well this was the line of conversation she'd get from Hester. Hester was entirely predictable that way. Hester was nice, everyone knew that. She never hesitated to volunteer to help with something. It didn't change whether she was at the Temple of Healing, or the Women's Institute, or some other gathering that needed what she called "willing hands". Ever since they'd met in one of the wards, Hester had been kind enough to invite Clara around for tea every fortnight or so, give her hand-me-down clothes, introduce her to other people.

But Hester hadn't had to worry about money. They weren't rich, of course. Oscar, Hester's husband, was something in the Ministry, a mid-level clerk who did something with supplies. Hester had never really specified what he did, but Clara had never really asked. It was work she'd likely have enjoyed, mind. Clara liked lists and order and making all the sums add up sensibly. But she didn't have the contacts to get a Ministry job either. Even during the War, it had all been people with connections, or people who'd already worked there, or both, like Oscar.

"It's, well." Clara swallowed. "It's not like you and Oscar. It's very new having him home."

"Surely you've had some time to catch up with each other? I remember what you were like when you got married, you disappeared for days. It's been, what, a fortnight? Plenty of time to get to know each other intimately again."

Some of that, right after the wedding, had been time in private. But his Mum had been right across the hall, and poorly, and it wasn't as if there was much privacy in the flat. Neither of them had known the proper charms to keep things really quiet. Even if they had, they'd both have been too worried she'd call out, needing something, and they'd miss it. What they'd done in bed, in those few days, had been something. But it wasn't enough to build a life on now.

Owen went out every day, not like some women whose husbands had come back from the War and hid inside. He'd spend time helping Master Thompson, then looking for other work. He was diligent. She had to give him that, but it didn't bring them any closer. If anything, it was more of a distance. He was doing things he didn't share with her.

Clara considered that particular line for a moment. Then, hesitantly, she looked up. "I think the wedding carried us through, the rush of it. But his mum was poorly, and he only had a few days of leave left, and - now, picking up is different."

Saying it out loud made it real, in a way it hadn't quite been yet. That made her flinch and reach for the teacup, to give herself something to do. "I go to work. He goes out and looks for work. No luck yet."

"Well, everyone needs shoes. I'm sure it will be fine." Hester dismissed the entire issue as needless worry. Clara wasn't at all so easy with it. She hadn't talked much with Owen about it, but she'd seen him counting out coins and pricing out leather one night. She didn't know all the relevant parts. It wasn't like pricing out a new variant for Aunt Lillian, what they should charge for it, but she knew what that expression on someone's face meant.

"He's looking for other work, too." Clara hesitated. "I've never really asked. I don't think Owen wants something in the Ministry. He likes working with his hands too much." Always keeping them busy, she'd noticed that, nearly the first thing. "But what does Oscar do, precisely?"

"Oh, goodness. Well, he's had that promotion last year. When we moved, it was just enough to make us properly comfortable now. And Doris, our help, well, she's delightful and skilled and knows just what's needed." That was right, they had a woman who came in three days a week for the heavy cleaning and some of the cooking. As opposed to Clara, who was doing all that and working, beside.

"Oscar works for the Treasury, of course. The Supplies division. Normally they're just involved with, oh, supplies for the Guard and the Penelopes, and all that. Other Ministry departments. But of course, during the War, they've had much more responsibility, and it looks like some of that is staying. Negotiating agreements with the incapables and their Ministry." Hester wrinkled up her nose.

People without magic. Owen had said very little about that. Clara had always lived among others with magic, and she knew Owen had, growing up in Trellech. But he'd mentioned, a couple of times, serving with people, most of whom didn't. Where he'd had to hide his magic, like everyone in Albion who'd made the Pact when they reached the age of twelve. Like Clara had too, of course. He'd been able to keep his boots a bit more dry, and his bedding a bit more free of pests. Though there were obvious limits to that, given the lice in the greatcoat.

"I suppose that's very important, yes. What kinds of supplies, do you know?" Clara was mostly just trying to make conversation now. She'd rather keep Hester off the topics like being bedded and children that were far too much for Clara's comfort.

"Oh, supplies. He doesn't talk much about the details. A bit about the wonderful people he's had a chance to meet. He got to do a tour of the warehouses at the Temple of

Healing. I told you that, I think, back when I was lending a hand."

"I do remember that." It had mostly gone in one ear and out the other. "Maybe they need a hand, still. In their store-rooms, or as an orderly or something? Or a handyman. I'll mention it to Owen."

"There, now. That's a proper thing for a wife. I'm sure he'd be glad to find something, and then you could stop working and keep house properly. I know it's a strain on you, poor dear."

Clara managed not to jerk her head up to look at Hester. She hadn't thought about that at all. Certainly, Aunt Lillian hadn't hinted at it, Clara would have noticed. Aunt Lillian was not, on the whole, a hinter. She'd say straight out what she thought. And all she'd been doing was encouraging Clara to go home a little early on slow afternoons. "I like my work." It sounded pale, entirely vapid. It was true, though. Clara liked making things be orderly, making sure the information added up, that they had enough stock of materials that Aunt Lillian could make what was needed. "I suppose we'll see."

It sounded weak, but Hester didn't seem to notice. "You should have a new frock or two. Something a bit more stylish. The War's over, we don't need to look drab. Now's the time to bring the brightness back."

"Money's still - well. Until he gets some work."

"Oh, I'm sure I've a thing or two you could make over. Or patch something together. I had that length of blue linen, the wrong shade for me, and Oscar doesn't care for it. Too close to the Guard uniform blue, and he gets enough of that at work, he says. But it would look well on you, and you could fill it out with some cream or white, bring out your complexion."

Clara had had only a couple of new frocks during the War. Well, new to her. Two of them had come from Aunt Margaret as Christmas presents, and Clara had remade them. She was wearing one of them now. Aunt Margaret had found them in a second-hand shop, and she'd had a great eye for colour, but they were getting worn now.

"If you're sure?" Clara asked hesitantly.

"Just doing my bit for the returning soldiers." Hester's eyes gleamed with a touch of teasing edging into mischief, before she pitched her voice sharper. "Thaddeus, no. You know Mama doesn't like that."

The children were behind Clara now, and she raised an eyebrow. "What's he up to?"

"A bottle of ink." Hester sounded disapproving. "Bring that here, Thaddeus. Do not dip your sister's hair in it. There we go, there's a good boy." She capped the ink without really paying attention to it and set it down on the table by her tea. "Do you want a biscuit, sweetie, for being a good boy?"

Clara rather suspected that had been Thaddeus's intention all along. He was not a dim-witted sort of boy. She waited until Hester had handed over one of the biscuits, before asking, "Are you doing much volunteering at the moment? There's the second set of the garden parties. You did such a fine job with the cut flowers last time."

"Oh, my, that was my news! Not the garden party, dear Clara, but I got an invitation for an interview to join the Vestigial Flowers. You know, they're the ones that see to the proper flowers for the Temple of Healing functions, and flowers for the shrines and such that aren't done by other people. Quite prestigious, of course, they only ask the right sorts."

Clara had thought at the time that flowers were

perfectly lovely, but that most men who'd been invalided back with injuries didn't care much what the flowers were. The Vestigial Flowers, as a society of women, had always seemed to her caught up on their own little rules and methods. Harmless enough, she supposed, but they weren't actually much use.

Not that she'd say that to Hester, of course. "Do tell me more. Have they told you much about the process?" That could keep them comfortably chatting for a good half hour. By that point, she really should get home and see about tea and setting up things for the next day.

CHAPTER 6
AUGUST 3RD, THEIR FLAT

Owen came home and put the kettle on, measuring out the nettle-mint tisane, rather than the actual tea. That was more dear, and he needed a drink more than he needed the tea specifically. He'd spent all day walking from office to warehouse through Club Row, seeing if anyone had work, or needed someone. He'd had a handful of comments about harvest, check back in a fortnight, but none of that helped now.

The money he got from the Army wasn't much. Enough to cover his food, give or take. He'd picked up, in his conversations, that prices had gone up a fair bit. He'd had to do the money conversions back and forth, but it was a shilling on the pound, nearer two by now. That made it ten per cent. He was used enough to doing the maths when it came to materials.

Which was why he was sitting at the kitchen table, about to drink a mug that tasted too much of greenness and mint. Not that the mint was bad, he'd have killed for the mint a year or two ago. And why he was feeling more than a tad guilty for the leather he'd laid out. It had been half his pay for the week. But Master Corwin had had some extra to sell on at cost. There was enough muted black leather to make a pair of cap-toe lace-up boots for himself, and maybe consider another pair too. It had been part of a special order, where Master Corwin had bought the hide.

Owen let his hands run over the leather, feeling the pliability of it, the way it gave under his fingers. He'd been oiling and stretching his old boots, but they still weren't where he wanted them to be, and the leather was scratched and worn enough to show.

And his uniform boots, well, the less said about them, the better. The right sole was disintegrating again. That made him pull them out, because he'd been wondering about that, and he'd not had his tools to fully explore them. He knew - he'd chatted up one of the supply clerks at one point - that they'd been made on a number of different patterns by a range of makers. His boots hadn't fit well, and no one much cared about that. Jack, the supply clerk, had said they cared more about hard wear than fit.

On the one hand, it wasn't like that was different from the rest of the uniform. On the other hand, it had offended Owen's sensibilities from the beginning. A man lived or died by his feet, particularly in the trenches, and that attitude wasn't on. His were well broken in. He'd had them since early in 1916, the older B2 pattern, with the horizontal line for better waterproofing. They'd been resoled twice and patched once.

But he could see how the sole was fragmenting around the sole studs and the heel plate. And the leather had been poorly tanned, all the ways it was giving way with cracks and damage now. Mind, they'd got him through four years of fighting, without his feet getting more wet than average.

Running his fingers over the rough spots, though, made

him quietly furious again. This was badly managed, is what it was. It wasn't expensive leather, of course, but good boots could be made out of cheaper leather, if it were prepared proper. He'd had to replace the laces every month or two, as they snapped and frayed, and a bit better quality would have changed that. Had, when he'd had a chance to buy his own on a short leave.

His fingers worked inside the back heel, where he'd rubbed his skin raw with a bit of thread that hadn't been pulled through and tight properly. A small thing, but he'd seen three men with infections from that inside a week, when they first got the boots. Then he'd twigged to it and worked out how to tuck the extra out of the way and patch it a bit. That had used a bit of magic, mind, when no one could see, to make the inside smooth.

It wasn't just the boots, of course. It was the tins of food, half of which tasted nothing like they ought to. Some of which were spoiled, long before they got to the troops, and some of which were just awful. The muck of the trenches. The way the decisions made no sense. Not that Owen had ever had training in warfare, whatever that looked like. But repeating the same thing that hadn't worked the last twenty times was the sort of thing he expected of a toddler, not someone with training.

He considered the food in the kitchen. He'd thought, when he first got back to Trellech, that his appetite would catch up with him. But no, everything tasted odd. Not enough salt, too much texture. They were ridiculous complaints. It wasn't like saying the bread was too fresh would make sense to anyone else, except another veteran. And none of them wanted to talk about it, at least none Owen had run into yet.

He picked up his tools. Owen had got wood, too, to

make proper lasts. He had his old ones, of course, but carving the wood would help him get the feel of things back in his hands. He'd always found it soothing. And he felt like his feet from before and his feet now were different, in some way he couldn't explain, even in his own head. So he'd settled down to take measurements.

Owen was finishing that up when there was the sound of the front door. Clara stood there for a moment, one hand full of a net bag with half a dozen small things in it. "Oh. You're home already?" She took in the table. "Have been for a bit?"

"No work." It came out more brusque than he'd meant to, but it wasn't as if there was an easy way to say he'd failed again. "I'll try again tomorrow." He hesitated. "Maybe something in a fortnight, for the harvest. I can ask about the hops, too. And Master Thompson needs a hand tomorrow, and he's insisting on paying a bit for it."

"That'd be Kent. Long journey." Owen couldn't read Clara's tone at all, whether it was disapproving or what.

"Gather the Edgartons will let people through their portal for it. By arrangement. But it'd mean being gone for a week or three." It wasn't great pay, either, though he'd get room and board in a shared cottage. It'd be somewhere he was actually doing something useful.

Clara nodded. "I couldn't go."

He hadn't expected she would, but now he gaped. "Didn't think you would. You've the shop." He then turned away, unable to face her, or what she thought.

She came past, behind him, into the kitchen, to put things away. "We don't have much for our tea. Bread, dripping, I got an early apple we can split, a bit of cheese. Eggs for the morning." She glanced at the table, which still had his materials out. "I can do a proper shop on market day, Thursday."

Owen flinched slightly. "Needed the leather. Here's what I've got left." He rummaged in his pockets, pulling out his coin purse and turning over the coins. She eyed it, moving one coin aside with her finger to count it up.

"Be a lot of dripping and bread, then. We need more sugar if you want it for your tea." She turned away, so that Owen could hear the sharpness in her voice, but not see her face.

If he'd been his father, there would have been a roar here, all about being the man of the house, and being the one who set the priorities. He wasn't his dad, he never had been, and he'd never wanted to be. The old man had his moments. He'd taken good care of Owen and Mum. He'd been a hard worker. That was why they owned the building, that and a bit put aside from Dad's dad, who'd died younger than expected.

But Owen couldn't do that. It wasn't Clara's fault they were skint. It wasn't Owen's either, mind, but it certainly wasn't hers. She was careful with the sums. She'd made bread Sunday rather than going round the baker. It was Owen who'd agreed the roof needed mending. That would take the rent from downstairs for the next few months, and had best be done before they got into winter on all counts.

He wouldn't roar. Even if it might make him feel better. Instead, he just let out a breath. "Let me clean up. Get out of your way for a bit."

She nodded once, and Owen set to work packing everything away. That was a bother, too. Before, in that dreamy golden nostalgic before, he'd had a workshop where he could leave things out. Where his tools were safe and sound, and he knew just where to lay hands on them. He hadn't needed to take ten, twenty, thirty minutes to lay things out before he started, and the same amount after he finished. Or to do it to Clara's schedule, so she could eat her tea at a reasonable hour.

When he came back from putting his toolkit away, she'd laid out a barren tea indeed. She'd made a pot, adding two precise sugar lumps to his teacup before she poured, then putting the sugar tin back on the counter. Bread, dripping, half an apple, a thumb knuckle of cheese.

They ate in near silence, bar her offering him the last slice of apple. Clara retreated to her chair, with a basket of mending, setting a charmlight so she could see better. Owen did his best to not disturb her, which meant he spent the evening reading the paper. It wasn't much of a life, for all it was dry and snug here.

At half-nine, she went off to change for bed, and they fell into the same awkward routine. Most nights, she curled up on her side, as if she was trying to take up the least space possible in bed. He lay there awkwardly, not sure if he should or could touch her, even in the small ways. They'd had sex four times now, and she'd been willing enough - kind about it, even. She'd been the one to ask him three out of the four times. But when they were done, she'd twist away from him again without much of a comment.

Most nights, he lay there for a good hour or two, counting out the time by the faint sound of the city bells. Some nights, he curled up on the sitting room floor again. Others, he eventually fell asleep, until he jolted awake the next morning when her alarm went off and she woke up.

There were worse lives, but he was fairly sure there were also better ones. And yet, he had no idea how to get one of those. Or rather, how someone like him got one of those. He wasn't even sure, honestly, what better looked like, in any sort of detail. A job that paid decently, that gave him some dignity. A world that meant Clara didn't have those furrows between her eyes of concentration and worry. Possibly a world in which he could make her laugh again, like when they first met.

But of course, they weren't remotely the same people as they had been then.

CHAPTER 7

AUGUST 10, THE APOTHECARY

Tuesday morning, Clara opened up the shop a bit early. Aunt Lillian had gone up north to her friend's in Scotland for a bit of quiet and restorative highland air. She did it most years, in the tail of the summer, before children went back to school, but the shop always felt empty when she did.

She had left the shop very well stocked and had made the usual arrangements with Master Luther and Mistress Salah for any request that wasn't on the shelves. In turn, Aunt Lillian would cover them for their own holidays in the winter. It worked out well on all fronts, though Master Luther had a rather more posh sort of apothecary business. Clara liked how they were companionable about it. Probably it was easier to swap that sort of thing with Aunt Lillian - competent but not at all flashy - than with a closer competitor.

It also meant that Clara was at something of a loose end. Life with Owen had settled into more or less a routine. She made a roast and loaves of bread on Sunday, to last through most of the week. They shared a bed, but precious little intimacy. In the morning, she made breakfast for them both, and then she came to work, and he went and looked for it. Entirely unsuccessfully so far, even the harvest work seemed to have fallen through. It had gone to people who were known, who had connections.

Clara was tired, to be honest. Tired to be the one to have to think about all the pieces. Doing the maths on how to make the food last was not at all what she enjoyed. It was better than going to bed hungry, because they'd run out of bread or something else filling, but that did not make it pleasurable. And whatever enjoyment they'd had with each other had gone like a puff of smoke. All the enchantment drained out of it. It had left what had been love and humour, a bit of crumbling clay, or the residue from a bit of alchemical work, whatever the word for that was.

At the same time, it wasn't horrible. They were having a difficult spell. She'd heard more than enough about it from other women before Owen had come home. And whatever else, he was at least kind. He hadn't yelled or slammed doors or broken crockery, or any of that. He didn't wake up in the night screaming. She wouldn't have held that sort of thing against him, it wasn't as if he could control his dreams, but she was glad of her own sleep.

He'd been considerate in bed, and it wasn't bad. But it also wasn't good. She was taking her contraceptive potion every day. She'd kept up with it all along, seeing as how it also made her monthly far more manageable. Aunt Lillian had a particularly good line in that sort of thing, and it was one that kept them in a steady trade. It wasn't too dear, and Clara would certainly cut more meat and sugar out of the shopping before she gave it up. She wasn't deft enough to use - or trust - some of the charms, and they didn't help as much with the rest of it, she'd always heard.

It was a quiet enough morning, anyway. Where she'd normally have taken a proper lunch break, upstairs in Aunt Lillian's flat above the shop, she stayed downstairs. She couldn't really eat at the counter, too much chance of something not good for one getting in the food by chance. Instead, she took ten minutes out at the back door, perched in the chair that overlooked the small garden.

All of that meant she was on the tall stool with a seat-back, a book propped open on the counter, when a man came in. She'd seen him come by a few times, but never when she was the one tending the counter. Usually around one or one-thirty, the way someone might come back from a longer luncheon.

"Afternoon, sir." Clara put on her best smile, the one that was free of any worries or concerns. "May I help you?" It was always a little delicate. It didn't do, in an apothecary, to make assumptions about what someone had come in for. It could as easily be a skin cream or a hair tonic as a potion for health or to treat some symptom.

The man blinked for a moment, as if not expecting to see her. "Is Lillian here?"

Which was also delicate, because Clara didn't want to say Aunt Lillian wasn't at home at all. "Her regular time off for the summer, sir. We're very well stocked, though. I'd be glad to bring out whatever you'd like to have a look at."

"Oh, yes, that's right." The man smiled at her, a generous smile, the way Owen had used to smile at her. He was older than she was, perhaps as much as twenty years. Well-established, she was used to weighing that up as quickly as she counted pills out for packaging. The man had good shoes, properly polished, not scuffed or worn at all. His suit was just as well tailored. Nothing flashy or to-the-minute, but more of a classic style. She could glimpse a pocket watch chain, which suggested a steady amount of money. "I'm Morris. Horatio Morris. I've a business down the way. I wandered into the shop, oh, months ago. There's a hair tonic I rather like."

Also a delicate question to ask about, because some of the tonics were for men who were balding, or women who were losing hair, or some such. And others were to add lustre and weight and silkiness, the kind of thing most people would want. He kept his hair on the shorter side, so whatever he did, it probably didn't benefit from the weight of the magic in the length. They had a tonic specifically for that, for the people who wanted all the history of their hair to lend weight to their enchantments. "Do you recall the name, sir? Or the colour of the bottle, that's how many people do it."

"Ah, aren't you thoughtful?" He bestowed it like a general blessing. "Your name, dear lady? And it's the purple bottom, with the shoulders to it, there."

That was one of the ones for good hair growth, not one of the more embarrassing options. The bottle had a curve to it, certainly, though if you'd asked Clara, she'd have blushed and thought it more bosom than shoulders. Then she realised she hadn't answered his question. "Clara P - pardon. Hubbard." She'd had the married name for long enough. Why on earth did she stumble over it now?

"Clara Hubbard." His eyes flicked to her hands. "Married?"

"Sir!" She made it a bit of an amused comment. She was, in fact, married, and she should not be a tease, for all sorts of reasons. Instead, she turned and moved the rolling step stool into place. She climbed carefully up, reaching for the bottle, then rearranging the others behind it to be properly in line and look as they should.

When she stepped down, he was looking at her approvingly. "Very tidy." He nodded at the bottle, and she could only assume she meant the bottle. She glanced at the price to confirm, though she knew it perfectly well. She'd priced out everything in the shop so many times now. "Anything else, sir?"

"Hmm." He tilted his head. "Perhaps some soap. Could you bring out half a dozen bars, the ones you like best, you think are Lillian's best work?"

Something in that comment made Clara tilt her head. "I've helped with the soaps, sir, and a few of the other things like that. Did you wish for a proper apothecary soap, with the enchantments and all, or just something that smells lovely?"

"Oh, bring out the ones you made. I'm looking for something for my housekeeper, as a little treat. I made rather a mess she's dealing with. And perhaps something for Cook, as well."

"Indeed, sir." Posh enough to have a housekeeper, not just - from the sounds of it - someone who came in for the day once or twice a week. And a cook. Clara reached under the counter, bringing out one of the clever little wooden trays. She'd talked Aunt Lillian into getting a couple after seeing them from one of the woodcrafters. They were a glowing cherry wood, and something in the colour made the glass bottles and tinted paper wrappings of their various items sing. It also made pulling items out of different cases much easier to manage. It wasn't just more dignified, she was far less likely to drop something, or need to scurry back and forth.

Clara took a moment to select several of the soaps. On a whim, she brought out the rather adorable little sample soaps they had pressed into carved moulds of flowers.

There was a rose, that one had come out well, and violet. Also the one that had half a dozen herbs in it, lavender and mint and hyssop and a little lemon. And then the spices. She added the sample jar of two of the skin creams, too.

"Here we are, sir. If it's for your housekeeper, I'm thinking she wouldn't want the more masculine scents. We have others that are more like heather and evergreen and juniper."

"Ah, she might like the juniper, dear old soul, but no, I think you are right. And it is still summer and a time for flowers. These are quite lovely. However did you get them into those shapes?"

Clara refused to babble here. "We use moulds, sir, for the shapes. The rose is very popular here, though it's a bit more dear on the price. The herbal one here, also very popular." And rather cheaper, given that several of the plants - the mint, especially - grew near enough like weeds.

He took his time considering, smelling each of them, glancing up at her for a reaction, then trying the next. In the end, he chose the rose, and also a small jar of the rose cream, when she suggested it might be a particularly nice touch. "You do have a lovely set of packaging. So many places, my former apothecary, it's all quite dire. Amber bottles, all the same, like little rows of soldiers. You've such colours here. And can you wrap that up in a bit of something pretty?"

"Certainly, sir." Clara busied herself with finding a small cardboard box that they'd fit in. She nestled the bar of soap against the box, packing a piece of deep pink tissue paper to hold the jar in place. All of that steady, she closed the lid and tied it in place with a bit of matching ribbon. "Here you are, sir."

"Horatio, please."

"Oh, I couldn't, Master Morris." Clara could feel herself blushing.

He handed over the coins for the payment, and added, "There's a bit extra, isn't there? Keep that, I don't need the change. I should get off, have a meeting at two I need to do a thing before."

There was, in fact, a bit extra, though not enough that she felt she couldn't accept. She felt herself blush again, but nodded. "I hope your housekeeper enjoys them, sir. Pleasant day to you."

Clara stared off after him, as the door closed behind him and the bell on the door fell still. The rest of the afternoon was a steady stream of custom. It was as if he'd raised the river to some useful level, like a lock did, making it easy for people to think of them. It was one of the better Tuesdays they'd had in a long time, in fact. By the time she locked up at half-five, she was feeling downright cheerful.

On her way back, she passed one of the flower stalls. Feeling the coin in her purse, she stopped and considered. There were a bunch of flowers, still good, but clearly on their way out. "How much?"

She had just enough, and she bought them in a fit of impulse. By the time she got home, Owen was seated at the kitchen table, having put together his own bread and jam for tea. He looked her up and down. "Flowers?"

"Yes." Clara turned away to find something to put them in, a proper vase Owen's Mum had kept a few, not that Clara had had them out much.

"Any reason?" Owen's voice was neutral behind her.

"We had a particularly good day at the shop, and someone told me to keep the change." She didn't turn round, fussing over them, and pulling off a couple of petals that were decidedly worse for wear.

"Last night, you told me how tight the money was. And now flowers?" His voice had taken on a much less pleasant edge.

Clara turned, her hands bracing against the counter. "Maybe we need a bit of pretty. Maybe it'd help." She didn't take the vase and dash it at his feet. She was better than that, but she pushed away from the counter, past him, and into the bedroom. He didn't follow her, and she hated that even more than everything before it.

In fact, he left her alone for ages. The bells chimed for six, then seven, then eight. The light was starting to fade when there was finally a knock. She'd long since curled up in bed, reading a tattered book she'd bought secondhand three years ago. Or rather, not reading it. It wasn't as if the words were sticking in her head at all, even if she knew the story. It was a telling of the founding of Albion, Brutus and the giants and the beautiful ladies who'd come out of mist and forests as Brutus and the others made their home.

There was a knock on the door. "Pardon." He came round to the end of the bed, but didn't try to get closer. "I'm sorry."

Clara couldn't look at him. She certainly didn't want to. And she didn't much want his apology.

"The flowers are very pretty. Look. I am sorry. You know if we could spare a little." That at least got her to glance at him, but she couldn't read his expression or his tone at all. It was rather like the book that way, going across her eyes and not registering as it should. "I'll sleep on the sofa. Next to the sofa. Whatever. Let me just get a few things."

He didn't say anything else as he gathered up whatever he needed, and neither did she.

CHAPTER 8
AUGUST 13, THE FIELD ON CLUB ROW

Owen frowned as he stopped in front of The Field. He'd never been in before. This was the club for people who'd gone to Schola and ended up in one of their houses. Horse, this one, that was obvious enough from the sign, as well as the name. The sign was nicely made, actually. Owen appreciated the craftsmanship, and it had been recently repainted. A white horse stood in a green field, with a swath of blue sky and a small herd of other horses grazing nearby. It looked like an idealised countryside, the sort that couldn't possibly be real.

But this was where he was supposed to meet someone who could help. Barry, who'd been in the regiment with him, had said this presumably posh Schola man would. Owen had come across Barry three days ago, purely by chance, near a pub. They'd had a drink, and it had been hard not to be jealous. Barry had got demobbed much earlier. He'd been a builder before the War, and that sort of work got priority again. Barry had been in glowing good health, newly married, and with money in his pocket. He'd paid for Owen's pint, for that matter.

Barry hadn't said much about the man, just that he could be found by asking at the front desk on a Friday afternoon. And if the man didn't have time then, he'd set up a time. The only other thing he'd told Owen was not to be surprised. That was exactly no help at all.

So Owen took a breath, and went up the stairs. He noticed that there was a ramp built out to the side, running along half of the building, then meeting the landing at the top. It was half-hidden by some fence work that made the appearance more uniform from the street, tidily made. At the door, someone in a green suit opened the door, bowing him into a foyer with honey-coloured wood, and murmured. "May I direct you, sir?"

Owen glanced around. The place wasn't nearly as posh as he'd expected. Oh, it was made well, and designed better, if anything. The woodwork was highly polished, but built for use, with bare floors rather than rugs or carpeting. He could hear people off to both sides, the clink of cutlery on plates. Owen let out a breath. "A friend of mine, Barry Wadlow, told me to ask here. That there's someone who might help with a bit of work, who's here on Friday afternoons?"

"Certainly, sir." The man at the door held up his hand, and another man, older - too old to have fought - came over. "Another one for Master Soltani, Greg. Could you take him through?"

Greg - or so Owen supposed he must be - just nodded. "Come this way, sir. He's in one of the smaller sitting rooms." They seemed to find this an entirely ordinary sort of occurrence. Greg led him down that broad hallway, past a couple of smaller rooms off to each side, and Owen refused to crane his neck to peer inside.

Some were quieter than others. One had a decided smell of cigars and cigarettes, which meant it was likely a smoking room. Another had what sounded like a billiards table or something close to it. Then they took a right, along the end of the building. Greg knocked, heard some sort of reply, opened the door. The room inside was much smaller, maybe the size of the sitting room at home, ten by ten or twelve by twelve.

Inside, a man was sitting at a table with a handful of papers in front of him. Owen thought he might have been looking out the window, before the knock on the door. It wasn't like he'd had a pen out to write. The sun was behind him, so it took Owen a minute to realise the man was decidedly dark skinned. He was a brown that matched the hues of the wood, more than anything darker. And he was wearing the sort of colours men simply didn't in England, a scarlet red and wheat gold. More common in Albion, those, but still not all that often.

"Another for you, Master Soltani. Do you need anything?"

The man tilted his head, as if evaluating Owen, and Owen felt ashamed at that, all of a sudden. "My usual, please. What do you like in a beer, then? My shout." That was aimed directly at Owen.

Owen coughed. He hadn't been going to have one, but if it was someone else's tab. "I like the Old Sprout, the newest one, if you have it on tap? Something dark if you don't." He could use the, whatever you called it, nutritive properties. But the Old Sprout brewery had been going since his grandfather's day, and the current batch, while weaker than before the War, wasn't bad.

"Be right back then, sir." Greg disappeared, leaving Owen standing in the doorway.

The other man kept tilting his head. "Do come in, have a chair." He moved suddenly, rolling slightly. "I bring my own." It was only then Owen made sense of what he was sitting in, a wooden wheeled chair, much less bulky than the hospital chairs he'd seen. "Would you be more comfortable in an easy chair or at the table?"

At the table, he'd be able to fiddle with something in his fingers, if he needed to. It wouldn't be nearly so exposed. "The table, if you don't mind." Owen cleared his throat. "Door closed?"

"Please. Greg will just be a minute or two. Who sent you along?" His voice was very cheerful, as if he talked to dozens of new people a day, and found each of them a delight in some way. That was no more real than the pretty picture on the sign was, Owen was sure of it.

"Barry Wadlow. We served together." Owen found he couldn't bring himself to say much, but then he offered his name. "I'm Owen Hubbard."

"Pleased to meet you! I'm Golshan Soltani. Do call me Golshan, near everyone does." There was a flashing grin. "Do have a seat. We'll save anything complicated for after the beer comes. It is a Friday afternoon."

Owen nodded, finally moving to sit in the chair. It, too, was more comfortable than he'd expected, with that same well-made polish through the building. Then he looked up at the man across the table from him, who was looking at him with that same curious expression.

"You're not a Schola man, clearly." Golshan's voice was pleasant, still, but there was a hint of bubbling laughter.

Owen looked down sharply. "No. Sir."

"Hey." That was immediate and sharp. No, not sharp.

Direct, but it didn't have edges. "I was a private in the trenches, just like you were. Well, to start. They bumped me up to Corporal, eventually. And I'll tell you a secret. Schola men put on their trousers one foot at a time like everyone else."

It made Owen blink that the man picked that particular idiom, but it meant he looked up. Golshan was leaning his elbows on the table, the sort of informality that posh blokes could get away with, but it looked entirely natural. "Not a Schola man, no. Apprenticed. I was a shoemaker before the War, had my own shop."

"There, that's a fine start." Golshan waved a hand at the space. "I live with a man who's a glorious carpenter and his wife, and their baby. I appreciate proper crafting, even if I care a bit less about the shoes for my own sake these days."

Owen coughed again. It wasn't the sort of thing one could ask about, even if the other person laid it out in public like that.

Golshan caught the moment, but before he could say anything else, there was a knock on the door. When Golshan called out "Come in," the door opened, bringing in Greg with a tray. He put a pint of the Old Sprout in front of Owen, and something that looked like cider in front of Golshan, and then a plate of sandwiches between them.

"Apple and cheddar." Golshan said. "Go ahead, please. As much as you like. The cider's up from where I live in Cumbria. They keep it on tap for me."

Owen couldn't resist the lure of the sandwiches, as it turned out. He took a bite to discover that they'd somehow found that perfect combination of the tartness of the apple and the sharpness of the cheddar, against a springy bread. It was the sort of sandwich that would be a stroke of luck to find at a pub tucked somewhere on the route of a long ramble. The one to remember ever after because of how perfect it was for the moment.

When he looked up again, Golshan was smiling more broadly, near sparkling with it. "My legs don't work anymore. Got shot in the back. The chair's a great thing, but one reason I'm here so often is they put in the ramp for me, without complaining, and a fair number of places have stairs. Had you noticed?" For the first time, his voice had an edge to it, but it absolutely wasn't directed anywhere near Owen.

"I had, um." He managed to muffle the sir. "Been going up a lot of them, asking about work."

Golshan nodded. "And then you ran into Barry. I was able to put him into a spot of work that seems to be doing well by him. That's why I'm here. Seeing if I can lend a hand. I know rather a lot of people, it turns out, or people who know other people. And we all need a hand up now and again. Especially those of us who went into the trenches, and now we've got to figure out a life."

Owen nodded, finishing that sandwich half before he looked up and reached for another. "I suppose. I've tried everywhere I can. Asked at the clubs, asked at the shops. My wife works in an apothecary, she's asked around. I don't have the skills, and I can't make shoes, and..." He snapped his teeth shut.

"I'm assuming it's something about space and funds for the shoes?" Golshan asked, leaning back a bit now, like he needed to be constantly shifting, even if his chair stayed in place. "Any children?"

"No. Not yet." Probably not ever, the way they were going. That would disappoint his mother's ghost and his grandmother's ghost, and probably a lot of other familial ghosts if they were paying any sort of attention to Owen.

"No space to make it - we own a shop downstairs, but the lease doesn't run out until Lady Day. And no money for hides and supplies and all that, or at least not enough to build a shop with."

Golshan nodded, considering, then shifted the pile of papers to pull something forward. "So, I know you can make it through the trenches sufficiently in one piece. Which means you can dig holes, duck often enough, have a fair bit of luck on your side. And you're patient enough to put up with a number of people being fools."

Owen had tensed at the beginning of that, but by the end he was laughing. "All that, yes. Not that that's much help."

"Any problem with sudden noises, more than the average?" Golshan flicked his fingers a little more. Owen considered that, munching on the next half sandwich.

"Depends on where I am, I think. If they're more or less ordinary or not." Owen frowned. "That doesn't seem like a useful answer."

"You said shoemaker. I assume that means you're good with a hammer and nails. Not long-term construction, I'm not asking about that. Handyman skills, though." Golshan leaned back again now, and Owen wasn't sure what to make of the expression on his face. There was something complicated there, under the good humour.

"Fairly. I did a lot of the repairs on the building that didn't need something special, before. I've been mending some things since I got back. Helping a neighbour across the way with odd jobs, he can give me a reference for that. Hammer, nails, level, neat painting. Fixed a door that was sticking the other day, sanded the top down. No lasting injuries, though my left leg yells bloody murder when it's going to rain."

Golshan nodded. "In that case, I have a place you should try. I know they're looking for someone. At least through to the end of January, possibly longer. Some day hours, some evening and weekend, it's part of why they've had trouble finding someone."

"What sort of place is it, then?" Owen couldn't think of anywhere legitimate that would be like that.

"One of the theatres. The New Ricardian, do you know it?"

Owen nodded. "Mum used to love the vaudeville there. Didn't go much to the actual plays. Good panto." He remembered that, in some distant time, that went with peaceful fields and grazing horses and wasn't at all real anymore.

"I used to work there." There was a flashing grin, all white teeth for a moment. "Ran backstage for the vaudeville, lent a hand in the theatrical weeks. They're good folks, having some hard times, and they could use someone who knows his work."

"You don't know I do." Owen challenged that assumption immediately.

"The way you talk about that door, you do. And I can see your feet. You've been tending old shoes well. They could use someone who knows when to mend and when it won't serve. And they'll interview properly. But I think you'd fit well there." He then grinned, if anything, more broadly. "And Barry talked you up, as it happens. Though I don't think he'd seen you for a bit then. Mentioned a mate who kept finding small things that made things better in the trenches, or behind the lines. Even when it didn't look to have much point."

Owen looked down again, and he couldn't argue with that. He certainly didn't know how to argue with someone who sidestepped every reasonable counter-argument he had tried to make. The man was reliably several steps ahead of him, chair or not. And it wouldn't do any harm to go to an interview. He had almost no experience of a theatre, other than helping around the edges with the Guild performances as an apprentice, but it was more than nothing.

"When?" He let out his breath in a huff.

"The weekend's their busy time and the whole place is dark on Mondays. Interview Tuesday, if that suits? I can send a message around. Are you all right for a few days, food and all? The other part of what I do is shame the Ministry into making sure people have enough to get by."

Owen hesitated. "It's tight, but we're managing. Especially if there's a bit of hope in the future."

"I'll send a note round to Orlando tonight - he's the overall manager, Orlando Hill. You'd be working under someone else. No one's going to dump you into figuring it out on your own. The pay's not grand, but they're honest about it, and if they've got extra hours on offer, yours is one of the roles gets first pick. And the people are decent. That counts for a lot." Golshan gestured at the sandwiches. "You said you're married. Want to take the rest home to your wife?"

"You're very generous." The 'sir' almost slipped out again, because there was something about the man that almost demanded it. Like he came from posh, even if he didn't look like it now. And his accent was nearly as plummy as some of the Schola types were.

"As I said, I shame the Ministry on the regular, and some of that goes into paying for food. We'll get Greg to wrap it up. You can pop by Fridays. I'm here from noon to five or so, or leave a message for me anytime and they'll get it to me fast enough, given Cumbria. You let me know how you get on, whether it's the New Ricardian or something else."

Owen looked down at the table for a long moment, then back up. "I will." He meant it. Though how he was going to explain this to Clara, he had no idea.

CHAPTER 9
AUGUST 13TH, THEIR FLAT

Clara was just about to put out bread and butter for tea when Owen came home. He opened the door, then set something down on the table by the door while he took off his shoes. He looked, honestly, baffled by something.

"Cuppa?" It was the least she could offer. They still had tea in the tin, even if it wasn't terribly good tea.

"Please. And I have sandwiches for tea." He tapped the thing he'd brought inside. "They're incredible."

That didn't answer any question at all, none of the ones she had. Clara swallowed hard. "Where from?" Then she looked him up and down. "You're not drunk, are you?"

"I've just had the oddest conversation." He shrugged out of his jacket, hanging it up tidily. Clara had to give him that. He was in fact tremendously tidy about his possessions. He didn't leave things strewn around the sitting room or kitchen or bedroom. Then he rubbed his face. "Maybe a bit tipsy. He bought me a beer, too."

"Who's he, when he's at home?" Clara put both hands on her hips, waiting for something that made sense.

Owen lifted his fingers. "Let me wash up." He brought the box over, a neat cardboard thing, with a horse stamped in green ink on the corner. "Here are the sandwiches. I've already had two halves. You should get most of what's left." Then he went off to the sink in the bathroom, and she could hear the water running.

She opened the box to find two sandwiches, prettily cut along the diagonal like something in a cafe, apple and cheddar, it looked like. The tang of the apple hit her almost immediately, and she turned to put them on a plate and the plate on the table. One sandwich for her, one for him. At that point, the kettle sang, and she turned back to pour the water into the pot and let it steep.

By the time she sat down at the table again, Owen had taken the other chair. She set the teapot down carefully, with the cosy on top of it, before glancing at her plate. There was now a sandwich and a half there, and half of one on Owen's plate.

"You've been shorting yourself." His voice was careful now. "No need to tonight."

"You—" She didn't know how to finish that sentence. Or start it, even beyond that one word that was more accusatory than anything. Clara looked away, down at the floor, out into the sitting room.

"You work hard. You're on your feet more of the day than I am. You should eat, too." His voice was somehow solid, in a way nothing since he'd come home had been. Then, there was a hint of a laugh, the way he'd been before, when they'd met. "Also, they're the best bloody sandwiches I've had in an age, and you should get to enjoy them as much as I did."

That made Clara look back at him wide-eyed. She had no idea what to do with that at all, and she was certain it showed on her face. She cleared her throat and did the only thing she could think of to do, which was take a bite. It was, in fact, amazing, all the best of those tastes mingled together. The sandwich somehow had more flavour than so many things she'd eaten the past year. It tasted alive, like glowing, like magic, and she didn't know how that was possible.

When she put the sandwich, he was leaning forward, chin in his hands, just watching her. Rather avidly, in a way that would be tremendously improper except for the fact they were married. "See? You should enjoy them too."

The tone in his voice, something with another kind of hunger entirely, made her flush before she looked away. There was too much there, far more intensity than she could cope with. It had been a reasonable day at the shop with no unusual customers, but there had been quite a few of them. Horatio Morris had come in, though one of the ladies from across the street had come by when he'd only been there a minute or two. It had been just enough time to make pleasantries and say that his housekeeper had loved the soap. When it was clear that Mrs Malcolm wasn't going to wander off quickly, he'd made his farewell and said he'd be back in a week or so.

All told, it had been a fine day. Mrs Malcolm had bought quite a lot in the way of cleaning supplies, which was both good for the till and something where Clara could make up more herself. Aunt Lillian had everything she needed, and those were a simple matter of proper proportions.

Owen coughed, calling her back to where and when she was, but at least now he was picking up his own sandwich. Half a sandwich. She tried to figure out what to say. "It is wonderful. Where - how? I don't know what to ask."

"A man from my regiment - do you remember me

mentioning Barry? I ran into him the other day, and he put me on to this bloke who helps connect people with jobs. Sets up in The Field, the Horse House club, down on Club Row. Awful posh, there's someone to open the doors, and someone else to show you where you're going, and all sorts of spaces." Owen titled his head. "Lots of polished wood-work, but not as posh as you'd assume otherwise? Not all gilt all over everything, like the opera house building?"

That, at least, was something Clara could nod along with. "And?"

"So I go up, and this man in a uniform - all green - gets the door, and asks me my business. Someone takes me along to a sitting room, and there's a man." Owen paused, frown-ing. "Not Indian, him. But something more like that? Soltani's the name, Golshan Soltani. He's got a wheeled chair, moves around on his own, not like those boats in the Temple of Healing where someone had to push. You couldn't even do it yourself if you wanted. There he is, bright as day, and he orders his usual, and asks me what beer I like, and chats. Few minutes later, back comes one of the staff with cider for him, and beer for me, and the sandwiches. All three of them." Owen frowned more at that, sounding somehow quite sad. "I don't think he had one, and there's a pity, isn't it?"

Clara blinked and nodded, before taking another bite of hers and chewing. It helped cover that she had no idea what to say.

"He asked me some questions. Long and short of it, he used to work at one of the theatres, the New Ricardian. Mum used to go regularly. They need someone to help out, handyman skills. I need to interview. I don't know what the pay is, but something is better than nothing. I don't know much about a proper theatre, but I had a few bit parts in the

Guild mummer's plays, before the War." He shrugged, but he didn't expand further on that.

"What sort of things, do you know?" Clara couldn't argue with the maths there at all. Some income beyond the pitiful sums from the Ministry would be a lot better.

"Mending things backstage, I think, and making sure things run smoothly. A chance to pick up extra hours, if there are some, reporting to someone else." Owen hesitated. "The hours, though. Mostly nights, I guess. On the other hand, it'd mean I could look for other work in the daytime. Do things around the place." His voice got a bit shaky on the other end.

On the one hand, if he was working late nights, they wouldn't need to talk to each other much. On the other, it would be awkward, being asleep and awake at different times. Third, though, it didn't matter. If they offered him a job, it was the best chance they'd had, and it wasn't like they could be choosy.

Clara looked up. "You should go interview, see what they think." She didn't spell the rest of it out. Either he'd figured out how much they needed this, or he hadn't, and she wasn't going to be the one to say it.

"Right. So I'll know more Tuesday, probably. Golshan - that's what he said to call him - said he'd send round a note. He seemed pretty sure they wouldn't find someone sooner. And I guess I'd have Mondays, whatever else, there's nothing at the theatre."

Clara nodded. "Not something I've gone to a lot. What sort of plays do they do?" She hadn't. And when she'd gone, Aunt Lillian had preferred the Rose, one of the other ones. Better refreshments, Aunt Lillian thought. Clara was certain that her aunt had something of a pash for the man who'd been their lead actor for a good two decades now, finally ageing out of the hero role.

"Mum used to like to go. Their vaudeville. They rotate, or at least they did. A couple of weeks of one play or another, then a fortnight of vaudeville shows, turn and turn about." He seemed almost eager about it. "Mum would have laughed and laughed."

Clara didn't know why. She focused on her food, working her way through another half sandwich, as the silence went on.

"I suppose we haven't had much time for those sorts of stories." Owen cleared his throat. "Did she ever tell you stories about when I was little?"

"Oh, plenty of story-telling." Clara had soaked them up, but Owen's Mum had kept to the same dozen or so. "But mostly the same ones over and over again?"

"Did she tell you the one about us being out for the hops picking?"

Clara shook her head. "That you used to go down fairly regularly. When everything closed up in August." That didn't happen much anymore, certainly not in Trellech, even right before the War.

"I found an orchard, some of the early apples, and went scrumping." Poaching for apples, near enough. "And I got caught - I was with a mate or two, and I was the slow one. Hand on the back of my shirt, holding me up, my feet swinging in the air. The man put me down, both his hands on my shoulders, and I went off and recited that bit from Carlton's *A Rose for a Rose*."

One of the magical plays, one nearly everyone learned in school at some point, seeing as how the content was more or less suitable for children. The more risque jokes went right over a kid's head. Aunt Lillian had laughed and laughed when Clara had first realised some of that, a good two years into her apprenticeship. She and Mrs Malcolm had been quoting bits back and forth and roaring with laughter, before they explained the bits of slang. "The bit about being a saintly child?" There was a bit where the hero came upon a small boy, who turned out to be one of the Fatae. The boy put on airs of being an angel, as if that were a thing anyone would want to claim to be.

"Just that. The bit that ends with 'And who would cry me false?'. I did it rather well, and the man let me go, so I took a step back and took off running. Mum always said it was proof of the power of the word." He was smiling now, more freely than she'd seen him do yet.

Clara offered a tentative smile back. "So you're not worried about being with actors?" Some people would be, she supposed. They were supposed to be temperamental, for one thing.

"Can't be worse than the trenches." Owen didn't seem put out. "I'll see what comes of it. Finish up your sandwich. I was going to do some sketches. Dream about what I'd do if I could get a bit more leather."

Her chin jerked as she looked up at him, but he meant the dreaming in earnest. "Give me a minute, then, and I'll come knit. We could both use new socks."

It was not, by any stretch of any definition, a romantic evening or a passionate one. But it was better than the past nights had been. And the sandwiches had been excellent. Maybe that was what her life was now, moments of light like that, fleeting and flying into memory. If so, maybe she could make do.

CHAPTER 10
AUGUST 17TH, THE NEW RICARDIAN THEATRE

S aturday, Golshan had sent round a note confirming an interview with the theatre manager on Tuesday, just after lunchtime. He'd included instructions to bring something he'd made and be dressed to tour backstage. It wasn't as if Owen had good clothes, or not really. One black suit for funerals. He hadn't worn it since Dad's. He hadn't made it back for Mum's, and that was going to haunt him for a long time.

The theatre itself was up near the museum, a few buildings down from the main intersection, nestled among other larger buildings and shops. There were several restaurants along the street that likely did good business before performances, and an ice cream parlour that likely had a grand time on matinees. He knew the other two theatres were nearby - not right across the street, but a bit further down.

He'd been told to go to the stage door, down an alley between the buildings. The door, when he found it, could use a coat of paint, but when he rang the bell, someone let him right in. "Mister Hubbard?"

"I am." Owen nodded. "Here to see Orlando Hill?"

"Come along this way." The other man was agreeable, a rather nimble man in his forties or maybe fifties. Ginger, fading to roan, and without a beard or moustache, very tidy in appearance. Owen might even use the word dapper and mean it. Maybe, he decided, the man had to be in his fifties for certain. He looked old enough not to have fought in the war, and moved like he hadn't. "I'm Edgar Watson, one of the dressers."

That was clearly a job title, and one Owen wasn't sure of. He swallowed, because there was a choice here. He could brave his way through not knowing things, or he could ask. "Pardon, dresser? I don't know much about the workings of a theatre, only seen it from the seats, and not so many times as all that."

That got Watson turning around with a sudden grin. "I help our leading man dress. Sometimes there are quick changes, the greasepaint and cosmetic charms need a hand. When I'm not doing that, I help manage the props and backstage, making sure everything's in place. Sometimes we need a spotter for something, or someone to flip this lever for that effect at this point in the script. It's all very much like a dance." He then continued along, walking through an aisle with curtains on one side and various racks of clothes and other items on the other. "It's changeover day, mind your feet. We could go the long way round, but best you see a bit of what we're like first."

Owen could more or less make sense of that, but then he put something together. "You mean we're going along the back of the stage?"

"Just so. Crossing stage left to stage right. That one's easy. It's the directions as we see it, from the stage, not the audience." Watson continued along the way, bringing them out in one of the wings of the stage, then through a curtained opening at the back. The hall ended in a little alcove, with a small table, a statue of some kind, and various small objects, a bottle of wine and some pinecones. Owen couldn't make sense of it, but Watson was speaking again. "Here are the offices. Orlando's there. We're on a first name basis, as employees, bit of extra polite won't be a bother now."

"Appreciate that." Owen straightened his shirt as Watson knocked.

"Orlando? Here's your two o'clock. Owen Hubbard." Owen hadn't given his first name, but he chalked that up to, well, whatever Golshan had said. Preparation, as well.

The office itself was a decent size, but it had that same slight shabbiness as the door on the alley had. It could use a coat of paint, a bit of beeswax on the desk. Nothing fancy, but it would shine a bit better. And some polish on the bookshelves, and maybe some elbow grease could take out the marks where someone had set down a mug, more than once.

Owen didn't want to be rude, so his attention immediately went from there to the man behind the desk. He was wearing a dark red flocked jacket, some sort of plush velvet. It was reminiscent of the fabric on theatre seats, actually, and Owen had to think that was deliberate. He seemed a little older than Watson, with streaks of a dignified grey at the temples, but he had visible worry lines, as well.

"Sir? Pleased to meet you." Manners, he could use his manners, and ought to.

"Ah, a pleasure. Have a seat, if you like? Look, to put you right at ease, I'd like a chat with you. Then we'll have you spend a few minutes with our chief carpenter, who keeps the building running, and also oversees all our set design, furniture, all that. If she thinks you'll suit, we'll give you a try for a few weeks. If that goes well, take you on at least through until the panto run ends in January." He named a number for the pay that was better than Owen had worried it would be, if less than he'd hoped. A good bit better than the Ministry payments, though, a couple of times over.

Owen nodded. "I, to be honest, sir, I don't know that I've got a good idea what the work involves. Golshan said he'd put in a good word for me, and he has, but he doesn't know my work either, beyond what I've said."

"Did you bring something you've made?"

Owen nodded once. "I made these for my Mum - she's several years gone, now. Just before I was called up. She wore them a fair bit, but they..." He looked up to find Hill watching him intently. "Here, sir."

It felt odd to be handing them over, but shoes were a craft that was made to be seen, but also to be felt. These were fine shoes, too. Nothing fussy or fancy, but two-tone black and a gorgeous golden tan, that set off the black nicely, and the stitching all looked like new. "Anything magic in this? Or rather, can I ask what is?"

"Not so many would spot it, sir. A lot of people think a shoe's just a shoe. A touch of it, to shape the last properly. And then more to encourage the leather to smooth and bend. Most of the charmwork's in finishing it up. I don't know a lot of magic, sir, but I learn what I use solidly."

"And you'd be up for learning a bit more? Light charms if you don't know them, both one that can follow you and one that will stay put. A few cleaning charms, having things on the floor's a hazard, so we need to clean up spills quickly."

Owen nodded. He still hadn't got an explanation of what the work would be. After a moment, Hill waved a hand. "Your job, to be precise, would be to lend a hand where we need it. Carpentry, under Maisery's direction and design. Putting other things together, doing repairs, if we need that, which we do. During a performance, a bit of stagehand work, moving things around where we need them. Possibly lending a hand in the wings, handing over what's needed from the props or helping with a quick change."

"Sir." Owen inclined his head. "And the hours?"

"It depends a bit on the week. Two weeks a month, we've a play on. That means making the sets, whatever we need for it, then the run of the play. The next two weeks, we've vaudeville acts that come through. Singers, illusionists, contortionists, a knife thrower or two." He sighed. "I do miss Golshan, he'd charm every knife thrower he ever met, and most others too. He made that whole line of things run smooth as silk, and that's no small thing with a lot of competing egos."

Owen nodded a little. "So the work changes, fortnight by fortnight." He could not deny that appealed, right now, while he was still feeling too unsettled for day-in-day-out work.

"Just so." Hill nodded, approvingly. "And day to day. One to nine at night on Tuesdays and Wednesdays - we have no shows, just rehearsals and preparation. A fair bit of that, you'd be making sets or whatever's needed for what's coming up. Mending things for later. Maybe getting some supplies in. Shows Thursday night through Sunday night, with a matinee on Saturday, that's a long day. Three to midnight those days, ten to midnight on the Saturday with a couple of hours off in the middle. We've an attic with cots if you want to kip, or you can go home, or whatever pleases you, so long as you're sober when you come back."

Owen snorted. "Not so safe, even if you've charm lights instead of lamps, I suppose."

Hill's eyes widened. "You see the key of it already. Theatre takes risks, it ought to, but better with the heart and the emotions than the body. It's hard to replace a good actor, we don't want any injury we can avoid."

Owen had a sense for a moment that this was not necessarily the usual thing. "Sir." He nodded. "Glad to see how that fits, then." It would be different work, but to be honest, he'd done his fair share of chipping in on all sorts of things in the trenches. At least here, no one would be lobbing explosives at him or sending him out to face guns.

"Excellent." Hill touched something on his desk, and less than a minute later, a woman appeared, noticeably on the older side.

She looked Owen up and down. "I'm Maisery. Come on, let's see what you know and what you don't." She was clearly a force of will. Owen found himself standing and following with a murmur to Hill. He was leaning back in his chair, looking deeply amused.

Maisery was a tiny woman, comparatively, the sort of fierce older woman who no one should ever take for granted. She had a work belt on over split skirts. He got a glimpse of several old scars on her arms, the kind that happened when a chisel or blade slipped while working. She led him into a long room that seemed to run along the back of the stage, on the other side of the wall from where they'd come across in the first place. There was a carpenter's workbench there, someone with a sewing machine somewhere within hearing distance, and the sounds of several other people chatting and working away.

"You set this up. How would you go about moving that bit of set to attach here and have it stable? You've a ladder, a few sawhorses with weights, and whatever else you can see here that you can pick up." She leaned back, crossing her arms over her chest.

Owen considered the challenge. He expected some people would leap right into moving, but he'd never been inclined to do that. If they wanted him to hop to on demand, they should have got him before the Army made him stubborn about that sort of thing. Instead, he took his time, looking at the situation, then walking around the back of the big set pieces. There, he found a couple of pieces bracing them, and what looked like tools to move them around. "Do these move with the levers here, or a charm, please?"

Maisery had followed him around the back. "Both. That crowbar there's charmed. The brace won't move without the bar in. Safety, you see? Put it in there, and then you can adjust."

With that information, it was easy enough for Owen to figure out how things had to move. Once he had a plan, he asked, "May I get a hand to get them into position?"

"May. Aren't you polite? I like that." A couple of minutes later, they were properly positioned, and Owen had learned how to connect them with a broad strip of thick woven linen. Not enough to hold anything together if the weight was on it, but enough to hide any visible gaps from the backside.

"There. You'll do nicely. You didn't rush, you asked questions, you asked for help. I can teach you how to do a specific task. I can't teach you how to do those things."

Somewhere in there, Hill and Watson had come in without comment. Owen supposed moving quietly was a good skill in a theatre. They were likely both wearing soft-soled shoes, too. Maisery nodded. "He'll do. Nicely, I expect. You able to work a bit today, or do we start you tomorrow?"

Hill chuckled. "Let me do the paperwork. If you're available, we could use a couple of hours today, getting the set sorted. Mostly holding things in place. Come tomorrow, and we'll give you a full day."

It felt like he'd tumbled into some fairy tale, but it was at least an agreeable one where people seemed to approve of him. Owen found himself back in the office, with Hill and Watson walking him through the agreements and what they meant, and what his salary would be. There'd be extra for approved hours over his usual. Or if he had a change of duties, like if he did front of house work before the show started if someone was out. Selling tickets or seating people, something like that, before going backstage for his regular work.

CHAPTER 11
AUGUST 19TH AT THE SHOP

On Thursday, Clara spent her day alternating between serving customers and dusting the glass bottles. Neither was enough to distract her from her thoughts. It was good that Owen had a job. The pay wasn't as much as it might be, but it was better than he'd been getting. And he'd liked the people he'd met.

But the hours were going to be strange. Decidedly strange. He'd been at work until nine the night before, the first full day. He'd come home just as she was getting ready for bed. On the one hand, it had been rather nice to have the flat to herself, entirely, and know that she would. It had felt like it had a few months ago, before he came home. She didn't have to explain what she was doing, or see if he needed a bit more tea, or, well, anything like that.

But of course, when he came home, he hadn't been ready to sleep. She'd gone to bed by herself. And when she woke in the morning at her alarm, he'd shoved a pillow over his head, and rolled over, grumping incoherently under his breath. She'd thought through a bit of what she'd need in the morning. Clara had laid her clothes out, but of course she'd forgotten about setting out her watch. She'd only managed the shoes because she only had the one pair suitable for work right now.

She expected to come home to dishes in the sink from his breakfast, and some unknown amount of bread and butter gone. Not that he shouldn't have a lunch before he went. But it meant she didn't know what would be in the cold box, tonight. She was still considering that problem and how to talk about it with him. She wanted to know what to expect for her own tea, for one thing. And to manage the shopping, since it wasn't like he'd take that on. She was circling those thoughts for the third or fourth time when the chime above the door rang out.

She turned to see Master Morris come in, smartly dressed. "Master Morris. Good afternoon. Pardon that I couldn't talk last time."

"You were properly helping another customer, and I had no particular business. Today, though, I wonder if you could be a help? Oh, you do look lovely, so suited to the summer."

"Certainly, sir?" Clara settled evenly on both her feet. She didn't feel lovely, especially given the fumbling this morning, but she had at least done her cosmetics in the bathroom mirror. But her blue dress was near five years out of date, it was from before the War, and the shape of her body had shifted. She was entirely aware her stockings had been darned, even if it wasn't terribly noticeable, and she could feel a loose thread dangling on the back of her leg.

"Oh, you needn't be so formal, surely." He came to rest his hands on the wood of the cabinet, barely touching the glass panels, leaning forward just a hair and looking directly at her. "And I am hoping you can help with a particular challenge. I'm hosting a supper party next week, a business supper. Surely you have one of those little devices that scents a room pleasantly, and perhaps a choice of scents? I heard someone mention there are scents that encourage different reactions, charms."

"Oh, yes." She felt awkward about not tacking the 'sir' on the end. "Something for a business supper? We have a small line of those scents, nothing, um." She flushed, and Clara had no idea why. "Nothing more compelling, I guess is the way to put that?"

"Why don't you bring out what you have, and I'll see if it suits." He made it sound simple, just to do as he asked.

Clara swallowed. "Some of it's in the back, sir." There she was, doing that again, there was no way to win here. "I'll need to get a few things out of a cabinet. It will take a couple of minutes." Everything was locked up out here that should be. There were protections on the counters. It should be safe enough. Aunt Lillian had made sure all of that was renewed before she went up to Scotland.

"Oh, I've got a bit of time. I'll let anyone who comes in know that you'll just be a minute." There was something about his ease and confidence that no problem would present itself he couldn't handle. Clara found it sparked more than a little interest in her. She ducked her chin and took that feeling - and her discomfort with it - promptly into the back.

Once she was there, she took several steadying breaths. She was a married woman. A married woman in a somewhat uncertain marriage, still, but everything was changing, had been changing, would be changing for a bit. That wasn't a reason to break her promises. She'd never liked the sort of person who would.

Only, well, she couldn't deny that the way Master Morris talked to her made her want something else. Something that wasn't a hollow shell of a marriage, something that had a bit of fun in it. She made herself turn to her work. First she unlocked the storage case with the keys in her pocket, then pulled out first the scent rods. Finally, she drew out a selection of the scents themselves.

Aunt Lillian wouldn't sell anything that had too much of a compulsion to it, though she knew how to make them. The ones they sold were all milder, an inclination at most. Setting the stage, there was a theatrical metaphor for it, but not forcing the actors to a particular script. There was the one they had going in the shop, that encouraged happiness and joy, hoping it would make customers think fondly of the place and want to bring that home. But it wasn't right for a business supper. There was the scent for romantic evenings, and that wouldn't do either. She wouldn't even bring that one out.

There was one for clarity of thought. It was popular with apprentices in the more complex apprenticeships. Alchemists could make their own, of course, but people doing more scholarly work found it useful. One of the Portal Keepers was very fond of it, and Healers liked it quite a lot. She hesitated, but then added the one some of the other shopkeepers liked that encouraged people to spend money. It was all spices and a bit of amber. Dreams of riches, that's what Aunt Lillian called it privately. She set all the little bottles on a tray, added half a dozen testing sticks, and brought them all back out.

Master Morris was still alone in the shop, and he was peering at the display on the other side of the room. He turned around as soon as he heard a sound from the door. "Ah, there we are. You were really quite quick. Eager to get back to me?"

Clara had no idea how to take that. It was exceedingly

forward. But he might have meant it entirely innocently, surely. And she didn't want to keep any customer waiting. "I'm sure you're a busy man, sir."

"Ah, well. Yes. Though I made a bit of time this afternoon. Now, tell me about these, do. What do they do? Which would you recommend?" She explained each of them, naming a couple of the particular scent notes, without giving away the specific alchemical recipe. She'd never do that. That was Aunt Lillian's creation. It got easier as she settled into the descriptions, and he listened intently, asking a thoughtful question or two.

In the end, he bought one bottle of Sharpest Wit and one of Abundant Blessings. Clara wrapped them both up carefully, adding a bottle and a dozen of the hollow sticks that would disperse the scent itself. "When you're done, sir, you can cap the bottle and set the sticks in the case. I marked the side, so you can keep them straight." She did that with a little touch of a charm, a silvery blue dot for the one, and a deep green for the other, to match the bottles.

"I'm sure I'll be back soon. I'll have to come tell you how well they work, of course. I could write up a testimonial for you. Your aunt, I mean. Though also for your service, this has been splendid. You're quite clever about all this, aren't you?"

It was another sentence she did not know how to respond to. She ducked her chin, trying to find words.

"Do you have a family you get home to? Or here?" He asked it almost casually, but it was rather a relief to say it.

"I'm married, sir, my husband was demobbed earlier this summer." There, that was a nice reasonable sentence that set expectations properly.

"Oh, good." There was something in his tone she didn't

actually want to interrogate, but he went on. "What does he do with himself, then?"

"He's got a job in a theatre." That seemed harmless enough to say. "Backstage, he's good—" No, she couldn't say good with his hands. He was, but that was right into blatant innuendo. "He's a good handyman."

"Ah, theatre needs a bit of that. Which one? I go to the theatre a fair bit." Master Morris asked it easily, and it wasn't like there were so many in Trellech.

"The New Ricardian." It came out curt. "He's only recently started. I don't know that much about it."

"Ah, well, there's some time to learn, isn't there? And you've certainly got a lovely job here, so helpful." He reached out a hand, as if to rearrange something on one of the displays, a bit presumptive. As Clara steadied the basket, she caught something in his expression she couldn't quite make sense of, like he'd meant to say something different. She couldn't imagine what.

"You're kind to say so, sir." She was saved from further confusion by another customer coming in. Master Morris picked up his items and nodded, strolling out as if he didn't have a care in the world.

Since Owen was going to be out for tea, and out til late that evening, Clara had made arrangements to go to Hester's after she finished work. The children were playing, but not in the same room this time. Clara got the chance to have her tea and sandwiches and biscuits and chat without too much interruption. Hester chattered amiably on for a bit. "The new girl's with them. Did I mention? Not a nanny, quite, but a help. Such a blessing, to be able to get a few minutes to one's self."

Clara couldn't imagine being able to pay someone to do that sort of thing. Which was a whole other challenge in her marriage they weren't talking about, but at least that wasn't urgent. Didn't need to be urgent. She had her potions. Maybe things would change so she could stop taking them, but that would need rather a lot of change, and a steady income.

Hester had quite a lot she wanted to talk about, all in that same vein, about how well Oscar's work was going. They had invited her to be on one of the minor philanthropic committees, and she was having a new frock for the occasion. To be fair, Hester had always been like that, but it grated more on Clara than it had sometimes, and she didn't entirely know why.

A good thirty minutes in, they'd gone through the sandwiches and were onto the stage of decorously avoiding taking the last biscuit on the plate. Hester looked up. "Oh, just listen to me nattering on. How was your work, dear? I hope it's going well?"

"I made a rather tidy sale today, beyond the usual. Someone who came in who's having a business dinner. He wanted some scents to go with it. Encourage the thing along. You know Aunt Lillian's line of those."

"Anyone I know, darling?" Hester reached for her tea, arching her fingers elegantly, like she practised it. Clara could never make her hands do that so easily.

If he'd come in for anything medical, Clara wouldn't have mentioned a name. They had standards, most apothecaries did. And it was a matter of public trust. No one would get their potions or salves or whatever if they thought gossip would spread all over town. But this wasn't that, it was household goods. And the soap had been too. "He gave his name as Horatio Morris. He's come in a couple of times now. Before, I think it was always when Aunt Lillian would be at the counter while I had lunch? I think, anyway." She'd meant to write Aunt Lillian about him, and get some of the gossip, but she kept forgetting to.

"Horatio Morris? An older gentleman, quite distinguished and well dressed?" Hester leaned forward.

Clara nodded. "That fits well enough. Though I suppose it might fit more than one person."

"Well, if it's who I think it is, he did very well indeed out of the War. Something about supplies." Hester would consider it crass to be too detailed about money, as she always was. She made reference to their prosperity by gesture and dropped in mentions. But Clara could translate her expressions, that this was more money than Hester dreamed of having. "Oscar's met him only the twice, even with his Ministry connections. All very formal, of course. Whatever is he like?"

Clara shrugged slightly. "He's been very polite." That wasn't the right word, though. He kept pushing a little. Leaning in, nudging things along. She supposed that went with being good at business, though. That kind of eagerness must make a lot of sales. She did that herself, too, by smiling and being pleasant, but men could do things women couldn't there. A different style of it, that was a better way to put things.

"And he's been in twice? My. I didn't realise your Aunt Lillian's wares were so enticing. I must come by, see if I could use a thing or two." Then she pouted. "You won't give me a discount, though?"

"No discounts. Shop rule." It was, too. Clara had put it in place, because otherwise half the neighbourhood would get things at cost, and that was no way to make sure the business kept going. Then she smiled as brightly as she could manage. "Tell me about what Oscar's up to that you can?"

That carried them through the rest of tea comfortably. Hester enjoyed talking about Oscar almost as much as she enjoyed talking about herself. Clara let the chatter wash over her, making agreeable noises at suitable intervals. When she finally set off home - just before Oscar was due back - she at least felt like she'd talked to other people successfully. It made coming back to a quiet flat easier.

CHAPTER 12

AUGUST 25TH AT THE THEATRE

"So, this is a music hall week, right?" Owen set the box of tools he was carrying down on the work-table, following Maisery along.

"Mm hmm. The actors are all up in, where was it?" She half turned over her shoulder. "Frank, where are they this week?"

"Bangor. Not a big magical community there, but they're doing a general show." Owen had seen the production last week, from the seats, last Thursday, in between being an usher. As Maisery had said, better he see what the thing looked like to the audience, and besides he wasn't trained enough to be useful backstage yet.

Not that it had stopped her planting him backstage on Friday night. It had helped, though, to know what was happening in the play, and when there'd be a flurry of things going on. He'd been in charge of opening and closing the curtains. He'd coordinated with someone on the other side of the stage who gave him signals with a little magical token. It was worn like a watchband that buzzed against his skin when he needed to do something. The whole thing had made him jumpy for a bit, but by Saturday he'd got used to it.

"They'll be back in a week and change. Yesterday was for cleaning up the stage, waxing it again, all that. Easier to do when we're not trying to put together a set on it at the same time, so we always do that on the first day of the changeover. Music hall doesn't need that kind of construction, so it's more figuring out what bits we need for what they want. We've got, let's see."

Maisery pulled out a list. "More magic, this one, than some. That'll be fun. Two singers, different styles, an illusionist with some instrumental backing, an adagio, stage magic, a comedian. Loosely themed around folk songs, looks like. That's nice, won't step on any toes for our panto. Here. Start sanding this down smooth, would you? Last time someone got a splinter pulling it out." She handed over a wedge, clearly meant to brace something on stage, a large triangular block that had two rough sides.

Owen immediately rummaged for some coarse sandpaper and got to work with it, bracing it in a vise on the workbench rather than scrabble to keep hold of it. Maisery nodded approvingly. Once he'd got that started, he asked, "Panto? And adagio? I mean, I know what a panto is, just I don't know what that means for the planning."

Maisery laughed, shaking the braid that ran down her back. "Sure you've seen adagio. It's a mix between dance and juggling. Usually a nicely built man tossing a slender young woman around. The group we've got this week is quite good. A married couple and her two brothers. She's tiny, and she's got exquisite balance. They toss her around the stage as if she's a bird."

Owen frowned at that. "Isn't that, well, dangerous?"

"What's art without danger, luv?" Maisery snorted. "Lots of risks in the theatre, and in music hall. The trick is taking the ones you meant to. They use charms for safety. They have a Healer on standby in case of a broken bone. They've been doing this, what, a decade now." Maisery titled her head. "You're married, you said?"

"I am." Owen wasn't sure what else to say about it, so his words came out clipped.

Maisery twisted on the stool she'd claimed. "The Perrels are good folks. Might want to have a chat with them. The two brothers are married, too, just their wives don't perform. One of the steadier sets I've seen in our line of work. Long line of performers, actually, though they're the first to do adagio."

Owen glanced away, focusing on the bit of wood he was sanding. There was still a snag there. "Are you saying I need to do that?"

"Oh, not an order. I care about you working with wood and mending things. But I'm also going to tell you about people you might like a chat with. They'll be here tomorrow for a run through. They don't need much for their act, just making sure the stage is clear. That's why they go on early, no change of something from a later act being on the stage. Dropped feather or something like could trip them up."

"I hadn't thought about it like that." Owen considered the complexities. "Or water, though I suppose there's not a lot of water on stage."

"Not this time, no. Though we've done an escapologist, getting out of a tank of water, in the past. And a couple of stage magic tricks with one. It's up there." She gestured at the ceiling of the large room, where he could see a piece of translucent something hauled into the rafters. "And yes, it's safe. I check the charms every day. Only place to store it. Doesn't weigh more than a couple of sacks of flour, right now, though it'd hurt if it came down."

That made Owen blink. "Charms?"

"Charms. Makes it much easier to handle. Besides the size, the charms for that make the material brittle, or at least so I had it explained to me." Maisery shrugged. "Right, panto. Obviously, we don't need to start from nothing. I had an American through here, before the War, didn't have any idea about it. Imagine!"

"What do they do there, over winter hols?" Owen shook his head. "Mum and Dad took me every year when I was little. And Mum and I would come, of course. Until the War."

Maisery nodded, then she asked, carefully. "She still around?"

"No'm." Owen shook his head. "Bad heart. She had an operation, I got leave for that, and she died when I couldn't get back again. Only child, Dad was already gone. Just my wife."

"Ah, I'm sorry to hear that. We like the kind of Mum who keeps coming to panto. Which is most of them, but there you are." She paused to open a jar of varnish and picked up a brush to work on applying that to a wooden bit she had set on the workbench. "Anyway. It's where we make our money for the year, reliably. And to be honest, we really need to this year."

Owen frowned. "That why the job runs to January?" He'd done enough of his own accounts to understand that type of planning. "What's the matter, then?"

"War shook a lot of things up. Obviously, lots of people not coming to the theatre, who couldn't. Who died, or were injured, who were over fighting, obviously." She gestured at Owen himself. "But also a lot of people didn't who were here. Maybe some felt it was disloyal, I guess, which I can see. Some didn't have the money. Some were too tied up in their grief, and we understand that too. But theatre, when it does its job, it helps people understand all those feelings and move a little forward with them."

Owen stopped sanding and cocked his head. "Even music hall?"

"Oh, sure. Take this week's show. The comic's got a great line in 'what I learned from folk songs'. Pretty sure he'll do that one this time. You know, don't go down to the greenwood. Stay home in May. Change your name if it's Janet or Margaret. There's a whole bit about Doleful Ghosts and how to avoid them." Something in that last comment made her stop and focus on the wood in her hands for a moment.

Owen hesitated before he asked. "Something about a ghost?"

"Oh, we've got those. Every good theatre does. Ours is normally very well behaved. Has a seat up in the balcony, in one of the tiny boxes stage right. He never shows at an actual performance if we sell the seat. But he's been, I don't know. Not A Doleful Ghost out of folksong, but not happy. If any ghost is happy. And there's a woman who likes the back corner of the costume shop, but she never does much. Sometimes you'll find something you thought you lost, somewhere you can't miss it, though."

"So, helpful, then. Both of them." Owen wasn't at all sure what he thought of ghosts, but if they were going to have ghosts, that was probably a sensible sort of ghost to have. He wondered if they came in types, like dogs, and some of them needed a job to do or things went badly awry. "And the panto?"

"Orlando's doing his best to keep things together. But some of our actors, the ones that filled seats, either fought in the War, or got injured. The Naples Scourge cut through us as much as anyone else. So we've got a set of actors where one of them really needs to give over to doing character roles. Then there's an unseasoned lead, and an ingénue whose voice isn't holding as well as we'd like. Panto could save us - we've got a fantastic dame. He's been doing it for two decades now. But we need the panto to do better than the last few years. By a fair bit." She gestured, and Owen got a sense that wasn't all that was a problem, but it was certainly all she was going to tell him about right now. "You've seen the faded paint. All of what we're doing is going into the front of house and all."

Owen frowned. "I could whitewash some things. If that'd help. Or paint, maybe."

"Paint costs money. No, we'll mend and make do. And maybe whitewash. That's an idea. But none of us knows if this is our last season here. I suspect that's why Golshan sent you to us. He knows a bit."

"Isn't he posh, though?" Owen frowned. "He sounded posh. And he went to Schola."

"Posh and having money are not the same thing. His family are all posh. He doesn't talk to them. Didn't much before he got hurt, does even less now. He'd be here helping, 'cept there's no way to have a chair backstage. Too many sets of stairs, you've seen that. But he's talked to Orlando. Pulled in a few favours about getting acts back to us and not somewhere else. And I think sent you because he liked the look of you, but if it all goes belly up, you have some other options. And we'd give you a good character, and all that."

Owen let out a long puff of breath. "Hoping to go back to shoemaking, sooner than later. But I can't do that yet, and I need money to set up a shop again, so." He waved a hand. "Ok. So the panto?"

"So we plan the panto well in advance. Asking our dame what he's up for. That's Howard. You haven't met him yet. Then someone has to write it. And there's a certain amount of coordinating with the other three theatres that do a panto, so we're not doing the same exact story. The Coliseum is doing a bit about Troilus and Cressida. They're going to get half a dozen annoyed letters in the Moon about how it's supposed to be a tragedy, not a romance. We did it two years ago. People expect there to be one, and we're not in the rota for another year. Maybe we'll figure something out. All round." She ran her hand through her hair.

"And what are we doing?"

"Brutus arriving in Albion, all sorts of lovely possible effects for giants. Giants are great for the 'look behind you' bits. You know how that goes. We do some of it with shadow puppets, some with illusionists. Our illusionist hasn't been lured away by anyone else, thanks be."

She nattered on about the performance from there. Another theatre had Arthuriana this year. That was deemed to be the easiest of the shows to bring in money, on the whole, but Maisery was dubious about their actors this time. They had a new dame who wasn't fully settled yet. And the last theatre was doing a bit of a fairy tale, Puss in Boots, another standard, but one that Maisery thought had been a bit overdone. Didn't speak to the moment.

"And Brutus does?" He set the second of the wedges down. "Done with these."

"Brutus, we can do a lot with finding ourselves in a new world that we don't understand, and how to make a go of it. All that finding ourselves on a new shore, and different challenges than we're used to. Seems a lot like today, doesn't it?"

Owen had to admit it did.

CHAPTER 13
SEPTEMBER 5TH AT A TRELLECH PUB

By early September, they'd settled into a routine. Clara didn't see Owen - at least not awake and coherent - between Wednesday evening as she was getting ready for bed, and Saturday morning. She was out, taking a packed breakfast with her, as well as a lunch, and she thought she only woke him up half the time. Sometimes he shared the bed with her. But at least a third of the time, maybe more, she found him curled up on the sofa or the floor in the sitting room.

Saturday, they'd have luncheon together, a main meal before he went off to the theatre. Sunday, she'd make a roast to see them through much of the next week. Monday was their only real day together, and of course she didn't get home until tea time or even later. Horatio Morris never came in on a Monday, she noticed, but he'd come in on a handful of other days, usually in passing on his way somewhere else.

This Sunday, though, she had a goal once the roast was packed away. There was a gathering at one of the local pubs one of her customers had told her about. It was for women whose husbands had come back from the War, where a woman might want to chat with others in the same position. They brought their knitting or whatever other handcrafts might suit a pub, apparently, so Clara had packed socks. She'd knit so many during the War she couldn't seem to stop. These at least had colour work, a glorious mix of greens and blues and yellows on a pale grey ground. Clara thought it quite cheerful.

The group apparently took over a room at a pub near the centre of Trellech, a little into the Crafter's quarter. Clara made her way in, and perched on a seat after getting herself a pint. She got out her knitting, listening to other women chatter as they came in. Most of them seemed to know each other, and she recognised a few faces. The customer who'd told her about it, Lucy, waved and settled with someone who was obviously a friend.

Right as the bells from the Healing Temple struck three, there was a general movement to look at one woman. Most in the room were around Clara's age, or older, but she was on the upper end of that, perhaps close to forty. "I see we have a few newcomers today. I'm Ethel, and we gather here because sometimes it's good to have company. We all have husbands who were in the trenches, and who came home, and sometimes that's not as easy as it sounds."

Something in the way she put it, the tone of her voice, hit Clara oddly. It was like a ringing bell, vibrating her. She paused in her knitting, taking a sip of her beer, while Ethel went on. "How we usually do this is go around and share a bit about what things have been like since we were last here. If it's your first time, it's always fine to just let others speak, but we hope you won't spread gossip from here about anyone. You all know why."

Clara certainly did know. The social threads were

awfully fragile, many places. She saw a lot of it in the shop. People came to the apothecary for beauty creams, of course, but they also came when things weren't going well. When they wondered why their husband no longer was interested in them in bed or anywhere else. When they had some ache or pain that wasn't enough to take to the Temple of Healing - if the Temple could even see them. Or when they couldn't sleep for dreams, or their husband couldn't, or their son.

One by one, the women spoke up. It was curious, listening to other people mention all the things Clara had noticed. How some men wouldn't sleep in beds. Or needed their boots next to them, or some other object. Not a gun, often, like you'd have thought, even if they'd had them, but something else. A gas mask made sense, or something shaped enough like one. But it was other things, too. The beds were too soft, apparently, even the beds most of the women here had, which were nothing particularly plush or luxurious.

And the foods. How they ignored perfectly reasonable foods, for no reason any of them could apparently explain. Owen was better there than most of them, apparently. But half the men the wives talked about needed their food cooked to indistinguishable mush.

It went on like that, with people commenting, and others chiming in here and there with nods of agreement, until it came round to Clara. She cleared her throat. "I'm Clara. My husband was just demobbed in July, and I still don't know what we're doing. We married during the War, rather fast. I moved in with his mother, when she was poorly. She died, and now he's come back." It got her a round of nods and sympathetic noises.

"Has he found work, or is that still, well, a thing?" That

was a woman across the room, with the sort of sharply managed auburn hair that Clara envied.

"He's got a job working for one of the theatres. Which is good, for the money. It was getting awfully tight. But he's out when I'm home, or comes home late, depending on the day. And on one hand, I know what to do with myself when he's not home. And on the other, it's not giving us much time to learn how to be together. Mondays, and a bit of Tuesday and Wednesday."

That got another murmur of understanding, though no one had specific comments. When the sound died down, Ethel nodded. "Thank you for that, Clara, and welcome." She went on to the woman beside Clara, whose husband had awful nightmares, but refused to talk about them at all.

It was curious what people talked about. More than that, how they talked about it. More than a few women mentioned their husband's temper or the way their first reaction was forceful, to say the least. Clara was grateful again that wasn't a thing Owen did. She wasn't at all sure how she'd react to it. She'd never talked to him about how her parents would argue. Or rather, her father would yell. Sometimes he'd throw things, sometimes sounds she'd never made sense of, from a room or two away. She'd been small. It was a strong memory now, but not one she could understand properly.

It wasn't like they'd had time for that kind of conversation before they were actually married. Or the privacy for it. She wasn't sure what she'd been doing, getting married. She remembered, sort of, how she'd felt then. Clara had been swept off her feet. Owen had been kind and funny, and she'd been in the middle of years of not having anyone notice her in particular, even before the War. It had seemed like a good idea at the time, that was all she could say for herself. And then she'd just kept putting one foot in front of another, helping Owen's Mum, and then going on by herself.

It wasn't enough, somehow. She felt like there was some sort of pamphlet or booklet that everyone else had got, somewhere between leaving school and becoming an adult. And she'd never got a copy. She'd never even heard of a copy. Aunt Lillian hadn't been much help. She'd been a widow on her own for near her whole adult life. She'd been pleased at Clara's wedding, she'd liked Owen. For that matter, she'd been the only person on Clara's side to come to the Halls of Justice for the wedding itself, given the timing. Clara's cousins and other aunts and uncles couldn't get the time free.

The meeting wound around the room, and then it turned into a general conversation about the poor job options for nearly everyone. There were plenty of complaints about the ongoing inflation and the cost of everything, and the poor quality of goods in the shops. They were common enough complaints for everyone, really.

But then one woman said something that made everyone pause and look at her. "I have such a hard time with the women who lost their husbands. Like having mine home should make everything else be better. Not a problem or a bother. That I don't still have worries about money, or the meat, or the shoes, or whatever else. That I'm not still wearing frocks from before the War, patched in three or four places."

That got a round of agreement, and the woman went on. "Not that I don't feel for them. But having a husband come back, who's different from the one who left, that's a thing, too. And there's precious little about it, not in the paper, or in the Women's Institute, or anywhere."

Ethel cleared her throat. "Well, that's why we're here, Ada. But you're quite right, it's a different experience. Just like it's different for our husbands, and for the men who were well behind the lines, with none of the same worries." She added, in Clara's general direction, and a couple of other newcomers. "My brother-in-law was like that. It's put me on the outs with his wife."

That at least wasn't a problem Clara had. She might well have liked more help when Owen's Mum was ill. She'd definitely complained about it enough at the time. To herself, because who else was there to complain to? But it meant she didn't have to deal with him having brothers or sisters who had their own opinions about things. She was beginning to think that was the better option.

Around five, everyone started wrapping up, putting their bits and bobs away. One of the other women came over, pausing by Clara's chair. "If you don't need to get back immediately, my husband works odd hours, too. It's such a bother to find people who are free when I am."

Clara blinked. "Sure. Clara, if you didn't catch it."

"Irene. My husband works for the Trellech Moon, the great big printing machines. Steady work. They took him back, thanks be, but he works overnight."

"Do you work?" It was a delicate question these days. Plenty of women in Albion did and had before the War. But there were those who'd filled in the necessary jobs during the War who'd been booted out as soon as the men came home.

"Secretary. Nothing fancy, just the filing and the typing and all, but it's steady and pleasant enough. Neither of my bosses have tried to grope me since Ethan came home. There's a good thing to come out of it."

Clara grimaced. "Oh, my. Hope they pay you well?"

It made the other woman laugh. "Just so. Well enough, now they keep their hands to themselves better. You?"

"My aunt is an apothecary. I handle things at the counter, and some of the bookkeeping." Most of the bookkeeping, honestly, though they had a proper bookkeeper go through it regularly. Some of the reporting regulations around poisons and specific other substances had necessary paperwork Clara couldn't sign off on by herself.

"Care to come round mine? I can do scones and tea and maybe a sandwich. I'm thinking we could both use a bit of a friend?" Irene seemed, if anything, much more lonely than Clara was, but Clara could use a friend too.

"Sure. Which way are you? Anything else I should know?"

"One cat, one dog, no children yet. Mind the last stair as you go up, it needs mending." That was easy enough, at least.

CHAPTER 14
SEPTEMBER 15TH AT THE THEATRE

Wednesday, Owen almost felt he had the rhythm of it. They were into the second week of the current run. The play hadn't taken too much construction. They'd reused a forest set that had been everything from the Forest of Arden to the hills of Scotland to the mysterious land of Brocéliande. This week, it was Sherwood Forest for a piece about Robin Hood, a comedy full of ribaldry.

"Trying out a couple of people for the panto." Maisery had said, amused. "See how their timing is, if they end up with too much ego. If their voices hold up. If we think they're too much of a pain to work with."

Owen cocked his head. "Is that a thing that happens?"

"Well, sure." Maisery turned, her hands on her hips, before she started rummaging by feel at something in her leather apron pocket. "If you'd been an ass, we'd have paid you off and sent you on the way. Panto, we're committed for the run."

"And am I an ass?" Owen wiggled his fingers. "I feel like I've wandered into the play we don't speak of." Which was

Shakespeare's *Midsummer Night's Dream*. He'd learned that one right quick. Sensible theatres apparently treated the play very cautiously. If it was performed - which was not often - it was always outside, and always somewhere with as close to nil association with the Fatae as could be managed in Albion. Which left a rather limited set of possible spaces, honestly. It was, frankly, one of the more sensible of the odd theatre traditions he was learning, considering the content.

"You're doing well, and I hope you know it. You take instruction, you don't argue, you're precise with your hands, and you swear inventively. I approve of the last one."

He'd also learned Maisery had as blue a tongue as any man he'd fought with, and didn't hesitate to use it when called for. So far, he hadn't called for it, and he intended to keep it that way.

"Right. So what am I doing today?" Owen stretched, hearing his shoulder pop.

"Sweep the stage, if you don't mind. Phil is out for a bit getting new stones for the light charms, and they're going to start rehearsal in an hour. They're running that bit from Act 2, with the fighting. Marian's cloak keeps catching on the tree at stage right, they want her to take it off earlier."

"Sure." Owen waited a moment to see if there was anything else. When there wasn't, he went off to the stage, working his way back and forth with the broad flat broom. He swept everything up carefully into the middle, where he could get it with the hand broom and dustpan at the end. As he moved back and forth, he kept getting a glimmer of light from stage right, one of the small boxes nearest the stage. He thought at first it was a trick of the light, but the house lights were half up, the stage lights all the way lit. It wasn't as if there were any windows to shine in.

More to the point, it kept happening, no matter where he was on the stage. He moved all the way stage left, into the wings a bit, and he saw it. Owen moved stage right, and as soon as he could see that box, there was the flicker of light again. He swept back and forth, several minutes' worth, and there it was again, as soon as he turned. He finished sweeping up, got the rubbish into the dustbin, and then went back along to the workroom. "All done. Can I go have a look at something in one of the boxes?"

Maisery was deep into her own work, smoothing some bit of prop out. "Sure. Don't take too long. I'll need your hands in twenty."

Maybe she assumed he'd take a cigarette break in there. They did that outside in the alley. Actors might smoke like chimneys, a fair number of them, but the workroom had too many things that could either go up in flames or where the smoke dulled the charmwork far too fast. He trotted along to the side stairs, making his way up.

There was the flash again, though this time, it was coming from down the slope, a seat nearer the aisle at the back than the stage. Then the flicker moved, just once, for all the world like someone raising a hand, before the air went opaque and then entirely transparent again. Something fluttered down on the seat, but it caught the light rather than reflecting it.

Owen hesitated a good ten breaths. Nothing else moved. Finally, he went over. On the seat, he found a silk flower. Simple enough, he thought, it wasn't bursting with petals. It looked more designed to be sewn to something flat, like the ones he'd used as decorations on shoes. The flower was a somewhat odd colour, though, a red-purple shading to gold at the tips. It wasn't unpleasant, the effect, but it wasn't remotely natural.

He glanced around again, but whatever had been queer in this spot wasn't there anymore. He picked it up carefully and brought it back down to Maisery. "I found this."

She blinked at it, and for the first time, he saw a moment of uncertainty on her face. "Where?"

"Box, um." He counted back. He still had to count. "Two. Stage right."

"That's the ghost, that is. Huh, wondered where those had gone to."

Owen didn't know whether to address the question of the ghost or the flower first. "The flowers?" That one seemed less likely to be too surprising.

"We make them by hand. By 'we', I mean there's someone the costume folks get to do it, as piecework. We reuse a lot of them, but sometimes we need a totally new colour, or moths got to the last set, or something. Not moths, they're not made out of wool, but you get the idea. Some of the dyes are, what's the word. Acidic. Makes the fabric brittle after a bit."

She flicked her fingers at the flower Owen was still holding. "That batch, the colour charms didn't take properly. We were never sure why. There's a whole range of colours of them, with the gold at the ends, but it looks horrid under stage lights, bright orange. So we can't use them. The whole box of them sat around for a while, and then it disappeared. Take it, if you like."

Owen hesitated. "And the ghost?"

"Bit of a flicker, nothing there, except, I guess, the flower? Yeah, that's the ghost. I told you he was well-behaved. Or we think it's a he. It's not like anyone's entirely sure." Maisery shrugged. "See anything else queer?"

Owen shook his head. "Everything's in good order in

the wings, I think. The props aren't out yet, of course." Then he hesitated. "Um."

"Um?" Maisery put her hands on her hips.

"Queer things? Moment for a question?" Owen hadn't figured out how to ask about this, but he had no idea if it was something he needed to know.

"Oh, now I'm curious. Go along, ask." Maisery stretched, more relaxed.

"The table, by Orlando's office, the end of that hall? Can I ask what that is, if I should do anything special about it?" He'd seen people - mostly the actors, not the vaudeville folks or the backstage folks, but some of those too - stop there. He couldn't see what they did. Their backs blocked the view. Whatever people did there, he hadn't wanted to interrupt or ask questions.

Maisery laughed. "Oh, that's the Dionysus shrine. God of the theatre. You're welcome to ignore it, or make offerings, whichever you want. Just don't interfere with it if you're not making an offering. He likes wine and women and song. If you want to leave something, wine, pine cones, ivy, grapes, apples, honey are the standards. It doesn't need to be much. Someone clears the offerings every day. Most all theatres have them, and we hope he smiles on us. We can use all the blessings we can get."

Owen nodded slowly. "Never done much of that sort of thing before, any way round." Mum had gone to services at the Temple of Healing now and again. It was a gorgeous show, the music echoed, and Mum had always liked a bit of a procession or parade. They didn't have anything against religion as a family, but also not much practise at it.

"If you're interested, ask Edgar to show you sometime. No need to if you don't want, or if it's not for a bit." Then she brushed her hands together. "You go ask him now if he needs a hand. Come back in half an hour. I'll need your brute strength then."

"You said that last time." Owen tossed it over his shoulder as he went off, grinning. She did that, and then he'd come back. She'd send him off on something else. He'd caught onto it a fortnight ago, but he didn't mind. He got plenty of walking in, and she made sure he got to know near everyone in the building, with one errand or another.

He found Edgar at the props table stage right, going through things one more time. His eyes were focused on the table. He held up his left hand as Owen came over, his right hand flicking over the order of the items, then changing the angle on one of them minutely. When he was done, Edgar looked up. "Thanks."

"Need a hand with anything?"

"No, no, we're just about set here." Edgar turned around. "Oh, except the table. They'll want that handy, just to put things on. Can you move that, no, it's unwieldy. Let me help." Edgar, he'd found, wasn't shy about helping, even though moving furniture wasn't anything like his job, technically.

Something about his voice caught Owen's ear this time. "You speak well, don't you?" He then flushed. He'd heard the same thing a few times in his apprenticeship, and it hadn't been meant kindly. From them, it had been him getting above himself, whatever that meant. Even though Dad had done well enough to buy his building, and Mum kept a good house, they weren't the sort of people who'd apprenticed out of the family before.

"Oh, I thought about going out on the boards, didn't you know? Took elocution lessons and all. But I turn out to be better behind the stage. A good dresser's beyond pearls, to those in the know, and the same with the props. We also serve who lurk behind the scenes." Edgar made a little flourish with his hand as he set the table down. "And I've been lucky in it, too. Good people to see to, interesting work, seeing Albion here and there."

Owen nodded. For people who liked a bit of travel, it must be an interesting life.

Edgar then tilted his head. "How are you settling in, then? Maisery's pleased with you, if she hasn't actually said. And proper pleased with Golshan. He's coming to see the show tomorrow night, I gather."

"Ah, I may see if I can get a moment to thank him." A few words seemed a very poor repayment indeed. It wasn't that his life had turned golden, and Owen certainly knew it might not last. But it was giving him breathing space, and work to do that he didn't feel helpless at, or hopeless about.

Edgar grinned. "Oh, he'll like that. He likes people, does Golshan. And he likes to see them happy." He looked Owen up and down. "You seem a bit better off?"

Owen nodded. "Getting my feet under me. People have been good about explaining." He hesitated. "Um. You see the ghost in box two?"

"Now and again. Has the dear thing been around again?" Edgar, Owen realised, didn't seem to insist on the ghost being man or woman.

"Maybe twenty minutes ago now, well, before that. But I got up there and found a silk flower." Owen shrugged. "It's like something out of one of those cautionary tales, you know the ones. Probably seen them on stage often enough."

"When we do a particular show for the kiddies, oh, yes." Edgar shook his head. "Nothing like that. It's, erm. Not a blessing, it's not so direct as that? But it's a sign the ghost approves, if you find things from them. They're never big, almost always fabric. There are theories about it. About ghosts, in general."

Owen felt his forehead crease up. "Theories?"

"Oh, yes. There's a whole line of lore that says ghosts are strongest near hidden treasure. But the ghost has been here a good two centuries that we know of, maybe longer. There's a good couple of decades of records that are hard to read, someone had awful handwriting, and no one's bothered to go through them for sightings. We've searched all over the place, over the years, and most of the panels have come down at some point too, and no treasure to be found. But we like our ghost."

"Don't annoy the ghost. Right." Owen felt this was one of the less likely sentences he'd ever expected to utter in his life. "How do I do that?"

"Take the flower to someone who'd like it. You, if that's you. Your wife, if she'd like a flower. Just somewhere it'd be appreciated. Makes for a happy ghost." Edgar turned away at that. "Help me with the table on the other side, since you're here? Save doing it later."

Owen followed along agreeably, though he was chewing on that inside his head. A happy ghost, indeed. Someone could be happy, right? He'd figure out something with the flower.

CHAPTER 15
SEPTEMBER 23RD AT THE SHOP

Clara stared at the silk flower propped in a chipped teacup as she had her breakfast. Owen was, for a wonder, still asleep in the bed, so she'd taken the chance to have a bit more in the morning than usual. He'd brought the flower home a week ago, and she still didn't know what to do with it. He'd made such a fuss about buying the real thing early on.

And now here he was, with a silk flower of a rather particular colour. She liked the colours. But they were the sort of thing that people like her didn't get a chance at. The red-purple was an expensive dye, she knew that. Even doing it by charm was touchy, if she understood right. That made sense. It was close to the Tyrian purple that the ancient Roman aristocrats would wear. Aunt Lillian loved the shade, but even she only had some bits of treasured ribbon in it, to go with other easier fabrics. She'd picked those ribbons off and resewn them on at least four different dresses or shirtwaists Clara had seen.

Then there was the gold on the end. That was apparently an easier charm. Aunt Lillian had a whole line in false gold being easy to conjure, but it didn't last. This looked to be holding up well. It glowed in the morning light, but she could see how it might do odd things under a stage light. Or she supposed so.

Owen was taking her to the theatre on Saturday. Or rather, he wasn't so much taking her as had arranged for a ticket. He'd be working, of course, backstage, and not able to sit with her. But she could at least see what he was doing, understand a bit more about the show. It was the second week of the music hall performances, and those should be fun at least. A distraction, at least, from a number of other things. Including Owen.

But what good was a silk flower, especially that colour? It wasn't like she could do anything with just one, except maybe add it to a hat. But if she did, she'd need a hat it went with, other ribbons to complement it, a host of decisions and purchases that she just didn't have time for. She liked the colour. The colour wasn't something she could have more of. And so it sat there, taking up space on a kitchen table that was too small for someone who wanted a working man's meal and anyone else. Lurking. Looming. Whatever you called a small object that didn't quite glow but certainly made its presence felt.

As Clara got herself out the door and on the walk to work, she had to admit that things were a little better. She and Owen had had a pleasant enough Monday evening together. She'd baked a raisin bread on the Sunday, and he'd appreciated it, properly. It had come out properly well, too. Something about the magic of the yeast and the afternoon sun on the bowl as the bread was rising, and the spices had come together perfectly. A good use of her treasured hoard of cinnamon.

The streets were settling down into the autumn

patterns. There were the usual patterns of children going along to their nearest grammar school. Adults were hurrying off to work, or having a relaxed morning bringing in the paper and getting going for the day. As she got through the centre of Trellech, there was the usual bustle. People were lining up for Portal Square, the newsboys crying the headlines, and the stalls getting set up for market day if they weren't already. The green grocer carts were already doing good business, and she stopped to pick up vegetables that would keep before all the better choices were gone. There was a good cabbage, some carrots, some fine-looking onions, a braid of garlic. She could make a filling soup with that with some flour dumplings and maybe some shreds of chicken.

Clara had no time to think once she got to the shop. It was one thing after another, first opening all the locks on the display cases and then rolling back all the covers, making everything tidy. Precisely on time, she unlocked the door and had three customers in the first five minutes, all popping in to get something before their own day really began.

After that, it slowed down, but she had several small groups of women come in and browse and not buy. Somehow that filled the time between opening and her usual current lunch time, at eleven. Right at eleven, Mrs Malcolm came by. "Want me to keep an eye on the counter while you have a bit of lunch, dear? My niece is helping us today - well, for the next few weeks - and if you wanted a minute of sit down. I could always sing out if you were needed for something."

"Oh, would you? That's most kind." It was on the chillier side today, so Clara took her lunch into the office and her own desk there. There wasn't much. It wouldn't take her long to eat, but it was a relief not to be constantly keeping one ear out. She'd been doing that at home, too, even when she knew Owen would be gone for hours yet. It weighed on one.

Only, of course, it wasn't like she could complain. Owen had certainly lived through far worse, when the thing he was listening for was a threat. And Aunt Lillian had every right to have a break. Even an extended one, as she was now taking. She'd shipped a crate or two of potions and salves down, based on the notes Clara had sent a fortnight ago about what they were beginning to run low on. It sounded like she wanted to stay up there some weeks more.

It had been something about her friend being ill, and needing a bit of nursing, but very little in the way of detail about what sort of illness. Aunt Lillian didn't care much for hands-on nursing, so that was a tad unusual. But if it was the sort of illness that needed teas and decoctions and infusions, well, there was no one better. Or if it needed a bit of alchemical potionry.

And as Clara had pointed out herself, she could sell the stock and run the shop whether or not Aunt Lillian was there. They were doing well enough, on the whole, though Clara still had to do the final numbers for the quarter, so she could turn the estimates in with her taxes for last quarter on Michaelmas Day. She'd been thinking she'd need to stay late or come in on the Sunday to finish that. It suddenly occurred to her that she could take the books home and work out the numbers in their own flat. Then she'd just need to confirm the amount with the Ministry and the Halls of Justice, and bring the transfer slip along to the bank.

That, mind, would mean leaving the shop closed for a few hours, unless, well. Maybe she could make it work. She came out from the office to find Mrs Malcolm talking too softly with Master Morris. Mrs Malcom turned. "Ah, I was just asking if I should get you."

Clara had a feeling that was not entirely the truth, but she did not know how to ask. Certainly not to someone who was doing her a favour, and where she was about to ask for another. "Oh, well, my good timing, then. You must want to get back, maybe, so kind of you to keep an eye out for me. I might pop across the road this afternoon when it's quiet. I was wondering about if you could help me with something next week."

"Oh, quite likely, dear." Mrs Malcolm gathered up her various things. She'd brought a small cloth-bound book with her, and a bit of knitting. None of them had put down the habit of knitting every time they could, really. And while the menfolk might need somewhat different socks, it wasn't as if socks weren't still needed. Just maybe with less attention to the Kitchener toe as an essential point of designing the thing. She was scatter-brained today, goodness.

As Mrs Malcolm made her way out, she looked back to find Master Morris watching her, rather focused. "She's an old bear of a woman, isn't she? Very protective of your time. She wouldn't fetch you unless I said what I wanted."

"Oh, my. I suppose, well. An apothecary, we're trained not to pry, even the counter staff. People come in with all sorts of personal matters, of course. That's why we have the little side office, or my aunt does consultations before and after our shop hours, sometimes. Though of course, often it's someone gets sent down here with a note from the Healer with whatever potion they want written out on a slip. Much more private, that."

"And that wouldn't be a help at all, now, would it?"

Master Morris said, his lips turning up as he laughed. "I don't have a tidy little note from Matron."

"Is there something that brought you in, in particular, today?" Clara remembered both her manners and her business needs, all at once.

"Oh, I just wanted a bit of pleasant conversation in my day. Starting on a bit of more, what's the word, fragile negotiation for a business prospect, and of course that's delicate. I've learned to keep my hands off while it is, but it takes such a lot of self-control."

Something about how he put that made Clara cock her head for just a moment, before she caught herself. "I don't know much about your sort of business, I'm sure. Running a shop like this is very different. I - did I hear correctly, sir, that you did quite a lot of larger manufacturing during the War?"

"Where'd you hear that, then? Though I suppose all you shop girls must have quite the little gossip network. And Trellech isn't a large city at all. We all run across each other, one way or another."

"Oh, I mentioned hearing your name to a friend. Her husband works at the Ministry. She was very impressed, and she's impressed only by a certain sort of thing. He'd met you once or twice, I think, but I'm sure you wouldn't remember him."

"I do meet a lot of people, it's true." There was the flash of the smile again. "And most of them, so tediously unmemorable. You, on the other hand, are quite the opposite. Or, of course, I'd not be in here nearly so often." Before Clara could say anything sensible to that, he went on. "I was planning on taking someone out for an evening, you know, supper and a show, and of course I want to look my best. Perhaps you could advise me on a cologne or a shaving soap. Anything in that line."

That was easy enough from the sales side. "Do you use a straight razor or one of those new safety razors, sir?"

"My man uses a straight razor." Clara half flinched. Of course, he'd have a valet or a man or whatever people like him called people like that. Someone who saw to his clothes and his person and kept all in order so that an important man could focus on other things. She turned away to hide her face, but also to grab one of the trays. He added to her back. "He likes a badger hair brush, and a walnut oil soap, but I've been thinking it's not as kind to my skin as it could be."

It meant Clara could pull out a few variations. "This one has a touch of charmwork in the making, sir, that gets a smooth and even lather. If your man's a traditionalist, maybe he hasn't tried something like this yet? I can give you a sample, enough for five or six days, and you can see how it suits?" Mirroring the language the customer used was a trick she'd learned very early, and it continued to serve well.

"Oh, that's generous, yes. And perhaps some sort of aftershave to go with it? That I'll pay for, of course."

She laid out the range of choices, and then the scents. These were unscented, to start, but she could add a suitable number of drops to help. "This one is the most moisturising, sir, and this one more for toning. I'm sure your man has a steady hand, but if you have concerns about cuts and nicks, this one heals them quickly." She glanced up. No, that was not a face burned by small nicks, like Owen's could be.

Not that she'd seen Owen shave, now she thought about it. He had both a straight razor and a safety razor on his bit of shelf in the bath. She had no idea how one asked about that kind of thing when it was a husband and not a customer. Now that she thought about it, he must be using a safety razor, and the blades rather longer than he ought.

Clara hurriedly moved to show off the scent choices. Once Master Morris had made his choices - a juniper that smelled pleasantly evergreen - she wrapped them up for him in a pretty package. "Do let me know if you like the soap, sir. We can of course adjust if you like."

"You're so thoughtful, dear. I'm sure I'll have a grand time tomorrow and look my best. I'll come back and let you know, oh, Tuesday, next week."

She nodded. She'd be in the shop, of course, like always. "Whenever's convenient, sir. There we go." At that point, there was Mistress Alden, in to get the cream for her joints. Clara had packaged it up neatly this morning, knowing she'd be in. "Mistress Alden, good afternoon. Is the weather treating you well today? Not too cold yet."

That carried her into the afternoon and to closing time, without much time to think further. Or, blast, to catch up with Mrs Malcolm.

CHAPTER 16
OCTOBER 15TH AT THE FIELD

On the Friday, Owen found himself with some extra time in the afternoon. He'd turned up a few minutes early for work, but two hours in, they'd finished everything needed for the rest of the evening. There were sets to work on, of course, but they could wait for Saturday or Sunday. Maisery had had to take an hour or two to go sort out a snarl with a supplies order, something they'd been supposed to get two days ago, and now no one knew where it had got to.

Last fortnight's play had done well enough, though apparently not as well as Orlando had been hoping. The play had been a comedy, drawing on Commedia dell'arte and someone named Molière's take on it. A French bloke, after the Pact but long before now, that was the explanation Maisery had given him. The costumes had been rather grand, even if they were a bit on the shabbier side close up. All shiny silks and paste gems. There had been young lovers, a pair of elderly crotchety men in a feud, someone who both dressed as and played the fool, and a handful of others. It had been a decent testing ground for new folks for the panto, at least. Three of the four had been offered positions for that.

The fourth had stomped off when Orlando couldn't - and wouldn't - offer everything she was demanding. That included a private dressing room, an allowance for meals from a fine restaurant, new costumes, and a dozen other things, all for a secondary role. Eleanor Hobbs, their leading lady, was not nearly so demanding. Oh, she was imperious, certainly. She knew how to use her words to get just what she wanted. But she also understood what was possible and what wasn't.

That afternoon, though, Owen had come by the office to find Orlando bending over a series of papers, and he'd heard just enough that he wanted to talk to Golshan. Something about a difficult probate, that was the phrase he wanted to have stick in his mind. And there was something else a problem, besides the supplies, something about a costume that had been sent out for special cleaning. So, when the opportunity presented itself, a few free hours, he said he'd be back later. He trotted off to that club to see if Golshan was in and not busy. Just like before, he was shown back to the same room, and there was Golshan. "Owen! Come in. Need a meal?"

"Could use some of those sandwiches if they're on offer. Tea, too? I'm due back at the theatre by six."

"Cider for me, the sandwiches, a pot of tea, and anything else that suits, please." Golshan waved the request off before leaning his elbows on the table. "Something the matter?"

"I don't know, that's the rub. Thought I'd tell you, and you might know. I don't know enough about what's normal, yet."

"People still treating you well, I hope?" They'd managed

a brief word when Golshan had come with two others, a married couple. Their first outing since their daughter was born, apparently, and they were the people Golshan lived with now. They'd been laughing and smiling, an easy comfort with each other that Owen deeply envied. Seth, that was the man, had been demobbed last summer, a year before Owen, and it was hard not to resent that too.

Only the man made it hard to resent anything. He wasn't greedy with his happiness. Maybe that was the way to put it. He wanted other people to be happy. Or Golshan's want for happiness rubbed off. It was hard to tell. They'd known each other since school, from something no one had really explained. That was another thing to be envious of. Owen didn't have friends like that, and it was certainly too late to make any in childhood who might carry through to whatever his life was now.

He found himself caught up in that. When he came back to himself and the room he was in, Golshan was watching him, head cocked to one side. "It was good to see you, what, a month ago? And it was grand for me to bring Seth and Dilly. He didn't want to come without her, and Linden, that's their daughter. She's still tiny. But Seth's got sisters glad to lend an evening to letting them get out of the cottage, so there we were. And Seth and I've always liked a story that has plenty of trees in it."

Owen swallowed hard. "I was thinking you were very happy. A kind of happiness I don't think is on offer to me, even if I'm better off than I was a few months ago. Or a few years ago, but it's not like that part's hard." He hadn't meant to say that, but it was true and he wouldn't take it back now.

"Ah, yes." Golshan didn't let his words tumble out this time. He paused deliberately. Something in the conversation had shifted for him from a game to something that had his entire focus. "Seth saved my life. I saved his. That's what got me the chair." His hand gestured at it. "It's what got me a home. My family didn't want me back, they shoved me in a care home. Non-magical, even. Seth got demobbed and came and found me. So we take our pleasures as we can these days, and shame the world for wanting anything else."

There was a fire burning there, something that Owen didn't know how to describe, and certainly didn't want touching him. It was too potent, too dangerous. It would reveal things Owen wasn't at all willing to deal with. He looked away, out the window, because he didn't know what else to do. When he looked back, Golshan was leaning against his chair, hands folded in his lap, then he waved one hand. "Pardon. We all get intense about certain things, I think. All right, what can I do for you?"

At that point, the food and drink came, and so there was a bit more of a natural pause. Owen claimed a sandwich, and Golshan did as well this time. Once he'd had half of it, and a bit of the tea, Owen tried to explain his thoughts. "I was going by Orlando's office, and he told me a little. That someone made an offer to buy the theatre and turn it into a cinema. He wasn't happy with it. But I don't understand, and I don't much want to ask anyone there, because I don't know who knows, or who it'd upset."

"And you don't like upsetting people, do you? I've been noticing that." Golshan said it thoughtfully. It wasn't a way Owen had ever described himself, but it was true enough. He certainly hadn't wanted to upset Dad. His Dad had worked hard, and he'd had a temper along with it, and Owen had never wanted to be the target. And Mum, he'd never wanted to upset Mum because she'd get all weepy and he didn't know what to do with it. He'd certainly upset Clara, and he didn't understand why half the time, but he didn't enjoy doing that either.

Owen shrugged slightly. "Suppose not." It came out gruff.

Golshan nodded. "I can explain most of it, anyway. So, each of the theatres has a small number of owners. They own the building, and either they run the theatre or they hire someone to do it. Usually it's a couple of people going in together, a mix of money and talent. Theatre's an expensive thing, done well, even if people know where they can cut expenses without damaging the immersion of the thing." He flicked his fingers. "Got that?"

Owen nodded. "And there's - four theatres?"

"Four and the Opera House, which isn't run the same way, people rent time there, a mix of the opera, larger orchestras, sometimes massive performances. There's a board that manages it, and the city has a say in it. Different. Anyway. The New Ricardian's had the same ownership, the same two families for a while now, down three generations on one side, and two on the other. Orlando's the second generation in his, and there was another partner, died two years ago." He didn't say of what, so it could have been sudden, or the Naples Scourge or the War or an ordinary sort of illness. It wasn't like those stopped just because there were new ways to die.

"So that's just Orlando, now?" Owen could follow that far.

"Just so. And Ferris's estate, which is tied up six ways, because the heir he named died just before him, it turns out, and so there's a mess. And not enough ready cash, even if the current heir wanted half a theatre. So what's the new part? The cinema?"

"I don't understand how that would happen. I mean, the theatre's doing well enough, isn't it? A bit of a struggle, but keeping things going."

"Let me come back to that. The cinema part, that's a bold move. We don't have our own movie studios in Albion, of course. All of that's non-magical, and it takes the sort of, what do you call it, artistic infrastructure to make it work. America's starting to work on a magical cinema, but not England. But there's also no full-time cinema in Albion, and if someone could get the films, there'd be an interest. Me, I think it'd be better to split it half and half. Just because something's new doesn't mean it's good. Mind, I've only seen so much myself."

Owen blinked at him. "More than I have, sir."

That got him a laugh from Golshan, the kind that had to fade out before the man went on. "Don't sir me. The care home, they arranged films several times. I appreciate a well-done physical comedy, turns out, but a lot of the melo-drama is entirely ridiculous. You can see the villains a mile away, and they look like me - dark and swarthy and mous-taches." Which was a fair description in one way, but nothing like the cheerful man at the other end of the table. "Anyway, some references wouldn't make sense to folks who are mostly in the magical world, just like some of ours don't make sense to them."

"Even before we get into things like what someone thinks about the Tudors. Or I guess Richard III." Owen was getting used to that. He'd picked up comments about plays that existed but that were never staged in Trellech.

"Exactly. Knowing your audience is key. Which takes me to the sales." Golshan considered. "I haven't seen ticket numbers, of course. But they're running a series of choices that are a good draw. Robin Hood and his Merry Men and his Marian always do well, unless the actual script is awful, which this wasn't. Commedia does well, though I suppose that brings up some cast challenges. What are they doing next, do you know?"

"Ariadne's Thread? I don't know that one, except it has a lot of walls for sets." It was funny what people told him about plays. Lots of twine on the props list, and some complicated costuming and illusion work, apparently.

"That's the Aphra Behn play, isn't it? One of her magical ones, though her others can be quite funny. Comedy's generally popular if you have people with the right timing. That play's a little more dear to the stage. Making a minotaur always is, but it's only the one. The rest of the set's straightforward, and the costuming too. So you make a splash with the visible costume for the creature. It looks fancy, but the rest of the costuming's cotton or linen tunics." Golshan grinned. "And if they're testing out an illusionist for the panto, a good time to do it."

Owen considered all of that. "I hadn't thought about most any of that. Mind, it's not like I know what goes into each play. You said something about the cast?"

"There's Eleanor, she's very good, and she's got quite a theatrical range. She's getting into her thirties. They need a new ingénue who can match her on stage, and that's been a trick, I gather. And Randolph, the long-time leading man, he's losing his touch. Too close to King Lear for comfort, I think I heard someone put it. Now I can't get the phrase out of my head, and isn't that an awful place to be in? He's fine with plays he knows well, still. But asking him to do something new likely won't go well. So they need a new big draw, someone younger and handsome, who can take on a hero's role. That Robin was a new fellow, wasn't he?"

"He was. He's got a good role in the panto."

"There you go. But his stamina - in acting, at least - is untested. I suspect he does very well in bed. He looks the type." It had a note to it that Owen wasn't at all sure how to read or reply to. "And he's not blonde, but he's not ginger. Ginger's a hard sell in a hero for some reason." Golshan shrugged. "And you can see how that plays out down the line, then. Because the success of the show isn't just one person, even the ones with their name on the marquee. It's how they relate to everyone else on stage, and a fair number of people off it. Anyway, the rub of it is that if Orlando can have a spectacular season, now things are getting back to normal, maybe the eventual heir won't want to sell to the cinema."

"Why would someone change their minds?" Owen was not at all good at this business planning. He thought Clara might be rather better at it, for all sorts of reasons, she'd handled everything about Mum and the lease perfectly as far as he'd been able to tell.

"Selling out, that's one and done, isn't it? You get the money, but then there's no more income. And it's not the kind of thing where you can expect half a dozen people bidding against each other. If they can keep making a profit on it, year over year, that's a fine investment, even if Ferris's heir doesn't want to be active in running the place. Ferris left most of the details to Orlando, other than wanting to understand what decisions he was making about the long-term plans. He'd just turn up at the shows, laugh and applaud, and send round treats for the actors and crew." Golshan obviously approved of that last bit.

Owen nodded slowly. "So what can I do?"

"That's a good question. Help as you can, be steady, and let me know if you hear more things? Might be I could lend a hand, or know someone who could. That's a lot of what I do now, introduce people."

Owen swallowed, then glanced at the time. "I should get back, probably. Lend a hand." It came out a little weakly.

"I'm glad you're there." That seemed entirely honest, and Owen blinked. Golshan went on. "They're good folks. So are you. I'm hoping you can all see this through."

CHAPTER 17
OCTOBER 18TH AT THEIR FLAT

Monday, Clara came home from the shop to find that Owen had just taken the kettle off the hob, and he had a plate of biscuits and sandwiches waiting. She glanced from the food to him, not sure what to make of it.

"You made tea?" She busied herself taking off her jumper. When she turned around, he was holding out the chair to her.

"I did. You'd meant some of the roast for tonight, yes?" He settled in the other chair. "The tea should be ready in a minute or two. It went in the pot just as you came in."

It was a quite reasonable tea. He'd toasted the bread for the sandwiches and made them with chicken and a bit of the pickle she'd made last week. Nothing wasteful, nothing wrong. Except she did not know what to do with this. She made her own tea; she had for years. Since long before they were married. "That's right. And the chutney goes well with it, don't you think?"

He gave her a flashing smile that was even more confusing. "You're an excellent cook. I haven't told you that near often enough."

It made her think of the complaints of the wives meeting on Sundays, how their husbands wolfed down food like they were starving, barely tasting it. Or others turned away from proper cooked food, as if the years of living on tinned mush had changed everything for them. It probably had. But all the posters and speeches about being strong had been about austerity measures, and the fact their men might die. They hadn't talked near often enough about life-changing injuries, or about all the small sharp wounds of how all their habits had changed.

The wives left behind couldn't show their love through food to someone who wouldn't eat it. Even if the reason wasn't personal, it still felt it. And there didn't seem to be anything that mended it. It was worse when nobody could even talk about it, because anything around the topic was edged with barbs and thorns.

But here was Owen, having made tea. She let out a breath. "Thank you for making tea. I wasn't expecting it." It was the truth, and he might as well hear that, too. Then she realised she hadn't responded to his compliment. "And thank you. Talking with some of the wives, I think a lot of us have realised that what you liked maybe changed? And then there's the problem of what we can get in the shops or afford."

"It must be a lot of work I don't know how to appreciate. But on Mondays at least, I'm glad to get tea together for you. You're working, and I'm not. And if I can be a bit more help with getting the roast together, or do a run to the shops in the morning before I go to work. You'd have to give me a list, what you want, but that's easy enough."

She looked at him, taking her time about it. "Why?"

"I should lend more of a hand around here. You've been very patient." Owen shrugged and looked at his own plate, taking a bite of sandwich. "This is your bread, right?" That was once he'd swallowed.

"It is. Nothing fancy. But the baker's getting more and more dear, and I can make bread easily enough." Clara took another bite or two. Admittedly, this one had come out particularly well. One could never quite tell with bread.

"I like yours better, I think. Though if you did some rolls, those would be good for this sort of sandwich, wouldn't they?" Owen reached to pour out the tea, adding a splash of cream to hers without asking. Just the right amount.

Clara considered. "I could do rolls. I've been doing two loaves, I could do one as rolls. They keep better, with the charms, than a cut loaf. I'll do that Sunday."

"Is that what you do, then? The roast and bread and all?" Owen shifted a little, leaning back. "I don't see most of that, not now."

"It's what I've done for a good long while. Since your mum wasn't up for the cooking. She had a very particular schedule, you must remember that." It was one of the first times she'd brought up Owen's Mum in weeks.

He laughed, rueful. "Oh, she did. And never let me forget it. You send the laundry out still?"

"That, yes. We really don't have the space for it, not without a lot of bother. It's a bit dear, but it takes so much time if you're out of the house all day."

Owen lifted his hand. "You're working hard. I'm working now. Let me know if we can't manage it, but I think that's a good use for what we make. And I've not picked up the more expensive vices, really. Not beyond a bit of beer or cider when I can."

She thought about that. He didn't smoke, or at least not much, which was curious, now she thought about it. Most of the veterans did. And he drank moderately, never tipping into anger or upset. She was lucky, and she knew it. Even if right now, she was also very confused about the state of things. "You've been very reasonable." She hesitated. "I could show you the account books sometime? When we can find time?" It was tricky, the two of them never having the same days off.

"I'd like to understand it better. But you've done a tremendous job managing it all." He tilted his head. "Has it been complicated all along?"

"It has. Shortages during the War, inflation. Figuring out what your mum had in the bank, in there. They didn't much want to talk to me, even after I brought the marriage papers. I appreciate they're cautious, but it was tricky. We had to get people to vouch for the marriage and all."

Owen frowned. "You didn't say."

"It didn't..." Her voice trailed off. It hadn't seemed worth bothering him with. "You had much bigger worries. And it wasn't as if you could have done much. They wouldn't have taken a letter. Too easy to forge. One of them explained that to me after."

"Huh." Owen nodded. "I'd like to go over the sums, but it seems like you're very good at it. I've done a fair bit of mending things around here, as I can, but is there anything else I can do with that?"

She shook her head. Clara had given him her list. That should be enough.

"Do you mind if I take over tending Mum's room? I'd like to go through some things. You needn't dust, or whatever it is you've been doing."

"Dusting, mostly." Clara let out a huff of breath. "It

doesn't take long. Once a week, ten or twenty minutes. An hour, if I dust under all the little objects, but that's only once a month."

"I can take that over." He nodded once, decisively. "And you take things round to the laundry? Can I do that, or do the hours not work?"

She considered that particular problem. It would be easier if Owen took it on. He would have less trouble hauling the laundry bag, and he could go when they weren't so busy. "If you wouldn't mind? I can let them know. They're just a block or two. Not too far."

"There." Owen looked quite pleased with himself. "And if there are other things. I know sometimes handing something over is even more work. I'm fairly confident about managing the laundry, so long as I'm not the one actually doing it. When it comes to washing, I can do uniforms, and all the bits that go with them, but that won't do for other things."

She half-laughed. "No. But what brought this on?"

"Oh, talking in the workshop. Listening more than I was talking. You saw the adagio dancers, right. When you came, they were mending a few things and talking. A woman, her two brothers and her husband, I told you that?"

"You did. And the other two brothers are married, too?" That had caught her attention, somehow, the way the three couples had to be living so much in each other's pockets. Not that their costumes had anywhere to put a pocket, even the men.

"They are. Anyway, they were chatting away, and someone asked them how they split things up. I hadn't really thought about how much of it was falling on you." He shrugged once. Clara was even less sure what to make of that than the rest of the conversation. It was on the one hand good that he'd realised. The sandwiches were quite well made, the tea was properly steeped. Having him take over the laundry would simplify things. But to have him do it because someone else explained, that also stung a bit.

There was that old proverb that had been stuck in her head. The one about how shoemaker's wives - or shoemaker's children, not that that was a thing here - went barefoot. The crafter was so focused on the craft and everyone else that those closest went without. It was true about her shoes, and had been for ages. It was true about other things too. And she didn't remotely know how to even bring it up.

"How are things at work? You'd been worried. Anything there you can talk about?" There, she'd change the subject. That would be better. Probably. Or at least it might be informative about his likely mood.

"There's a man wants to buy out the theatre and turn it into a cinema. And that would be a shame. Pots of money, I guess. But it would be so many people out of work. Not just me." Owen spread his hands. "Though I care about that. But everyone else. And not everyone's got skills that can pick up and go do something else. I feel more confident now I could get other handyman work and do it well."

"Do you know what sort of man? Or what sort of money?" It was an idle question, but sometimes there was gossip. Who knew, she might hear gossip herself, maybe.

"Something to do with supplies. Making money on the back of the trenches." He went stiff then, hard-edged. "The sort who didn't care about stinting on materials or the making. So we got boots that leaked, and food that had gone spoiled in the tins, guns that didn't fire. All sorts of things. And it kept happening. I don't know which sort of thing he made, but none of that rot's good."

Clara held up her hands, feeling a wave of anger and

frustration coming at her. If what he was saying was true - and it must be. She'd heard other stories, though never with details - he had every right to be upset. "I - it." She stalled. Apologising would be very British of her, but this was, in fact, absolutely not her fault. Even if the instinct to apologise was just as embedded in Albion.

He stood, going to put the teapot back by the kettle again. When he turned back, he let out a long breath. "Didn't mean to do that to you. Forgive me?"

She nodded once, murmuring a simple "Yes."

"Maybe a walk before the evening?" He made the offer cautiously, as if he didn't know what she'd do.

"Ah, been run off my feet. They're aching." She shook her head. "You go, if you'd like. I'll put my feet up and read."

Owen nodded once. He cleared the dishes and washed them, while she put on warm socks and her slippers, and then he left her to her book.

CHAPTER 18
OCTOBER 20TH AT THE THEATRE

Owen finished his immediate work Wednesday afternoon in good time, and Maisery sent him off to see if Edgar needed a hand.

"Isn't Edgar up north or wherever with the actors?" Owen asked, as he tucked his toolbox away.

"Nah, came back yesterday. He's having a look at the panto supplies, seeing what we need to mend or make now we're settled on a script. Go ask him about it, see what he could use some help with. I won't need you until tomorrow."

Owen shrugged, snagged a cuppa from their little break cart and drank it down. Then he trotted down to the costume room, where he heard some noises. Edgar was half into one of the massive wardrobes, bent over, so he was only visible from the waist down. Owen cleared his throat, loudly enough to not be startling. "Edgar?"

"Oh, moment!" There was rummaging inside the wardrobe, then Edgar reappeared, holding a bright pink dress, very much the colour of fuchsia. "This won't do at all, but can you hold it? I want something behind it. Or did you need something?"

"Maisery sent me down to help you, so I might as well be your coat rack as much as anything else." He hesitated, then added, "She's in a mood, about something, more about materials we should have had? I don't think she wanted to take it out on me."

Edgar grimaced at that. "Glad to have you." He didn't comment on the rest of it, which said a lot by itself, the running tension the senior theatre folks all seemed to have now. "Fair enough. I'll hand you a few other things, then." He produced after a moment a violently purple evening gown, then a set of panniers made from an extremely energetic chartreuse. Finally, he came out with his apparent goal, a beautifully trimmed tabard and cloak of deep crimson. "There we are. There's armour back there somewhere. Hang those up, would you, wherever you can?"

"For Brutus, that?" Owen nodded at the tabard and cloak.

"Just so. Easier when your hero stands out on stage. I need to have a rummage for something for our Innogen. It needs to stand up to it, but, well, there's the rub. Eleanor's getting a little old for it, not that I'd say so near her. But she's no longer an ingénue."

Owen turned to hang up what he was holding, so he could come back to take more. "Is Eleanor playing Innogen, then?"

"She'd rather not, actually. There's a rather nice role in this one for Diana. You know how some of the pantos have a fairy? We have a goddess in this one, one tied to the land. Perris - you met him, didn't you? Does our illusions and effects. Anyway, he has a really nice line in shadow puppetry. She comes on stage, and behind her you can see a silhouette of a great antlered deer and a bear and a boar and all that."

"Huh." Owen could see how that'd be effective. "All right. But if she's Diana, she can't be Innogen. How does the story go? I've heard it before, I mean, school primers."

"The way our panto goes, the story starts when they land in fair and verdant Albion. Cliffs and ocean and all that. Diana has been on stage already, to tell them where to go, and then she pops in and out." Edgar shrugged. "We're stealing a bit from a Merovingian legend, actually. There's a whole sequence where Brutus goes to sleep and has a dream, and sees a wild animal outside, and it's all very funny and advances the plot. Three different quests, anyway. The last one is the giants, who don't want Brutus to stay."

Owen cocked his head. "That seems tricky to make into a panto comedy? Though I see how some of the staging could be interesting. So we've got Diana, instead of one of the Fatae."

"Just so. Honestly, when there's the whole Good Fatae and Bad Fatae pair, it's a lot. I know it's traditional, and they can have such a grand time chewing the scenery in the best way possible. But I always do worry we're going to do something to give offence to the proper Fatae. Whether we mean to or not."

Owen considered all of that entirely above his pay grade, honestly. That was what other people were for, to make sure there weren't insults to the Fatae or, really, unspecified others. Though he hadn't really considered the theatrical implications of that. "Does someone check?"

"More or less. There are a set of things we've got permission to do. Plays in the standard canon, particular treatments of the Fatae. Some of it goes through the

Ministry. Sometimes they get one of the Council to have a look and sign off. We can't do anything that looks like that sort of ritual. If we mention offerings, there's always something strange and not quite right about them. Just in case people try to get ideas."

"Huh." Owen considered that. "Like, um. Oh, we saw one when I apprenticed that had the offerings be milk and honey and a perfect apple. And everyone knows it's not an apple."

"Exactly. But you wouldn't want to make an offering in a play and have someone show up in the middle of your act. For one thing, it would entirely discombobulate all the blocking." Edgar made a joke out of it, but Owen could see the problem. Not that it made it easier to talk about it.

"So, Eleanor's playing Diana. Who's the dame?" An important question in a panto.

"The cook. Classic role, really. All bustling in at a serious moment with some new treat. There's a good chance for a funny bit with the things she pulls off a tray, you know the sort of thing, all puns and wordplay. And she can chase someone off the stage with a pot and a spoon. You get a nice little smattering of camp life, and her trying to push her son up into a better position because of her proximity to the heroes."

Owen grunted. "And the son?"

"Iawn. Who played Robin, you know him."

"Ah, right. That'd be a good role to give him a tryout. Not the main character, but something substantial."

"Exactly. So we have Madeline for our Innogen, and she's new. Randolph as Corineus, who's a bit older than Brutus, still a fierce warrior, but not the young hero. And we're getting in Theo Robbins for Brutus." Edgar said it like Owen should know the name.

"Theo?"

"Oh, don't you follow theatrical gossip at all? I suppose you wouldn't. Went to Schola, dear boy that he is. He's one of the Nine Muses. That's the society that focuses on the arts. Lovely voice, singing and speaking. He's been making quite a name for himself on the London stage, but he agreed to do the panto. His mum owes Orlando's wife a favour, I think is how that worked, but you didn't hear it from me."

Edgar admittedly knew quite a lot of gossip, and wasn't shy about sharing it, but Owen had noticed already that very little of it was nasty. He shared the good parts about someone else, the things you wanted to know about them. What they were good at, what you should ask them about, all of that. "So that's a win for us, then? A chance of keeping things going a bit further?"

"Oh, yes. And he's got a crowd of admirers. We'll likely want your help keeping things manageable at the stage door when he's ready to leave. You're sturdy enough."

Owen flinched. "I suppose."

Edgar caught it almost immediately. "A problem, dear boy?" This time, that was applied to Owen himself. Edgar was generous with endearments, in an easy way that Owen still didn't know how to read. Friendly, absolutely.

"I'm still not much for crowds, I suspect. But if you want me to loom a bit, I can probably pull that off."

"Ah. Yes. Let me give some thought to that. Are loud bangs a problem for you?"

"It depends, on the whole, if I think they're aimed anywhere near me." Owen was pleased he kept his voice steady and his tone light. He didn't have it nearly as bad as some of the other men he'd seen and talked to. But he didn't trust himself not to react as he had in the trenches. It would take a long time for all his jagged edges to wear down. It wasn't as if he could take sandpaper to them.

"We'll give you plenty of warning. But there's a bit of a battle scene, clanging metal and all that, and an arrow striking someone. You can watch the whole thing when we first rehearse it, with the script in hand. Would that help?"

It probably would, honestly, and Owen nodded.

"Besides, having someone watching's a help. Orlando's eyes can only be in one place, and Maisery's back stage for that part." Edgar shrugged. "At any rate, we're getting Theo. We'll make good use of him. He's doing us a grand turn. Maybe we'll convince him to do a show a year, one play or another, if we keep the place going. It would do everyone some good."

"And maybe find some other people to fill in the gaps?" Owen considered. "I had tea with Golshan, Friday. We were talking a little about the, what do you call it, filling out parts."

"What we really want, honestly, is to find a stream of people who don't necessarily want the lead role. That's harder to come by." Edgar buried his head in the wardrobe again, coming out with a golden yellow frock, then something in deep green. "Oh, this might do for Diana. I think we wanted something sleeker for Innogen, and maybe blue. Or maybe green. We'll see."

Owen considered, as Edgar bent to his task. When the other man's head emerged again, he asked, "Do you ever watch the guild shows?"

"Not very often, dear boy. One of the great splits of the dramatic."

"I don't know all that much about it. I've only ever had bit parts before the War. But they're a ritual drama, of sorts. A mummer's play, isn't that the word for it? A different kind of story, sure, but there are men and women who, I don't know the word. Step into the part. Inhabit it properly. And you could hear how well they project their voice, and see if they hit their marks, and if they draw attention to them the way you want here."

Edgar turned, leaning back against the side of the wardrobe. "You might just have an idea there. You're right that it's a different kind of theatre, a different style of it, but some things are eternal to both. Do you know the schedule?"

"They're rehearsing now for the spring and then for the Midsummer Faire. Two different stories, usually, but the same people for the year. Something for the autumn too, but that's not always a play. I hadn't re-upped my guild dues." Not enough money, though he might scrape it together in a week or three. "But I could go round, ask about that, and ask about the plays."

"Would you, dear boy? It's an avenue we've been entirely ignoring. It's not just marching on stage, going 'Behold the moon, under my light is the linen spun' or whatever nonsense fits? I mean, you make shoes. What stories do you tell in your ritual dramas, then?"

"Well, there are the elves and the shoemaker, for one. There's a handful of stories? Sometimes about a battle, the nail in the boot, the care about it, being the thing that matters." He caught a flash of something as Edgar pulled it out of the bottom of the cupboard. "Is that a boot? There's something on the heel."

When Edgar handed it over, Owen could see that one nail was coming loose, and that just re-hammering it wouldn't do any good. It had worn away where it had been holding. "Can I take this home and fix it properly? Bring it back tomorrow? This is no good. It'll catch and scar the floor every step."

"Oh, would you? Spare us sorting it out. Or bring your kit or whatever around tomorrow. We can have you go through the lot. Buckles, too? We don't want one of those giving way in performance. I need to check the shoe sizes, figure out what we need."

"I know some of the fitting charms. They won't make it entirely a different size, but I can get a better grip on the foot without binding." It had been ages since he'd done those, but he remembered how they went. And maybe he could practise on Clara's shoes tonight or something of the kind.

They left it at that, a pleasant conversation about how many pairs of shoes needed looking at, and where to set them up.

CHAPTER 19
OCTOBER 22ND AT THE SHOP

Clara was out from behind the counter, working on cleaning the glass on the display cases. It had to be done regularly, people would lean their hands on it. Aunt Lillian had invested, years ago, in charmwork that helped keep the glass clean. The charms were beginning to wear a little now. The glass was still easier to clean without streaks, but Clara had to tend to it every couple of days.

The problem was doing it when the store was open just encouraged people to stop by at exactly the wrong moment. And she didn't much want to come early or stay late. It was getting darker in the mornings and certainly in the evenings. She found it a little eerie to be in the building with no one else when it was dark. She didn't want to light up rooms she wasn't in, but if she didn't, it felt like something was in the corners waiting. Like a child's nighttime terrors, or rather like her own from a particular age, or so she'd been told.

It was also a tad undignified to be cleaning, with the

soft rag in one hand, and a spray bottle of the cleaning solu-
tion in the other. But she'd done everything else she needed
to, including unpacking the latest shipment from Aunt
Lillian and putting it all away. She'd fully restocked the
shelves, first rotating the older stock in. Some of this shipment had a finicky shelf life. A good nine or twelve months,
all of it. Aunt Lillian didn't make up stock of things that
would spoil before they could be sold. She'd do that on
demand, normally. Or right now, they had an agreement
with the Temple of Healing to run older stock down there
when there was still a month on it.

She'd have to do that tomorrow, probably. Even if it was
a Saturday, the shop would be open in the morning and
early afternoon. It wasn't as if the Temple of Healing closed
up outside of ordinary business hours. There would be
someone at the receiving door who could sign the receipts.

Clara was bending down when she heard the chime of
the door behind her, rubbing at a spot on the glass at about
knee height. She couldn't imagine who'd done that. No,
wait, Mistress Wellmount had been in with her grandchil-
dren, and one of them was just about that height. The
bottles in that display were rather pretty colours too, a
rainbow designed to catch the eye, echoing another set up
at an adult's eye level in the case above.

As she turned, she heard an appreciative chuckle. "I was
beginning to wonder if you ever came out from behind your
counter. Good afternoon, Mistress Hubbard. You look very
well today." His eyes drifted down, then back up to her face,
or near enough to it. She wasn't at all sure how to interpret
that.

"Master Morris." She nodded. "Pardon the cleaning,
just let me put the things away." She ducked around the far

end of the counter, putting a bit more space between them. Slipping the bottle and rag into the cabinet under the sink, she washed her hands. The cleaning supplies left a rather acrid scent behind, and it went badly with showing off other items. She rubbed a bit of skin cream from the jar by the sink in, tucked her hair back behind her ear, and came back out.

Master Morris was glancing around the shop again, as if seeing what had changed. He'd been gone for a fortnight. He'd come in to say he had some business travel to do, not to worry if she didn't see him. She hadn't been going to worry, so continuing to not worry was quite easy, really. He'd been a good customer these past months, but there were a good number of other steady customers. One built a reliable business by spreading your wares around, not just in one place.

"Sir." She settled her fingertips lightly on the wood of the cabinet. "I hope your business travels went well?"

"Oh, yes, quite." Morris gestured at the space. "Goodness me, I don't think I've ever explained what I do, have I? Not really. It was seeing your feet that made me think of it. Your shoes, pardon, you have such lovely ankles, but they don't do you any favours."

Clara couldn't stop herself from glancing down at her feet. Her shoes were a bit worn, in the way that polish couldn't quite fix. And there was a scratch on the heel of the right one. Surely he hadn't spotted that. It wasn't like people normally looked at her feet. Certainly Owen hadn't, and he had some professional reason to do so.

"Ah, there you go. Now you're self-conscious. But I notice shoes, that's one of the things I make. Well, my factory." He said it the way some people talked about their children who had done something slightly clever. Clara was never sure how to respond to that particular coyness. Praising someone for having a factory seemed ridiculous. It was even more silly to praise the factory for doing the thing someone had designed it to do.

"Shoes?" That just sounded daft.

"Boots, during the War." He sounded even more proud of that. "We had one of the larger contracts for it, actually. General supplies, not just magical, but we were able to take some, oh, not shortcuts, but efficiencies, due to magic. It let us undercut the other bids. You must understand that, surely, a shop like this. Every bit you can save off the cost of an item adds up, when you're making hundreds or thousands or tens of thousands."

Clara tried to get her head around making tens of thousands of anything. At best, they did dozens, and small numbers of dozens at that. "That seems like a great deal to manage."

"Oh, yes, it is. And was. And now, of course, we're retooling for other things. Army boots being not nearly so much in demand, though of course there's a standing army, some still aren't demobbed, and all that. So we were looking at the designs for women's shoes. Children's. All that. You really must let me bring you a pair to try. I can send for whatever size."

Clara had no idea what she thought of that. A moment or three later, she realised she had no idea what Owen would think of that.

Master Morris took her silence for agreement. "Your size, dear?"

Before she could stop herself, she responded to the question. "A six." She did not have large feet, rather average, really.

"Grand, grand. I should have something in a few days.

I'll stop by then. Or let you know, at the very least. I do hope you've had a pleasant time in my absence?"

"Oh, yes." She gathered herself up. "My husband's working at one of the theatres, I think I mentioned. He arranged a ticket for me. That was a delightful evening. Music hall, but some very entertaining performers."

"I'm sure." That had a note to it that was a tad patronising. As if he himself was not the sort of person who went to music hall performances. "That was, you told me, yes, the New Ricardian." There was something smooth and slippery in his voice for just a moment, but she couldn't make sense out of it.

Then he went on, as if nothing were unusual. "A fine theatre with a good history. At any rate, the shoes, I forgot to tell you the most interesting thing. Of course, we're fully mechanised, with only a few steps done by hand. All the enchantment work is done before the leather and all goes into the machines."

She frowned. "I thought that could cause problems? Wasn't there a story in the Moon, I don't know? Several years ago." Right around the time she and Owen were married, she'd been decidedly distracted.

"Oh, not for the right sort of person. All entirely managed. That's why they've got me on hand, to make sure that sort of thing isn't a problem." Something in that rang hollow. Then he went right along, rolling into something else. "If your husband's working at the theatre, that must be rather inconvenient hours." Clara didn't begin to know how to respond to that. When she stayed silent, Morris tilted his head. "I'd be delighted to take you out to supper sometime. Quite public, of course, whatever you felt comfortable with."

"I, well." She swallowed.

"Do say yes. I've rather a lack of pleasant conversation in my evenings. All work and no play, makes Jack a dull boy. And Jill a dull girl."

Clara managed to gather herself. "I'm afraid I'm still sorting things out at home. There's rather a lot, with my husband back. Rearranging the space and all. And with both of us working, not so many times we can move things around." She swallowed. "Perhaps sometime in the future."

"I'll keep asking, then." He smiled, broadly. "I suppose your diligence is quite enticing, too. And certainly your aunt must appreciate it no end. I hope she's doing well and will be back in Trellech before too long?"

"The friend she's helping is doing better, but it will be a few weeks yet, at least. And I think she's rather enjoying the mountain air." Clara cleared her throat. "Did you come in for anything in specific today?"

"Oh, yes, quite. Let's see, let me look at my little list." He pulled a notebook out from his inside jacket pocket, consulting it. "My housekeeper wondered about cleaning supplies. Could you show me, oh, something like that spray for the glass you were using? Or something for metal polish. And a wood polish."

That, at least, Clara could do without fear of stumbling over her own tongue. She got out samples of everything, asked the usual questions about scent, and had absolutely no qualms about selling him on the more expensive polishes. They did, in fact, work better. You paid for what you got, but they also had a better profit for less fuss on Aunt Lillian's end.

When he left, a good quarter hour later, she was pleased with the sales for the day, but still unsettled a bit by the whole experience. First, it was ridiculous that someone like him would come look at someone in a shop for company. Second, she was married, even if she wasn't at all sure about the state of her marriage. And third, surely there were people who were more willing to keep such a man company. He wouldn't keep asking.

CHAPTER 20
OCTOBER 25TH AT THE FLAT

Owen had tea ready again when Clara came home on Monday night. She blinked at him, as if she hadn't expected him to do such a thing twice. Then she kissed him on the cheek, companionably. "Will it keep if I wash up? I was moving some packing material around. I feel like there's dust all through my hair."

"Absolutely." He could always start the kettle up again. "Thirty minutes?"

She nodded absently as she went off to start the bath running, then to the bedroom. She came out a minute later in a dressing gown. Owen realised, all of a sudden, he'd never seen her, not since he'd come back, without a layer of the armour of her clothes, unless she were already in bed. It made him swallow hard, and then let out his breath. He still didn't have an idea what he was doing with her, what he'd done wrong or clumsily. It was being an apprentice all over again, but this time without anyone to look to for guidance.

Even at the theatre, there wasn't much help. Orlando was married, but he never talked much about his wife.

Maisery was a widow, details unspecified, and he hadn't dared ask anyone about it. Edgar was a bachelor. As he said, his hours and travel were entirely unsociable to anyone decent. The Perrels were an example of a marriage, but they all - all three couples of them - were so close they weren't much of a model Owen could use. And Master Corwin and his wife had been a model of how to run a business, but not how to be close. Intimate.

He hadn't wanted a marriage like his parents. They'd settled into reasonable fondness by the time he was paying attention, but tempers had flared, and especially if something wasn't done the way Mum wanted it. He'd hoped for something else, with Clara. Only now he felt like he was on one bit of ground. There was a bridge to where she was, but he didn't know how to get onto it or if it would bear his weight. Whatever he thought he'd known wasn't much help.

And it wasn't like he could even put most of it into words. She didn't blame him; she didn't snap at him. He'd heard bits of that, when he'd gone round the Veterans Club for a beer, now and again, or standing in line when he'd had to report he wasn't working. Owen, in his turn, tried to stay out of her way, to move to the couch or the floor of the sitting room if he thought he'd be too restless. He wanted to be considerate. It seemed the least he could offer her.

While he waited, he did a bit more tidying in the kitchen. He'd been hesitant to move anything around, other than to pick it up and clean under it and put it right back. Mum had been very firm about that sort of thing. Clara might not be, but she did most of the cooking, and she surely had reasons for where she had put things, even if they made little sense to him.

While he went over the woodwork with a damp cloth,

to get whatever dust had filtered onto it, he considered the curtains. They were a rather faded cotton print in pinks. He remembered Mum putting them up when he was about ten. It had made her smile, but he'd never thought it suited the kitchen. Too dim, somehow. Being around the theatre and the bright colours had made him think differently about it, and so had seeing Clara come and go. She favoured brighter colours.

The silk flower sat in a little glass in the centre of the windowsill. Clara had put it in an old jam jar with a slight crack, too elderly to be used for canning again, she'd said. He thought that added a bit of colour, but of course, it didn't go with the pink of the curtains at all. He was still staring at it when he heard Clara come out. She came up behind him and cleared her throat. "Something the matter?"

"Would you mind if I changed that up a bit?"

She blinked at him. "The curtains? Your mum was so fond of them, I didn't want to change them." It was a very considerate sort of answer. On the other hand, it made him tilt his head.

"Can we talk about that a little? Over tea? Here, let me get the kettle going again." She came around beside him, then to the chair he'd had waiting. Her hair was in a loose braid, charmed mostly dry. Or he assumed it was a charm. She'd put on an old dress, the way there were signs of wear, but it was a glowing teal, and it brought out her eyes. "I like that colour on you." Now he'd said it, he felt completely clumsy.

She blinked at him. "You do?"

"I'm finding I like the bright colours. The silk rose. That dress. A lot of the costumes, of course, they're bright so they stand out, and so are the sets. After years of beige and dun and grey and mud, it's..." He shrugged. He couldn't put into words how much he'd hated that, and the colours that were worse. Those were the blood colours, or the ones that were the pale green of illness or the burning red of infection.

"Oh." She glanced at the curtain. "I didn't want to change anything." She repeated it, like it was some charm for understanding.

"I'd noticed." He grimaced. That came out sharper than he'd meant. "I mean. I think I understand why? But Mum's not living here now. You are. We are. We could make some changes. I—" He stopped, then just gave up and let it come out in a rush. No playwright would ever give a character this sort of muddied speech, but it couldn't be helped. "I appreciate you didn't want to change things while I was gone. But would you be all right if we did now?"

Clara's shoulder twitched. "If you like. I'm not very good at that sort of thing, though. And I don't - with Aunt Lillian away, I don't have time to think of anything new."

Owen frowned at that, then poured the boiling water. It had still been hot. The kettle hadn't taken long to come back to the boil. "Like your head is full up?"

She nodded once. "And I can't spare the thinking about it or asking what you've done, or anything like that."

"How do you feel about me asking you about a couple of choices? When I figure out things? I can buy fabric, I suppose. I know how to sew. Nothing fancy, but shoes need quite a lot of sewing, and putting curtains together is just hemming and making something to hang them from." He glanced up. "A pocket along the short end for the rod, right?"

She looked up too, and when she looked back down, their eyes met. He found her half-smiling, and he smiled back, encouraged. "Like that. Sure. There's a couple of decent fabric shops, not too dear. Or I'm sure the theatre can tell you the good places."

"It'd make a good conversation. I'm sure people have opinions. And I have some time, when I'm just sitting around, I could do a bit of sewing. I don't know how to use a machine, but by hand's easy enough."

"I have a machine. I've made most of my own clothes. But—" Her shoulder twitched. "No time. No money for new fabric."

That made Owen blink. "Did I know that? Had you mentioned?"

"Probably not?" She looked away, reaching for a sandwich. Chicken and chutney again, with a sliced up apple. "I didn't know you were interested, I guess." She sounded tired now.

"I was thinking, when you came in, how you always look so put together. I don't know how to describe it, just —" Owen ducked his chin. "I do notice."

There was another flicker across her face, a bit of a smile, a bit of something else. She picked at her food for a moment, nibbling at one slice of apple. "Perhaps we might, um. Some time in bed, tonight?"

"Oh." He paused. "Oh! I'd like that, yes. If you're not too tired?"

There was a twitch of her shoulder. "You must have..." Her voice trailed off. "I want to be fair to you."

Owen was not at all sure how to answer that. Yes, he wanted more time with her. Intimately, if they could figure that out. Yes, he liked when she smiled. But he wasn't sure how to explain what he wanted, mostly. He couldn't get it to make sense in his own head. How could he tell her anything that made any sense?

They ate quietly, and then spent an hour or two in the

sitting room. She knitted a bit, and he offered to read bits of the paper out loud. That went quite well, really. So much so that by the time she looked up at the clock, he'd forgotten the time. "Perhaps we might?" She just glanced at the hall.

"Um. Yes!" She put her knitting away, and he folded the paper up. He could finish it tomorrow morning, or there'd be another one, of course. There was an ongoing bit about a mysterious house, from right after the Pact, and they kept discovering new things in it. It was a bit like some of the stories about finding Egyptian tombs, but much less full of mummies. Or even, apparently, ghosts.

He followed her into the bedroom, and she began to undo her dress. He bit his lip, then reached to touch her hand. "May I?" She hadn't let him before. Now, she blinked, wide-eyed, before she nodded once. He took his time, feeling the shape of the buttons, the horn they were made of, the way they slipped through well-worn button holes. He let his fingers brush the cloth, then her skin, as it became visible.

When she was mostly undressed, he leaned to kiss her, doing his best to take his time and let her respond. She wasn't hesitant, exactly, but she seemed almost shy, as if she weren't sure what to do. Or at least, what to do with him. He knew other men had come home to find wives and fiancees and sweethearts had put their hearts in other hands, or their bodies. He didn't think she had, but he didn't know what to do with how things were.

A few minutes later, they were on the bed, with his clothes shrugged off into a neat pile. Owen had done his best to find what pleased her with his touch, but he felt somehow clumsy. She seemed happier with it than before, though, and when he finally pressed into her, he could feel she was hot and damp, clinging to him. As he began to move, he felt her shift under him, the way one of her legs came up around his hip, or her body arched.

He thought she found her own pleasure, finally, but by the time that happened, he couldn't think much about anything except his own. When he'd finished, trying not to just collapse on her in a sated heap, he felt her hand come up to brush his shoulder. He nuzzled at hers, since it was right there, then rearranged himself a bit more comfortably. Once he lifted his face again, he could see her just drifting on the bed.

"Good for you?" His voice cracked at the end, and he cursed inside his head.

"You're kind." It came out as almost a whisper. Then she cleared her throat. "I suppose you must enjoy it quite a lot?"

Owen swallowed. "It feels very good to me. To be close like that. Besides everything else." He didn't know how to explain to her how it had been years of not being close, or not being able to choose to be close, or who you were close with. Not having any real autonomy about what his body did at all. "You can always tell me no."

Clara turned her face away, and he worried he'd said the absolutely wrong thing. Then she looked back at him. "You haven't asked, but I'm using a contraception potion." He hadn't, and his hand instinctively went down to touch her stomach.

"Oh." He frowned. "I hadn't thought to ask." He'd assumed, maybe, but right now he couldn't even figure out if he'd assumed she was or she wasn't. Before he could stumble through other words, a flurry came out of her.

"As we are right now, do you really think we could manage a child? The hours I'm working, the hours you're working, the money we don't have? And an apothecary with a lab in the back's no place for a baby, far too much that could go into a mouth the wrong way."

"Hush. Wait." It came out wrong again. "It's fine. That makes sense. If things change, we can talk about it." He glanced down at her body, then back up. "I'm glad you thought of the potion. You seem to think of quite a lot."

She made a small incoherent noise he couldn't interpret, then shifted. "I should sleep. I've a lot to do in the morning." It put an end to the conversation, certainly. He let her rearrange onto her side, before settling to curl up behind her. She didn't object to that, nor to the arm draped over her. He found himself half-waking when she got up, a whole night in the bed, without restlessly moving somewhere else, or just having to get up. Then he burrowed back down into the warmth to sleep for a bit longer.

CHAPTER 21
NOVEMBER 3RD AT THE SHOP

Clara was polishing the wood again at the end of the day, trying to find something to fill the time or at least distract her from her thoughts. Still, or rather, it seemed like an endless task. Master Morris had been in right after lunch, with a box of shoes for her. He had insisted on her trying them on right away. She'd taken them off again promptly, as soon as he'd gone away, and now they were lurking at her from the corner of the office where she kept her handbag.

Near the end of the day, Clara heard the bell ring and looked up. "Agnes." Agnes Evans didn't come in often. She had a busy work life, but she'd known Aunt Lillian for ages, and her own aunt and uncle lived not far away, around two corners. She was a bit older than Clara herself, into her middle thirties, but they had enough in common to enjoy chatting when the time allowed.

"Clara. Your aunt's still away? Aunt Edith was asking."

"Still in Scotland." Clara agreed. "Anything I can get down for you?"

"A bottle of Auntie's tonic. And you made a note last

winter about something that might be worth trying when it got chilly again. For her rheumatism. Is that something I could get, or is it something that needs the apothecary at hand?" Agnes was very attentive to the proper regulations, both by inclination and by profession. She worked in the Trellech Moon's morgue, so she read and indexed all the many ways that sort of thing could go badly wrong.

"I did. Let me consult the notes. Would you keep an eye out, though we've been quiet all afternoon? Just take a minute." They kept quite good records of that sort of thing, at least for regular customers.

For one thing, it wouldn't do to suggest a tonic that would do badly with another, or some other medication. And for another, sometimes things were seasonal. It had got warmer just as Aunt Lillian had got comfortable with the salve and pills she'd been working on with Master Luther and Mistress Salah.

Clara went back to the bound volumes in the back. They were sorted by last name, though of course not alphabetical within the volume, since people did not come into the shop in tidy orders. She checked the index and then flipped to the page. No contraindications, and Aunt Lillian had noted both the salve and the pills as worth trying, but one at a time. Both might be too much of the active part, even with some charmwork to make them effective.

Those were all kept in the workroom, so Clara went and counted out twenty pills and gathered up a small container of the salve. "Aunt Lillian's notes say not to take them both together, not regularly. The pills act on the system, but there's a risk of bleeding. If she notices any bleeding - a cut that's sluggish to close up, or her gums, or anything like that, she should stop taking it immediately. The salve works where you put it, with a smaller general effect, but it's somewhat safer."

Agnes nodded. "Just now she's hurting everywhere. One a day?"

"Start with that. You can go up to two comfortably, if it's tolerated, but not more than that. If it works, we have more, of course, but no sense in selling you a lot if your aunt can't use it."

"How much do I owe you? And no, that should give us a couple of weeks to figure out what's useful. You know how it is, better some days, worse others, without any rhyme or reason most of the time. Most untidy." Agnes waited for the sum, then counted out the coins. "How are you doing, keeping things going by yourself?"

"Well enough, actually, though I get a little lonely, no one around all day." Clara hesitated. "Can I, do you mind if I ask a favour?"

Agnes leaned back, peering down her glasses for a moment. "You never have before. Can't say I'll say yes to it, but I'll hear you out?"

It was fair. More than fair, really. It wasn't really proper for Clara to ask for something like this. But something had been nagging at her, and she didn't know how to get more information. "Is there, um? I don't even know how to ask. Is there a way to find out more about supply chains and poor materials during the War?"

Agnes's chin went up and her eyes flashed. "Oh, is there ever! Any particular kind of supplies you have in mind? You'd best narrow it down some, or I'll have a stack of paper as tall as the building, at least."

"Shoes." It escaped from Clara's mouth before she could think about it. Then she looked away. "Shoes." That came out softer.

When she looked back, Agnes had tilted her head. "Something specific then. A name you can give me?"

Clara shook her head sharply. She wasn't supposed to talk about customers with other customers, even in this context. Not really. "Shoes. Someone who did well out of it, if that's any help."

"Not as much as it should be, unfortunately. Too many people profiting on the backs - or the feet, in this case - of our valiant menfolk. And womenfolk, too, I've heard horrors from the women who went over as nurses, actually. We were thinking about a story about it, more specifics, but we haven't found the right sort of case. And nothing's fully made it through the courts yet, not with a judgement we could bring out and explain."

That seemed rather wrong to Clara, but she certainly didn't know how the Halls of Justice worked, not behind the scenes like that. "Bribery?"

"Probably not on our end, on the legal side? But people making settlements, certainly. And those are often kept private. For one thing, if the amount gets out, it messes up the negotiation for anyone coming after."

Clara nodded, uncertain now. Agnes rubbed her hands together, then tugged on her gloves to gather up the packages. "I should have something for you in a couple of days. I know where all the files are, just depends how busy we are, when I get a chance to make a few copies and write up notes."

"I didn't mean for you to go to any trouble." Clara winced. "I mean, you're very busy. And you're doing something important, helping make sure people can find the information they need."

"You're also someone looking for information you need. Even if you're not saying why. Besides, I know where things are. It's not hard. And you've been steady and kind, you're part of this neighbourhood. If you could borrow a cup of sugar or a few eggs, why not a few minutes of my lunch or tea break?"

Clara spread her hands. "If you're sure."

"Now I am. Back in a few days. Maybe Friday, maybe next Monday, but if it'll be longer than that, I'll leave you a note. Now I should get off to Auntie and Uncle, and see how she likes the new things." Agnes nodded once more, then was pivoting on her heel and back out the door.

No one else came in during the last few minutes. When Clara heard the clock strike, she finished up, and took herself back home. It was a Tuesday, so the flat was dark, and she busied herself putting a few things away, tucking the shoes well into the back of the wardrobe. She was sure Owen hadn't rummaged in there, and he wasn't likely to.

She was, in fact, still awake and in the sitting room when he came home at half-nine. He came in rather quietly, as if he'd expected she'd be in bed. "Up a bit later?" Owen seemed in a good mood. He was smiling.

"There's a bit of bread and cheese and an apple if you want it? I wasn't very hungry for tea."

"Ta." He went off to the kitchen, and she heard him washing up, then he called out, "Come sit and keep me a bit of company?" There was a tiny pause. "If you weren't in the middle of anything?"

She grimaced but went to join him, settling down in the other chair. "A good day at work, then? You seem in a good mood."

"Doing pretty well. It's a play they've done before, regularly, and I gather Randolph adores it. *King Lear*. All very tragic, but the scenery is interesting, and the costumes are in good order. And they all know the play backwards and forwards. Gets good crowds, I guess, too."

"So, that'd be..." Clara considered. "An easier week for you than most?"

"Exactly. Mind, we're getting deeper into what's needed for the panto now." He chatted on about that agreeably, for a good ten or fifteen minutes. Costumes, of course, and she had some interest in that. She understood putting things together out of cloth, anyway. The sets were more confusing to her, especially since Owen tended to gesture, get distracted by his tea, and then forget what he'd explained and what he hadn't. But she gathered there was a sort of balcony or cliff or something. They had shadow puppets to make the giants the right size, and plans for a deeply comic sort of battle sequence.

She couldn't ask how he felt about that, about making light of a battle, after having seen quite a few of them. He seemed happy enough with it. Maybe the fact it was so far distant, so obviously a story, made it an entirely different class of things in his head. When he finally finished, she smiled. "It sounds intriguing. And making do with what you've got for materials, that's clever."

"Well. Necessary. But paint's not that much more expensive if it comes in bright colours. Mostly. Depends on the pigments, of course. But there are some that take charms well, and they've got someone who'll do all that, so it glimmers and shines in the lights."

"Rather a lot to keep coordinated." Clara swallowed. "Can I ask about something really different?"

"Of course." He answered easily, which made Clara feel all the worse. She'd been meaning to ask about Master Morris, and the shoes. But now it came to it, she couldn't. She thought that someone who made shoes by hand - even if he hadn't recently at all - would have opinions about factory shoes. And moreover, she was beginning to think that the factory didn't make good shoes. Clara couldn't explain why she thought that. Just that something about the leather felt wrong, or something about the soles on the floor, even the brief time she'd had them on.

She shook her head suddenly. "No, never mind. You enjoy the rest of the tea. I think I'll wash up and go to bed. I've got a lot to do in the morning."

Owen blinked at her, but didn't ask anything further. "I'll do the dishes, of course. I've got a few things to work on. Let me know if they're too noisy?"

Clara nodded as she pushed away from the table. She bent to kiss him. She could do that much, at least. Then she went off to the bathroom to braid her hair and wash her face and all that for the night. She was a coward, and she knew it.

CHAPTER 22
NOVEMBER 4TH AT THE THEATRE

Owen spent the afternoon at work on solitary tasks, more or less. He mended the hinge on one of the doors, just needing a hand to get it rehung after that. He tacked down the carpet on the balcony stairs to make sure it would stay safe. Two of the chairs in the orchestra had armrests coming loose, and another one had a spring coming through the padding. He couldn't mend the last one quickly, but he could swap it out for a different cushion and tack the new one in place.

None of it was terribly challenging, as Golshan had said originally. It didn't take much in the way of specialist knowledge, just his skills in hitting small nails and tacks accurately enough with a hammer. It also felt good to keep the place a little more in order. From time to time, he glanced up at the stage, where they were doing auditions for additional roles in the panto. They'd settled on the main cast, of course, but there were a good dozen supporting roles that still needed people, as well as a chorus who could dance.

Half the people up there were, well, not doing terribly well. Singing and dancing at the same time was a gift not everyone had. Owen certainly didn't, so he couldn't judge people who didn't either. But he also had more sense to get up on stage and pretend he did. He'd been told he had a decent voice, both speaking and the sort of singing. Just the singing that went into work songs or a bit of a hymn or chant or whatever you called it at whatever church or temple you might go to. But he also felt he had two left feet. Even if he knew better, given how well he knew his own.

Mostly, he shrugged it off. Perhaps Orlando and the others evaluating them would find some way they could be part of things. Certainly, that was part of it. Having a part in the panto was apparently a treasured goal for some of the amateur dramatic societies. Owen had certainly heard some of that from the Guild performers, even if that was a very different kind of acting. And singing, for that matter, though mostly the dances were either processions or the sort of traditional circle dance most people had been doing since they were tiny tots.

As they finished up auditions for the day, Owen did a pass through the balcony, making sure everything was tidy. Maisery had been busy all afternoon fixing one of the bits of cliff needed for Lear that evening. The rehearsals had gone well, apparently; it was not only a play most everyone knew well, but nothing new in the staging, or at least nothing new that involved Randolph.

That worried Owen a bit. Not that the man was ageing, and not as glorious as he was. That came to everyone, if they were lucky enough to live so long. And the theatre was doing their best to take care of him, to make sure there were parts he could still thrill in. But there were so many things that could go wrong backstage, if something were moved into the wrong place. Edgar was on top of it, as was Randolph's dresser, and the other people who kept an eye on things backstage, but still.

As he made his way along the side, Owen caught a glimpse of that curious glimmer again. This time, it seemed almost like something was moving or pointing, the way you'd get a flash of light on a wristwatch or a bangle at the wrist. Not that he had much experience with either, and he wasn't sure why it came to mind now. He had his Dad's pocket watch, battered as it was now.

When he got to the ghost's box, he found the seat down, even though he knew the springs were good. Sitting on it were a pile of silk flowers. A third, maybe, were the purple shading to glowing gold. But the others were a sapphire blue, and a teal - not colours he thought Maisery had mentioned.

"Am I supposed to take these?" Owen asked the theatre, forgetting there were people down on stage, still.

The sound from there went suddenly silent, before Orlando called up, his voice carrying like any theatre impresario who could both project from the diaphragm and use a sound-amplifying charm. "Something the matter up there?"

"Sorry, sir. Nothing wrong." Owen called it back down and then glared at the seat. "Well, am I?" That was a whisper, and wouldn't carry, or so he hoped. The seat twitched once, and Owen sighed, unfolding his handkerchief - it was nicely clean and folded. He tucked the flowers into it before tying the corners together to make a little bundle. Mum had done that with his lunches for school, once upon a time. She'd tie up the tin that held whatever he was eating in a clean cloth he could use as a napkin.

Now, he brought them down to the workroom, undoing the knots and laying them out on the bit of bench he'd claimed as his own. Maisery looked up from the other end, where she was doing some sort of tally. "What's that?"

"They were on the ghost's chair. Different colours, though - the purple, but here's blue and teal."

Her eyes went wide. "I thought all of those went somewhere else. Huh." She came over to peer at them. "The colours look well together, though. None of the oranges or reds, that'd look more like sunrise. This is more, I don't know. A vivid garden?"

Owen considered. "I was saying to Clara last night that I liked the brighter colours here." It was entirely creepy to think that the ghost might have known that. A respectable theatre ghost ought to stay in the theatre, not wander around listening to opinions about decorating a flat.

Maisery waved a hand. "Well, you take them home, then. Not like we've a use for them, as I said. Might have a few more bits of ribbon, actually, from that batch, if you want that?"

Owen looked at the flowers, which sat there, very unhelpful. Then he considered the curtains in the kitchen. "If it's not a bother?" He'd picked up some plain white muslin the other day, on the advice of several of the theatre folks. It would take dye well, they said, or a bit of sewing.

"If I don't find it the first two places I look, I'll stop." Maisery looked cheerful, as if having something she could hunt up was a help. The ribbon turned out to be in the second place, in the back of a drawer in the costume shop. "All right if I take this, Alice? It's the one the dye took queer."

"Oh, that? Gladly. Who wants it?" Alice turned around

from where she was working at one of the sewing machines.

Owen cleared his throat. "Me." Alice intimidated him, more than a bit. She was something like sixty, and she ruled the costume shop with an iron fist in a beautifully decorated velvet glove. She was scrupulous about waste, and about making sure the pins didn't get tracked around. Both of those were sensible, but the way she did it sounded like Owen's Gram had when he was little. He always felt he'd been caught with his hand in the biscuits out of turn.

"And what do you want it for, then?"

He hadn't intended to explain, but asked like that, he couldn't duck it. "Making some new curtains for my wife. I thought a bit of pretty might be a thing. She likes the brighter colours, and I do too."

Alice looked him up and down. "Huh. Well. Bright we can do. Let me think about if there's other scraps you could do something with. You go ahead, take those. You can sew, then?"

"Yes'm." Owen spread his hands. "Fabric's a lot easier on the fingers than leather. I can't do anything fancy, but I can manage a straight hem. Not a machine, though."

"You watch yourself, or I'll be borrowing you from Maisery." She made it sound like a cheerful threat. "Off with you. I need to finish letting this down by tonight. Albert shot up another two inches." He was playing one of the secondary characters, a lord with sweeping robes and a cloak.

Maisery tugged him off by one arm, then dumped the ribbons on his desk. "There you go." Right around that point, Edgar pushed the workroom door open. "Tea? We have some biscuits and such left over from the auditions.

They always get a decent spread for that. It keeps everyone much less cranky."

Owen wouldn't turn down free food, at least anything decent. He snagged a scone and a chocolate digestive biscuit and a few bits of cheese, as well as a cup of tea from the urn that took up half the cart.

Maisery, who had precedence in the asking, piped up immediately. "So how'd it go? Any hope?"

"Enough, I think. Several promising, though all of them will need coaching to cheat properly." Edgar added to Owen, "That's talking to someone on stage, but being turned enough to the audience so they can see you. Better acoustics, too, besides the fact that staring at someone's shoulder or arse is not usually the part you want to be looking at."

Maisery snorted. "Speak for yourself. I do like a man in a short tunic and hose." She tilted her head. "Well, some men."

"And you can see all you like of that from the wings." Edgar shrugged, amused. It was obviously an ongoing wrangle. "Anyway. Need to see how they are on the stage, but there's a chance some of them might be worth keeping around."

Owen considered. "That's a thing you're thinking about, then, not just talent?"

"Well, if we have a future - I hope we do - then yes. But it's not just about talent. There's one woman was here, and she was all up on her high horse about getting treated right. Orlando's remarkably patient with that sort, without giving an inch. But I was the one had to make it clear she was standing in the way. And if she stayed there, she'd get bowled over twice in three minutes. She sniffed at me."

"And you told Orlando after, I'm sure." Maisery nodded approvingly. "One of those posh sorts?"

"Didn't go to any of the Five Schools, apparently. Educated at home, local dramatics." Edgar shrugged. "That sort has been coddled from before she could walk, and that's never good for anyone. Catch me wanting to work with anyone like that. The ones that go to Schola or Alethorpe— those are the two we tend to get going into theatrical lines of work." He said the last aside to Owen. "They usually have some discipline about it. And they're used to not being the best or at least used to not always getting their own way, I will say that."

Owen snorted once and refilled his teacup. "And the others?"

"One of them, that Umbert? Unfortunate name for an actor, but he was really quite pleasant. Checked with me about if there was anything he should know to avoid causing a problem, real careful about setting props down exactly in the right place. He's had a bit of physical training too. He knew what to do with a sword besides flail it around, though I don't think he's an actual fencer."

Maisery grinned at the expression that must be on Owen's face. "Edgar's a treasure in sizing people up quickly. Orlando relies on it. And how they treat the backstage staff makes a world of difference. Bet you Umbert gets a good offer, then. But yeah, needs a different name, if he's going to keep going with the theatre. Uneuphonious, Umbert."

Before anyone could say anything more, they all heard a call down the hall. "Edgar, is there more tea?"

Edgar waved. "Let me take this out to the ravening hordes. Owen, when you're done, could you sweep the stage again? You're always so careful with it."

"And watch that loose charmlight. I was thinking I

should have a better look at it tomorrow, but a bit of a sticking charm should have it hold for tonight." Maisery added it quickly.

"You're a wonder. Yes, both of those, please." With that, Edgar took off back down the hall with the cart, and Maisery patted Owen on the arm.

"Off you go, then. I'm good until we open up for the night."

CHAPTER 23
NOVEMBER 4TH AT HESTER'S

The following week moved on in the way Clara had come to expect. Aunt Lillian had sent another crate of various bottles and salves and powders, and the same vague answers about when she was coming back. At this point, Clara wondered if it was going to be after Solstice and the New Year.

She didn't much like the idea, but it would be awkward for Clara no matter what happened. No tucking up with Aunt Lillian and a few others in the upstairs flat above the shop and trying to stay up all night. No making their way to the pre-dawn services at the Temple of Healing and a procession down to the river, or all the food they cobbled together for that. Whatever she did, it'd be with Owen, or waiting for Owen to come home, or something.

Agnes had brought by a sheaf of articles on Monday. Clara hadn't had a chance to read them until the Tuesday, of course, because Owen had been home and the shop had been busy enough she didn't want papers out. Especially not where Master Morris might catch a glimpse of them.

The articles both told her new things and made everything else much more confusing.

The folder Agnes had given her held twenty different articles and a few sheets of notes. Copies from the original, probably made with a magic Clara had no idea how to do. They were typewritten, but with none of the indentations on the pages Clara had expected. And the ink wasn't quite black, but a slightly muted dark grey-brown.

It wasn't as if the contents helped, either. The articles talked about five or six different suppliers of shoes, because no single provider had been able to turn out enough. Most of them were non-magical shoes. There was no charmwork in the footwear itself, but the factories relied on charms and enchantments to keep the machinery running smoothly. Or more safely, theoretically, but apparently that was doubt-ful. At least, that was what the articles suggested, that the safety protections had failed, that the enchantments had damaged materials. And that several of the lot had been using shoddy materials to start and using magic to cover enough of it up until they went through inspection.

Clara was chewing on all of that still by Thursday, when she went along to Hester's for tea. Tea and listening, because Hester wanted to talk, barely letting Clara get a word in edgewise. The children were grand and brilliant, despite three interruptions involving Marigold's hair and Thaddeus's ink bottle. Clara had to give him points for consistency, at least. And of course, Hester wanted an audi-ence for every minute detail of officially becoming one of the Vestigial Flowers at luncheon.

It sounded rather tedious to Clara, whole hours of sitting around and making small talk. Or of listening to someone talk about some pet project that had a dubious benefit for the rest of the world. Though, to be honest, she wasn't in the habit of having personal projects, not since before the War. It had been an endless cycle of work, of volunteering, and then of knitting or rolling bandages or whatever except for a few minutes with the paper every night.

She must have failed to say something properly, because Hester nudged her sharply. "I say, Clara, you're not even listening."

Clara rummaged back in her head - shop work had given her that skill at least. "Something about, pardon, was it Mistress Halloway? And the development of a flower in her garden. You know I can't follow the plant details as well."

Hester sniffed, partially mollified. "You've been very quiet, haven't you? How are things, then?"

Being asked straight out wasn't any better at all. Especially not when Hester had that particular tone. "Owen's busy at the theatre. It's going well enough, I gather. They're gearing up for the panto."

"Oh, that's right, you said they were doing Brutus and the giants." Hester sniffed again. "We were going to go to Puss in Boots."

Clara hesitated, but Owen had said the news was out last night. "Oh, hadn't you seen the posters up yet? They've got a rather grand young man to play Brutus. He was in the Nine Muses at Schola. You know how they only take the best. And he's been making his name in the London theatre. But he's coming back for a stint in the panto."

"Oh. Well." Hester fanned herself with her hand briefly. "I suppose we could give it a try. Good-looking enough for a hero?"

"I gather there are shoulders involved." Clara leaned forward a little conspiratorially. "If you go up by the theatres on a walk tomorrow, you'll see the posters. I haven't been by yet, but Owen brought a playbill home, one of the test prints. Quite fetching. And quite a talented young woman, for Innogen, she has a lovely voice."

Hester sniffed again. "Well, I suppose. And one wants to be a support."

"I appreciate that." Frankly, it felt condescending and rather awful, but Clara wasn't in any position to complain about someone turning up at the theatre. Every bit would apparently matter. It made her want to change the subject, though.

"I was wondering a bit more about Master Morris, actually. If you don't mind being a bit of a help."

"Ooh, has he been round to get something again?" Clara had, honestly, not told Hester about most of the visits. Something in her had made it clear that was a bad idea. Clara couldn't tell why, or even what was bothering her.

"I've been trying to figure him out. He's come round a couple more times, small purchases. But he's—" Clara frowned. "I want to say he's flirting, but he knows I'm married."

"That doesn't stop some men." Hester looked her up and down. "You're out of practice having men around. We all are."

Clara nobly refrained from pointing out that Oscar had, by and large, shared Hester's bed throughout the War. Or if he hadn't, it was because the two of them had separate beds by choice, not because he was posted anywhere further away. She was sure - Hester had complained about it - that he'd had to stay at work some nights, or come home terribly late and left before dawn. But he had, in fact, been around a remarkable amount throughout.

"That does not mean I want to be flirted with."

Hester considered her. "You dress well enough. You've a lovely slim figure, too, and for the current fashions, even. You could make yourself another dress." Another dress would not improve this problem. Clara was entirely sure of that. One that flattered certainly wouldn't, and at the same time, she refused to change what she was doing because someone else was taking more liberty than he ought.

"But you said he's well off?" Clara was still chasing that around. His name hadn't come up directly in any of the pieces Agnes had handed over, but it wasn't like Clara had named him specifically. She wondered if that made a difference. But it was boggling to think they might have people indexed by name, as well as profession or whatever. At least most people. A factory owner might have money, but it wasn't like he was one of the Council or always in the papers for some bit of gossip or philanthropy or whatever. Now she thought that through, though, maybe she was entirely wrong.

Clara got terribly tangled in her thoughts, then. She didn't know how to measure what Master Morris was, never mind what he wanted with her, and approximately all of it made her uncomfortable. Well, beyond the part where he paid for his goods promptly and had never asked her to run a tab. Before she could dig herself deeper in that hole, Hester coughed, pointedly. "Clara, honestly."

"I've just thought of something I ought to tend to at the shop before I go home." It brought Clara back to herself sharply, then she stood ungracefully. "I'm sorry, Hester. Another week."

Hester pouted, rather effectively, honestly, it almost made Clara sit down again. But she wanted to look at the papers again, and, well. Be by herself, that was what she wanted, with no one jogging her elbow.

That was not to be. She'd planned to cut across Agnetian Way to their less grand bit of town. She'd been walking along, rather briskly, when she heard someone call out her name. "Miss Hubbard?"

It must not have been the first time, because she could see several people around her looking behind her. She turned, pausing under the street lamp. Approaching - in a quite posh overcoat and hat - was Master Morris. Very smartly turned out, and more polished than she had seen him so far. "A delight, Miss Hubbard." Using that form was ... well, she should take it as an insult. She should be Mistress, for being an adult, even if he didn't remember she was married.

"I beg pardon, I was coming from a friend's." She gestured vaguely. "I hope you are well, Master Morris?"

"Oh, much the better for seeing you. You're such a bright spark, aren't you? And you exist outside of that delightful little shop of yours. Do you need to be anywhere urgently?"

There was no good way to answer that. If she said no, he'd likely offer something she wasn't at all sure she should accept. Or worse, he'd tempt her with something she couldn't bring herself to turn down. Her tea was going to be a bit of bread and cheese and weaker tea than she'd like. If she said yes, she suspected he'd press about what it was. She swallowed. "It's been a rather long day, and tomorrow will be as well. I was on my way home."

"Oh, I was hoping I could persuade you to come out to

supper with me. I know a lovely little place, quite delight-ful, French cuisine, just around the corner from the Grindlay Bank. Do say yes?" His voice took on a pleading tone, and that made her even more uncomfortable. Surely no one sensible actually wanted her company that badly. She was not anything remotely special.

Clara shook his head. "I really do need to get home. I've chores to tend to, they won't do themselves."

It took him aback, stalling him visibly for a moment. "Ah, I suppose you'd not have the sort of staff I do. May I walk with you for a bit, then?"

She didn't know how to put him off, really. "As far back as Trivium Way. I've an errand on the way home, and I'd rather not bother you with that."

"Every little morsel is a delight, my dear." He offered his arm, and after a hesitation, she took it. That was proper enough. He tucked it close in against his side, so her fingers pressed against his chest, even though there were layers of camelhair coat and his suit under it. They walked along a block or two before he leaned his head down toward hers. "I'd be delighted to show you a good time. You do know that, don't you? Far more than shoes."

Clara stiffened. She could feel herself do it all through her shoulders and back. "You flatter, Master Morris. I couldn't possibly. For one thing, I'm married. For another, not with someone I know via the shop. It's. It's not the done thing." If the gossip columns had it right, adultery was in fact a frequently done thing, but maybe he'd understand how she meant it.

"Oh, I'm going to keep trying to persuade you." Just the one sentence, but then he left her at that, completely polite again, when she indicated she had to turn off. She busied herself going into one of the message offices to send a note up to Aunt Lillian before they closed. The bustle in the shop and the lights made her feel a bit better. She walked out the door with a couple of women who were chattering along about the market day. They seemed glad enough to include her.

CHAPTER 24
NOVEMBER 4TH AT THEIR FLAT

When Owen came home that evening, he noticed immediately the lights were still on in the sitting room. Fully on, too, not just the table lamp. That worried him, the way that the sudden silence of the guns had worried him in the trenches. It suggested something was about to happen and he wouldn't like it one bit. He tried to reassure himself that it wouldn't actually be artillery fire, but that did not actually help.

It did mean he was quiet when he opened the door. Not that he wasn't usually, but he hoped it was just that Clara had fallen asleep on the sofa. She hadn't. She had shifted her chair so she'd see if anyone came in the door. When she saw it was him, she let out a little sigh of relief, then pulled a shawl around her more tightly.

"Are you all right?" It was the first thing Owen could think to say, even though it was fairly obvious that she wasn't. He wasn't the most observant man, he knew that. Even more so now he'd been around theatre folk, who were emotive to a fault, whatever their other habits.

She shrugged first, and then she shook her head. Just

the once, left to right, before she pulled the shawl even tighter around her, straining the yarn visibly. Owen closed the door behind him, then locked it.

"Did you see anyone outside?" Clara's voice cracked in the middle.

"No. Not the last two blocks. It's near half-eleven. Can I make you a cuppa? You had that chamomile, didn't you?"

She shook her head again, just a twitch. "Tea won't help. I tried tea."

That was indeed rather a bad sign. Owen paused to take off his boots and hang up his coat and scarf and tuck his gloves in the pocket. Then he crossed over to where she was sitting, to perch on the solitary footstool. He didn't quite want to touch her, and she certainly didn't reach for him. "Are you scared there was someone outside?"

"Yes. No. It's foolish." She looked away from him, but she didn't move other than that.

"Someone specific?" Owen felt completely at sea here, which was a fitting enough metaphor, because he'd only ever been on the open ocean going across the Channel to war and back.

Clara didn't answer that. Her stillness was indeed as eerie as the silence of the guns had been, and it made his own heart beat faster in a way he didn't like at all. After a moment, he stood. "I'm going to make myself a cuppa. And a hot water bottle for you?" He offered it cautiously.

"Wouldn't turn it down." Something in her tone made him sure it would help, and she hadn't been able to think of it or ask for it. He had no idea what had got her that locked inside herself, but he at least knew a bit of what to do with that. More warmth, someone to make ordinary noises, to be present. That would be a start. He'd done it for others in the trenches often enough, or behind the lines, and they'd done it for him.

He made a point of small noises as he bustled around in the kitchen, humming softly at one point. Mostly, he just let the sounds of the kettle and the mug happen as normal without trying to muffle them. He put plenty of water in the kettle, then rummaged for the hot water bottle, and the cosy that went round it. That took up quite a few minutes, especially since he rinsed out the dishes that had been soaking while he did so. Then he washed his hands again, to get the last of the grease from the evening out from under his nails.

Owen came back with a mug of tea for himself - chamomile lavender, which Mum had kept for such occasions. He didn't dare risk a slug of medicinal brandy. He didn't trust himself with it, not with things in a delicate way. He handed over the hot water bottle, and Clara immediately cradled it against her chest, under the shawl. She made a small noise as she did so, what might reasonably be called a whimper, and that worried him all over again. Not that he'd actually stopped.

Once he was settled on the footstool again, he cleared his throat. "It's clear you're scared of something. Is it something I should be scared of, too?"

She froze like one of the rabbits who'd dart out of a garden and go still as soon as a predator was too nearby. She didn't answer him, and he thought after a moment that she honestly couldn't.

"Can we play animal, vegetable, mineral, magical?" It was the childhood guessing game, a pleasant amusement when you needed to kill time. He'd played endless rounds of it in the trenches, though without the magical part.

That made her blink, but then she nodded once.

"Right. Animal?" She nodded. "Vegetable? Mineral? Magical?"

The second and third got a shake of her head, a clear no, the magical question got a yes.

"A ghost?" No, again. "Magical animal?" Another no.

Clara hugged the bottle a bit tighter against her, her shoulders rounding. He could see the way the tension was unbalancing her. He was used to seeing that - or at least once, in the time before - with leather. With leather, you wanted that, in some cases, so the shoe would have proper shape.

That left a fairly obvious answer. "A person?"

She didn't move for quite a long time, maybe thirty seconds. Then, all in a rush, she stood, pushing the chair away behind her, rushing in a swirl of shawl and skirt around it, toward the door, jamming her feet into the shoes. But he'd locked the door, and she had to fumble to open it, enough time that he caught up with her.

He didn't think before he reached out, both his hands on her upper arms. He didn't want to hurt her. Gods, no. But he was terrified now that she'd hurt herself in her rush to be anywhere else. That whatever had upset her so much really was a risk, and she was going to go run right into it. He'd seen that kind of utter panic before, but he'd never expected it to come roost in his own sitting room.

Clara didn't try to fight him. That was some small comfort. She went still, first, other than the quivering he could feel beneath his fingers. Then she half-collapsed, something like a faint, against him. Owen's breath caught. He frantically did his best to make sure she didn't hit her head, that he caught her in time, that the weight of her was steady in his arms.

Only then he had to decide what to do. After a moment,

he managed to get her fully into his arms, cradled like a child, and took her off to their bed. She'd pulled back the covers at some point earlier in the evening. One of the other water bottles was already in there to warm up the sheets. Owen considered, then managed to get her tucked in. He didn't have the magical gift for warming a bed properly. His attempts always came out splotchy. But he could go fetch the other water bottle and tuck it in beside her, after he'd pulled up the sheets and blankets all the way.

By the time he came back, she was only barely stirring, which gave him time to sit on the bed, perching where he could watch her. She came out of it scrabbling for a moment, as if she were fighting off some dream or nightmare. Like he did, more nights than not, even if he tried not to have her notice. He didn't try to hold her in place, but just braced one arm so that she couldn't hurt him much if she lashed out.

Fortunately, miraculously, somehow, she didn't. She came back to herself, enough to flush a bright red, and to turn away from him, pulling the blankets nearly over her head. Some part of him was sure leaving her alone was what she wanted. Clara couldn't have been more clear if she'd used words. But he also thought if he did so, it would be a great wrongness. Not the sort that could be sorted out in the third act of the play, but the sort that was the hinge point of a tragedy. What he did now mattered, it would change everything, and he had no idea what kind of play he was in.

Cautiously, he put a hand on her shoulder, above the blankets. "You're scared." Naming it couldn't make it worse, surely. "I'd like to help."

He felt her shoulder shake, not quite violently enough to move his hand. Then, muffled, she spoke. "Why?"

"You're scared." He let his breath come out in a huff. He didn't know her, not like he thought he had. But that didn't mean he didn't care about her. If nothing else, they shared the flat. They shared a bed, for goodness' sakes. It wasn't much of a marriage, but without her, he'd be a lot worse off, in all sorts of practical ways. Even if he didn't know what he felt about the rest of it at the moment. "And I'm here. You're not going to make me run off."

She made a sound under the blanket, something that could have been a laugh or a whimper. After a long moment, she rolled onto her back, still tucked under the bedding. "You won't like it."

"I don't know what I think. Except, except." He let out a long breath. "I don't like you being scared." Then, as if there was a wall of water breaking through a dam, he went on. "We loved each other. I know that. I don't know what you feel now." He certainly didn't know what he felt now, not that he'd say that right in the moment. He had more sense. "You took care of Mum. There are all sorts of reasons I'd want to help. It doesn't matter which of them are the right ones. They're enough." He swallowed. "You're scared, and you've been alone with it, and I want to help."

He thought it hadn't done any good. And for a long time, far too long for any sort of comfort, she didn't move. Then, finally, carefully, she spoke, near enough in a whisper. "There's a man who's been flirting with me. Making it clear he'd like - he'd like things with me." She didn't say more than that. She didn't spell out the flirting, or what he'd offered, but Owen could fill in the gaps. Enough, anyway, to be going on with.

"And?" He didn't want to press, but after the quiet went on, he had to say something. "Did he hurt you?"

"That's what you ask?" It came out sharp and surprisingly loud, Clara pushing up on one elbow for a moment before she collapsed back on the bed. "Not if I - if I did anything?"

"You're scared." He kept coming back to that, but it was true. If she'd just felt guilty, he was sure it would have looked different, come out different. He didn't know what she'd actually done, if she'd liked being flirted with. Though it probably was reasonable she would. She was an attractive woman, he certainly had noticed that right off, and again every time he got a glimpse of her. But she was also loyal and clever and funny and intensely practical in a way he found tremendously reassuring. "What happened tonight?"

"I ran into him on the way home. He's come into the shop every week or two. Just often enough." She swallowed. "I don't know. I've been trying to find out a bit more about him. And I." She stopped, meeting Owen's eyes for a fraction of a second. "I am scared."

"Scared he'd hurt you?" Owen was trying to get a feel of the shape of things, and it was like swimming through mud. "Something else?"

"He's got a lot of money. Influence, too, probably. I mean, I assume so. He owns a big factory." Then she looked away, off into the corner, as far away from him as she could look without fleeing the bed. "A shoe factory."

Owen was not at all sure what to do with that bit of irony, though now it definitely felt like he'd wandered into some sort of melodrama. "Oh." He had to say something, and that was a lousy sort of something, but it was what he had.

"He asked me out for supper tonight. And he took my no, but he said he'd keep trying to persuade me. Only then I kept looking over my shoulder, even though I made an excuse to get away from him, so he wouldn't see where we lived. I don't think he knows that?"

Owen nodded once. "That was smart of you." He let out his breath in a long huff. "I'm, honestly, I don't know what to think of it. But I'm not angry with you." He felt jealous, more than a bit, but that his was to deal with, not hers. "Anything else I should know?"

"He gave me some shoes. He insisted. They're in the back of the wardrobe. I - I couldn't get him to take them back, but I couldn't wear them, either. That's it. I promise that's it. Talking in the shop, he'd buy things, the shoes, tonight." It came out of Clara in a rush, the sort of frantic edge to it that made him rest his hand on her shoulder again.

"I believe you. Let me stay with you for a bit. Read, maybe? Just be here. You need to sleep. May I look at the shoes sometime?" He felt he could learn quite a lot about the man from his shoes. If he couldn't, he should go burn his own lasts.

Clara let out a little whimper, but she nodded. "It'd be kind, if you sat. Read, maybe?"

He bent down to kiss her forehead before thinking better of it and stopping halfway there. "Let me pull out the shoes and get my tea. I'll be up a bit more, most likely." He went off to do both those things. First he found a pair of fashionable women's shoes and took them out to the sitting room, before reclaiming the hot water bottle and his tea. Once he came back, he read to her.

The book she had out from the library was apparently terribly popular. She'd got a bit in, so he picked up in chapter seven. It was unpromisingly labelled "Bernard's Idear", and it began with two characters sitting around. "After Mr Salteena had departed Bernard Clark thourght he would show Ethel over his house so they spent a merry morning so doing. Ethel passed bright remarks on all the rooms and Bernard thourght she was most pretty and Ethel began to be a bit excited. After a lovly lunch they sat in the gloomy hall and Ethel began to feel very glad Mr Salteena was not there. Suddenly Bernard lit his pipe I was thinking he said passionately what about going up to London for a weeks Gaierty."

Owen cleared his throat. "What is this?"

Clara coughed once. "Very popular. It's very funny, actually? The author wrote it when she was nine, and it's - a friend suggested it. She has very odd ideas about how adults do things? If you can get past the spelling. I like hearing it out loud, though. It's funnier?" She hesitated, then added, "And you have a nice reading voice."

The goal of the reading was to help Clara settle down and go to sleep. If this was what that needed, well, he could read a ridiculous chapter or two. It was, at least, somewhat reassuring that he was not so daft about romance as Bernard appeared to be. By the time he'd got to the end of the book, Clara had almost fallen asleep. He set it down on the side table, and she rolled over, her breathing smoothing out a minute or two later.

CHAPTER 25
NOVEMBER 5TH AT THEIR FLAT

The next morning, Clara woke with a start. She remembered dozing off, with Owen sitting on the bed beside her, not quite touching, just the weight of him on the mattress. In the middle of the night, she thought he'd come back, but she wasn't sure. Now she was alone in the bed, and she flopped onto her back.

It was mortifying. That she'd been that scared, for one thing. Master Horatio Morris might be something of a creep. Certainly he was pushy. But she couldn't say, in the light of morning, why she'd been terrified. Worse, she'd confessed to Owen. Either she should have told him the first time something happened. The shoes, at the least. Or she should never have said anything.

It wasn't as if they had a habit of confessions to each other to build on. She did with Aunt Lillian. She knew how that worked. No two people were always smooth together. Sometimes they were oil and water, not mixing. Or water and fire, alchemically speaking, and what happened in the middle state was spitting steam. But she and Owen had none of that. They'd been doing cordiality quite well, she thought, but this was nothing like cordial.

As she lay on her back, she heard various small noises in the hall. She'd expected he'd be asleep still. On the sofa, or beside it, since he wasn't in bed. Instead, there was a careful knock on the door. "You up?"

Clara couldn't think of what to say to that except the obvious. "Yes?"

Owen pushed the door open, and he had the small bed tray, the one his Mum had used. It had been in her room still. "Thought you could have a bit in bed first?"

It was a kind thought. A wonderfully kind thought, actually. He'd put a mug of tea on the tray, the little silk flower in its teacup, toast, and two eggs. Not quite how she'd have fried them, but quite properly cooked. She blinked up at him as he set the tray down carefully. Before she could say anything else, he added, "I thought I might walk you to work, if you don't mind?"

"You need your sleep." It came out without her permission. "Don't you?" Then she flushed, embarrassed. "That isn't what I meant to say. Thank you. For last night. For this." It wasn't remotely enough, but she didn't know how to put what she was feeling any better. She could at least be polite while she was incoherent.

He gave a little smile, the one she'd fallen in love with, to start. "I like being a help, turns out. I got a few hours in the night, and I'll have a nap when I get back. I don't need to be at the theatre until three today."

Clara considered arguing with him, but he was a grown man, and it wasn't like he shirked going to work. She looked down at the food, then back up at him. "Thank you." Then she tucked in. It wasn't as if she exactly had an appetite, but tea and eggs and toast weren't hard on a touchy stomach, and she did need to eat.

Owen gave her a moment before he stood. "Your lunch is all packed. I'll be ready when you are. Thirty or so?"

She nodded without quite looking at him. Eating in bed felt like a ridiculous luxury, but by the time she'd got the food into her, she felt a bit better. The tea, even more so, he'd put two lumps of sugar in. She went off to the bathroom to wash up and do all the ordinary morning things, and when she came back, the tray had disappeared. She could hear him humming slightly in the kitchen, and the splash of water.

Right on time, she was ready to go. She looked much more put together than she felt, honestly. But her bright blue frock and a nicely trimmed hat at least drew the eye away from her own face a bit. She hadn't felt up to doing anything fancy with her hair, so it was in a low bun, puffed out a little so the hat would stay put. When she came out into the sitting room, Owen was fully dressed, jacket and all, and looked up at her. "You look a picture. May I carry your bag for you?"

Another thing she hadn't expected. It was a proper satchel, because of the lunch and the other things she carried, not a little decorative handbag like Hester made a point of carrying around. "If, I mean. You don't have to?"

"I want to, please." Owen offered his hand, but there was something gentle there. Far more gentle than she deserved. She handed over the satchel, and he slung it over his shoulder, apparently ready to go.

She turned to find her winter coat, which was not nearly as sharp as the dress. "Why are you like this? So kind? Why aren't you upset with me?" It was easier to say it when she wasn't looking at him, but of course she couldn't stare at the wall forever. She had to turn round.

He'd taken a small step back, hands by his sides, rather than reaching for her. "You haven't done anything to be upset with. I mean, I wish I'd known a bit sooner, so you weren't alone with it. But I understand you need to be pleasant to customers. That you're holding up a lot of the weight of the shop, and it worries you. You feel responsible to your aunt. And you're worried about money, that part we've talked about."

Clara let out a little huff of breath, but she could only nod at that. "Doesn't explain why you were so - the breakfast this morning. Now."

"We're rather a mess, aren't we? I can't spend a night in bed reliably still, even with you there being - well. You. I have a job, but there are worries there. And we've just been stumbling along. But I remember falling in love with you. Certainly remember how a letter from you, over there, made the whole day better."

That, well, just shamed her again, and she had to turn away for a moment, pretending to straighten her coat. "I haven't been much good since you came home."

Now, he reached out, a touch on her arm that made her jerk for a moment before she stopped and let him rest his fingers. "Do you want to figure it out?" Her face froze, her shoulder stiffened. He must have seen some of that. "Not a conversation for today, no." He took his fingers away. "I'm still not upset. Promise. I won't press. We've got time to figure out whatever we want to figure out. Right now, you need to get to work so you don't worry about the time."

That much was entirely true. She wanted to be angry with him, honestly, but he was being entirely sensible. She was the unreasonable one, made of spikes and guilt and frustration, and she didn't know where to begin with it. Clara took a deep breath. "To the shop, yes." She glanced at him sideways. "Thanks for not pressing." That was all she could manage to say, but maybe it was enough.

He got to the door, letting her go out first and locking it. Then he went down to see if anyone was lingering on the street as they came around through the front gate. No one was. There were just the ordinary neighbours doing what they did in the morning. The walk to the shop was fine, too. Owen didn't fuss about making conversation. Just a few comments on shops that had changed since the War, once they got into the areas he'd not been in for that long.

One of her shoes started giving her grief as they crossed one of the main streets, and she had to stop and adjust the buckle. Clara caught Owen watching closely, but after a second, he just offered her his arm for balance. Nice and steady, that was. She didn't hesitate to lean on it once he'd offered.

Finally - it certainly felt like it took forever - they were at the shop. She unlocked the wards, her hand on the tile that did that. Apothecary shops had to be particularly careful, of course, with all the dangerous things they stored. Everyone knew that a broken window would alert the Guard immediately, or any attempt to mess with the wards. It was one of the things built into their budget, the fees for the upkeep of the wards and the testing that went with it. Only once she'd done that did she unlock the door itself before opening the door.

Everything was as she'd left it the day before. She took a couple of steps in, automatically going to put her bag down, before she realised the problem and turned around. "My bag? Do you want to come back to the office for a minute while I set up for the day?" She locked the door behind him, out of habit, and he then trailed her back to the office space. Clara made all the ordinary little gestures of the morning. Her lunch went on the table, her notebook for the day went on the desk, she had a glance at the calendar.

When she looked up, Owen was standing there, leaning slightly against the doorframe. "Everything all right?"

She nodded once. "I - thanks for walking me. The company. But you should get home, get some sleep?"

Owen hesitated. "Your shoes. Do they bother you?"

They were shoes. She'd never had shoes that fit her particularly well. The ones Master Morris had given her fit badly, but in a different way she didn't have words to describe. She shrugged. "They're old."

"Can I have a look at them some night?" He seemed insistent about it. On the other hand, he knew shoes. Not that she'd ever really seen that, directly. She'd heard a lot about it from his Mum, who'd been very proud. He'd made his Mum's shoes, of course, but by the time Clara met her, she wasn't doing much walking.

"If you like?" Her voice cracked on the last word. "I mean."

"I'd like. I won't do anything without checking with you. Just want to see what might be a help. You spend a lot of time on your feet."

She couldn't argue with that, either, even if she had a stool for the quiet bits of the day. Suddenly, on impulse, she came back around the desk to kiss him on the cheek. "Thank you. Go off to get a nap in. I should be asleep when you come back tonight."

"I can get free for a bit when you're done for the day, if you want me to walk you home. You just send a message round."

That cost money, and she'd have to admit she couldn't

manage herself, and surely they both knew that she wouldn't do any such thing. She just nodded, though, because it was easier than saying any of that. "Have a good day?"

"You too." With that, he finally turned and went out. She followed him to get the door, locking it behind him again. Once that was done, she could begin her day the way she was used to.

CHAPTER 26
NOVEMBER 9TH AT THEIR FLAT

Owen didn't have a chance to talk to anyone at the theatre on either Friday or Saturday. Getting ready for the evening show, and then the challenge of the matinee followed by the other evening show meant they were all moving full speed backstage. They were like some automaton, each whirring past the other with their own specific tasks and obligations. Owen liked having a place in it, he'd found, but it didn't allow for other conversation.

He hadn't heard anything at all from Clara on Friday, though he mostly hadn't expected to. By the time he came home at midnight, there was only a single lamp on in the sitting room. She was tucked up in bed and he couldn't tell if she were sleeping or not. He peered into the dimness before turning around and going and looking at the kitchen table. On the back of an old receipt, she'd written, "Going to bed. Thank you for this morning. C."

Which was not at all informative as to her state of mind in general, nor was it much in the way of useful communication. He could see she was in bed. On the other hand, she needed sleep. He did too, but he had things he wanted to do before he did that.

There were the shoes, for one thing.

He'd tucked them back behind his own kit, so they wouldn't be out in the open. Now, he settled down on the floor, under the lamp, so he could get a good look at them. Machine made, yes, he could see all the places that showed. Pegged together, of course, using some machine to force the upper and the sole together, rather than the far better quality a competent shoemaker got with stitching. But stitching was slower, and there was only so much it could be automated, especially once the shoe was taking form in all dimensions. That was vulcanisation on the sole, too, which Owen was quite dubious about.

For one thing, magic played poorly with it. It insulated too well, that was the problem. And in a shoe, if it wasn't properly applied - it hadn't been here, he suspected - it could flake and peel. The shoe could pull apart, or worse.

After a moment, he stood to go gather up Clara's current shoes, to compare them. He could see why she was having trouble. The heel had worn unevenly, especially on the right, and he could see where the shoe hadn't done well with how she walked. A little twist to the outside, he expected. It made his hands itch to set up a new last, but he'd need to get some measurements to do that. He'd have to ask her. Somehow.

Owen wasn't at all sure what she'd think of that, honestly. She hadn't told him no this morning. Frankly, she hadn't told him no since he got back. Not if it wasn't about the budget or what money they didn't have. But she hadn't said yes terribly often, not directly. They'd both been making assumptions, maybe, and Owen wasn't sure what he felt about that.

He turned the machine-made shoes over, looking for a maker's mark. There it was, in the rise of the instep, where it wouldn't get worn down. An elegant stamp, embedded slightly in the arch, a swooping HM. There couldn't be that many shoemakers with that combination. Master Corwin would likely know. If not, he'd certainly know where they could look it up. He'd stop by on his way to the theatre tomorrow.

The next day, they ended up with a good hour between the afternoon work and the time to get ready for the evening show. Not enough time to go home, nor enough for a pub, really, not with some of the work they'd need clear heads for. Edgar snagged a cup of tea and waved Owen to a seat in one of the back hallways. "You look like you've been thinking."

Owen nodded. "A bit, yeah." He frowned. "Do you know who it is who's after the theatre? Buying it, I mean?" Orlando hadn't mentioned the name where Owen could hear, or at least not clearly. And Golshan hadn't known it either, or hadn't shared it.

Edgar tilted his head. "Are you worrying about that? You've not been here long. And you've some options, don't you?"

"Depends." Getting enough materials to actually start a shop of his own was going to take some doing. He could - literally speaking - bootstrap himself if he could get some commissions and find a place to work that wouldn't mind sawdust and such. The back room downstairs, for example, even if he leased the front out to someone else for a bit longer once the current lease ran out in March. "It's not cheap, setting up properly. And I don't have a workspace to use, to do a few here and there."

Edgar nodded once. "And the theatre?"

"You all are good people. And I might—" Owen hadn't been going to get into it, but maybe he should. "Look, I came across something else, and I'm trying to figure out if it's connected. Or how. Do you know the name?" He pressed more, leaning forward as he did.

"Morris. Horatio Morris. Owns a factory of some kind. Wants to turn the whole place into a cinema, just a cinema, not like Roberts and Glory, who are a cinema half time."

"Newer's not always better." Owen looked away. If he'd been in the trenches, he'd have spit. Avert ill luck, but also a commentary. He wouldn't do that here, of course. "His shoes are lousy. Badly made. Cheap."

"His shoes." Edgar's voice had a hollowness to it for a moment. "He makes shoes?"

"He does." Owen cupped his tea in both hands, looking into the liquid so he didn't have to look up. "He's been making a fuss at my wife, it turns out. Getting a bit more so."

"Ah." That sound was a lot harder to make sense of. When Owen glanced up, Edgar was setting his tea on a crate and crossing his arms. "How do you feel about that?"

"He scared her. Don't like that one bit. But he's a customer at the shop she runs, and a steady one. An apothecary, but she runs the counter. It's her aunt who makes everything." He flicked one finger, then went back to holding the teacup. "He gave her a pair of shoes. That's how I put it together."

"I can't decide if I like the confirmation that he's a cad, or think it's one more worry. Probably both. May I pass that along to Orlando? He might have some ideas of more he can do with that information. The man's got money, though, bushels of it. Fancy house up in the good end of town, you know. One of the ones that looks fancy for show. Too much visible gilt."

"Is that gilt as in gold, or guilt as in shame? No never-mind, the man's shameless." Owen couldn't hide the bitterness now.

"Hey." Again, Owen looked up. Edgar was leaning forward. "That was clever wordplay. But you're right. He is. Is your wife all right?"

Owen shrugged one shoulder. "For the moment." He didn't have a clue to explain how he felt about that. Edgar wasn't married, Owen knew that much. Like he knew Maisery was a widow. Going to either of them about a marriage he didn't know how to explain felt rude. And he couldn't explain how badly he felt it was going, because he didn't have words for it himself.

But Thursday had made him worried for Clara, very worried. And also he'd felt tender, and fierce, and confused, all in a jumble. He'd absolutely wanted to put himself between her and danger, but at the same time, she hadn't really said she wanted that. He'd been fighting for her, for the safety of everyone in Albion and in Britain, while he was in the trenches. But it turned out that didn't translate from the abstract to the very specific at all well.

At the same time, no matter how awkward it was, or his feelings were, she'd been scared. And that wouldn't do. He took a breath and let it out. "It's hard to talk about. Do y'mind if I go make a circuit?"

"No, that's fine. I'll be here a bit if you want company later. Til, hmm. Half five, then I'll have to make sure the props are set."

"I'll come lend a hand with that, if nothing else." Owen left his teacup and plate on the cart, and then went up to do a round of looking at the balcony. He'd checked everything that afternoon, but he had a nagging thought about it. When he got upstairs, he started stage left, moving clockwise. There were customs about that sort of thing, and this was one that went far beyond the theatre proper. As he circled, he could see the shimmer again, but this time it wasn't in the usual box. It was along the back wall of the theatre, as if gesturing through the wall. He frowned. "Are you trying to show me something?" Owen didn't pitch his voice loud. There were people down backstage.

The light blinked, or rather the shimmer did. It wasn't a light source, exactly, more a shift in reflection. Owen got within five or six feet of it, and it bobbed along, into the foyer outside at the back, where the stairs came up on either side. Fire exits were a thing, even in - maybe especially in - a theatre as old as this one. The shimmer went through the double doors as if they weren't there. When Owen opened one, it had gone off to the left, then up the side stairs, into the attic area.

Owen had been up here several times. It was where the smaller, more portable items were stored. Not costumes, so much, certainly not set pieces or furniture. But the smaller props, in trunks and crates that could be brought down as a group when needed, or sorted out into types of objects. It wasn't the cleanest or tidiest space, but it didn't smell of mice or worse.

The shimmer paused a quarter of the way along. The wall must be the back of the theatre, the wall that ran up between the foyer and the balcony. It was sturdy brick, whitewashed not terribly recently, so it was now a dingy beige.

"Is there something here?" It felt slightly ridiculous to ask a shimmer, it wasn't as if he was going to get information. "In the wall?"

The shimmering bobbed once and then produced a series of silk flowers from absolutely nowhere. There were a dozen this time, showering down, followed by a string of loose petals, all with that brilliant gold tip, in every shade of the rainbow. They dropped into a pile on the floor, and then the shimmering vanished through the wall, as if marking a specific point.

Owen stared at the wall. There was nothing that remotely suggested anything like a covered doorway or window or any such thing. And whatever it was would be ten or fifteen feet in the air from the other side, if he remembered right. He considered, then patted the half-apron he was wearing. There was a grease pencil in there, and he marked the area carefully, with bold strokes, covering the area the ghost had gone through.

Then he stared at it. For quite a few minutes, he thought. When nothing else changed or happened, he piled up the silk flowers and petals into a small basket and brought them downstairs. Edgar was still on his crate in the hall, now joined by Maisery. They both stopped talking and looked up at him. "More flowers?"

"Is there something that used to be on the other side of the stage left attic? About where the crates of balls and shields are?"

Maisery frowned. "Not that I know? Why?"

"The ghost." Owen spread out his free hand. "He, she, I don't know. Went from the back of the house through the foyer, up the stairs, and then through a bit of wall. I marked it."

Edgar glanced at Maisery. "There is that bit of lore that you get ghosts where there's some sort of treasure. I've never put much weight on it, personally, because we've always seen our dear ghost in the box. Never anywhere else.

I don't know of anything that would be there. I thought that was an original wall."

Maisery shrugged. "We can pull out a copy of the blueprints, sometime, and figure out what might be there. It's a thick wall, though. Load bearing, for the ceiling and the balcony on that end."

There was no sort of useful exploration possible in the time they had before the evening performance. They certainly couldn't go demolishing even part of a load-bearing wall without a lot of planning, either. Owen shook his head and took his profusion of silk flowers off to his workbench until he was ready to go home for the night.

CHAPTER 27
NOVEMBER 16TH AT THE SHOP

Clara had relaxed a little. She'd had a quiet Saturday to herself after the morning in the shop. And it was Owen's long day at work, so they'd barely had time for a conversation. Certainly not anything complicated. She'd done a fair bit of mending, and realised she was running a little low on black thread. She'd added that to her list for errands this week. It was no good running out when she had to mend a skirt or sew a button on.

Sunday had been quiet as well. Owen had slept in, and she didn't really grudge him that. She certainly wasn't using the bed. Clara had been up and about quite early, unable to stay asleep for some reason. She'd gone out in the afternoon to the meeting at the pub. This time, she had been quiet, saying near nothing until everything broke up at the end. At the end, she'd caught Irene's eye.

It had been a few weeks since they'd chatted, but Irene promptly invited her round. Clara felt this was a tad uneven. She made herself a note to bring some nice soap - the stuff that had some cosmetic issue, but was perfectly good - with her next time. And maybe to pick up some pastries or something. A couple wouldn't be too dear.

They'd had a good chat. Clara had worked up the nerve to ask about something Irene had said that first day, about Irene's bosses groping her, before Ethan came home. Now, she kept thinking about what Irene had said, that some people - men, more than women, but it wasn't just men - took advantage to see how far they could go. That it was a game for some of them. They didn't care much how it felt on the other side.

It didn't solve the problem of Master Horatio Morris, not one bit, but it gave her more ways to think about it. Irene had encouraged her to at least write to Auntie Lillian about it in specific. After all, maybe there was something Aunt Lillian knew about him, especially if he'd been as good a customer as he kept implying.

Thinking about how to do that had kept her busy most of Monday. That, and dusting the shelves, of course, they seemed to pick up no end of dust between Saturday and Monday. That evening, she'd had a pleasant enough evening with Owen. He'd read out loud while she sewed, then she'd done the same while he worked on something made out of wood. Whatever it was still had a fairly formless shape when he was done for the evening.

Of all things, he'd asked her to read the beginning of The Young Visiters over from the beginning. He had been right. It was a particular delight to read out loud, to make the ridiculous sentences sound serious, and the serious ones sound amusing. "She ran out of the room with a very superier run throwing out her legs behind and her arms swinging in rithum.", for just one example. It was not the way people normally left rooms. Or entered them, for that matter. And she was fairly certain that was true among the Great Families, as well as her sort of people.

It gave them something to talk about, at least. The book took place, more or less, in 1890, a few years before Owen had been born, and more like seven before Clara's birth. Their parents had been adults, though, or near enough. Mind, it made her laugh, to think of Owen's Mum being anything like Ethel in the book. She had been an intensely practical woman. While she might have liked a good hat or pair of shoes, she'd have chosen steady, lasting colours rather than flash or garish combinations.

All of it meant that Clara was thinking hard while she was tending the counter on Tuesday. They were not bad thoughts, but they were complex ones. Owen had been kind, kinder than she expected, on Thursday and on Friday. He'd been funny the previous night, putting on voices. He said he'd been picking up something from the actors and actresses. And he had a good voice in general, a comfortable rolling baritone that resonated.

Clara, on the other hand, felt she had a tendency to shrillness that she did not want to encourage. She didn't enjoy hearing it, and she was sure no one else did. When she'd been volunteering, she'd kept to something softer and lower, like a proper nurse should have. Clara was stuck on that thought, the question of voice, when the bell above the door rang. She was looking up, smiling, before she realised who it was.

"Master Morris." She made herself continue the smile. "Not your usual day!"

"Ah, I couldn't help stopping by. Such a pleasure to run into you last week, a delight, truly. I hope your husband is well?"

It was a question that surprised her, and she wasn't

sure how to answer it. She didn't particularly want to imply Owen would be out that night - though it was Tuesday, he should be home by six. She could even go meet him at the theatre if she wanted. It wasn't too far out of her way.

"Very kind of you to ask." That wasn't any kind of answer at all, and she knew it. "We're both well. Busy, but that's all to the good."

"And he was overseas?" Morris came and leaned on the glass, getting closer to her, or as close as he could get without the display cabinets in the way. And smudging them, she'd have to clean them all over again, specially. Blast the man.

"He was. Demobbed in July, so we're settling into things as they are now." She didn't want to tell him more details, but that much seemed harmless. Mostly harmless.

"Indeed." He glanced through the glass as she turned away to tuck something under the counter. "You're not wearing the shoes I gave you. I hope there's no problem."

There were, in fact, several problems with them, not that Clara was going to say that, either. She really wished she'd already written to Aunt Lillian about the man, and had got back some sort of sensible answer that would help better decide what to do. Or, while she was wishing for impossible things, that Aunt Lillian would walk out of the back room and take care of all of this for her. Men did not do this sort of thing to Aunt Lillian.

Mind, that was sensible, since Aunt Lillian knew all sorts of ways - approved ones, even - to cool a bit of lust as easily as inflame it a bit. The latter was one of the more prosperous bits of their trade, on the whole, since people were willing to pay well for it. The Healers kept a tight lid on the more effective recipes, to make sure they wouldn't do too much damage, but that didn't mean they didn't exist. Clara didn't much see the point, honestly, in inflaming things, not from her experiences so far.

"Oh, no. But the pair I'm wearing, they're broken in." She'd almost said that Owen liked them, but that would have been a lie, and it stuck behind her teeth, anyway. She didn't think he'd much liked them, but she hadn't been able to figure out why, or how to ask about them. He'd fixed the buckle, though, doing something to stabilise the strap so it didn't pull and gape oddly. They did feel more comfortable now.

And they were, whatever else they were, broken in, as fitted to her feet as any shoes she'd ever had were. Imperfectly, but hers. Rather entirely like the rest of her life, honestly. She cleared her throat. This was hopeless. "Did you come in for anything in particular from the shop today?" There, that was reasonably lacking in plausible innuendo.

"Oh, well, yes. Besides your company to brighten my day for a little. Did you have more of that aftershave, or what were the other scents?"

That meant she was in for a good twenty minutes of him going back and forth, she thought. And she was. He never quite crossed the line from hinting into suggestion, never mind proposition, but she kept feeling like it was a very near thing. Rather like all the alchemical instructions to have things at a simmer, not a boil, where someone had to watch the pot like a hawk. Or the ones that were insistent about stirring, or there'd be glop on the bottom of the pot.

They were at least fifteen minutes into it when Mrs Malcom came in. "Good day, Mistress Hubbard. When you've a moment? There's something I'd like to discuss, about the shops along this way, that affects all of us." Clara smiled back at her and went back to getting Master Morris to make a decision with good will.

Fortunately, his pattern held true here, as well, when it made things easier for her. She'd noticed he didn't press if there was someone else around. He dithered between two bottles for a little longer, bought both of them in the end, and waited while she wrapped them up. "I'm sure I'll be in again soon, Miss...tress Hubbard."

"A good day, Master Morris."

She waited until the door was well and truly closed and she could see him a good few steps down the street through the window, before turning to Mrs Malcom. "Thank you for your patience. What can I help you with today?"

"Oh, my dear. I came to lend you a hand. He's been by quite a lot, and I got the impression - do tell me if I'm wrong - that you're not entirely comfortable with it. We all have to put up with customers who aren't entirely who we'd choose, of course, but there is a line."

Clara froze in place. She couldn't stop herself. "That obvious?"

"To me, yes. To him, I'm certain not. Or if he notices your discomfort, it's because he enjoys it, and that's even worse, isn't it? Look, dear, I came over to say we could set something up so that one of us in my shop could hear when he came by. Either something you touched when he came in, or one of those - you do have one of the charm stones that let you hear in the back room?"

"We do, but it's set for upstairs, for when Aunt Lillian takes her lunch."

"Well, then. I have a stone here, you touch it, it will let us know in our shop. And it's the three of us there, so chances are very good one of us can come step across in a minute or two's time. Touch it several times if it's urgent, it makes a little chirp. Like a bird, they told me, though I think it's not a very articulate bird."

Mrs Malcom chattered along amiably, and Clara let it roll over her. The idea of having someone come and interrupt was terribly tempting, but she wasn't at all sure she could or should trust it. It was one more thing she should tell Aunt Lillian, and one more thing she wasn't sure she could. It would be a sign Clara wasn't managing, and that was no good at all.

"I couldn't presume." Clara let it out a bit unevenly.

Mrs Malcom looked her up and down. "You go make yourself a cup of tea in the back room. I will tell you if anyone comes by. Take fifteen minutes or so. Come back when you've done that." It was not quite an order, but it was implacable, and Clara knew it would be easier to do what she was told rather than fight.

Fifteen minutes later, she had to admit the tea - and a sit down - had in fact helped. She didn't feel nearly so raw. She came back out after washing her hands in the sink in back. "You were right, Mrs Malcolm."

"Winnie, please, dear. If we're going to plot together, we should be on first names, don't you think?"

Clara's mouth quirked up. "Plotting?" Then she added. "Clara. As I'm sure you know. You seem to know quite a lot."

"Well, yes. We've had our shop near as long as your aunt's had this place. And you've done well with it here. She never was terribly good at the paperwork if it isn't a recipe. But we're glad to lend a hand. Well, me in specific. Alice and Florrie are excellent young women, but they wouldn't do to distract someone like him." The emphasis was clear.

"And you are?"

"I, my dear, am the sort of woman he'd like to ignore, and can't quite. And I've had enough experience of the world to know what to do with that. I can smack a hand down at ten feet with a glare. I have sons and nephews, for one thing, always wanting to sneak a bit more from the tea table."

The image made Clara smile, almost despite herself. "If you're sure. I - it feels very uneven. Ma'am. Winnie."

"Perhaps you might have a look at our books, and see if you can simplify how we keep our records? Make it work better? That would be a true kindness, and no end of help." Winnie said it right out, as if she'd had it in mind from the beginning.

"You could have asked," Clara said, a bit weakly. "I'd be glad to."

"You could have, as well." With that, she left the stone on the counter and swept off, leaving Clara gaping at her back.

CHAPTER 28
NOVEMBER 17TH AT THE THEATRE

Owen was perched up in the balcony when Maisery found him. He was sitting down, apparently at leisure, but of course he was supposed to be there. Howard and Iawn were on the stage, working out one of their first scenes, and trying to get the timing right. Owen was keeping an eye on the lighting, and how it reacted.

Not that he was touching it. That was far above his pay grade and his skills. But the lights could be trained to follow specific actors on the stage. Maisery had explained it as something having to do with sympathetic magic. Something in the light, linked to something the actor or actress wore. Usually it was pinned into the cloth at the back of their neck, so it could be removed quickly for scenes that needed that. It would not at all do for a character who was sneaking to be brightly lit, at all.

At the moment, the lighting didn't need much help. Howard wasn't all dressed up, of course, but he was wearing the Cook's Apron. That was a spreading length of thick fabric painted with patterns that nearly jumped off the stage and shouted in the audience's eyes. As it were. Owen was aware he was mixing metaphors, and he didn't care at all.

Maisery glanced at the stage and frowned. "We're going to have to get Iawn to buck up. He's being timid, and I didn't think he had it in him."

"Howard's doing a decent job setting things up, though."

"Well, Howard's broken in I don't know how many actors in that sort of role. Dozens, probably. We don't usually keep them in it for more than a year or three." Maisery snorted. "But Iawn's not cheating out enough. His shoulder is not the interesting part of him."

Owen raised an eyebrow. "And he's supposed to be interesting with his arse?"

"He certainly was in *Robin Hood And His Merry Men*. He's got good legs for hose. If we keep going, we should look at a historical that'd give him a good part." It was - and this is what Owen found interesting - a purely aesthetic evaluation. Maisery had an eye for what looked good on stage. Owen had heard Orlando checking in with her, and she would pull up details he'd never spotted, even when he'd been right next to her the whole time.

Owen watched a bit where Howard produced a series of increasingly odd food ingredients from the apron. "So how does this work, then?"

"It's a bit more complicated story than some. There's the whole quest sequence." Maisery considered. "In the first scene, Brutus and the other Trojans - so to speak, they're all two generations down, of course, but we're not getting into that. People will know it. They land, and Brutus and Innogen are refusing to talk to each other. Cook gives a monologue that sets the scene and has a bit of funny stuff. Then Diana appears, makes vague prophetic noises in rhyme, and disappears in a puff of shadow and smoke, just as the giants appear."

"And there are the illusions, and also other things?"

"Just so. Those little alchemical twists. They're like Christmas and Solstice crackers, you pull them, and the magic pops. Only instead of getting a paper hat and a not terribly good joke, you get a bit of magical effect."

Owen half-laughed. "I'd forgot about crackers, did you know?" He'd been noticing that more the last month. There were a whole host of things from his life before the War that just dropped out of his awareness, unless something brought them up.

"You talk to Perris. And the new guy, who's working with him. What's his name? Hector. I heard he does nice ones, at a discount for minor flaws - they'll still pop, just the wrapping's not perfect or something of the kind. Paper hat, decent joke, small trinket, as I understand it." Maisery leaned back, letting out a sigh. "Anyway, Cook and Jack need to carry a lot of the humour. And I think Iawn's not feeling so comfortable with the improvisation, reading the audience, as we hoped. Blast."

Owen nodded once. "And then there's the quest sequence?"

"Just so. Diana comes back, trailed by a whole herd of shadow images of animals. That bit's very impressive, Perris already showed us, it's why we've built a lot of the show around the illusion work. Brutus has a dream and has to get three objects. An enormous turnip, an egg of purest gold, and a flower of whitest down."

"What's that even supposed to mean?" Owen's voice

got a bit louder, and he snapped his teeth shut. "Sorry. The turnip I understand, I suppose."

"Any enormous root vegetable is great for jokes. It is a key understanding in the theatre." Maisery said it mock-solemnly, but her eyes were dancing with it. "And the egg of purest gold is classic, and the flower is for punning at the end."

Owen raised an eyebrow. "All right."

"Anyway, Brutus and Corineus go off hunting for the items in one direction, Innogen and Jack go the other way, and there are various minor adventures. We see the giants popping up here and there, and being silly more than scary, that sort of thing. Brutus finds the turnip, Innogen finds the egg, they're both stumped about the flower. Cook goes on about whether or not the turnip is really big enough. We have all sorts of slapstick humour about dropping the egg. It gets tossed around, a game of keep-away, a chance to do a bit of audience back and forth about whoever has it. And all the while, Cook's making up a big pot of stew and demanding various ingredients. You know, total chaos, hopefully very funny."

"Hopefully." Owen eyed the stage. "Howard knows what he's doing though, right?"

"Yes. Bless him. He's solid as a rock as the dame. But this isn't one of his favourite roles. He'd much rather be doing Puss in Boots or maybe Cinderella or something like that." She tilted her head. "Possibly it's that he does better with other objects for his humour than turnips. There is probably only so much scope you can get with a turnip. Anyway, that's act one, finishes with a big song and dance number, everyone troops off stage."

Owen nodded. Howard and Iawn had paused, both of them going to opposite sides of the stage to get a drink, rather like boxers going to their corners. That was not the mode they wanted, surely. "And the second act?"

"For the second act, we have everyone waking up, and suddenly there are giants. Do not ask why no one notices the very large giants thumping around near the camp. It's panto. Logic often does not strictly apply."

Owen laughed at that. "Did I say anything?"

"No. But you were going to." Maisery looked over at him, mock-stern, before her mouth cracked into a smile. "They need to find the flower, of course. Then we get a nice chase scene with the giants, and the audience getting to shout 'He's behind you!' and all of that. That's all in the timing too, but I'm less worried about that part."

"Right. That seems, I mean, a chase scene. That's going to be tricky, getting people on and off stage in the right order without banging into each other in the wings."

Maisery chortled. "See, we knew you'd pick this job up fast. Just so, if that's the first thing you were thinking."

"Are the giants shadows or illusion, or something else?"

"Huge paper mache puppets, with illusion to make them look more impressive."

Owen went still at that, looking out toward the balcony. He saw that flicker of light again, and cordially ignored it. He could feel the way his hand had tightened on the arm of the seat. Maisery went on for a couple of sentences that didn't make it into his ears, not in any way that made sense. Then she stopped and asked something he didn't make sense of either.

"Pardon?"

"Is something the matter?" Maisery's voice was more careful now.

Owen still felt frozen. It was ridiculous that talking about puppets, of all things, made him lose track of everything. He shrugged, the shoulder on the far side from Maisery.

"Something is the matter." Maisery shifted, the seat creaked. "Fetch you a cup of tea?"

Owen hesitated, but then nodded once. She levered herself up, and he could hear her footsteps going up the balcony steps to the foyer. She'd be a minute or two. Despite it being the heart of Trellech, the tea was a good two minutes away.

He watched the flicker of the ghost, leaning back into the seat. The ghost didn't scare him. Most things didn't scare him anymore, honestly. Or if they did, it was different than it had been. Certainly, the ghost was bobbing around some distance away. And it hadn't seemed to want to cause harm any time before. Something in the pattern of the shimmer seemed a little different, though. As if the form were a little more solid - something between a flicker of light and an illusion, maybe.

Maybe he'd ask Perris how illusions worked properly. How they made people see things that weren't actually there. It wasn't like anyone here seemed to know anything about ghosts, or what they meant.

He leaned his chin on his hand, elbow on the arm of the seat. Maisery came back up, balancing a saucer on top of one of the mugs of tea she carried, with half a dozen biscuits on the saucer. "Here." She left an empty seat between them, giving her space to balance the saucer on the other armrest. "You all right?"

Owen shrugged, but he was a bit better for the time. "Sometimes it catches up with me. What the last five years were like, how everything here is a kind of ordinary I've forgotten about." He reached for one of the biscuits, but he didn't take a bite before he said, "They made paper mache forms for sniper targets. Rigged it so it looked like someone was smoking. Pull the target down, see where the shots came from, and you know where the sniper is."

Maisery went absolutely still for a long moment. "Well. Blast." She rubbed her face. "That kind of thing get you a lot, then?"

"Enough. It's fine. Mostly." He grunted once. "It's the ones that surprise me that are bad."

"Does the smell of it get you?" Maisery was frowning. "They're going to start making the puppets next week."

"Don't know, honestly. We'll find out. Tuesday?" Owen reached for his tea, which was at least soothing.

"Tuesday. If it does bother you, tell me. We have other things you can do for a few days."

Owen nodded, then flicked his fingers toward the ghost's box. "No one knows why we have a ghost? No lore about some tragic death?"

"Nothing we know about. The theatre's been around a long time, under one name or other, and the ghost's been here most of it." She grimaced, nudged one of the biscuits on the plate, indicating he should have the third. "You want the rest of the plot?"

He let out a long breath and reached for the biscuit. "Ta." Then he nodded. "Might as well."

"So Brutus and Innogen have not had a happy romance, but at this point in the story, they get caught together, and have to think their way out of it. And that goes pretty well for them. You know the sort of thing, where they both do asides to the audience about 'I hadn't realised!' and 'There's something there!'."

"I can see that working. Again, a lot of it's in the timing."

Maisery nodded. "The two of them, I'm less worried

about. Besides, it's easier to do the Innamorati than it is the comedy. Melodrama and romance don't take the same sort of timing. A lot more of it is in the posing. And Theo's grand, and Madeline is doing well with him so far. Helps that Theo's not got the ego he probably could claim about it."

"I thought he was still in London?"

"He's come a couple of Mondays when their theatre's dark, to run lines with Madeline, and get a good sense of things going. Done a little checking on the staging, too, since there's so much fighting in this one. Can't risk him getting hurt, so that takes time to block out." Maisery leaned back again with another creak of the seat. "Anyway, that ends up with a food fight, which is going to be a tremendous mess. And then we go into the last bit. A closing thing from Diana, in front of the curtains, so we can do a quick clean and everyone can do something about their costumes, then a final song. About three-fourths of it will be an illusion. But cleaning up the stage after is our job. Mops and all."

Owen grimaced. "That part doesn't sound fun."

"We're pretty good at it now. The illusion work means the costumes are pretty safe, but there are still things that need sweeping up. We mostly use something like an aspic jelly to anchor the illusion. Not the most pleasant, but it bounces and you can sort of sweep it up if you're not too vigorous."

"I don't think I've ever been asked to do 'not too vigorous' sweeping before." Owen shook his head. "The things you all think are normal."

"Oh, come on. You like us, don't you?" Maisery was suddenly laughing. "For all you're still figuring us out."

Owen swallowed. "Yeah. I do. And you've been proper

kind. " He stretched. "I want to stick around, turns out. I don't know a lot else, but." He shrugged. "Suppose we should get back to work."

"That's my line. Do your own part." She was laughing though, as she stood up, taking her plate and mug with her.

CHAPTER 29
NOVEMBER 19TH AT THE SHOP

Clara was tidying things up. They were half an hour from closing time, and Owen had said - or maybe just implied - he was going to come by and walk her home. She hadn't seen Master Morris since the sixteenth, and honestly, that was just making her nervous. He often went weeks without stopping in, so she couldn't assume he'd given up. And yet, she kept worrying he'd come through the door.

Just as she thought that, there was some noise outside the door. Not just someone coming in, the ring of the bell. Not Master Morris, probably, then. He walked in like the entire place was at his disposal, and as if everyone inside - well, Clara - would be soon enough. That was what made her uncomfortable, actually. Now she had got round to this side of thinking of it. He didn't ask directly, generally, so she felt she couldn't say no more directly than she already had. And she particularly didn't know what ways he could be extremely difficult, where he could throw his weight around. They didn't need a scandal about the shop. Well, she didn't, and Aunt Lillian certainly didn't.

While she was still thinking about that, someone got the door open. It was a pleasant woman, a bit older than Clara, maybe. She was wearing a rather pretty brown frock, even through brown wasn't a colour you said that about very often. But this was like the soft grain of wood. It made her eyes gleam, and balanced off against her hair and her hat, which had a broad green ribbon that somehow seemed to bring everything together.

A moment later, she was joined by a man in a wheel-chair. He was darker skinned, wearing the sort of fiery red and orange that no one with Clara's complexion could possibly get away with. Another man, behind him, apparently making sure he got in the door fine, was blond and rather broad shouldered. Clara blinked, then remembered her manners. "Good afternoon. May I help you?"

The man in the wheelchair wheeled himself forward, with a cheerful. "I do hope you're Clara Hubbard? I know your husband, Owen. Golshan Soltani."

Clara blinked. "You got him his job." She remembered the name. Or she might not have remembered the name without prompting, but she remembered the sound of it. Then she caught herself. "Pleased to meet you. And we're very appreciative, I hope he's said?"

"Oh, he's doing very well there. They seem to have got the better deal of it." Master Soltani looked very pleased with himself. "These are my friends - I live with them - Seth and Dilly Wain. We thought we'd stop by. Partly because I'd love to talk to Owen at some point. And partly because we were in town, all three of us for once, and I'd heard about the shop." He leaned forward, something that felt conspiratorial, and shouldn't have, given the angles. "We like spoiling Dilly with lovely soaps and things for the bath. And I can't say as I mind them, either."

The other man - Master Wain - snorted at that. "He's in a mood."

The woman, though, was looking at Clara thoughtfully. "Please, do call me Dilly. I've heard a bit about you from Golshan. Do be informal with him, too. He shakes off formality like a wet dog, and then it gets all over everything."

Clara blinked several times. "Ma'am. Sir." She cleared her throat. The man in the chair - Golshan, she tried it on in her head - made an encouraging gesture. "Golshan?"

"There you go!" He seemed utterly delighted, as if this were some great gift. "Anyway. Is there a chance we might catch Owen today?"

That put her on the spot, a bit uncertain. "He thought he might come meet me, but it wasn't a sure thing. It's..." She glanced up at the clock. "Twenty-five minutes until I close up?" He hadn't met her very often so far, given their different schedules. It wasn't like she knew for certain that there was a routine. Then she frowned. "You have our address, though?"

"I do. But I didn't want to just show up. And I gather you've got stairs there."

They did. This was true. And the front of the shop was at street level here. She nodded once, unsure what to say. Dilly grinned, as if something in that amused her. "Also, I do actually have an apothecary question. We've a daughter, she's still nursing, and do you have a salve that actually does any good?"

Dilly seemed to have no worries about saying it in front of both men. Plenty of women would, even in front of their husband, but if Golshan lived with them, well, maybe she had got used to it? Clara nodded. "I can pull out some different options for you. Um." She glanced from Dilly to the men. "May I ask a few questions, or would you rather do that privately?"

"Oh, I don't mind either of them listening. They like knowing things, actually."

It meant Clara could at least fall into the explanation. The salves were all lanolin based, safe for a baby, but some were more solid, and some more like a lotion, and of course there were different properties. This one was more soothing, this other was cooling, this one was good if there was a blockage. Dilly was easy to talk to, remarkably so.

As they finished up, and Dilly chose all three of the salves Clara had thought might be useful, she grinned. "We're in a particularly good mood. Seth just had a promising couple of sales - he makes wooden furniture and things like bowls and boxes and all that. And Golshan and I had a lovely time harassing a particularly annoying office in the Ministry. That's what we do once or twice a week, do our best to shame them into doing the right thing. Or at least making themselves more accessible for appointments."

"This one," Golshan said, fitting himself into the conversation smoothly, "Is the Veterans Office. The more administrative office is up three flights of stairs, in a building where the lift only works reliably one day out of three. So we make them come down to talk to me. Or sometimes whoever I'm with. They hate it. It's a delightful challenge." His eyes were gleaming, and Seth leaned to pat him on the shoulder.

"Dill-my-love. You are getting soap, too, or something for the bath. And if you insist on picking things out for us, you can do that too." Seth seemed deeply amused at the whole thing.

Dilly lit up. "Soap. And bath oils or whatever you have,

please. I'll take my time." Clara set the salves by the register, and pulled out the samples of the soap, the bath oils, and a bit of lotion. Dilly settled in to explore it, taking her time, which meant Clara could look up at the men again. Or across at them, at least.

"Is that what you do then?" Clara was trying to make sense of some of this.

"Help veterans who need a hand? That seems to be my line of work. Sometimes people pay me. Seth's father is setting up a proper charitable arm for donations and all. One of the good things about having gone to Schola is getting the word out about that kind of thing." He said it easily and casually.

"Also, my Mum and Dad between them know near two-thirds of the Ministry, and where enough skeletons are buried to make people just a little nervous." Seth's voice was a comfortable burr, and Clara blinked at him. He shrugged. "Mum works dealing with food. Managing shortages, recipes that you can use if you can't get the obvious thing. Thirty uses for the turnip you may not have considered."

That made Clara giggle. She realised that must have sounded odd a second later. "Owen told me a bit about one of the running jokes in the panto this year. A turnip's involved."

"Turnips are hilarious vegetables until that's all you've got to eat," Seth agreed.

Clara turned that over in her mind. She hadn't known who to ask this about. But there was no one else in the shop, nor anyone terribly likely at this point. And if Seth's parents knew the Ministry, and Golshan went and called them out regularly, and both of them were veterans to boot, well. Maybe they'd know. "Can I ask a question? About something sort of delicate?"

A bit to her surprise, it was Seth who nodded. "Please. If we can't help, maybe we know someone who can. That's mostly himself, here, but one of my sisters teaches at Schola, there are my parents, there's the people my other sisters know..."

Clara gathered her thoughts as best she could. "It's - there's someone I've come across. And I wonder what war profiteering is. What it means if it's, um. Not weapons or anything."

"Making money on supplies?" Seth's question came out quite sharply. "Rather a lot of that with things. Boots that got holes almost immediately. Spoiled food, because the tins weren't sealed correctly. All sorts of issues."

Golshan was nodding along. "Not everyone. And some of it's, what's the word. Understandable. New techniques for making things, in large quantities, don't always work, or some supply chain failure happened. But decent people didn't get rich from cutting corners on other people's lives. Some people did." There was a sudden fierceness in him that made Clara shiver.

He seemed to catch it, and said, more comfortably, "I'm glad you're a decent person. Though of course you are. But we do know some people to talk to. You'd need to be willing to share what you know - a name, numbers if you have any, whatever information you have."

Clara hesitated. "What does that involve, please?"

Seth had shifted forward. He exchanged a glance with Golshan. Something Clara couldn't read at all.

Golshan went on, without missing a beat. "There are magics in the courts that make it clear if you're telling the truth, or someone else is. So long as you have sincere reason, you're sharing what you know, you're not trying to mislead or get someone else in trouble, you have nothing to worry about. If you're concerned about retaliation or something like that, they have ways to keep things private. I don't know a lot about it. You should talk to Volans, though. Seth's father."

"Um?" Clara felt like she was entirely out of her depth now.

"Dad's an accountant. He knows how the finances run, what things are suspicious or look suspicious and are actually fine." Seth shrugged. "Also, he's really easy to talk to. I'm not even biased. Everyone agrees."

Dilly looked up from where she'd sorted some of the soaps into mysterious stacks. "Entirely true. Seth, love, give her his info? And can we give him yours?"

"Yes. Um. I suppose?" At that point, the door opened, and Clara froze up for a moment. But then the person came in, and it was Owen. He stopped in the door, just far enough they could see him clearly. "Owen. Um. Golshan and this is Seth and Dilly Wain? They came to see if you were going to come by."

"We've had a bit of a financial blessing as a household, and I want to pass it around." Golshan said cheerfully. "Would you make me some slippers? I don't need much in the way of soles, but I'm particular about the rest of it. And please, dear gods, something with some proper colour?"

Owen looked as startled as Clara had felt. "Possibly?" he said, then he cleared his throat. "I'd need some measurements."

"That the sort of thing you can do now, or should we arrange a time? Dil and I will be back in Trellech. What, Thursday, right?"

"Thursday is for harassing the Temple of Healing about

advertising their services better, yes," Dilly said, agreeably. She added to Clara, "We have a schedule, but half the time Golshan gets distracted and forgets what day it is, never mind what day it's going to be. It's fine. Can I get these three, please, and these two oils?" She turned over her shoulder. "Neither of you look, you hear? Mine to distribute when I see fit."

"Yes'm," came from Golshan, and a "Would I, love?" from Seth. Clara shook her head, and settled into wrapping them up all pretty, making a note of the costs as she did so.

While she did so, Owen had sorted out something. "I can do it now, but better on Thursday, when I've got my tools. Somewhere I could meet you, a cafe or something?" They made arrangements, and Clara ignored that part. As she finished ringing everything up, she looked up. Seth was grinning at her, "If you're looking to establish yourself, come the spring, I'd be glad to help you with sorting a plan for it. Dad too, quite likely. He's the one who got me sorted when I got back about all of that. Fees and taxes, of course, but also where there might be help with things."

Owen cleared his throat. "I'll let you know?" He seemed as unsure what to do with the offer as Clara had been about the profiteers. That was reassuring, somehow. That she wasn't alone in her confusion.

Dilly came forward to pay for her things and grinned. "I'll likely want more. For presents, too, once I've had a chance to try these out." There were a few more pleasantries, and then the three of them went out the door, leaving Clara and Owen blinking after them. And Clara still had to clean up and manage all the small tasks for the end of the day.

CHAPTER 30
NOVEMBER 25TH AT THEIR FLAT

Owen got home close to midnight on the Thursday night. It had been a long day. He'd ended up meeting Golshan - and Dilly - at the Field to do the fitting, since they knew there would be space.

He wasn't sure what to make of them. They teased each other in a way that felt entirely relaxed. It certainly had an intimacy to it that Owen wanted himself with Clara. At the same time, it wasn't like he could expect that, or make it happen, if she didn't want to.

But he had kept coming back - in the midst of the rehearsals and then setting up for the music hall that night - to the way Dilly looked. Happy. Not just happy, the laughing sort of happy, though it was that too. But she looked really contented. She'd brought her daughter with her in a sort of sling. That apparently made her happy too, splitting her attention between the baby and the conversation.

At any way, he'd got the measurements for Golshan's

feet, rather carefully. The man had feeling in his feet, apparently, though that wasn't necessarily the case. But it made it more important to have slippers for some protection against bumps, or cold rooms.

Better yet, they'd been crystal clear that Owen should have a deposit that covered the materials. More than covered, as it turned out. Golshan had wanted something in reds and yellows. When Owen went round to the Corwins, Master Corwin, by sheer luck, had a lovely bit of golden yellow he'd bought for something and then couldn't use. And he'd had a rich red he'd been willing to part with, at his cost.

Between the two, he'd have enough for a pair for Golshan, comfortably. And possibly, maybe, a pair for Clara, as well. The yellow would go well with several of her frocks, and he could pair it with black, or maybe even something startlingly colourful, like a bright blue. Not the same way as Mum's blanket, where somehow the colours should have worked and they didn't, but the same quality of colour.

It made him wonder what sort of decorative things she liked. A bee sprang to mind, the way that she was constantly working, thinking about the future, in a way that he had trouble keeping in his head. He could only do his best not to mess up her planning. They hadn't had another bad fight about the money - she'd been entirely in the right. But he'd been very careful not to mess up like that again, or get in her way about it. She'd been very good about telling him what was fair game for meals and snacks.

Which reminded him that there was a bit of cheese and bread and maybe an apple he could have. He settled at the table with his sketches out. For Golshan's shoes, he wanted tongues like tongues of flame, licking up from the toecap, over the vamp.

The soles didn't need to be much - and, in fact, better if they had no heel. Apparently, that might catch, in ways that could be uncomfortable or even dangerous to Golshan. It had been Dilly who explained that in a no-nonsense tone. He could move himself in and out of the chair, for various reasons. But it relied on his feet being where he intellectually expected them to be, or staying where he put them. A heel catching spoiled all of that.

Once he had the sketches, he began laying out the proper measurements. He'd need to work on the last, first of all. And one for Clara, too. He meant to make her more than one pair, if she'd let him, so he might as well do the last properly and save it.

He went and got her shoes from the entry hall, setting them on a bit of old newspaper. He grabbed some more of the paper. There was a charm he'd learned that let him use newsprint to make a temporary shape for the shoe's last. Though of course that wouldn't help with how they actually fit her. He'd have to judge that from the fit itself.

Owen turned the light on overhead, so he could better see what he was doing, then he worked through it piece by piece. First the newspaper got stuffed in, as full as he could, without stretching the leather out of shape. More out of shape, they really weren't very good shoes.

Then the charm, to turn the paper into a solid form. Once he had that, there was another to split it in half, so he could ease the heel out of the shoe, then the toe, before joining them again.

That meant another charm, to see where the leather had been stretching, plus a close examination of the soles, to see the wear. By the time he was done with all of that, it was half-five. He'd need sleep, but at this point, there wasn't much reason to go to bed.

Owen contemplated his options. He could go for a bit of a walk, but the wind had been picking up when he came home, and that didn't seem very pleasant. He didn't have to be out in the chill, even if the flat was on the cooler side now.

In the end, he got out the curtains. He'd hesitated, but then he'd begun sewing the silk flowers he'd collected on, laying them out first to see how the patterns went. With the newest pile of them, he had enough to have petals trailing down the edge of the curtain. Then he could sew a loose pile of them along the bottom hem, right where they'd be visible. He'd measured twice, after all.

Owen had learned to listen to the small sounds that Clara might be waking up. And besides, he'd been keeping an eye on the time. Half an hour before she woke, at half-six, he did go out, bundling up long enough to go get a paper from the corner.

Then he put the kettle on, starting it so it'd be just about ready when she was up and about. And the toast. He couldn't forget the toast. When she came out, sleepily tugging the dressing gown around her, everything he'd been working on was back in its proper place.

Except for the leather for Golshan's slippers, on top of the workbox.

Clara rubbed her face. "Oh. Morning?" Then she blinked. "Have you slept?"

Owen looked a bit sheepish, he suspected. "No? I got into working on the design for Golshan. It's an interesting challenge, without the rigidity of the shank for structure. And wanting something comfortable that won't rub when it's on a foot that's not moving much." Then he gestured. "Come have a seat? I can make you an egg, and here's tea and toast."

She cupped her hands around the mug and inhaled it. "You didn't have to." It was as if she was trying to make sense of something.

"I wanted to. At least once I realised it was almost time for you to get up. I'll get some sleep as soon as you head off. It's fine."

"You shouldn't short yourself. It's not good for you." It was an almost automatic comment, but Owen heard an edge in it that wasn't there before. Or that he hadn't noticed before, anyway. "And a hard-boiled egg is fine. I'm not very hungry. If we have one?"

They did, and so Owen got that for her, and the last of the jam, and set that down, before taking the other chair. He hesitated, but he would not learn more if he didn't ask. "You worry about my sleeping?"

Clara took a sip of her tea, and said, rather tartly. "I worry about you not sleeping. To be precise."

Owen couldn't argue with that. "Can I ask why?"

That required a longer sip of her tea, cracking the egg and peeling it, and having a bite or two. Then, slowly, she glanced at him, then away. "I don't know what we're doing. Together. But not sleeping's a way to, a way to get hurt."

He hesitated, then remembered something she'd mentioned only once, very early on, the kind of thing you glossed over because it was far too complicated for the moment. He frowned, fingers twitching to be doing something while he worked through this. "Your parents, you said?"

"Not sleeping's dangerous." She glanced up, then took pity on him, and gave him an explanation. "Out on one of the fishing boats, not far from Forvie, and - things went wrong. Not them, not sleeping, but the ocean doesn't care. Especially not when a storm blows up."

Owen took a breath, and then carefully reached out a hand to cover hers, ready to pull his fingers away if she didn't like it. He could feel her skin, the way she was lightly trembling, but she didn't move. "I'm sorry. And more sorry that it worries you." He considered. "Are there things in the shop that could help?"

"Maybe." She didn't look back at him, just down at a spot on the table. "What kind of not sleeping is it?"

"The Temple of Healing would have given me a sedative, but I hate them. They make me feel too slow. And that's dangerous. Was dangerous. Here, it wouldn't matter." There wasn't terribly likely to be a crisis in the flat.

"But where you were?" Clara saw it immediately. He loved that in her. "And some of your head's still there. Your reactions."

"Yes." Owen cleared his throat. "Might always be, to be honest. And I don't want to wake you, when it's bad in the middle of the night, when I can't stay asleep." She looked up once at that, then back down, as if she couldn't entirely make sense of it. He went on, "Maybe we could figure out something. I've been going through Mum's things. Making a bit more space."

She nodded once. "Whatever you like, there." Clara was annoyingly vague about her own preferences. Owen resolved to have another look and see what could be packed away to make more space for them both. "I could write to Aunt Lillian about the sleep. Or could you write up a note, and I'll stick it in?"

"I'll have something for you by tomorrow morning when you wake up." Owen could do that. It was a specific task. "And honestly, last night, I got caught up in the work. And I missed that, you know?"

"They were very determined about getting the shoes,

weren't they? And being helpful. I see what you mean about Golshan, though. He's very fierce, even when he's being kind? Determined."

"Just like that. And Seth and Dilly aren't exactly faint of heart. I'd only met them briefly at the theatre, and Golshan was catching up with other people, too. But I guess - he told me more yesterday. Seth had a really big commission, the kind of thing that's going to make it much easier to get more." Owen knew how that went. "And so they wanted to share some of that around. If things go well, I might do shoes for Dilly and Seth, too."

"What does Seth do, did you say?"

"Makes furniture. Ordinary things, nicely made. But the fancy one that got them the money, that's a bed that has charms on it. Changes the height, warming, cooling, things like that. I guess there's some posh veteran needed it, needed something that'd suit the house, so it's got fancy inlay and all. But what he wanted was to be comfortable."

"Huh." Clara pushed the last bit of her toast around to get the bits of jam that had fallen off. "So crafter, like you."

"He went to Schola. He knows a lot more fancy magic for it, I bet. But a similar sort of apprenticeship, it sounds like. He wasn't there yesterday - working on something - but Dilly came with Golshan, and she was chatting. She said he'd likely be glad to talk me through setting up a shop when we've got the space again."

Clara looked up at that, then nodded once. "Seth's father should be in touch sometime. Maybe tomorrow, when he's got time to catch up. I don't know what I want to do about that yet, but talking with someone who knows more, I guess."

Owen could ask more about what made her decide to see about reporting it. But that felt far too delicate, like the finest thread that could snap if the stitches pulled the wrong way or tugged too hard. Instead, he just nodded. "I could walk you to work, but I do need the sleep, too."

"You sleep. It's daylight, I'll be fine." She stood then, bending to kiss him on the cheek. "Sleep well."

CHAPTER 31

NOVEMBER 27TH AT A PUB IN CUMBRIA

Saturday afternoon, Clara waited her turn in Portal Square. She hadn't taken a portal in what felt like months. Longer, when she counted, more like a year and a half, and not much in the several years before that. During the War, of course, the Healers and Ministry had priority, and she'd got out of the habit of being able to use them without a lot of planning.

Now, she only had to wait twenty minutes or so, and that was mostly because they'd been bringing livestock through who didn't appreciate the journey. The attendant set the portal for the address she'd been given in Cumbria, and waved her through.

Clara found herself in a pleasant little square, with dirt roads leading off in several directions. She glanced down at the directions in her hand and followed the map. If the portal was at her back, then the inn was up the road here. She came over the crest of the hill and found the inn, just where it was supposed to be.

It must have been a coaching inn at one point. The road looked significant, but as if it didn't get much travel now.

That made sense for the portal, too. She remembered being told in school that some of them were in odd locations now. The busy roads had changed over the centuries, with the addition of trains and other options for goods.

Clara also wasn't very used to country inns, not since she'd become an adult. But she more or less knew what to do now; go in, and look for Volans Wain. He'd said he'd meet her, and she was a good twenty minutes early. Plenty of time to get something to drink and maybe a little food, and to get her notes in order.

The inn-keeper was an older woman, who reminded her cheerfully of Aunt Lillian, only taller and a little rounder. "I'm meeting someone in a bit, ma'am. Could we have a table that's a bit out of the way, easier for talking?"

"Ah, you're the one meeting Volans, then? This table, right over here. There are some charms to keep the noise out, and keep your chat quieter. You just touch that if you need something, since we may not hear. A pint, dear, or something else?"

Clara didn't have much money to spend, and she must have looked a little uncertain, as the woman added, "He's got a tab, you're welcome to add to it. He thought a pint might suit you, and we've got a great steak and ale pie today he's very fond of."

Clara let out her breath. "If you're sure? If he's sure?" Then she cursed herself for sounding so uncertain about everything. She was a grown-up, a married woman. She should be able to make decisions. At least about a fairly simple meal.

"Oh, quite sure. He does the books for me. It'll come off his tab. Drink now, food when he comes?"

"Please." She could nurse the beer for a bit. That let her get a grip on herself, and by the time the older woman brought the pint, she'd laid out her files where she could find them. The beer, apparently, came with little bread twists, and something like a mustard sauce to dip them in.

By the time she'd explored that, she checked the time, just as an older man came in. He spoke briefly to the innkeeper, and then came directly to the corner. "Mistress Hubbard?"

"Master Wain?" Clara ducked her chin. "Please, call me Clara?" She wasn't sure what to think about being formal, but she was fairly sure she couldn't keep it up. "You're doing me a favour. I hope I'm not keeping you from something else?"

"Seth and Dilly and Golshan live down the hill, a little past the portal. You're keeping me from my granddaughter, but she's currently napping, so not very much. I will have plenty of other times to admire her while sleeping, I'm sure." He nodded. "Poppy told you I'm glad to feed you, I gather."

"Yes, sir. It's very kind."

"It's about a quarter of an hour of my work for her, which is just fine. I expect you and I will take more time than that, but I'm glad to help someone out. And especially if what Golshan told me turns out to be true." Volans settled back, and Clara contemplated him for a moment, now she was not quite as much on edge with waiting.

He must be in his late fifties, maybe mid-sixties, with salt and pepper hair and a beard. He was dressed comfortably, with a jacket and trousers rather than working clothes. They had an ease of fit that wouldn't suit a formal office, and a tie that suggested Dunwich rather than Schola.

He let her look, not rushing her, before adding. "Let's get the food before you get into the details." There was something about his patience, about the way he wasn't rushed, that made her wonder what Owen would look like at that age, if he'd be as easy with himself or anything around him. She was quite sure she probably wouldn't be, and that just made her wonder what Mistress Wain was like.

Before she could think better of it, the question popped out of her head. "Can I ask about your family, sir?"

"No need to be formal, and yes, of course. You've met three of them, then, though one by marriage and one by adoption, near enough. We've seven children, two of whom are married with families of their own. Lia's our eldest, about two miles back that way, past the portal. She and her husband Cephus have five little ones now, ten down to the baby in arms. And I suspect they're thinking about a sixth. Then there's Or - Orcus. He works in research at the Ministry. Then Seth, and he and Golshan have been near enough inseparable since their first term at school. First week, I think. Golshan spent a lot of holidays with us."

Clara got the sense there was a lot of history there, and not at all anything she could ask about. Volans went on, steadily. "Then Thesan, who's the Astronomy professor at Schola now, and she loves that and the stars. Then Allie, who works for one of the book publishers in Trellech, and Cel, who's learning to be a serious sort of cook. Our youngest, Archie, is still figuring out what he wants to do with himself. And my wife works for the Ministry, also food, but making the most of what you have, the best preservation charms, that sort of thing. She went to Alethorpe, but our children all made it into Schola. Seth's very sharp with his carving and the charms that go with it." There was absolute pride in that.

Clara felt that was an awful lot of people. She had

cousins, certainly, but seven children. "Did, um. Did Archie fight?"

"Called up once he left school, but he'd only got as far as training before the War ended. And after Seth and Golshan being over there, well. We worried a lot." Volans tilted his head. "Dilly mentioned you married your husband during the War. He was in the trenches."

"He was. It's been - I didn't know him before, you understand? We met when he was injured." She couldn't decide now if that made it better or worse. If she'd loved the man he was before the trenches, before the endless risk and threat, he might have changed. She'd met him in the middle, in a space where nothing was certain or settled. She hadn't fought, not like that, but she was beginning to think she hadn't been any better off than he was in some ways. Battered by the world.

Some of it might have shown on her face, because Volans tsked gently. It wasn't mocking or upset, just him seeing something that had settled into place. "And you've got all the other worries. Ah, here's Poppy with the food." Volans kept her chatting, gently, until she got halfway through the slice of meat pie, which was excellent. Far better than Clara managed herself, she didn't have any sort of gift for a pastry crust.

Finally, though, they had to get onto the topic. Volans settled back. "So, what is the actual concern here?"

Clara swallowed hard. "There's a man who's - who's taken an interest in me. He knows I'm married, he doesn't care. He has a factory that makes shoes, but I've heard a few things that make me wonder about how he made his money. Owen's not said much about it, but I gather the shoes, the boots, could be awful."

"They could." Volans agreed. "And you think there's

something off in the figures? Over-charging? Saying they were charmed properly, when they weren't? That sort of thing?"

"Something like that. I don't know how to describe it. Part of me wants to like him, and part of me wants to run the other way." She put her hand to her mouth. "I didn't mean to say that."

Volans leaned forward, deliberately. "One of the truths of the world, Clara, is that certain kinds of evil are compelling. They get what they want by being charismatic and likeable, by offering things that please. You're sharp enough in what you do, you can see both sides of the coin at once. Plenty of people don't, for whatever reason."

She hadn't thought of it that way at all. It made her swallow hard, then take a cautious sip of her beer. "I haven't known what to do." She admitted it without looking up. She couldn't bear to.

"You talked to Golshan about it. That's enough. This is the kind of thing I want to help with. For my boys who were over there, and everyone they know, and everyone who didn't make it back." His voice was all sharp, the dark of a forest filled with wild animals who would do what they thought best, no matter what. Then he coughed. "Also, flawed accounting offends me. On entirely other levels. May I see your notes?"

She passed the folder over, eating the rest of her food carefully. Volans thumbed through the pages, once, to get a sense of them, then went back over them more slowly, just like she would have. He pulled out a notebook, scratching several things into it.

Finally, he nodded. "This is all public information. Good sources, too. What you'd need for an investigation is something more. Him admitting to shortcuts, to knowing about problems. If you're willing to make an oath in the court, and share what you'd heard."

"That would be enough?" Clara hadn't known what to do with that. "What, what would it mean?"

"Well, for one thing, it'd mean he wouldn't get any more contracts from our Ministry. Not from the London Ministry folks, either, most likely. They don't know about our tools, but they do trust us when we say something like that. There might be fines, too, depending on what the records actually say. It's boots, not guns or medical supplies, which might be more directly life and death."

"But an army marches on its feet. And its stomach." Clara felt a little giddy. "Someone might actually do something?"

"Possibly. If you're brave enough. Or someone is. Do you want to think about it some more?"

"I don't have to do anything in advance. Prepare anything?" Clara's mind was whirring around now. She suspected she could get him talking if she asked the right questions. If she didn't have to have him somewhere specific, be too much in private.

"Enough for the oath. And they'd rather not have potions, even the memory ones. They can work with it, but it's easier unaltered, apparently. I don't know the details, exactly." Volans shrugged.

"I don't know how to thank you for this." Clara let out a breath. "I really don't. You've been so kind."

"I try to live up to my children, it turns out." There was an old humour in it. "I'd be interested in talking shop about your record keeping. When this is all sorted out, perhaps you - and your husband, if you like - could come for supper. I gathered from Dilly you run things in the shop on your own, the business side?"

"I do. I'm sure I could do it better. You must know more." Clara hesitated again.

"Running accounts for the Ministry's very different. I do bookkeeping for a handful of people on the side, including Poppy and Seth. But a shop's a different set of expenses, and so is handling longer-term inventory. I've had a couple of people ask about it. I'm sure I'd learn a good bit from you. Not right now." He held up his hand. "When you're all sorted with this."

Clara looked up and met his eyes then. He was there, just patient and steady. Again, it made her wonder what Owen would be like at that age. She let out a slow breath. "When this is sorted."

"Grand. Let me amuse you with a few stories from the office, and when you're ready, I'll walk you back to the portal."

CHAPTER 32
DECEMBER 1ST AT THE THEATRE

The second week of rehearsals for the panto seemed to be going unevenly. Not that Owen was experienced with it, mind. He was reading the reactions of everyone else. Maisery seemed decidedly on edge, while Edgar was a little more relaxed. Under all of it, there was an undercurrent. There'd been no movement about the finances of the theatre, and Orlando looked a bit more frayed every day.

It wasn't solely physical. There was something in his eyes that Owen had seen too many times in men who'd been on the Front for far too long. Those were the people who would shatter sooner than later under the pressure. The sort of people where he could only hope that when they did, others wouldn't get hurt, too. Owen had heard bits and pieces of comments, that there was more pressure to buy out the other half of the ownership, or to have funds to fight properly in the courts, the sort of thing that needed specialists and accountants and solicitors putting in a lot of time beyond the ordinary run of a business case.

He couldn't make sense of why there was such a pressure to sell. Or why Horatio Morris, curse him, was so intent on it. From what Owen had picked up, it could just be that he wanted more money, without doing any real work - and while making things awful for people who wanted that work. Or maybe he wanted an obvious source of income that wasn't tangled up in war profiteering, who knew. It'd be a savvy choice, if the man was angling for more social status. Or at least, that's the way the plot in a play would go, for the villain of the piece.

On the purely practical level, things were also uneven. There was a lot of rearranging things backstage every time Orlando changed any of the blocking. They'd tried some scenes a dozen different ways now, and each change meant figuring out where props had to be. The turnip, for one. Or rather the turnips, since there was the real turnip, the heavy turnip, the light turnip, the enchantable turnip, the glowing turnip, and the enormous turnip.

Owen had not realised that the success of the theatre depended quite so much on the humble turnip. But here he was, trying to decide if they needed spares of them, and if so, who was going to make them. He could do most of them. They were wood, but the light turnip was paper-mache, as was the enormous one. He was standing there, staring at them, when Maisery tapped him on the shoulder and gestured him to the side hall, closing the door to the stage behind her.

"Yes, Maisery?" Owen immediately stood to attention. It was still instinctive for him. And the thing of it was, he liked and respected Maisery far more than most of his commanding officers during the War. For one thing, he was fairly certain she would prefer him not to get killed. That was, in fact, not something he'd been at all sure of in the trenches.

"We just had word Theo's able to come down for the night's rehearsal. We weren't planning on it. Soon as they're done with this bit, can you reset for Act Two, Scene One, all of it? I've got to run an errand for Orlando. Edgar's keeping an eye on Randolph to make sure he doesn't wander into the middle of the last of the set painting."

That would do no good. They were in a state where they'd smudge as soon as anyone looked at them, apparently. Theatre sets, Owen had come to learn, were simultaneously shouting what they were and extremely fragile, in entirely unexpected ways. He could put his hand through a pile of rocks if he got the wrong angle, or bring down an entire village street by leaning on the wrong rope. "Sure. Five minutes?"

Maisery silently opened the door, listened for ten seconds, closed the door. Judiciously, she said, "In about eight if you need to run and get anything."

Owen nodded and took off without another comment. If he had to reset everything fast and on his own, he needed his notes, a swig or two of water. And maybe thirty seconds at the shrine for a bit of blessing and good fortune. He swooped into the workroom, sidestepping as someone was about to come through with a rack of costumes. They were doing fittings for the chorus after the usual work hours tonight, which would mean even more chaos down at this end of the hall. His notes were right where he'd left them, so was the bottle with his water.

Two minutes later, he was at the shrine. He didn't know what words other people said, if they said them. He'd seen actors and actresses in all stages of dress and undress at this point, right side up and upside down. And a few times a bit more in their cups than was strictly sensible. Asking about what people did at the shrine, that was too intimate, though. Certainly for him, he was still new here. But he bowed once, murmured the most basic sort of prayer, a "please let it go right tonight," and promised to bring in a bit of scone for an offering tomorrow. It was all he had to work with, and it wasn't much.

Right on time, he was backstage. Orlando called out, "Preset, please."

"On it." Owen made sure to call it back clearly, and he set to work. All the set pieces for this could be handled by one person, fortunately, or rather, they could at the moment because they were still waiting on the full set. Instead, there were two stand-ins to be rolled into place, the cyclorama to be set at the back. That would be replaced before the panto proper. The large muslin panel was a bit beaten around the edges, yellowing in spots. For now, though, it would take up the space it needed.

He paced forward, placing the movable parts of the set where they should be. Then, of course, he had to add the little charms that kept them there. This stage, like the other venerable theatres of Trellech, had a raked stage. He hadn't properly considered what that meant until the job here. The angle wasn't strong - half an inch per foot, just enough to bring out the footwork and highlight the choreography. It gave them a bit of an edge in the display of the thing over the newest theatre in Trellech, and one of the others. That one had reset the stage flat just before the War.

It seemed a silly thing. Owen was coming to realise that all the illusion of the theatre was built on a very pragmatic understanding of how the eye and ear and mind brought everything together for the best effect. If he stumbled over his feet now and again still, so long as he didn't put an arm through a bit of set, everything was fine.

Now he checked the placements one more time. There

were little marks on the floor, and those helped, but it was hard to tell which was which, with the current production still running another week. That small red X marked one side of the dais. There, this blue one was where the rock ought to go.

Finally, he had to go set the pieces for the giants. The paper mache torsos and heads and arms would reach up from behind the scenery, to go with the illusions proper. That went well enough. It had turned out to be the scent of the thing that was a problem. Now it was dry, the paper mache didn't unsettle him quite as much as it had. It helped that these were painted a particular shade of blue-green that apparently took illusions better than some, for all some considered the colour a trifle unlucky.

Owen finished up five minutes early, while he knew several of the actors were still getting themselves together. He took one last look from backstage as Theo Robbins came out. He had a sword belt on, with a stage sword on it, but he moved well with it, remembering it was there. Not everyone did that, Owen had noticed.

Theo seemed lost in thought, murmuring something under his breath. Lines, probably, they did that a lot, all of them, like the words fell out of their heads if not repeated at regular intervals. Which, for all Owen knew, was probably true. He wasn't the one on the stage. He wasn't going to judge however they got through doing that proper.

After a moment, though, Theo looked up. "Evening. You're, um...." He paused, as if counting through names. "Owen, was it?"

"You've an excellent memory," Owen agreed. Theo had to be a hair younger than Owen himself. He certainly looked better, like he'd been well fed for years instead of only just starting to catch up to that idea. But he was smiling, showing a bit of the charm that beamed out over the audience from the stage. "Owen Hubbard. I've not been here long, though."

"Longer than I have," Theo considered, then swung himself to sit on the edge of the stage, legs hanging over the orchestra pit, such as it was. They didn't have room for a big one, but there'd be musicians there next week. Right now, it was just the piano standing in. "Edgar all right?"

"He's fine - he was," Owen hesitated. Saying the truth wasn't kind to Randolph. "Making sure Randolph is ready."

"He's a fine old actor." Theo said, his voice quieter. "Not what he was, but being able to be on stage with him, that's a thing I never thought I'd do. He played all the big roles when I'd come with Mother and Father when I was a kid, and in school." There was something warm and kind there. "Did you see him in his prime?"

"I did. Mum and I would come along quite regularly. The panto, but other things too." Owen hesitated, then sat down, a few feet away. Might as well take a load off his feet while he could. He'd be back about being active again as soon as they got started. "Edgar's got a good eye for what's needed in the moment. I don't know what we'd do without him." Owen hesitated. "Or you."

"Ah." That got a smile, boyish and charming. "I'm a bit of a deus ex machina, aren't I? Swooping in at the last moment. That's a theatre term, originally, did you know? In the Greek theatre, it was actually a bit of machinery with a god in it to cap off the play. Coming down from above or rising up from below the stage, depending on how celestial or chthonic things were." He leaned back on his hands. "I haven't played a god yet. Some day, probably."

Owen was not at all sure what to say to that. Any of it, though, the last bit in particular. Instead he stared off out over the seats, before he said, "It matters a lot. That you were willing. Gives us a chance."

There was a silence, a potent sort of silence. Then Theo said, his voice far more intimate. "It matters. Keeping these places going. Besides, I want you to be here in a year or two, when I can come back and do something else, a grand drama or a tragedy. Panto's great fun, but I have range. I want to show it off."

Owen looked up, blinking. Theo went on. "Also plenty of ego, but it's a hell of a career for anyone who doesn't. I figure I can use it to do some good - like here. And maybe it'll give me a chance to do things down the road." Then they heard voices behind them, people coming out onto the stage. Theo rolled up. "Hey now, leave the set where it is. We'll want that in a minute. Evening, I'm Theo Robbins, pleased to meet you. I'm Brutus, in this thing, of course. Sword and all, see."

He made it sound easy, being agreeable and amiable and on point with what he was doing. Owen took his cue as well, and stood up, brushing off his hands. Before he could duck backstage, there was another comment. "Owen, can I have a minute? Everyone, this is Owen, and if you mess with the props backstage, you'll make him very unhappy, and that'd make me unhappy. And Orlando, too. So let's not, right? Owen, is there anything else they ought to know right now?"

"That way's downstage, don't trip?" Owen suggested. "And mind the turnips. You want the right turnip for the job, remember."

Theo laughed, more than the joke probably ought to have had, but it brought everyone along. After a moment, Owen added, "The props are all set up. I think Orlando said he wants to run the bits with those of you who are hiding.

Then the ones who pick up rocks, then put the rest of it together. The set's not all that firmly fixed, so running into it could shoot it off into someone else. We don't need any actual broken legs or wrists or whatever." He leaned down to knock on the wood of the stage, while several others made aversion gestures with their hands. "Anyway, I'm stage right, there, if you need anything. Ta, Theo."

Theo picked up again, into a cheerful chat about what to expect from the scene, what he was looking forward to. He went on about how they could help make Madeline and Howard and Iawn all shine, as their various characters came out and got into the fray. He'd got on to a bit about what they could do in the background when Orlando called out. "Places! Places everyone. Act two, scene one, from the top."

As everyone trooped into the wings, Owen got ready to pay attention to everything. Not only his own direct cues, but all the unspoken rhythms, to do his best to predict what was needed as they went.

CHAPTER 33
DECEMBER 9TH AT THE SHOP

It was more than another week before Master Horatio Morris turned up again. Volans had followed up with additional notes and information, so Clara understood what kind of information the Guard needed to do further investigations. She read through it all, three times, until she was certain, and then she waited.

One part of it was the question of getting someone else to overhear. She'd swapped one of the enchanted stones for the back room with Mistress Malcolm, across the way, and they'd tested it, both directions. She had one of theirs, though of course with two apprentices, it wasn't like they needed help minding the shop or lending a hand.

They were permitted, so long as they were in the public part of the shop, with no particular expectation of privacy. Not near where Aunt Lillian did consultations, of course. Even if Aunt Lillian wasn't doing any of those at the moment. But by the register, Clara's realm.

She waited and waited, and waited. Aunt Lillian showed no signs of returning before the holidays. Yesterday, Clara had had a note confirming that, along with another crate of items. They were well-stocked for the holiday shopping, including the seasonal soaps and a new set of salves for chapped lips, and another range for hands. Aunt Lillian had found a lovely blend of scents, something with orange and pine than smelt glorious.

Sales in general were doing well, though. It had been a rough few years that way. Clara had had a plan, when they first thought the War would be over by Christmas, for all sorts of things that made good, simple gifts. The soaps, of course, but a line of salves, a collaboration with a candle-maker. Aunt Lillian wasn't a perfumer, but she had a knack for things that smelled good that were also useful, how to combine the properties and the ambiance.

Only then the War had gone on. 1918, they'd been run off their feet, trying to keep up with the demand for influenza remedies. It wasn't just making up new stock. It had been all the precautions for keeping the disease out of the shop, as best they could. Clara had served most customers from a table at the door, where the fresh air was a help.

Last year, they'd finally moved past most of that by the holidays. But of course, it wasn't as if Clara had anything particularly festive in mind. Inventory in the shop, Boxing Day and through to the first, was not terribly exciting, even if she did like knowing exactly what they had on hand, where they were running short.

This year, though, things were going quite well, considering. The small bars of soap were selling as fast as Clara could put them out. They made good gifts for a friend, or for a stocking, or something of the kind. And it wasn't as if soap went bad quickly. If they did have extra, the Temple of Healing would buy it up, if at a significant discount.

She was going through the lists one more time, her

notebook spread out on the counter, when the bell on the door rang out. Clara only had a moment to gather herself, closing the notebook over her figures, before she had to smile and make herself pleasant. She brushed her fingers over the charmed stone, feeling the slight tingle of magic that indicated it was active, something like the buzz of a bee. "Master Morris."

"Mistress Hubbard. I was hoping you'd have a moment. I keep coming by, but it's obvious from the street that you've been quite busy. I hope all of that is treating you well?"

Clara did her best to hide her expression - or hurry it along to something more pleasant. She was beginning to think that actors and actresses had terribly difficult jobs, far more than it looked. "Well, we are quite busy, Master Morris. I may not have terribly long to chat today."

He grimaced, just briefly. "Ah, well, I suppose, a working woman. Your dedication to your work really is notable. The girls at my factory, why, they're always chatting when they should be minding the line."

Clara felt that was as good an opening as she was going to get. "I was talking to someone, sir, about - well, not really understanding how factories work that way. Would you be willing to tell me a little more?" She wondered if this was laying things on too thick.

"Oh, my." He looked flattered. "I had no idea you had any interest. There you go, surprising me." Master Morris stepped forward, leaning on one of the glass shelves. She almost reflexively asked him not to, but of course, she had to let him. She had to make this look good. Sound good. Whatever.

"Oh, of course I'm curious. How a business works, that matters. Though ours is nothing like yours, I'm sure."

"Goodness, no. You rely on handcrafting, of course. And that's worthwhile, of course. But it's not going to keep pace with the modern world, now, is it? The incapable, the non-magical folk, they make do with factories that make all these tonics and whatsits. Now, mind, I do like that I can come to you, and you can make it up in a flavour I like, or scent, or whatever. More or less for the asking, if it's available. That's something you can't get out of a factory."

"I suppose, sir." Honestly, Clara liked knowing where the potions she took came from. If it weren't from Aunt Lillian, she'd find some other apothecary she trusted. Where she'd met them, could shake their hand, see a glimpse of their workspace. Whether they were tidy or slovenly. Though, to be fair, a number of the apothecaries she'd met were orderly in their workspace and nowhere else. Aunt Lillian's rooms certainly bore that out.

"Well, let's see. The trick with a factory, of course, any big business, more than one or two people." He nodded at the shop. "Is that you need to look for efficiencies of scale. Each person doing one job, over and over, for example, lets you move faster than one person doing all the steps. And there's much less training needed."

"Wouldn't that be a problem, then?" The first part slipped out before she thought better of it. "Maybe I'm missing something. But wouldn't it be harder to catch if there was a problem somewhere? If each person only knows their part of it?"

He went silent for a long moment. "Oh, I suppose that's possible. But that's why many people have someone to check the quality at the end. Someone experienced, who knows how it ought to fit together."

Clara thought that was foolish, honestly. Perhaps it was that she spent so much time around an alchemy lab and a stillroom. But if an oil was spoiled in the second step in the process, it certainly did no good to carry on with it to the tenth. It was a waste of time and materials, for one thing, even without questions of contaminating other aspects.

That must have shown on her face somehow. "Something the matter, then?" His voice had a slight edge to it.

"Oh, just thinking how very different it is. I'm used to needing to stop if something goes wrong in the first step - or anywhere along the way. It must be very different. But you make sure everything's done properly? It seems so easy for something to slip."

"Oh, don't you worry your little head about it. Besides, it's shoes. If something goes wrong with a shoe, it's not the end of the world now, is it?"

Clara felt that was entirely wrong-headed, but this time she managed to cover it by turning away to cough. "Pardon, bit of dust in my throat. And you provided, you said, quite a lot of shoes, to the army? Fancy, my husband might have worn something you made."

Again, spreading it thick. Owen hadn't commented on that part of it, and she hadn't wanted to press in more detail. Hadn't known how, either, if asking would disrupt the delicate sort of balance they were managing.

"Oh, he might, I suppose. Quite a few pairs of boots on the ground." Morris chuckled to himself, pleased at the bad pun. "And I did quite well out of it. Of course, it's not the done thing to comment about that, when we were supporting the fighting men."

But he said it anyway. That hadn't slipped past Clara. She was finding it a little easier to deal with him now, honestly, now that she had a goal. "I suppose it must be an awful lot of work. I know we have a lot of paperwork. Not just the fees and taxes and all that, though there's that too. Permissions and certification of the spaces."

"Oh, I suppose. I don't handle that at all." Morris waved it off, even though Clara felt that certification was more of an issue in a factory than in many places. It made her wonder suddenly how many injuries there were, how many more than there should have been.

"My. You must have - you must have rather a lot of people working for you?"

Morris beamed at that. "Enough I can come have an enjoyable chat with a beautiful woman." She was not the only one in the room laying it on thick. That was pure blather. Her head twitched a little. "But yes, we've quite a large staff. I've a dozen people reporting to me, and dozens to them. Of course, I don't handle the small daily things." He waved a hand. "Easy to hire if someone leaves, by and large. That's the modern way, inter-changeable."

Clara hesitated. None of this was entirely incriminating, but Volans had made it clear they might not get that. What they wanted was enough to be able to dig deeper. She was considering whether that was the case when the bell over the door rang again.

"Mistress Malcolm." Clara couldn't decide if it was a relief or a frustration, honestly. "Did you need something? You remember Mrs Malcom, Master Morris? She has the shop over the street."

"Do pardon my interrupting, dear, but one of my girls - Alice, poor thing - just burned herself on one of the lamps. Not terribly bad, but you have that lovely cream that takes the heat out, right away. Might I get a tin?"

Clara nodded, automatically, and went to get it, then to take the coins Mrs Malcolm pushed across. Given that excuse, the other woman couldn't linger, but she leaned in, murmuring, "Need another excuse, dear?"

Clara cleared her throat. "Perhaps I'll come over and check when we're done here? I did volunteer quite a lot in the wards. I'm glad to make sure it doesn't need a proper Healer's touch."

"Oh, that would be a kindness, dear. I'll send Florrie over in a minute to keep an eye on things." There, that would give Clara a sufficient excuse.

She blinked up at Morris. "Perhaps another time?" Even saying that much was a trick.

"Perhaps next time at the end of your day, and you'd permit me to take you out to tea? But you must certainly lend your skills. A light touch, I'm sure, will do a world of good." He nodded, touching the brim of his hat, and went out, holding the door for Mrs Malcolm.

Two minutes later, Mrs Malcolm was back. "That man is a piece of work. Are you alright, Clara, dear? You seemed to be trying to keep him talking."

Clara opened her mouth, then closed it. Then, carefully, she managed, "He's not a nice man, is he? Nor a kind one. I was hoping to get a bit more information for, well. Reasons. Can you trust I have a good one?"

Mrs Malcolm looked her up and down, hands on her hips, then nodded once. "Lillian says you have a good head on your shoulders. No reason to doubt her. Or you. But you let me know if you need more help. Or another person here. I don't like him."

"He's entirely too charming. Like nothing sticks to him." That made her wonder if it was, in fact, some sort of enchantment that kept people from paying attention to all those warning signs. There were such things, at least there were stories of them, but she couldn't imagine why he was here, if he had a thing like that. "Thank you, again. Can I give you something for your trouble? Another tin of salve, or something of the kind?"

"Oh, let me have a look. Your seconds, of course. The things you'd not sell out of the counter."

"Just so."

CHAPTER 34
DECEMBER 15TH AT THE THEATRE

There were no shows this week at the theatre. The entire place, all the effort of everyone who worked there, was given to preparations for the panto. Rehearsals and getting all the last pieces of the set and the props and the costumes together were all anyone had time for. Opening night was on the 22nd. When all the posh folk were out at fancy parties for the solstice, the ordinary folk would have somewhere to be full of light and laughter, music and dance.

Though the dancing seemed a little less certain than anyone would like. Owen had been assured this was relatively normal. A bad dress rehearsal was good luck, even. It was different with an audience.

Owen suspected that some of those were people desperately hoping the superstitions were true. Or that they'd hold true this time. Yesterday's rehearsal had been a mess. Two of the dancers had collided with each other when they both went the wrong way getting off stage. Bess, the woman who did the makeup, had thrown up her hands at the bruise and black eye and sent them off to see the Healers.

That, in turn, had Orlando worried about money, far more visibly than usual. Not that the Healer expense was large, but he was counting every coin, no matter how tiny, now. Edgar and Maisery hadn't commented on that, not to Owen, but they were both tightlipped about it.

There was a particular pleasure today, though. Clara had got someone to keep an eye on the shop for the last hour, so she'd be able to come round and watch a full run of the rehearsal. Owen kept an eye out for her, between moving things around. Or all the other tasks, checking the wheels on a bit of set that were squeaking, and the dozen other things that needed a handyman's attention.

Perhaps a quarter hour before the rehearsal was set to start, Edgar poked his head back behind the curtain, velvet folds framing his neck. "All set? There's a woman waiting for you, I assume your wife?" He was cheerfully teasing.

"Clara." Owen let out a breath. "Can you tell her I'll be a minute or two?"

"Oh, of course. She brought gifts!" That was very cheerful, and Owen was suddenly unsure what sort of gifts she'd brought. He finished up his work, checking it over twice. A tripping hazard, that wasn't a thing he'd allow. All the cables that moved the curtains were well out of the way, all the supplies that could be put up out of the way were.

He let the actors and actresses gathering in the wings know everything was set. He came out from between the curtains for a change, since he needed to tell Maisery and Orlando, too, and they'd be out in the seats. Not alone. Clara was sitting there, leaning in to hear something Maisery was saying, with Edgar on Orlando's other side.

Then she caught sight of Owen, and there was a smile.

A real one, an honest one, the kind that crinkled up her eyes as well as her mouth. As he came around, ducking into the seat beside her, he could see Orlando had one of the cardboard boxes Clara wrapped things up in, balanced on his knees.

"Your wife is a delight, Owen. Why didn't you say?" Maisery beamed. "And she's brought us useful things."

Owen blinked several times. "Yes?" That sounded completely idiotic.

Clara patted his hand, then left her fingers there, resting lightly. "We had some bruise cream and liniment that'll need a new home in a couple of weeks, and we're unlikely to sell it all. I checked with Aunt Lillian. Don't worry."

Owen hadn't been going to say a thing about that. He could, however, say something about the gift. "That's proper, generous and useful. Plenty of bumps and bruises and strains. Did they tell you about the black eyes, then? I didn't get a chance last night."

"They did, so a touch of foresight, or something. I was mostly thinking of bruises other places, you've complained of a few."

The others let them chat back and forth for a minute or two before Maisery cleared her throat. "Clara, you're welcome to keep your seat here, but Owen and Edgar and I should probably take our places for the runthrough. Tea, though, after? We can give you tea and festive biscuits, at least. One of the chorus is a baker's daughter. Her mum sends round the seconds to keep us well fed."

"I'd like that very much. If you're sure I won't be in the way here?" Clara glanced at Orlando.

"No, I'd like some company. And fresh eyes, I've seen and heard everything so often I don't think any of it's funny anymore."

Clara tilted her head at that, the way she did at Owen, when she was thinking. Owen hesitated for just a second, before leaning to kiss her on the cheek. "I'll be out for at least a few when we're done with the runthrough, all right?"

She smiled another of those crinkly real smiles at him, and nodded. "As long as it needs."

The runthrough went... Well. It went. The first half of the first act was smooth enough. He could hear Clara's laugh a couple of times, echoing in the theatre. There were a small group of others, scattered in ones and twos or threes in the orchestra seats. A couple of people would be up in the balcony, making sure everyone could be seen and heard.

They had to stop once to adjust the sound amplification charms. That was not Owen's line of work at all. It meant resetting the scenery back to the beginning of the scene, which he did easily enough. They got through the end of the first act, but it was a bit shambling by the end.

Maisery sent him out to bring Orlando a cuppa and see if Clara needed anything. When he ducked into their row, Clara was talking animatedly, with her hands moving. "It wouldn't take much. Turning away from each other, just a bit, taking half a step. The way that Brutus and Innogen both think they know what's right, instead of working together. It's almost there, just. Too subtle, isn't it?"

Orlando grunted. "Probably." He waved a hand at Owen. "Ta for the tea. Can you tell Madeline and Theo I've got a note for them? They should try it as we go into act two."

"Of course, sir. Clara, do you want a bit of tea?" Owen paused, just waiting to see if she needed anything.

"Brought my own flask." She lifted it up, agreeably.

Which meant he could make his way backstage, through the maze of dressing rooms, and let both Madeline and Theo know Orlando had a note. It got them up on stage promptly, and Owen listened to Orlando explain what he wanted. A turn of the shoulder, a half step away, all the little signs of people who did not want to be closer in any way.

It made him shiver once, and then he turned back to his work. They'd be starting the second act in a few minutes. He had to make sure the scenery was where it needed to be and that no one had done anything foolish like lock it in place backstage.

The second act was a lot rougher. Brutus and Innogen were doing much better with a round of aggravated frustration with each other. Finally, the chase with the giants began in earnest and they had to work together or risk being stomped under foot. The illusions were going off well, he thought. He could hear the small audience making all the proper sounds. "Look behind you, there he is!" echoed around a satisfying number of times.

The last three scenes were shambles, though, as best he could tell peering from his spot in the wings. He thought that Brutus and Innogen had a more solid sort of conclusion, with a kiss. Theo and Madeline had some quite real chemistry with each other, if that was how the word went.

They were going to take a break, though. The people doing the lighting charmwork had to reset, and Perris, the chief illusionist, needed to coordinate with his second, apparently. It meant that a number of the cast and crew accumulated themselves on the stage or the steps leading up or the first orchestra seats. Someone brought out the trolley with an urn of tea and another with stacks of biscuits and some sandwiches. The younger members of the cast, there were about six boys and girls to fill out the sense of a whole community, took over one end. They were tossing a woollen ball with ribbons back and forth.

They were all chatting easily enough - no one was in a foul mood, actually. All of a sudden one of the younger girls, perhaps twelve, pointed up at the balcony. "What's that?"

Everyone looked. Of course they did. There was the shimmer, but much brighter this time. It flickered several times, coming back brighter and stronger with each beat, like it was a pulsing heart. Clara had settled next to Owen, her legs dangling off the stage.

She was frowning now, up at the figure. The ghost. Might as well call it what it was. Last time, it had disappeared up the stairs, but right now the ghost was in her usual box, though there were flashes. Suddenly, Clara grabbed his upper arm. "Do you know semaphore code?"

Owen blinked up at it. "Do you think?" It was hard to tell without actual flags, but as he looked, the patterns seemed to make sense. "I know it, but I'm rusty."

"I know some. And who was it I was talking to? Jacob, you said your da does ocean rescues, do you know a bit?" Theo was the one who had spoken up. He stood, coming over to crouch down behind Owen, one hand resting on Owen's shoulder with a brushed by, "You don't mind?" Owen shook his head.

Another of the young men in the chorus came over and peered up. "If we put our heads together."

Maisery had been down in the seats, but she stood as well. "I think we've got a book that has it in. We needed it for one of the plays a few years back. If you get it wrong, the people who know it mock you." She took off at a good clip, angling for the offices and the bookshelves.

Owen nodded, and then did his best to focus on the

movements. After a moment, he cupped his hands around his mouth. It wasn't like he had one of the sound charms on him, after all, and called up. "Can you go slow, please?"

The light flickered once, then again, and then it began again. The ready position, then letter by letter. Between them, they called out the letters, each by each, and someone called out that they were writing them down. They got to the end of the sequence, got the position that indicated the end of the signal.

"Help in wall. Papers. Please."

"Wall?" That was Theo's voice. "What wall?"

Owen cleared his throat. "I know which one. I think. But it looks like solid brick. And I don't know if it's, I mean." He pointed. "It's up there, ten feet above the balcony level. There's storage on the other side."

Another one of the chorus cleared her throat. "My da's a bricklayer. I could have a look?"

A man, several people down, said, "Done some building in my time. I know the charm for if it's load-bearing. The wall."

Owen glanced out at Orlando, who was leaning his elbows on his knees, looking somewhere between fear and overwhelm. Owen had seen that expression so many times, in men about to go over the top, men who had heard one order too many. Too much to process.

"May we, sir?"

Orlando let out a long sigh. "Take Maisery with you. Don't destroy my theatre, please."

Everyone, for some reason, was looking at Owen. He cleared his throat. "Not all of us. There's not a lot of spare space. You two," he said, nodding at the two who knew the construction work. "Maisery, of course. Theo, Jacob, if you want?"

"Me." Clara said it, as crystal clear and carrying as any of the actors did. "Just." She swallowed. "Me. Please."

"Of course." Owen took a breath. "Let me get the big mallet." He stood, jumping down from the stage the couple of feet to the ground, and went off to find that. By the time he came back, a small knot of people were standing waiting for him by the doors to the foyer. Someone, sensibly, had got Theo and Jacob to take off their outer coats and given them smocks to protect the rest of their costumes.

"Right. Let's do this."

"If it were done when 'tis done, then 'twere well it were done quickly." Theo said it with a slight quirk of his mouth. "As the Scottish play says." It was not considered bad luck here, but Owen supposed Theo must have learned the other customs rather well by this point. He nodded once - the sentiment held, honestly - and led the way to the stairs.

CHAPTER 35
DECEMBER 15TH AT THE THEATRE

Clara was not at all sure what she'd got herself into. Watching the rehearsal had been interesting, seeing what it was like before all the polish was on. That made her feel better, honestly. She'd been missing the times chatting with Aunt Lillian while she was trying out something new. Or when they were talking over how to lay out a label design, or which type of bottle would suit a particular tonic.

The rehearsal stopped and started. She had more sense than to interrupt the theatre owner, also in this case the director, or at least the one making final decisions. But Orlando - as he insisted she call him - asked her opinion several times, and she could tell he was paying close attention to what she found amusing or moving.

At the pause, she watched how he talked the two leads through their scene. That was interesting to watch, even if she couldn't hear all of what he said. Both of them had leaned in, but there was a moment where she thought the heroine, the woman playing Innogen, was going to complain. But then the man playing Brutus had shaken his head, just a titch, and she'd subsided and listened.

Whatever Orlando had said had helped. They played up their frustration with each other in the second act in a way that was the right amount of over the top. Clara wondered if that was the right word. Or especially here. Owen wasn't the only veteran, of course. She'd figured that out fast enough when there'd been a loud noise backstage and near half the male cast had jerked around, and a few of the women.

And now there was a new bit of chaos. Following a ghost was, on the one hand, ridiculous. On the other hand, it seemed like a very insistent ghost. A very visible ghost. A remarkably communicative ghost, overall. Clara had waited for Owen to lead the way. He knew where they were going, and he knew the space in general. She trailed along at the back, not sure why she was coming along, but sure she needed to. It wasn't just Owen. There was something tugging at her, like a thread from her breastbone along a path she couldn't see.

They made their way, the five of them. Owen and Maisery went first, and then Jacob, and Theo. Now she'd got a handle on the name. He glanced over his shoulder, trotting up the stairs as if he did this sort of thing every day. "You're Owen's wife? Pleased to meet you." He had the sort of smile that ought to be in cinema acting. It had a charismatic quality out of all proportion.

"Clara. And you. I liked how it went, the second act."

"I did too. Playing up the frustration, that gets a better resolution." His grin flashed broader, somehow shinier. "Also, it's more fun." Then he looked up the steps. They were coming up to the attic level now, around the turn of the stairs.

Owen brought them over immediately to an area of wall that faced back toward the theatre itself and gestured. "This is where I saw it - her - last time." The greasepaint marks he'd left last time were still there, of course, framing a space more or less the size of a door.

Theo took it in with a long look. "You know there's lore about ghosts."

"That there's treasure of some kind." Owen folded his arms, visibly uncomfortable with something. "What are you saying?"

"Hey." Theo's voice got easier, not quite conciliatory, but smoothing things over. It didn't make the hair on the back of her neck rise up, like Master Morris did. But she could feel a little twining something, making her want to agree more than was probably sensible. "I'm in London these days. Ghosts all over the place, in the older buildings. And often enough, the treasure's right. Sometimes it's gold or gems, but sometimes it's knowledge. A burial, a set of papers, who knows? Do we know how thick the wall is?"

Maisery cleared her throat. "I had a look at the plans. It should be a double layer wall. Wall, space, another wall, bracing between them. So there could be something between the two. Or shoved into one of the interior bricks. The plans we have weren't clear about what's where."

Jacob - younger, less certain - half held up his hand, like he was still in school. Maisery nodded at him. "Is there a join or a seam in the wall anywhere? Or do you know how long it's been since there were any renovations here?"

"Good question." Maisery furrowed her brow, thinking. Clara was still getting a sense of her, the way she was brusque and no-nonsense, contrasting with the stories Owen had told about her kindness and humour. Clara hadn't seen a lot of that yet, and quite possibly wouldn't. "Do you know how to tell?" That was to Jacob.

"There's a charm, for if there's a hollow behind the wall. For nailing things, you know? I know it. Give me a minute to figure out how it goes with brick. It's been a while."

They stepped back. There was a brief flurry of consulting, and then they let Jacob get up close. He leaned over the crates and boxes of materials, humming something under his breath. It was a tune with a melody, but one that didn't quite stick in Clara's memory, like it went in and out her ears, leaving nothing in its wake. Then he tapped, precisely, making a ring with his thumb and index finger on his left hand, and tapping with his right index finger. They could hear the sounds, then, like bells. Sometimes they were higher pitched, with an echo, sometimes lower with a sort of muted thump.

After a minute, he said, "Does someone have a wax pencil or chalk or something?"

Maisery produced a stick of chalk from the apron she was wearing handing it to Owen. "You've got longer arms." Which he did. Owen moved to where he could make marks. They were little Xs and Os, like a tabletop game of naughts and crosses, but not nearly so orderly.

In the end, they found an open space where they'd been considering, with the little X marks making parallel lines down, a few feet on either side. "Best guess is this is an open bay inside there." Jacob said. "But I'd not bet on it, or not by much. The mallet might be too big, maybe a chisel? I could see if we could get a brick or two loose. It looks like the mortar's crumbling here. Quick job, when they did it, maybe, it didn't set properly."

Maisery frowned. "Give me just a minute. I'm sure

there's one of the toolkits up here. Just need to find it." She went off to the far end of the room, waving a hand for Owen to stay when he took a step after her.

He glanced at Clara. "What do you think? You wanted to come up."

"It's where the adventure is?" The line fell flat as soon as she said it. "I - something in me wants to be up here. I'm not sure why."

Owen nodded at her once, as if he wasn't sure about it either. She certainly wasn't. She was being entirely truthful here. But then he held out a hand to her, and she took it gratefully.

Theo had found a bit of furniture - some sort of table, a bit battered. "Not newlyweds, then? I know what that looks like on stage."

It was a ridiculously personal question, and an entirely reasonable one. Owen squeezed her hand. "Married during the War, while I was on leave. I was in the Temple of Healing, she was volunteering on my ward, and of course I had the good sense to fall for her." He glanced at Clara, then focused back on Theo. "She was patient. She didn't lose her temper, even when she had excellent reason. And she had.... I love watching her do things with her hands."

Clara blinked, then without realising she was doing it until her hand was halfway outstretched, put her left hand out in front of her, fingers spread. Owen squeezed the right again. "I liked how Owen made everyone laugh. Even when he was still recovering. And he always had something in his hands, too. He'd do little wood carvings, simple toys."

"What'd you do before, then?" Theo swung his feet, and for all he must be in his later twenties, he looked absurdly boyish.

"Shoes. I make shoes." Clara's chin came up at the verb

tense. She hadn't known he was doing so right now, beyond the ones for Golshan. Owen glanced over, and his mouth quirked up, the same impish smile she'd fallen for, back then.

"Shoes. Huh. Would you talk to me about a pair, maybe? Something to wear when I've been on my feet for hours, on stage, and everything aches?"

Owen hesitated, and now it was Clara's turn to squeeze his hand. "Sure." It came out a bit rough, as if something caught in his throat. "Glad to talk about it. I'd need a deposit for materials."

"Oh, sure." Theo clearly had no problem with that. Before anyone could say anything else, Maisery came back with a toolbox brimming with handles. She quickly produced a chisel and a smaller hammer than the massive mallet Owen had carried up.

Ten minutes later, Jacob had worked loose a patch of wall, perhaps two feet by two feet. They'd had to move all the boxes out of the way, and Theo and Clara had stacked them wherever they fit. Maisery called light into her hand, and then knelt and peered into the hole. "Oof. We've had mice in here at some point. But here, what's this?"

She brought out a closed wooden box, the kind that people kept papers in. Technically, not quite a safe, but much the same if you were magical. "If it's blood-locked, we'll be out of luck," Clara pointed out.

"You familiar with them? Can you tell? Have a look?" Maisery handed it over to Owen, who looked around and then set it on the table Theo had been using as a bench. "Here, there you are."

"We use them for documents. I know a couple of the standard opening charms. There are specialists who can do more?" But she settled down to get a good look at it. Same model as the one Aunt Lillian used. That put it back about what, forty or fifty years ago. "There was a thing, oh, 1875, I think? People pilfering secrets, documents they shouldn't get their hands on. But these, there's a set of ways you can open them. It'll alert whoever set it, maybe, though."

"It's in the theatre. Everything here that's not specifically marked out is fair game for Orlando and the other owner to handle. Well. Was. When the probate goes through. If we're lucky."

Clara was not Orlando, but that felt like enough permission to let her go forward. She gave the undersides of the lid a good look, twisting the box carefully to make sure there were no hidden needles or metal to catch on. Then she ran her fingers along the underside. The first pattern she tried, her fingers pressing into the slight indentations, didn't work. Neither did the second, third or the fourth. The fifth, though, something gave. She could feel the click under her touch. The lid opened visibly a moment later. There was a dark crack showing the line between the base and the top.

Her hands were shaking as she began to lift the lid. Owen was right there, picking it up carefully by the edges and setting it on the table, top down. They all stared at the contents. Faded, browning in spots, but those were some sort of formal business papers.

"This is for Orlando, I'm sure. This is ... this looks like an ownership agreement? And this is some sort of inventory or record. I think that's a property deed? My Aunt Lillian has similar sorts of things for the shop. Only why are these up here?"

Maisery shook her head. "Let's take these down to Orlando's office. If you don't mind, Clara, going through them with him? If there's a legal issue, having two eyes on it for the courts might be a good thing. Me too, probably, or

Edgar. We'll see who he wants. Multiple witnesses that nothing was removed or added. Can you close it up and open it again?"

"Now I know which it's set for, yes." That meant they made a little procession down the stairs, through the back of the theatre, Maisery going ahead to explain to Orlando. His eyes went wide, and then he sent one of the younger crew off at a run. By the time Clara and Owen made it down to him, he was saying, "Best have the solicitor around, or a clerk from his office, too. Just to be on the safe side."

He looked caught in the midst of something. The papers could be amazing news, for all Clara knew. But they could also be catastrophe. Unexpected papers were like that.

CHAPTER 36
DECEMBER 15TH AT THE THEATRE

There ended up being quite a crowd in Orlando's office. A quarter hour later, Theo had got all the cast back out on stage. Randolph was very helpful, actually. Theo was getting them all going on working through making the big scenes look good. Owen ended up going back and forth, running instructions from Orlando to the other backstage crew. Edgar had disappeared off to the stage door to wait for the solicitor or whoever showed up.

By the time the solicitor got there, Orlando was pacing. The box was sitting on his desk. He'd cleared everything off to an unsteady pile on the side table. Clara had tucked herself into a corner, not taking up space. Maisery was next to her, talking quietly. Owen couldn't decide if he should stay, or where he should stand.

After a moment, Maisery waved him over. "You helped find it. Soon as Edgar's back, we'll toss a coin for who's here, and who's out there with the chaos."

Owen couldn't help a bit of a smile. "You cheat at coin tosses." She did, too.

"And he knows it, worse luck. We'll get someone else to flip it." Maisery shrugged and went to hover by the door.

Owen shifted a bit closer to Clara, as the others all went back and forth a bit, and Orlando went out on stage to check on something. "You all right? You rather got dropped in the middle of it."

"So did you." It sounded sharp for a moment, then Clara cleared her throat. "Sorry. I - I was having such a good time. And this isn't bad, but I wasn't expecting it."

"None of us were." Owen pointed out. "As a script, it's not very well foreshadowed, not that I actually know all there is to know about that sort of thing in scripts."

Orlando heard it as he came back and laughed. It was not the most reassuring of laughs, but it was something for Owen to hang onto. "In terms of pacing, it's about right for a twist at the end of the second act. The third would be a resolution, of course. And we can't say the ghost hasn't been about. You've seen him or her quite often."

"Her." Owen said it, almost without thinking. "Pretty sure. Not just the flowers, but that didn't hurt?" He then hesitantly reached to brush Clara's hand with his fingers. "You sure you want us here?"

"I do. If there are financial papers, I'd like another set of eyes used to that sort of thing on them. And you're not entirely neutral in this, but you're new to the theatre, you've served with distinction in the War, all that won't hurt." Orlando looked up. "Besides, you fill out the casting nicely. In this play we're improvising. The older genera-tion." He gestured at himself and at Maisery. "And you're not Innamorati, seeing as how you're married, but you'll do well enough for a romantic couple."

Owen felt this was perhaps a bit more of a stretch on the casting than he'd like to claim. At that moment Clara shifted her fingers and squeezed his hand. She didn't say anything, and that wasn't a lot of communication to be going on with. But she didn't drop his hand, she didn't stop touching him, and she leaned a little closer. "Glad to stay." She was speaking to Orlando. "Though I'm not an expert bookkeeper. I could introduce you to someone, though."

"We'll see if we need another formal set of eyes on it, or what. I don't even—" Orlando ran his hand through his hair. "There are all sorts of things it might be, some much better than others."

Finally, what seemed like ages later, and was only about half an hour, Edgar came along, escorting someone who could only be a solicitor, even without casting notes. He had a suit, a briefcase, and glasses perched on his nose. "Your man got me at home. We were just about to go for a postprandial walk. I gather it's urgent?"

Orlando nodded. "Rather, yes. And it might need some attention before the Courts open tomorrow." He swallowed hard. "We'll pay for the time, of course."

The solicitor looked around. "Who's all this? My clerk should be here in a minute or two." Edgar made introductions all round, and the man peered at Clara, and said, "My wife likes your soaps, and she said you're very orderly. You're the one who knows how to open the case." Then he remembered that some of these people didn't know him. "Harold Wallace, of Doyle and Wallace." He considered. "May I, Orlando? The desk?"

"Oh, please." Orlando waved a hand at it, and Wallace set down his briefcase, opened it, and pulled out a few papers. The next few minutes involved standing around awkwardly, since Wallace was visibly waiting on the clerk. No one apparently wanted to say much of anything. Finally, though, a prim young woman was shown in, and she promptly pulled up a chair to the edge of the desk, took out a notepad, and asked, "Potion, sir?"

"Please." Wallace added to the room, "A memory potion, since we hope this might be some use in Court. One of the approved ones, of course."

Orlando winced slightly - likely at the cost - but he nodded once. "Best it were done right. Go ahead."

Wallace glanced around. "Who's staying as witness, then?" Maisery and Edgar had apparently sorted themselves out, and she ducked out the door to go back to the stage and keep things moving there. "Mistress Hubbard, would you do the honours and open the case. Then take out the papers as Miss Helling gets a look at them as they're stored. Make whatever stacks seem logical to you as you go, like you would if you were sorting out other accounts, and we will go from there."

Clara nodded. Owen squeezed her hand one more time and let her step forward. She stood in front of the desk, took a breath, and then her fingers slipped along the sides of the box. They all heard the click of it, then the box opened, and she pulled out several stacks of files, setting them on the desk in four different piles. Her fingers brushed over one. "This feels like it has a seal on it." Then the other three. "Two folders, one stack, tied with string."

"We'll start with the seal, if you can let me look." Clara stepped back, wobbling very slightly, and Owen stepped up to take her elbow. She smiled at him, but she was focused on the desk again immediately.

Wallace turned the packet over to reveal paper wrapped around a small stack of papers, and sealed with a great wax seal. He bent over to peer at it. "Glass, please."

Miss Helling, the clerk, handed over a magnifying glass, and then a small metal case. Wallace peered at the seal first, then opened the case, revealing an intricate set of tools. They might have better suited a watchmaker or a jeweller. He took up one in each hand, tipped like larger needles, coming to a point, and touched them both to the seal simultaneously. It glowed a brilliant green for five seconds, and then the seal seemed like it came free all at once.

"That's a proper seal of the Courts, which indicates it was made and recorded. That's a good sign, at least, that proper procedure was followed."

He thumbed through the papers, then looked up. "Let's look at the others and come back to this. It's promising, though." He then went through the other stacks. "These are copies of financial records of the theatre, your fathers." That was to Orlando. "And more recent. Nothing you don't know about, just from the other side of things."

"The first, then?" Orlando's voice cracked just a little as he talked.

"Yes." Wallace was a bit curt, Owen thought. Wallace picked up the packet, moving the other parts out of the way, and laying it out so he could flip the pages over easily. He ran a finger down the text, bit by bit, silently. He stopped twice, went back and reread something, then flipped the page, going on steadily from there. It took him a good five minutes to read through everything, then he looked up. "There is good news, yes."

"There is?" Orlando had, in the interim, reclaimed the chair by his desk. Now he stood again, to peer over at the files.

"The current will in probate is unclear. I am now..." He flicked his fingers at the detached seal, "Fairly certain it's a forgery. With the seal and the registration information in the Halls of Justice, we can make sure we're looking at the correct copy. But this one says it stands unless and until a new will is formally registered using the same methods as this one. And the one under probate wasn't. Just the more usual witnessing."

"So why did it end up here?" Orlando asked. "Is that one a fake? Did Grant forget about this? But how do you forget about shoving something in a wall? I must say, this is not the best written plot I've seen in my life."

"Perhaps he worried about having a later will suborned. Or you did say, didn't you, that he had a couple of difficult relatives living with him?"

"More than once, yes." Orlando grimaced. "What's the date on that one?"

"1905. September 5th."

"Oh, that was one of them." Orlando sank down into his chair again. "I don't know the details. Papa was still alive, he didn't get into it with me. Grant had pneumonia, I think. Certainly a long recovery. Something with his lungs, anyway. He had to go away somewhere warm for six months, for one thing. He must have done that before he left."

"And then hidden it later? When he was worried that people in his house would have found it?" Wallace was tapping his fingers on the deck. "You've got the family names, yes?"

"Oh, you know them." Orlando reeled off several, faster than Owen could make sense of them. "The same that are pushing the current will. And who I think want to sell." Then he paused, as if this were the fearsome bit. "What does it say about that?"

"That if this will hold, it means he has no direct heir for the theatre, and you inherit the lot, including money for his half of the share. So, free rein to act as you see fit, some money." Wallace held up his fingers. "Mind, I don't know how much of that there will be. But you'd not be held back by a silent partner."

"A very loud and unwilling trio is more like it. Like ugly stepsisters out of some fable. Or panto." Orlando pulled out his pocket square, dabbing at his forehead.

Clara hesitated, and Owen squeezed her hand again encouragingly. "Can I ask, sir, what that means about the aim to buy the theatre?"

"That's going to be a good question. If he's keeping tabs on the case - and he might well be - he'll know when I file the documents tomorrow morning. Which I intend to do as soon as the Halls of Justice open, we're just within the window for an adjustment without problems for the next hearing." Wallace glanced up. "You know something about the man, then?"

Clara nodded once, her lips tight. "I do." She hesitated, then added, "He's been talking to me, I run my aunt's apothecary. I thought his attentions were more personal, originally, but I did mention my husband got a job at a theatre, and now I'm wondering..." She flushed and Owen squeezed her hand again tighter. "I didn't tell him anything detailed, I didn't know it myself, but he kept asking."

"Might want to have a word with the Guard just so they're aware. Could you meet with them in the morning?" Wallace glanced around, and Owen thought he was rearranging a dozen pieces of information in his head. "I know theatre folk keep odd hours."

"I've got to open the shop, sir." Clara's voice had shifted into the cautious polite tones she'd used with Owen, early on. "I need to be there from half-eight at the latest."

"I could ask someone to stop round, then." Wallace said. "Or arrange to meet you at the end of your day. A message, either way, shall we say? I won't be talking to anyone until half-eight, so it'd be ten or later."

"Sir." Clara seemed to be doing columns of maths in her head. "That will do, I suppose." Then she added, more earnestly. "I want to be a help, just I need to be there, and... " Her voice trailed off.

"We're near enough done here, at least for the moment. Helling, if you could get the notes done first thing, I won't need them immediately, but we'll want the proper reports in as soon as can be." He began to pack his things up.

Orlando gestured. "Owen, if you'd like to walk your wife home, we can spare you for a little. Barely, of course." He made the last into an obvious joke, flagged like a stage fight.

Owen wasn't going to argue at all. "Come along. We'll get you home, yeah?" It had gone dark out, well since, and Owen did feel better knowing she wasn't alone with it. By the time they got halfway home, she was chatting a little about the parts of the play she'd seen. At the door, she stopped and kissed him. "See you when I see you. Thank you for walking me home."

He let his hand rest on her shoulder for a second. "Walk you to work in the morning, come back and nap after."

CHAPTER 37
DECEMBER 16TH AT THE SHOP

T he excitement on Thursday night meant Clara had slept poorly. Owen had been up and waiting when she woke up, bleary and wanting to be unpleasant to the world. None of it was his fault, though, and she refused to take out her mood on him. It left her uncertain what to say.

He walked her into the shop, before going off to catch a nap before going back to the theatre for another full run-through. He'd be out until nine, possibly later, depending on what needed mending or adjusting once they'd done that.

Clara also didn't know what to do with the entirely unspecific comments about time. She opened the shop right on time, flipping the sign on the door to 'open', and making sure the lights were on, visible from the street. Then she settled on her stool behind the counter, slowly working through the inventory notes. She kept herself to work she could easily double-check later. Right now she didn't trust herself to count things correctly the first time, and she definitely didn't trust herself to handle breakable bottles.

There was a steady stream of customers through the morning, one or two at a time, never so many as to be overwhelming. Any other day, she'd have been pleased at the sales. A number of the holiday items were selling brilliantly, especially the scented oils that made the house smell like pine and juniper, or like baking spices and vanilla. They were popular choices for modest gifts, unlikely to offend and not the same as everyone else's. The bottles were handsomely styled, as well, gilt against the coloured glass that Clara and her aunt had negotiated for what seemed like years ago, last spring.

It did not actually occupy Clara's mind enough. That was the problem. There was a part of her braced for something to happen, and given the decent luck of the past few days, it was bound to be something unpleasant. Mostly, of course, she was braced in case Horatio Morris got it in his head to show up. There were enough people in and out that he probably wouldn't. If he didn't over the lunch hour, probably not until late in the afternoon. Probably.

Besides, the solicitor had said she wouldn't hear anything before ten. That had been some small help at nine in the morning, and it was absolutely no help at all at half-ten, eleven, noon, or one. Nor any of the minutes in between, when she checked her watch warily between customers.

It wasn't until half-one that anything out of the ordinary happened. There was, just as the clock down the street was striking, a small procession into her shop. Four people, two men and two women, once she could sort them out. One was a very elegant woman who must be in her fifties or sixties, with an exquisitely tailored Guard uniform. Clara didn't begin to know the terms for half of it, but the effect was compelling. She was clearly senior.

With her was a younger man, also in Guard uniform, paying close attention to her, and then two others. One was a woman, carrying a bag of some kind, quite a large one, slung over her shoulder. The other man was in a wheeled chair, but it wasn't nearly as nimble as Golshan's had been. The woman with him had to push him, to get him into the shop.

"May we have a few minutes of your time, Mistress Hubbard? And perhaps close the shop for a few minutes? We shouldn't need more than fifteen or so at the moment."

Clara blinked, then swallowed hard. "For what reason, please?" She tried to keep her voice even, and it wasn't working. She could tell.

"May we speak privately?" The older woman pressed. "I'm from the Guard, here." She dipped her fingers under the line of her collared shirt, bringing out the pendant she wore on a chain, then stepping closer to the counter to show it off.

Clara was trying to decide what to say, how to respond. She wanted to be a help, but she did not care for the brusqueness, not one bit. The man in the wheelchair spoke up then. "Do pardon Captain Donovan, we've had a terribly busy morning. We really do only need a few minutes. No one saw us come in, but better no one wanders in to buy..." He gestured. "Actually, those soaps look delightful. Can I have a look when we're done with our actual task?"

It at least gave Clara something more to go on. "And you're from, sir? Master?" She wasn't sure of the proper form of address.

The Captain sighed slightly, and Clara hurriedly said, "If you wouldn't mind flipping the sign, let me just put this away." She felt that manners suggested she offer them tea. Did one offer tea to people from the Guard who turned up on almost no notice? It would take several minutes, though. She'd finished the last of the kettle at lunch and hadn't put on something fresh to keep warm. In the end, she closed the ledgers, put them on the desk in the office, and came back out to find all four waiting on her.

The older woman cleared her throat, looking for all the world as if she'd been scolded by one of the others. Clara couldn't imagine who would dare, honestly. "I beg your pardon. As Griffin said, it's been rather a morning. I am Captain Donovan, also Lady Genvieve Donovan, of the Guard. This is Guard Archibald Donovan." She did not explain what relation he might be, though Clara could see something of a familial resemblance, especially around the nose and cheekbones, all quite strong. He was rather strikingly handsome with blonde hair and classical features that would do well on a stage.

Clara nodded uncertainly.

"And this is Griffin Pelson." The man in the chair, given the nod and grin Clara got from him.

"Call me Griffin, please. We are not in my particular realm at the moment. We are in yours." He waved a hand and said, "This is Lucy Kemp. We're with the Halls of Justice."

The younger woman nodded once. Not a bob or a deferral, the way Clara would have done, but she was also rather clearly the junior of the party.

"Now, we understand you were involved with finding the will and other paperwork last night?" Captain Donovan went on briskly.

"Yes, ma'am. Captain."

"Either is fine." The older woman did manage half a smile at that. "You're not in any trouble. You've been an interesting amount of help. I should have started with that. Pardon, I'm not usually the person who does this kind of interview."

"By which she means," Griffin said, breaking in. "That we've spent all morning being imposing at people, and she forgets to turn it off." It was a good natured teasing between colleagues, or at least that's how it was supposed to go. The way Clara might tease her aunt, or the way people at the theatre had teased each other.

Captain Donovan sighed. "You go on then, Griffin."

"As we've said," Griffin picked up smoothly. "We've been talking to people all morning. Right now, Horatio Morris is making some interesting moves, but we're not entirely sure what he's up to. He's withdrawn money from his bank, he's made several other calls related to business, but he isn't in his factory, nor is he at home. His staff there say he's gone for a few days, expected back Monday morning."

"Sir." Clara frowned. "I - pardon, I don't know what you've been told."

"That he's been something of a bother and a worry to you, sometimes more than that." That was Lucy Kemp. "And yet, that he might turn up here, when he's avoiding other usual places. We think - though we can't be certain - that he doesn't know you know he's connected to the problems at the theatre." Then she added, "Oh, and it will take a bit for the proper hearings. However, Griffin and I agree, along with several other offices of the Courts that the will you found does look in order. A resolution that's good for the theatre is likely as soon as we can do the formalities. I like their shows best, mind, I want to see them go forward."

"Ma'am." Clara felt overwhelmed and after a moment, she tugged the stool behind her so she could perch on it. "But why are you here?"

"In part to tell you that, but also to ask a rather large favour. If Morris does not reappear where we can find him for a conversation by Monday morning, would you be willing to send round a note, encourage him to come by? We can help you with the wording. Something like having something for him before the holidays, or even, if you think it's something you'd say, that you have some news from the theatre he might want to hear."

Clara immediately shook her head at the second bit. "The first, maybe. Or a comment about the shoes he gave me. He was very, um." She waved a hand. "Do I have to write it now? What if he comes by? I don't. It isn't safe. He scared me." It all came out in a rush, and then all Clara could do was hug herself.

There was a brief silence before Griffin spoke up. "It must be very unsettling. And you just want the shop to run smoothly, of course, and your other customers to feel at ease. People don't buy much when they're nervous."

She looked up at that, and he added, brightly. "Shop-keeper's son. I do know a fair bit about how that goes. Your sign said you're not open on Saturdays right now, yes?"

"Normally, no. But I'd been thinking of opening tomor-row, for the holiday sales. Last minute, you know how it is. There's several sales and specials down the street, and all the shop window displays." She hadn't done much of one this year. They were difficult to put up by herself. Just some lights and evergreen boughs.

"Well, how about this? We can lend you Archibald to lurk around and be helpful today and for however long you're open tomorrow. He can walk you home as well, if you'd prefer that, or to wherever you choose. If Morris does come by, he can summon more help, very quickly, as well as his own skills. And he can be a hand in the shop."

Clara frowned at the younger Guard. "Do you know anything about working in a shop?"

"No, Mistress. Other than having shopped in them." He had a lopsided grin when he relaxed. "But I'm good at getting things down from tall shelves. Perhaps as an excuse, I've a source for some extra decorations. You could say I was helping with that. I did bring a change of clothes with me. You could say you'd borrowed me for a day or two to lend a hand when it's busy. I'll duck in the back or whatever you like when people come in."

Clara considered it. It would be helpful to have someone else around, and she had been feeling like the decorations weren't up to scratch. Archibald added, "I'm quite good with both light and sticking charms for the decorations, too."

"All right." Clara let out a slow breath. "What do I have to do?"

"A spot for Archibald to leave his journal open - a bit of table or shelf will do." Captain Donovan said. "And then just sort out when you want him here."

"And Monday?" Clara made herself go forward to that idea.

"Ah, Monday, we would like to have some people in place. Do you mind us seeing your back room, whatever it looks like, so we know what we can work with?"

People didn't go back there. There was space, but it was

Aunt Lillian's domain. But Aunt Lillian hadn't been here. As if he'd seen all that written on her face - maybe he had - Griffin cleared his throat. "We don't need much space, and we're glad to make oath on not touching whatever you don't want us to touch."

They had an argument for everything.

"And it may be we don't need it. We are trying - pardon, the Guard is trying - a range of other methods. With a bit of luck, we won't need your help at all on Monday. In which case Archibald will trot round and let you know first thing." Griffin's voice was cheerful, relaxed, as if he wanted her to be easy about this, too. Though Clara had caught the look Griffin had got from Captain Donovan, that made him make that correction.

"I don't really have a lot of choice, do I?" She hadn't meant to say it out loud, but there it was, sitting there in the room like an elephant. Uncomfortable, large, and opaque, or at least she assumed that all three were true of elephants, she'd only seen them in the London zoo a few times, on outings.

Griffin leaned forward in his chair. "You do have a choice. We hope you'll do the noble thing, because we'd like very much to see justice done here. And..." His voice trailed off. "No, that's not fair."

"What isn't fair?" Clara found herself with her hands on her hips, leaning forward to match him.

Griffin cleared his throat. "No promises on this one, but we understand from your own information that it's quite possible Morris was involved in war-profiteering. If so, if we can get a judgement that gives us access to his business paperwork, we might be able to do something about that. Distribute ill-got gains somewhere more useful, for example."

Clara grimaced. "That is unfair. What am I supposed to say to that?" Then she paused. "What sort of distribution?"

"Money for veterans services, maybe. Grants to people with foot injuries, caused by the boots - that would be a long process, but we could do more to help. Your husband might have some ideas about it, I'm sure, and there are other people we could consult. A simpler version might be turning it into grants for getting businesses up and running. Something of the kind." Griffin waved a hand. "We're counting chickens well ahead of eggs, there, but you see the sort of thing."

"Unfair," Clara said, then she sighed. "Moment, and I'll put the case up so you can come back." The centre of the cases had a wooden shelf that went over. She folded that over the glass top of the case next to it, carefully, then moved things out of the well. She'd been meaning to redo that display for something festive. She could do that with Archibald's help this afternoon, probably. That done, she gestured them through into the back room, holding the curtain between the two back.

Lucy bent to murmur something to Griffin Pelson, then came around. There wasn't quite a bounce in her step, but she was eager about something.

As Griffin came by, he was chatting amiably. "We're rather imposing, aren't we? And this must be all of a sudden for you. Oh, yes, this will do fine. We really won't be difficult, I promise. If we do need the space Monday, the idea is that we'd wait back here, with two nice strapping Guardsmen in case of trouble."

Captain Donovan picked up, just as smoothly as she was circling the worktables. "In which case, Griffin will bind him to tell the truth, enough to take him into custody. And then we should be able to do something."

"And you can't tell me what, exactly."

"Not without more information, no. But this should be - if we don't get him before that - be enough to get us to that. You really are doing a lot of people a favour, as well as yourself and the theatre." Captain Donovan peered around. "Can Lucy take a few measurements? It won't affect any of the charmwork here. Not usually your realm is it?"

"My aunt's. She makes all our goods, but she's away, yet." What Clara would tell her about all this didn't bear thinking about, but it wasn't something Clara could do much about until it was all over. Writing in the midst would be far worse. "And - you won't touch anything?"

What Lucy was doing was apparently, in fact, just measurements, though as she finished up, she said, "There are some stones I'll bring on Monday, additional protections. Mostly for your shelves, that everything will stay put, even if it's jostled."

"Oh." Clara swallowed again. "Is that likely?"

"Probably not, but we like to be careful. It's a, what's the word for it, Griffin?"

"Preservation." Griffin said. "We want the passage of justice through us to not leave chaos in its wake. So when we need to do work somewhere like this, or someone's home, we like to make sure there's as little damage as possible. It does work quite well. The stones help map the spaces it affects."

Clara didn't know what to make of the fact that was a standard thing. But given the number of glass bottles on shelves in the shop, she could only be glad. "And if something does break?"

"We'll recompense you for it. Both in replacing it, at what you'd have sold it for, not just material and labour cost, but also covering the cleanup." Captain Donovan spoke up promptly. "Again, not terribly likely. You might want to pack away anything that would be dangerous if it was mixed, or keep it well separate, if there's anything like that. But you're an apothecary. I'm guessing you already do that."

"Yes'm," Clara said promptly. Accidents did happen, and nobody wanted a shelf coming down or someone's elbow sweeping across several bottles to cause problems. "We keep those sorts of things well apart."

"There you go. Now, Archibald, can you go round and see about decorations? We'll pay, Mistress Hubbard, but you can keep them after."

"Yes'm." Archibald snapped to attention. "Pine, and what else?"

"A bit of mistletoe, if you can get it, it will help anchor one of the charms best. We can work with pine, if not." Captain Donovan cast an eye over the front shop. "Aim for reds and golds, I think, for ribbons, if that will suit, Mistress?"

Clara felt rather like things were unfolding fast around her, but that suited the season and it would look smart in the shop against the wood and the charm lights. She just nodded.

"There we go, then. Any other questions? I'll stay until Archibald gets back, and then we'll leave you to it. Griffin, Lucy?"

"We've everything we need." Griffin said, amiably. "If someone could get the curtain for me."

Clara swallowed. "Um. Can my - if it's Monday, could my husband be here? Back here waiting?"

"Of course." That came from Griffin, who'd been about to wheel through the door. Then he raised an eyebrow at Captain Donovan, a little behind Clara's shoulder. "You know you were going to say yes, Genevieve."

"I was. Just. We'll be a bit crowded."

"Cosy, before the holidays," Griffin said. "I bring my own chair. You needn't find a place for me to sit." He chuckled, and then wheeled off through the door, with Lucy following him.

Captain Donovan shook her head. "He's in something of a mood. This is the kind of puzzle he rather likes, that needs a creative touch, not just the routine rituals. Here, may I sit down here and stay out of your way? You're looking a little like you could use a cuppa."

The term, the way Clara would put it, sounded odd in Captain Donovan's accent, but Clara couldn't deny it. "Would you like one, ma'am?"

"Oh, please. It was such a morning. I'll just be here. I've a book. Sing out if you have another question. When Archibald comes back, I'll leave you to it. He really is quite competent, not that I say that to him directly often. It gives young people ideas."

On that note, she did in fact take out a book, setting it open and appearing quite happy to read. Clara bustled around with the kettle, and by the time the tea was steeping in the pot, she felt a little more settled. She went and flipped the sign, and three minutes later, her life was full of a stream of customers again. Archibald turned up an hour into it, with a large basket overflowing with boughs and mistletoe and things tied up in bows. Getting the decorations set up took the rest of the afternoon between the other demands of the shop. By the time Clara locked up, the place looked entirely up to her standards of festive decoration, and she felt marginally better about the whole thing.

The four of them had asked, after all. They'd been

careful to explain what they wanted, and to protect the shop and Clara. And she did very much want Horatio Morris to stop being awful to rather a lot of people. That went above and beyond her own minor problems, in the scheme of things. If she was lucky, they'd track him down well before Monday, and that would be the end of it.

CHAPTER 38
DECEMBER 20TH AT THE SHOP

Sunday evening, there had been a note saying that they'd like to proceed on Monday. It hadn't been long, the note, but it had the proper Guard seal and Captain Donovan's signature. More to the point, when Clara turned up at the shop Monday morning, there was Archibald, waiting.

"Good morning." He looked a little apologetic, actually. Then he smiled, turning on the charm, but differently than Morris did. "Is this your husband? Pleased to meet you, sir."

"Owen, this is Guard Archibald Donovan. Archibald, Owen." She glanced around. "Um. Come in?" Clara unlocked the shop. Everything was as they'd left it on Friday. "Do I send the note now?"

"If you would. Would you normally drop it in the post, or a messenger?"

"Post. If it goes out now, it should get to him in the half-ten run, don't you think?" Clara did the maths on that, but it wasn't going far. "Assuming he's home."

"We believe he returned a few minutes ago." Archibald tapped the bound journal he was carrying. "Most useful, the journals. Here, write something up, and I'll take it along."

Clara went into the back office, Owen following her, a bit uncertainly. "Are you sure you're comfortable with this?" His voice was a bit uneven.

"Are you going to tell me not to?" Clara looked up from where she'd found a notecard and a pen.

"Goodness, no. Just. If you want to tell them no, I'll back you up. Or whatever you want." Owen spread out his hands. "Not a thing I'm used to dealing with. And you aren't either, I think? I hope?"

Clara had to pause at that. "You wouldn't know." She tried not to make it an accusation, and she mostly succeeded. "This is more than usual. But we do have difficult customers. Usually, though, it's older women who really want an ear, and will stand around for hours chatting and not letting others shop. Entirely different sort of problem."

"What do you do with them?" Owen glanced behind him. "Not the Guard."

"Aunt Lillian has a list of clubs, the Women's Institute gatherings, that sort of thing. The library has some discussions, or there are people knitting for the Temple of Healing. Usually we can nudge them toward one of those, and then they can chat to people and be doing some good." Clara snorted suddenly. "I can't see Horatio Morris doing much of that, no."

Her laughter seemed to ease something in Owen. "Well, no. All right. You send the note off, and I'll stick around, and whoever else is coming will show up, and we'll be right here. Good?"

"Good as it's getting." Clara finished the note with a little flourish of her pen. She'd thought a lot about what to say the last two days. It was brief, just a greeting, then 'I have something for you, before the holidays, could you perhaps stop round today?'. To make it more certain, she noted she'd be closed for Tuesday and Wednesday for the Solstice proper. After Clara sealed it up, she paused to kiss Owen's cheek. "I'm glad you're here." Before he could say anything in reply, she went out of the office, handing the card in its envelope to Archibald.

"Back soon, and the others should be along in a quarter hour or so. They were just finalising things at the Courts." He trotted off, moving briskly. It left Clara to look around the shop, and she was adjusting the displays when the other three came in. Key to the whole thing was a wicker basket in the gap in the cabinets. It was packed with light, unbreakable things so it could be whisked out of the way when needed.

"Here we are, then. There are two more Guards, in street clothes, outside. They'll be handy as soon as he comes in and make sure he can't get out. Do you mind if we lock the door to the back garden, too?"

Clara shook her head, but fumbled over finding the key for that. It took her a good few minutes to settle down again. By half-nine, everyone was tucked away in the back room, including Owen. They had chairs - she'd scrounged up two more. A charm of some sort blocked the sound. Clara did her best to go about the day as usual. A bit early, she perched to eat her lunch for as a short a time as she could, constantly aware of the charms that let them hear what she was doing.

Just as the Temple bells were striking half-one, the door opened with a chime. "Mistress Hubbard. Oh, my, this is festive. Is that mistletoe, even? Goodness, I didn't expect that." Master Morris was all charm, all smiles, all ease. But it felt, somehow, slimy. Much slimier than before she'd seen how Captain Donovan was, all sharp competence.

Clara opened her mouth, trying to figure out what to say, before her voice caught in her throat, and she coughed. Before she could do anything else, the shop was suddenly full of people. One of the Guards came in from outside, one from the back door. Archibald was vaulting over the basket and table next to Clara, using the top of the display to boost him along. The front door of the shop swung open, and she couldn't see exactly who had come in.

Master Morris was backing up, without looking, away from that, when he ran smack into one of the Guards. One took his right hand, the other took his left, then they rearranged so his hands were behind him. When Clara could get her eyes to focus - she'd moved to the side, behind the glass cabinets - Lucy was moving the basket and table out of the way. Captain Donovan strode out, followed by Griffin in his chair, and behind them all, there was Owen.

He came right over to her, arm around her waist, and she leaned into the warmth. Master Morris was sputtering now. Captain Donovan prowled around him, like one of the great cats; Clara had seen the zoo, and a bit of cinema footage of them both. Then the captain nodded at Griffin.

From his seated position, Griffin lifted his hands, clapping them together once and then saying something in a language Clara couldn't follow. His voice rang as clearly as bells, as if there was something more behind it than just his body. It felt like things clicking into place, like clockwork. Or like the way Aunt Lillian knew when a potion or salve or whatever she was working on shifted that last step when it was done. That, and there was a shimmer of something else, a pressure and weight, but not uncomfortable. Not for her, anyway.

"Justice is present, Captain. Proceed." Griffin's voice wasn't deference. It was peer-to-peer, in a way that seemed complicated, somehow. But Captain Donovan nodded back, and then launched into a series of what seemed like routine questions. Name, date of birth, place of residence, profession, businesses. It should have been ordinary, if a little peculiar, but part way through, as they got into the businesses, Morris started sweating, visibly. Sweating, stuttering, turning his head from side to side, as if he were coming near to choking.

"It's worse if you fight it." Captain Donovan's voice was almost a purr. "You know what you've done. If you don't admit it now, it'll be worse at the trial. You know that. You know just what you've done."

There was something almost primal in it, like she was indeed a cat who'd pounced on her prey. Master Morris took a step back. Then Griffin did something new with his hands as Lucy walked around behind Morris and Captain Donovan. The words came more easily then, question and answer. Once they'd run through the simple things, what should be simple, Captain Donovan took him through a dozen questions about his business. From there, she pinned him down into admitting he'd deliberately taken shortcuts on boots for the war effort, that he'd knowingly sent boots that failed out into the trenches and so many other places.

She asked another couple of questions, then lifted one finger. "No. That can wait for your trial. Silence him and take him, please, Guards." They bustled him out of the store, and that was going to cause gossip on the street. Clara just knew it.

Once that was done, the door closed against the world, Captain Donovan turned. "Mistress Hubbard, you have been exceedingly helpful. As you may have gathered, the charges are quite widespread. War profiteering, but we also came across evidence, thanks to your information, of abuse of workers at the factory. Stealing pay, unsafe conditions, that sort of thing, and various other violations of law. Moreover, we have excellent evidence that he was actively interfering with business at the theatre, or doing his best to, so he could take control of it. Interfering with orders and deliveries, that sort of thing."

The younger Donovan chimed in, "Orlando Hill, Captain."

She nodded briskly. "Just so. We'll be going along to let him know the good news at home shortly. Mistress Hubbard, we will request your presence to give evidence at the trial. It will be a few weeks. After the holidays. Someone from the Court," again, another tiny pause, "Lucy, in fact, will prepare you for what is involved. We will make sure there is someone who can tend the shop in your absence if needed. We appreciate your help, a great deal, in providing the illumination of justice and helping make things right." Again, that had a sound of a formal ritual to it.

Then the smile cracked wider. "And now we'll get out of your hair. It's fine to tell your neighbours and customers the basics. Namely that you learned Master Morris had been involved in some illegal dealings, that you properly brought it to our attention, and that they can watch the papers for the case."

Clara appreciated that. She nodded, unable to find words to say anything. Five minutes later, Lucy had gathered up the stones that had anchored the magic, picked up their various bits and pieces from the back room, and was holding the door. A minute after that, they were all gone, leaving a gaping silence.

Owen's hand shifted on her back, fingers spread. He

glanced up for a moment - they'd moved back into the door frame. "I would like very much to kiss you. You were very brave, and very steady. Then, if you don't mind, I'd like to go along home, and see to a few things. Unless you'd rather I stay the day until you lock up?"

Clara blinked. "The kiss, yes?" Her voice cracked. "And ... go along." It was a couple of hours yet to closing. She'd have people in and out to gossip. Maybe someone would walk her back. She didn't want to juggle what Owen heard or didn't hear, or the fact he was there, all at the same time. That was too much.

He pulled her closer against him, taking his time with the kiss. When he finally pulled back, she felt something she didn't know how to describe, besides simply wanting more. More what, who knew? Then he kissed her forehead. "You'll see. Come home when you close up. I can't be in two places at once, or I would. Take a cab, if you need to?" He pressed a coin into her hand, enough to cover a carriage back to the flat.

With that, he squeezed her hand, and rather purposefully took himself out the door.

CHAPTER 39
THAT AFTERNOON AT THEIR FLAT

Owen knew just about how long it should take for Clara to get home. He'd set everything up carefully. The new curtains were hung up, the brightly coloured silk flowers curving up in an arc, like they were something out of a lush garden. They stood out against the white fabric beautifully, like he'd hoped. The bedroom was tidy. He'd laid out their tea on the best plates, he had the teakettle ready.

And the other bedroom was ready, too. Though he couldn't let himself think about that too much. He'd give it away on his face, almost certainly. That wasn't where he wanted to start.

Just about the point when he was starting to actually get worried, the door rattled, then opened. Clara came in, looking absolutely done in. He considered and said. "Tea will keep. Do you want a bath first?"

Her mouth opened, then closed, then she nodded once, and drifted into the hallway. He waited until she was in the bathroom with the taps running, then picked up her discarded clothing and set it in the hamper. He checked the bed one more time, cushioning and warming charms, then went back to settle at the kitchen table, cupping his hands around a mug of black tea.

She took her time, and that was fine. Except for the fact Owen was getting antsy. That was his own fault. He had to remind himself of that. He was doing something he hoped she'd like. Several things. Rushing her would be a thing she didn't like, so he wouldn't do that.

Finally, though, he heard her come out of the bathroom and go into the bedroom. A few minutes later, she came out into the kitchen wearing a housedress and a dressing gown over it. The dress was a bit worn, he thought, but a bright teal, and the dressing gown had a cheerful print in yellows and reds. He suspected some people would think it clashed, but he liked it.

She stopped dead at the entrance to the kitchen. "What's that?"

The curtains. "New curtains. The flowers are from the theatre, a batch they couldn't use. And you liked the one I brought home."

Her mouth opened and closed several times, then she came closer. He reached to stretch the curtains out to show the full effect. "If you hate it, we can take them down."

"You made them?" She tilted her head. "When?"

"Plenty of time when you were working or asleep, and I was awake." Owen said, amiably. "And sewing's quiet."

Clara snorted at that, then came closer, turning the fabric around to look at the stitching. "I didn't know you could do such fine sewing. Very even."

"Easier than shoes, those. The silk wanted to curl up a bit. It's slippery? But much easier to get a needle through."

308

Owen had found it an interesting challenge. He'd not sewn much on fabric since early in his apprenticeship, when he was learning how to use a needle properly. Or in the trenches, doing his own mending, which was an entirely different sort of thing.

She took a step back. "You did this? Why?" A different question.

"Because we should have - you like colours. I like colours. We should have colours here. And then there were the silk flowers, the ghost gave them to me."

Clara's mouth twitched up, and then she was smiling. "Well. If a ghost gives you flowers, I suppose that's something you can't ignore." She looked at the curtains, then back at him. "You really went to all that trouble?"

It wasn't a great deal of trouble. That was the thing. It was something simple. All right, a fair bit of sewing, but he'd found it soothing. "We should make the place ours. Come, sit down, you must be starving. I got a bit of cheese and the scones you like, and there are apples, if you want to make cheddar apple sandwiches."

She nodded, busying herself with making up a sandwich for herself. She ate in silence, though with small pauses where she put the sandwich down and looked around, then went back to eating. He didn't interrupt, other than nudging the sugar for the tea over, or checking if she wanted the last bit of scone.

Finally, she looked up and met his eyes. "I don't know what to expect from you right now."

"I think neither of us has known that, right?" Owen had to feel his way with this. He'd learned, somehow, complicatedly, how to talk about this, when it was tight spaces and dangerous work at the theatre. He'd learned how to do dangerous things where you had to trust someone in the trenches, but talking about it was harder. Or so he thought, anyway. On the other hand, they needed to sort this out, or what did they have? "Seeing you, today. Well, before today. I fell in love with you for good reasons. You're sharp, you notice details, but you - I love when you smile. Or laugh. The way your mouth curls, the way your eyes are."

She flushed, rather deeply pink.

"And you don't know what to do with me saying that. Right." He rubbed his face. "The thing about the theatre is - seeing lots of people figure out how to tell people things. On stage, of course, but backstage, too. How to make the, the back-and-forth work. And it's different for everyone, isn't it? We never really had a chance to find ours. Not enough time. Too many other things to worry about."

Clara nodded slowly. "I suppose."

Owen stood, then came to kneel on one knee. A traditional pose for something they'd already done, but it seemed the one that suited. "May I court you again? Properly? Give ourselves a chance to find out who we are together?"

Her eyebrows went up. "Very theatrical."

"Very much in earnest." He could feel his hands start to tremble. He knew, he'd known for weeks, somehow, that he needed to do this properly. That doing it properly meant knowing she could say no. That there was a real chance she would.

She looked down at his hands, not his face, then very carefully took one hand, then the other, her fingers curving around them. There was the wedding ring, matching the one on his hand, simple and plain. Mum had insisted. "What did you have in mind?"

Owen swallowed hard. "First, I'd like to take you to bed. Make sure you have a grand time." He looked up, flushing. "I'm not sure if you have, since..." His voice trailed off. There was absolutely no good way to have this conversation.

She flushed and looked down. "I'm - it hasn't been bad?" Then she tried, her voice suddenly so soft he had to lean forward to catch it. "I think it could be better, though."

"I will do my best. Pay all the attention to what you like. Try a few new things?" When he met her eyes again, she was smiling. "All right. And then I have some things to show you. So we should make sure you can walk after."

That got a raised eyebrow. Then she was laughing. "Were you thinking that was your challenge? No." She swallowed. "All right. Bed. Then whatever you want to show me."

Owen stood, wobbling only slightly. Actors, again, made this look easy, getting up and down with grace and heroic poses. Then he bowed, offering her his arm. "Shall we?"

She barely hesitated before standing. "Leave the dishes. I'll wash them later." It was just crumbs left, nothing that couldn't sit out. Instead, he drew her along to the bedroom, walking backwards and bumping the door with his shoulder to open it.

Both of them were shy at first. It wasn't their first time, but it was. It was his first time doing his best - he'd admit it to himself now, and to her later. Not too much later. He fought with the desire to do what they'd done before and instead started from first principles. From the way his fingers brushed her skin, how she reacted to it. He'd trained his fingers, long ago now, to feel bumps and ridges and places that needed to be smoothed, and he called on all of that.

Owen didn't even begin to nudge her clothing aside for minutes. Tens of minutes, it felt like, just tracing the edge of her collarbone, the line of her hand and her wrist. He bent in to kiss her, willing his mouth to be as deft as his hands. She let herself relax more and more into the bed. He could feel the tension shifting. As she settled on her back, he found a way to stretch out beside her. Now he was pressing against her left hip, leaving his right hand to wander and begin to undo her robe. The dress buttoned down the front. That would be easy, too.

What he found, as his fingers worked their way through undoing buttons and folding fabric back, was that she was quiveringly responsive. He didn't have a wide experience to compare it to, but compared to his experience of her before, certainly. Taking his time, he traced the curve of her hip, the shape of her breast, like he'd work leather. Firm enough not to tickle, but gentle enough he could feel every piece of it.

By the time his fingers dipped between her legs, he was nuzzling at her breasts, kissing whatever part of her was within reach. Owen had to trust that he would sort out the touch, and as she arched and spread her legs more, he could only assume he was doing something right. He lifted his head to watch her as his index finger slipped inside, to see her arch her head to match the rock of her hips and moan. A minute or two more, another finger, and she was shuddering against him, given over to her own pleasure.

He didn't think it was the first time he'd managed it, but it was far more obvious, far more certain, than anything he'd known with her before. Only then did he begin to undo his own clothing, alternating more kisses and touches along her skin as she caught her breath with peeling off his own layers. When he stretched out against her side, she shook her head once, no.

He couldn't make sense of it and blinked at her. "Clara? Love?"

Clara shifted, then nudged his shoulder. When he glanced down her body, flushed as it was, he saw she'd spread her legs, made room for him there. That almost brought him off, honestly, embarrassingly easily. He swallowed hard, turning it into a kiss on her shoulder, then on her mouth, before he rearranged himself. She was soaking wet now; the heat radiating from her.

Part of him wanted to drive into her, but that wasn't what he was going to do, no matter how willing she seemed. Instead, he got his hand between them, arranging himself so he could rock against her, bring that pressure to bear. It felt amazing to him, endlessly so, without being so much it would push him over. More kisses followed, more brushes of his fingers on her nipples, on the spot he'd found on her neck that made her shiver with delight, just below her ear.

Only when she was shivering again did he finally move, notching in the right place and pushing in. Everything was heat and pressure and just perfect, shoe and last meshing perfectly in every way. Personal, the way it should be, what made sense for her and for him and the moment, all coming together at once. The mere thought of it made him speed up. It drove him to rock his hips as he filled her, then let out a gasping sound as he pulled back so he could it again. Over and over, until her hands were clenching on his back, until her legs had come up around his hips to hold him deep and close.

Three more thrusts, and he finally felt her begin to clench around him, giving herself over to it. He sucked hard on her neck, for sheer need. He managed to hold on for another few seconds until everything was too much in all the best ways and he felt himself explode in his own shattering climax.

They came to rest with him still half in her, one of her legs cocked up around his hip, the other sprawled on the bed beside him, his body draping across hers. He couldn't bring himself to move for what must have been minutes, when they were both coming back to themselves. Only then could he roll to one side, his hand automatically cupping her hip and his thumb playing over the skin.

"Grand time." It came out softly, barely a whisper. "Give me a bit."

"All the time you like." He settled his head against her shoulder, not bothering to move more or try to find a blanket.

Some time later - he'd heard the bells go at least twice - she finally stirred. "Think I can walk?"

That made him laugh, more or less into her shoulder. "You'll want your dressing gown. Slippers for the first part." But Owen rolled out of bed, pausing to stretch a little. Then he turned around and offered her his hand. "We're not going far."

She stood, letting him lead her, discarding her dress and pulling the dressing gown around her and doing up the belt. It left a deep V of her skin delightfully visible. He suddenly wondered what that would be like as a decoration on a shoe, the way it was smooth lines and curves all at once. He tucked her hand into the arm, and then crossed the hallway to what had been Mum's room.

Clara stalled. "Owen?"

"Take a look." He opened the door and watched her. That was what mattered here. He knew what she would see. He'd packed up all of Mum's trinkets, he'd gone through them. Some had gone to the jumble sale or the second-hand shop. He'd kept one trunk of letters and photos and other things he didn't want to part with, but it was tucked in the attic space.

Now the room was freshly whitewashed. He'd repainted the bed frame a matching white after sanding out the rust on a few spots. There was a teal chair he'd picked up in trade for a bit of work from one of the actors. The footstool shouldn't have gone with it, but somehow did, in a purple. The bed was unmade, but he'd put a couple of newly fluffed pillows on it.

Clara squeezed his arm. "What - what did you do?"

"It's our flat, love. We should make it our own. It's a bigger bedroom. I thought - and if I can't sleep, I could be up, not disturb you."

She went still and quiet for a long moment, then stood on tiptoe to kiss his cheek. "What do you want to do?"

"I want us to have a wander sometime, see what we could get for sheets and blankets. Make it up properly. Both of us. I've got a little money set aside now. I've got a decent idea which shops might have things."

Clara swallowed, then leaned her head on his shoulder. He shifted to let his hand curl around her back, holding her closer. "I like that. You really did all of this? For us?"

"Us." Agreeing with that felt like the skies opening and the sun pouring through. "I have another thing I'm working on, but it's not quite done yet. Let's save that. You sit in the chair, tell me what you think about the room, and let's talk about what we'd like in here. If we could find it."

"Wishing." Her voice had turned very thoughtful now.

"We do know some people talented in making things, you know. Might not be entirely an illusion."

That made her laugh, and then she pulled away from him to sit in the chair, cross her ankles on the stool, and look up at him. There was the smile he'd fallen for, in the Temple of Healing, something impish and delightful and delighted. Maybe they could really make this work.

CHAPTER 40
DECEMBER 20TH AT THE THEATRE

The opening night was a delight. Clara had found herself tucked into a box with Golshan, Seth, Dilly, and Seth's parents. They'd brought Golshan's chair up through the lift used for moving items to storage. When she'd nervously turned up, not sure what to expect, all five of them had welcomed her in. Arca, Seth's mum, was kind and warm, and made Clara miss Aunt Lillian rather a lot. There had been food to share, gossip about the actors, and Arca and Volans keeping up a cheerful chatter about various holiday amusements.

No one asked her much about the bother with Horatio Morris, except for one thing. Volans had leaned over, not long before the panto started, to say, "You did a fine thing there. Gather it's all coming together. Now, how about in January? We see if we can find a time when you can show me a few of your clever ways of doing things."

He'd timed it perfectly. There was only enough time for her to stammer something about being glad to - she was - before the lights dimmed once, and the audience tucked themselves into seats. It was interesting to Clara. She knew how the show went, she'd seen most of the dress rehearsal. She'd certainly heard bits and pieces about the rest of it from Owen.

Seeing it all together, with all the illusions and the charmlights and the full orchestra, that was an entirely different thing. From the moment that Jack strolled out on stage, in front of the curtain, laying out the story, she was entirely enraptured. Part of her kept thinking of how they were making all those scenes work, but the rest of her was caught up in the story and the magic - both the figurative magic of the story, and the quite real magic making everything work.

More to it, everyone seemed to be absolutely on, as the phrase went. It was like bottles glittering in the sun, everything lined up perfectly in the shop. Everything went sharply right. Jack and the cook - Iawn and Howard as the Dame - bantered back and forth, teasing, even improvising, she was sure. Not that she'd memorised the whole script. But they were easy about it, almost casual, the way a son and his mother would tease, or so Clara supposed. The way Seth had teased his Mum, before the show, though that had been less on the edge of bawdy puns and wordplay.

After a song that nearly brought down the house at the end of act one, she'd been laughing and grinning so much her face was fit to ache. Seth caught a look at her, then said, "Hey, Dill. Let's go get the refreshments and bring them back."

"One of the privileges of a box," Golshan said, cheerfully. "Treats all round." He tossed Seth a couple of coins.

Seth caught them neatly. "Our treat, Clara, don't even try to argue. Mum and Dad will win, and if they didn't, we would."

Clara looked at all of them, made a weak protestation of "I couldn't."

"You can." It came in unison from all five of them, with Golshan continuing, "It's by way of a celebration, anyway. It's a year since Seth and Dilly brought me home, near enough. You're helping me celebrate that particularly fine anniversary. Night out for the family. One of Seth's sisters is tending the babe. Besides, Seth's doing much better with his sales. Dilly and I had a signature win with the Ministry, and that's before we get to Mum and Dad." He used the names casually, as if it weren't anything special, but Clara caught the look in his eyes, and certainly the way Arca and Volans turned to look at him and smile back. It made her unsure what to say, so she folded her hands in her lap.

Arca asked Golshan something that Clara didn't quite hear, keeping up an amiable conversation that didn't require any input from anyone else. Volans leaned forward, looking out at the stage. "Does your husband enjoy being backstage?"

The question startled Clara out of her thoughts. "Yes." It came out like she wasn't certain, then she repeated it, more sure. "Yes, he does. He likes figuring out how to solve problems, I think. Shoes are a particular kind of problem. This is a different kind, but also important."

"They were very good to Golshan here, so I suspected someone who likes solving problems would do well," Volans said, amused.

Before Clara could say anything, Golshan's laughter cut in. "I'm also good at causing problems." He sounded absolutely delighted at it.

"Not so many as you keep claiming." Arca snorted.

"How many plates did I break?" Golshan asked. "And not like the ones here, that are mostly illusion."

"Plates mend," Arca said. "And you notice we still keep the good ones out of the way most of the time. Easy enough to do." She glanced over at Clara. "I find taking people as they are more interesting than trying to change them, anyway. The decent ones. That's the thing about panto, isn't it? You've a story that barely holds together, most of the time, but there's a happy ending and good triumphs, and somehow it's still entirely satisfying."

There was a lot in that, really. Clara was still thinking about it when Seth and Dilly came back with a cardboard tray full of treats. There were roast chestnuts sliced through the bottom to peel, little marzipan sweets charmed all sorts of shapes and colours, three different kinds of spun sugar, bottles of lemonade that Seth produced out of the pockets in his coat. The box was full of the contented sounds of eating and drinking. People were sharing, with an "Oh, try this one, it's a great mint," until the lights flickered again and called everyone back to their seats.

The second act was even better than the first. There was the whole glorious hide and seek sequence with the giants. She knew most of them were made of paper mache and shadows and illusions and she still shrieked every time one popped up. And of course she did her bit in yelling out "He's behind you!" when that was the thing.

The whole arc of the romance held together, too. The actors had all made it look much more real and solid. And Theo Robbins, as Brutus, absolutely held everyone in the palm of his hand when he started making glorious, over the top, ridiculous apologies to Innogen. That was a new bit. Owen had told her it was coming, but not anything about it. First Brutus produced a flower, then a gold crown, and finally, when that hadn't really melted Imogen's heart, he told her something in a whisper. She dramatically stepped back, with a "Say that again?"

"I'd fight dozens more giants for you... but I'd rather not have to!" Brutus laid it out as if the nonsense - even in the context of the panto - was the grandest gesture. Something in Imogen cracked, so she flung herself at him. He picked her up, twirled her around, kissed her soundly, and that went right on into the final dance. They made the most of the choreography, barely wanting to stop touching each other, until they ended up arm in arm for the final bow.

They had to wait for the rest of the crowds to file out, all burbling over cheerfully. Golshan leaned forward. "Full house, or near enough. Bet it will be completely full tomorrow, when word has got round. That Brutus, Theo - he's really good. Not just a good actor, though that helps, but he's got a real knack for keeping the audience happy. He'll go a long way, and if Orlando can get him back next year, they'll be well on the road to success."

Finally, though, the crowds had cleared. They could bring Golshan down in the set elevator, cranked mostly by magic, and stood around for a few minutes. Eventually, Owen came out, looking still a little out of breath. "Maisery's told me I should take you home. I'll do my bit tomorrow." He then added shyly, "Got a bit of a solstice pressie for you."

Clara made her goodbyes to the others, promising to find a time to talk accounting and bookkeeping in the new calendar year. They walked together up to where Clara and Owen broke off to their flat, rather than toward Portal Square. Clara tucked her arm through Owen's, content just to walk and be quiet. He kept looking at her, smiling, when she caught his expression. He let her go in ahead of him once they got up the stairs to the flat. "You up for one more good thing tonight? At least I hope you'll think it's good?"

"Yes?" Clara felt awkward and uncertain again, even though Monday night had done a lot to help her feel more like they were doing this together.

"Come into the centre of the room, close your eyes." She did, putting her hands over them for good measure, and refusing to peek. Clara could hear him moving around, then he came back close to her. She could hear him breathing. "When you're ready."

She opened her eyes to find a cloth out on the side table. Sitting on top of it were two perfect leather shoes, made of purple and blue leather, tied with a matching purple ribbon. They weren't ridiculously decorative, but they had a dip, where the toe cap met the body, like a curve of a flower petal. She reached out hesitantly. "For—"

"For you. Made to fit you, if I know my work." Owen had stepped back, his hands behind his back.

"Will you help me put them on?" Clara could do it herself, of course, like she'd done so much in the past years. But she didn't want to. She didn't need to.

He beamed at her, and then pulled a chair over where she could sit comfortably, before bending down to unbuckle her current shoes and then slip the new ones on. No new shoe was ever entirely perfect, but this was near enough as to be like something out of Cinderella. The curves fit brilliantly, she could tell already the toes wouldn't pinch, she had space to wriggle her feet.

"There are charms, to be more comfortable when you're in the shop all day. And against slipping. If you want a pair to go out dancing in, I'll make you something else. Here, are those snug? Take a few steps, see what you think."

She let him offer his hands, let him pull her gently

standing. Then she couldn't resist picking up one foot, then the other, looking over her shoulder to see what they looked like. A few steps had her twirling - no, she wouldn't slip, but she could pivot, if she went at it deliberately. "Dancing, is it?"

"We could, some night when I'm not needed at the theatre. If that's the sort of thing you'd like."

"You know," Clara said, after a moment. "I'm not sure what I like anymore, things like that. I like pantomime, very much. I like your theatre. I adore these shoes." She then took two steady steps forward and kissed his nose. "I love our bedroom. And I most decidedly love you."

Owen picked her up and swung her around. "And?"

"And I should take these excellent shoes off so we can go to bed." She kissed his nose again for good measure. "Whenever did you make these?"

"Finished them this morning. I could use sleep, too. After the other thing."

Clara laughed, and then stepped back to undo the buckles. She stepped out of them before tugging at his hand. "Bed. Now. Got a present for you in the morning. It'll keep."

EPILOGUE

Clara let herself in downstairs. The shop felt different already, knowing there was someone about upstairs. Aunt Lillian had sent a note around yesterday, saying she was back in town. Come by Sunday for tea. Bring her husband, if she liked. Well, Owen was busy. The theatre was preparing for a post-panto season, cheerfully.

They'd had nearly full houses all through the run. A fair number of people came to pine at Theo, apparently. He was, honestly, the sort people did that with. Kind, mind. She'd gone round the theatre on the weekends, helping with a bit of mending or something else simple while Owen worked. She'd enjoyed the camaraderie, and even more how they cheerfully included Clara, not just because she came with Owen.

She'd begged off today, of course. Clara had sent Owen off with a packed supper. They'd finished up fitting up their new bedroom enough to sleep in it comfortably last week,

324

and she expected she'd be asleep when he came home. They'd work something out, she hoped.

After checking to make sure all was well with the shop, a matter of instinct and routine these days, she opened the door at the back that led upstairs. "Aunt Lillian?"

"Come up, come up, Clara dear!"

There was the smell of something with spices in the air, like Aunt Lillian had been baking. When Clara got to the top of the steps, the sitting room was a riot of warmth, both physically and metaphorically. Aunt Lillian had the fire going properly. There were scones waiting on a tray, the teapot was steaming gently. But more than that, it felt homey. Aunt Lillian turned around, a beautiful knit shawl with cabled designs pulled around her shoulders, in a deep heathery blue.

"It's so good to see you, dearest. Come, sit down, you've taken such good care of the place. I had a look at the books last night. You've done wonderfully. And I have new stock with me."

"Aunt Lillian." She cleared her throat. "You're back for a bit?"

Her aunt, bafflingly, blushed. "Yes. And I owe you an explanation. More than just an explanation. You must be wondering why I was gone so long. But before that, are you well? You look very well. There are roses in your cheeks, and you're smiling."

Clara blinked, but she supposed she was, wasn't she? "Things are much better now. Owen and I are doing very well, but it took a while to figure ourselves out. And we're not nearly so worried about money as we were."

"Were you, dearest? I thought you said his job was going well?"

That let Clara explain the whole saga of the theatre,

about how he'd had such trouble finding work. And then, when he did, how it might have disappeared without much warning. She didn't go into all the details, certainly not about how many nights he'd spent on the floor. Nor about they'd barely been passing in the dawn and night. The story of discovering the papers made a much better tale, though, and by the end of it, Aunt Lillian was smiling.

"Ah, that's a fine thing. And you're settling in properly, being married." There was a little quirk to her mouth. "Was there anything else?"

"There is, but - perhaps give me a minute?" She didn't want to follow talking about more pleasant things with talking about Master Morris's arrest.

"Ah, well, then. Let me fetch my knitting. You have another scone." Clara did that, it gave her something to do with her hands. It took a few minutes for Aunt Lillian to get herself properly settled, knitting in her lap. She was perhaps halfway through something that might be a cardigan. "I was gone a long time, because, well." She paused. "You've not asked about my personal life. Not in years."

"Of course not, Aunt Lillian. You didn't seem..." She hadn't seemed to have one, honestly, except for the long-dead husband and the friends in the neighbourhood. And whoever she visited in Scotland. "You didn't seem to want to talk about anything like that?"

"No, I didn't." In someone else, it might have been harsh, but here it was very gentle. "I've had a friend - another woman - for many years. Since we were in school together, actually. But she had to marry for family reasons, and then after her husband died, she had to take care of her parents." Aunt Lillian wrinkled up her nose. "Very old, very crotchety. Very set in their ways."

Clara nodded, a bit uncertainly.

"But we were still - ah, well. We never stopped being in love, even when we were married to other people. We didn't do anything that - how to put this. We never had the chance when our husbands were alive. It was all letters and occasional visits when I could. But now her parents have both died, and she doesn't need to concern herself with their disapproval. They could be very nasty, the way words cut all the ways that hurt most. I'm convinced her mother practised hours a day to be able to do it. She had a knack for always hitting on the worst thing."

Clara nodded again. It seemed the thing to do.

"And, well. I went up to visit. But then she got quite ill. The sort of thing that was one part surgery, and one part was her being very weak, for quite a long time." Aunt Lillian held up a finger, keeping her place in the knitting with her other hand. "She's doing much better now. But it was very clear that losing her would have - well. We admitted what we'd both been feeling all those years. She needs to finish up some business, but then she'll be moving down here. In with me."

Clara blinked several times, then asked carefully. "As your partner? In the shop, too?"

"Ah, that's where we should talk through the details. Her skill is about where yours is. Capable to help with the simples, she can certainly help with the prep work, though she's got a bit of arthritis in her hands these days."

"So not the mortar and pestle, then, or too much fine chopping." Then Clara ventured. "It explains why we've such a range of salves for aches, too."

"Exactly. But she could take over measuring things out, or some of the inventory." Aunt Lillian looked up and tsked. "I'm going about this all wrong. You still have your job, darling. We wouldn't dream of doing anything otherwise.

But if there were things you wanted to do that were less in the front of the shop, we'd have some time for that now. Or something else you'd like. Because Effie would be available for some of that. We could even work out a proper apprenticeship in accounting or something of the kind, if you wanted, I suspect."

Clara rocked back in her seat a bit, her feet coming off the ground, even. She curled her arms around her stomach. "Oh." It felt like a tremendous change, being knocked off balance all over again. "I. I had been wondering if there was a way to have a day off on Monday. Because Owen's working evenings, some later than others. And the weekends, of course. And..." Her voice trailed off weakly.

"My goodness, of course. Just Mondays?"

Clara considered that. "I like going round to the theatre on Sundays to help out. Saturdays, they have the matinee, that's much more busy, though I've helped a few times when they need an extra usher or someone handling tickets."

Aunt Lillian considered. "Well, how about you have Sundays and Mondays off, then. Would you still be willing to have the shop open some of Saturday, maybe? Or we could spread out your hours the other days."

Clara did some quick math in her head. "Saturday afternoons would be good. And some time in the late morning for inventory and so on?"

"See, there we go. Was there anything else we should sort out in the business?"

Clara looked down at her tea. "There's - we've had rather a time of it with a particular customer. He's been arrested now, for other reasons."

Aunt Lillian paused in her knitting. "Who, dear?"

"Master Morris. Horatio Morris." Clara looked up, nervous again.

"He's the one you were talking around? Oh, goodness, you should have said. He's got a reputation. Did he - um."

"He didn't do anything to hurt me, not directly? But he made me very uncomfortable."

"He's only a good customer when he's on the prowl somewhere. I thought that was what Winnie Malcolm was on about, but she seemed to assume you'd named him to me. Honestly, Clara." Aunt Lillian tilted her head. "No custom's worth someone making you feel badly. I'd have told you as much. Well, I am telling you as much. Shop rule. None of that kind here."

Clara ducked her chin, flushing now. "Oh. May I excuse myself a minute, please?"

"Of course, dear." Aunt Lillian's knitting picked up again, a steady click as soothing as the sound of the knife on the cutting board or the pestle grinding things down to grains. Clara went off to the loo, mostly to wash her hands and her face. And gather herself, that was true enough.

When she came back, Aunt Lillian had refilled her tea and put another scone on her plate. And one of the fancy biscuits. "Are you all right about things now, dear? You said he was arrested?"

"Arrested and his trial's next week." She grimaced. "I'll have to go in that morning, in case they need my testimony? They probably don't, but the Guard wasn't sure. They overheard most of it. But he was bragging about the way his factory ran, the things he skipped. It took a bit to coordinate with the non-magical side, I guess?" She hadn't been entirely sure of the details, and even Mistress Kemp hadn't been able to explain it terribly well.

"Ah. Well. Good riddance. He threw his money around."

Aunt Lillian considered. "How much of his money did we get out of him, anyway?"

Clara blushed again. "Rather a lot, actually. And do you know anyone who needs a pair of shoes? Otherwise, they'll probably go to the costume stores at the theatre. My size, not horribly made in an absolute sense, though Owen's got a whole list of things that are badly done in them?"

"Maybe. I'll ask around. I'll take a bit to get back into the flow of the gossip. All right, then. You've settled in with Owen, you smile proper now. Have me round for tea some Monday, maybe?"

"He's been very much fitting up the flat. You'd scarcely recognise it. He repainted the kitchen chairs last weekend. They're very bright and cheerful now." A resonant purple, to go with the curtains, though the table was white, even if they often had a cloth on it now.

From there, well, that was a much easier conversation. By the time Clara left, a good hour later, she was in a far better mood, and certainly far more certain of what the future looked like for her. Maybe she would see about an apprenticeship in the more involved sorts of bookkeeping, or in some particular part of the apothecary work. And Owen thought he could start making shoes again, by commission, when he had some workspace. So they were turning the other bedroom into a space he could use, with a daybed for when he needed to sleep there.

But he'd actually spent most nights with her, so far. Now they had the bigger bed and a different space to be in. It had made a difference, apparently, that it wasn't his old childhood room. That just meant Clara was bound and determined to try things, if something wasn't working. And that, on the whole, seemed a fine principle for her life. Plenty to be going on with.

IF YOU ENJOYED *Shoemaker's Wife* and would like to read more of this series, please sign up for my mailing list to get all the latest news and fun extras.

Your reviews (on whatever review site you use) are much appreciated, too!

Read on for more historical details about this book.

AUTHOR'S NOTES

Thank you so much for joining me for *Shoemaker's Wife* and a glimpse at life in Trellech! As always, the greatest of thanks to my editor, Kiya Nicoll, for many excellent suggestions (and all the editing), as well as to my early readers. They all helped make this a much better book.

You can find connections to other people, places, and events of my books in my authorial wiki (found at bit.ly/celia-lake-wiki or from the links on my website). Several secondary characters who appear here also appear in other books, so let's start with that before we get into the details of each chapter. You don't need to know their backstories to make sense of *Shoemaker's Wife*, but if you want a bit more of them, here's where to explore.

Shoemaker's Wife gives us a look at Golshan, Seth, and Dilly beginning about eight months after the events of *Casting Nasturtiums*. That novella (found in the *Winter's Charms* collection) is a friends-to-lovers polyamorous romance that begins when Seth goes looking for his best friend after Seth is demobbed in the summer of 1919. Seth and Golshan have been friends since they were 13, and Dilly has her own affection for Golshan.

Griffin Pelton appears in *Point By Point* in a minor role, and he's getting his own romance later in this series, in a book that will be focusing on the magics of Trellech's legal system (and Trellech itself) along with jewellery making and jet carving. As I write this, it doesn't have a title yet, but it should be out around August of 2024.

Edgar Watson appears briefly in *Country Manners*, another of the novellas in *Winter's Charms*. That one takes place about a year after *Shoemaker's Wife*, when Edgar has left working for the theatre, on good terms but wanting a bit more of a regular schedule, to take up as valet to Giles Lefton. (I am contemplating whether there's a romance in the offing for him in that time period, too. Edgar's a delight, and I do love his particular form of competence.)

On to the book!

First, let's start with the theatre. My father was a theatre professor, so I grew up around and sometimes tucked into odd places in a university theatre, seeing all kinds of shows from the time I was remotely old enough. It left me with a great amount of respect for the process, as well as far too many opinions about staging, direction, the proper way of doing things, and what makes a scene work than anyone really ought to. At least not anyone who isn't actually doing theatre regularly. (I had a series of small roles when my father needed a conveniently scheduled child actor for things he was directing. As well as some time playing in the pit orchestra for high school productions and turning my hand to a little bit of stage management.)

All of this meant that when I sat down to write this book, I spent a bit of time poring through a couple of theatre history resources, and trying to figure out what

Albion's cultural divergence from the non-magical community meant for theatre. Albion, frankly, mostly didn't care
about the artistic impact of the Restoration in nearly the
same way (and while Shakespeare is obviously in their
repertoire, they would not have been focused on the
creative output of the Elizabethan court.)

The result is a mix - some plays do very well in Albion,
others are rarely or never performed. Albion's satires and
comedies tend to come from Albion playwrights as well,
because the beats that are funny (or that are on the nose for
the moment) are a bit different than those in London or
elsewhere.

For those who aren't familiar with the British panto (or
pantomime) tradition, it is very much its own particular art
form. It does owe something to the comedic (and also satir-
ical) works of forms like commedia dell'arte, combined
with a lot of topical humour. If you're curious, YouTube
does have a number of performances (of varying levels of
professional staging).

It has a number of common traditions. Pantos these
days are most usually based on some sort of fairy tale - Puss
in Boots, Cinderella, Jack and the Beanstalk and so on.
There's often a Good Fairy who pops onto stage to help and
perhaps a Bad Fairy who's part of the challenge of the plot.

There is also a long tradition of cross-dressing, both by
the Dame (traditionally played by a mature man), and a
breeches role (traditionally played by a woman). The
latter's often a young man who serves as narrator and/or
the hero. In many cases, the character the Dame is playing
is his mother. There is, however, a lot of possible variation
in terms of the parts assignment here, and I've taken some
liberties to adapt for Albion's stage.

There's a lot of historical reason for all of this, and some of it works better than others in our current conversations of gender, identity, fictional roles, and so on. There's also a lot of academic, experiential, and other discussion about this in various forms, if you want to explore more about it.

Onto the notes by chapter.

Chapter 2: From 1860 to 1916, soldiers in the British Army were required to have a moustache. This, obviously, causes some complications for men of Albion, who tend to prefer being clean-shaven for reasons of magical contagion concerns. (It's easier to fully shave, and dispose of the bits in a magically appropriate way, also various of them have thoughts about disease and hygiene.) Anyway, that was lifted in 1916, in part because gas masks in the trenches were complicated when men had facial hair (which had generally become less common among British men by the 1880s.)

Chapter 4: There was an entire process of demobbing. People would be sent back to a camp in Britain, where they'd wait for a period of time (usually somewhere between a week and a month) while the final paperwork was processed, and they made arrangements for whatever they were doing next. Once they were formally demobbed, they were given a train ticket (or money for one), often a civilian suit of clothes, and sent off. They were expected to turn in the great coat local to them once they'd arrived, and would then also (at least in 1920) qualify for thirteen weeks of payment.

If I did my maths right, using inflation calculators, 24 shillings a week at 20 shillings to the pound (so 1.2 pounds) comes out to about 69 pounds or 78 dollars today. (I did the maths during the drafting of the book, so it's based on November 2022 currency conversions.) Not enough to cover all your expenses, though it'd certainly help with basics. Britain is in the early months of a major inflationary cycle at this point, too.

Chapter 6: Of course Owen paid particular attention to the boots in his uniform. As he mentions, there were a handful of common patterns, and some of them lasted better than others. The issues he mentions are all things that came up repeatedly in commentary from the period.

Chapter 8: As Owen is aware already, beers after the Great War were notably weaker than before. Other beer-drinking habits had also changed, with porter becoming decidedly less popular, and lager and bitter (draught pale ale) were more popular. There were fewer varieties available overall.

Chapter 10 : One of the questions I had to sort out an answer to is "just how big is the theatrical base in Albion?" Trellech is a city of 20,000-25,000 people (depending on how you count: some people work in Trellech and live outside it, some residents are seasonal). But they're also a central location for all of Albion, with easy transportation for a significant portion of that population via the portals.

The end result was four theatres, plus the Opera House which has a different range of productions, and a number of troupes doing some amount of touring. The touring was extremely common in theatres of the period. There are of course a whole host of amateur theatrical groups, one-off productions done outside a long-term theatre schedule, etc.

Chapter 12 : The vaudeville acts are more or less as Maisery explains them. You can find some period videos (or nearly period) of adagio acts on YouTube if you do a little searching. Adding the term "gymnastic" or "acrobatic" will help you filter out all the other musical uses of the word. British Pathé has a recording from 1933 under the title "The Dance Acrobatic", for example.

One of my ongoing favourite sorts of humour is people listing all the things that happen in folk songs that you should not do. Don't be named Margaret or Janet. Don't go down to the greenwood, or any navigable waterway. There are a lot of iterations of these, but my standby is a post called "Folksongs Are Your Friend" on a blog called Making Light, posted in 2005.

I also had to do some thinking about what themes and stories are popular in Albion's creative arts. The legend of Brutus is in fact one of the possible origin stories of Britain. Arthuriana (in its many and varied forms) and fairy tales are also regular themes.

Chapter 14 : And of course, which plays are sensitive is a bit different in Albion than in Britain as a whole. You may well be familiar with the theatre folk custom that you never say the name of the Scottish play in a theatre (*Macbeth*. I'm typing it, and I'm still wincing a little.) Albion doesn't actually care as much about that one. The play that causes problems is, as noted, *Midsummer Night's Dream,* because of how strongly associated it is with fairies and the Fatae, and might get their attention.

Chapter 16 : Aphra Behn is a real person, but she's also a great example of one of my favourite methods of worldbuilding, aka "wait, this person has dropped out of documented history for a bit, were they doing something magical?" She appears on the scene in very early adulthood during the English Civil War period, becoming one of the first English women to earn her living by her writing. She was a poet, author, translator, and playwright, as well as probably also being a spy. There's very little known about her early life, and she also disappears from the historical record for a few years as an adult.

Obviously - if you're me - she had made the Pact, and

was part of Albion's society. There are, obviously, therefore some plays that are performed regularly in Albion not known to non-magical audiences.

Chapter 17 : Laundry is eternal, isn't it? Households in Albion have a variety of methods of dealing with it, but it's all fairly labour-demanding. Even with magic. In this period, it's still quite common to send laundry out, even for working class or middle class households.

Chapter 18 : Theatre has a long history of Guild pageants and mumming plays, telling a fable or morally relevant story or one related to the organisation putting the thing on. They often involve stylised characters or archetypes, and some set and costuming to support the story (but not a lot of elaborate set building, since they'd often be performed outside or in a multi-use space.)

Chapter 19 : I am just noting here that the phrasing given in this chapter for "All work and no play" is in the original punctuation.

Chapter 20 : The reference to the mysterious house is the plot of my *Wards of the Roses*.

Chapter 21: Agnes Evans, met in this chapter, appears in *Point By Point*, which has a bit more of the Trellech Moon's morgue. *King Lear* is a well-known Shakespearean play, based on a bit of ancient British myth. It's a cautionary tale about the challenges of age and making good decisions. It is also a classic role for actors who are getting toward the end of their career, and the comments about Randolph here are not entirely kind.

Chapter 22 : I couldn't have a theatre and not have a theatre ghost. There is a very long and grand tradition of theatre ghosts and other spooky events. As noted, ghosts in Albion are often associated with some sort of hidden treasure (coins specifically hold magical energy in ways that make that more likely, as discussed briefly in *Fool's Gold).* I also just wanted a generally friendly theatre ghost, unlike some of the depictions we get in other sources.

Chapter 24 : *The Young Visiters* is in fact a real book, and it came out in 1919 (though it was written in 1890.) I was introduced to it by my father, and then met one of my life-long best friends during a session of reading it aloud in the social room of a convention hospitality suite. It is abso-lutely hilarious in that mode, especially if you swap around who's reading regularly.

The chapters are short, the spelling is horrendous, and the childhood assumptions about Victorian adult life are also hilarious. The 2003 film version also has some wonderful acting, and is also hilarious though in slightly different modes (since it can rely on visual absurdity). Once I realised it had been published in 1919 - and immensely popular - I couldn't resist having it appear here.

Chapter 26 : Owen is fairly straightforward when talking about the changes in shoe manufacturing in the period. Some of those changes came about with factory manufacturing, some were due to processes like vulcanisa-tion (a more flexible and waterproof sole, arguably, but with other limitations.)

Chapter 28: Why are turnips funny? They are funny for me because I grew up watching the British comedy series *Blackadder*, which takes place through multiple periods in history. Turnips feature particularly in the Regency series, and well - as Maisery said - you can get a lot of mileage out of a root vegetable.

Chapter 32: The magical green screening here is inten-tional. But mostly because Welsh does in fact have a colour word - glas - that is about a quality of shimmering colour as much as it is about the shade of blue or green. It seems a fine background for illusion work.

Chapter 34 : There was a requirement in many Great War units for a certain number of people in the unit to become adept in using semaphore, since it was used extensively for signalling during combat situations. Semaphore and the number of people in the infantry who learned it.

Chapter 36: For those who like to make connections between characters, the Doyle of the solicitor's office is Lucy Doyle's father. (The solicitor of that name is referenced a couple of times in other books)

Chapter 37: Captain Donovan appears at the end of *Wards of the Roses*, and Griffin in *Point by Point*. Griffin will also be getting his own romance later in the Mysterious Arts series as I mentioned earlier, so we'll be seeing more of him then.

Thank you again for joining me for this journey and a glimpse into the theatrics of Albion. The next book in the *Mysterious Arts* series is *Perfect Accord*, focusing on perfumery and alchemy. It will be out in February of 2024.

Also by Celia Lake

The Mysterious Charm Series

Outcrossing

Goblin Fruit

Magician's Hoard

Wards of the Roses

In The Cards

On The Bias

Seven Sisters

The Mysterious Powers Series

Carry On

The Fossil Door

Eclipse

Fool's Gold

The Hare and the Oak

Point By Point

Mistress of Birds

The Mysterious Arts Series

Bound for Perdition

Perfect Accord

Charms of Albion

Pastiche

Sailor's Jewel

Four Walls and a Heart

Land Mysteries

Best Foot Forward

Nocturnal Quarry

Old As The Hills

Upon A Summer's Day

Other stories

Complementary

Winter's Charms

Forged in Combat

Learn more about the world of Albion and future books at my website, celialake.com. Additional information linking characters, places, and timelines is available at bit.ly/celia-lake-wiki

Sign up for my newsletter to be the first to hear about future books and learn about fascinating bits of research. Happy reading!